FINDING JUNIPER

CINDY THOMSON

Theresa,
Cindy Thomson
2025

EMERALD
PATH PRESS

Finding Juniper

by Cindy Thomson

Emerald Path Press

ISBN: 978-1-7367131-3-6

Edited by Jamie Chavez

Proofed by Michelle Levigne

Bible quotations from the King James Version, public domain

Cover design by Cindy Thomson

Background photo by Cindy Thomson

Letter illustration by Carterart on Vecteezy.com, pro license

Girl illustration Photo by Iurii Melentsov on Unsplash, free license

For Eileen Thomson, a storyteller with paint, hugs, and smiles.

CHAPTER 1

P atrick

Early April 1950, Golden, Ohio

Patrick stood at the mailbox and examined the envelope in his hand. Addressed to Paddy Doyle and postmarked Ireland. Who back there had anything to say to him after all these years? His mother had been dead for decades. He flipped the letter from one hand to the other. A long-lost relative? A distant cousin, perhaps. Patrick slid his finger under the seal and removed the paper inside. The handwriting was crude, so unlike the florid script written with a fountain pen on the outside. This was a child's pencil scrawling. Peering at the words, he had to steady himself against the mailbox post. He glanced up and gazed at rows of budding green stalks dotting the cornfield across the way.

The one thing. The only thing that could ever make him return to Ireland was written on the paper. But was it real? Could his child have actually written this?

To my Da, whoever you were,

You left me. I want you to come back and say why. Why did you go away, Da? Because I am not a boy? I'm ugly? Too dirty? Too sick? Too poor? I wish you'd come back but you can't. If you could you won't.

I want you to come back.

A.J.M.

He'd made a promise, but that was thirty years ago. He had wanted his child, but she had not survived long enough to have written this. The paper looked old, but what if she hadn't written it?

That was it. No name. A joke? A cruel prank? If wee Juniper had written this, it must have been before ... before she'd passed. While Róisín was still alive her letters had stopped mentioning their child. The girl could not have survived the terrible destitution over there. Patrick had tried not to think of it. Too awful to imagine. He glanced back down at the letter. Who would take something the child had once written and post it to him now?

Patrick kicked at the weeds encircling the weathered mailbox post and ran a hand through his thinning hair. The words scalded his heart. He'd been in America so long now, lived a whole other life with a wife and child. He'd put aside the hurt Ireland had caused him, buried it in the depths of his soul.

A chill shook him, carrying memories he'd tried to forget. Patrick grasped the front pocket of his overalls. *No, Juniper. I did want you!* The news that she had longed for her father made his pulse race, made him wish for a drink ... no, he wouldn't go there, had been sober since '26. It made no sense that old longing would come back after all this time. He was cured of the bottle.

Rubbing his temples, Patrick glanced up at the sound of an automobile engine. His daughter Mardell was home from her job. Wiping the dampness from his eyes, Patrick stuffed the paper into his pocket as the Chevy Styleline, the car he'd bought a few years back from a friend, pull into the dirt-packed driveway. The smell of spring—damp earth, young plants, Ernie's cattle up the road—would forever be associated with the day Patrick Doyle had to face his past and had to keep it from his younger daughter.

He needed a drink and yet he couldn't. Especially not with Mardell here. With shaking hands he offered a small wave as she drove past him.

He'd have to divulge the sister Mardell never knew, the life he had wished away. She'd read the trouble on his face and know something was up. Where to start? Ireland, the First World War, the Irish Civil War … all the despair those things had brought. Mardell had only been told basic, benign things. Mardell was an innocent girl who had only known the fresh country air of the American Midwest. He'd wanted to spare her the details. There was so much to explain now. He needed time to sort out what to tell her. And how. Oh, how he wished he didn't have to. *I want you to come back.*

While Mardell prepared dinner, something she'd taken on since her mother died, Patrick retreated to the living room. Opening the top cabinet on the dresser, something Americans called a china cabinet, he retrieved a small silver flask he'd kept for Ernie's visits and took a gulp of Irish whiskey. He'd limited himself over the years. A couple of drinks when his friend came by. Ernie was a busy doctor so those visits had not been frequent. Paddy had controlled his drinking. When Veronica was alive he'd hardly ever imbibed, but having a toast to the memory of loved one was an Irish tradition he'd observed. He'd kept a bottle in that dresser since the funeral, just for emergencies, although he hadn't expected to need it. Never even thought about it much. Nothing like the old days. He hadn't dreamed he'd get this letter, though.

Over a dinner of cabbage rolls, Patrick mustered the nerve to tell his daughter a bit about his life before he met her mother.

"Why haven't you talked about this before?" Mardell asked. "I've always wondered, but what's brought it on now?"

"Didn't see a reason to. Your mother and I thought it best to look forward not back. You know I was born in Ireland and left right after I got out of the war." He huffed. "Getting out took a while, you understand. So it was late 1919 when I left." The letter burned in his pocket like a lit match.

Mardell nodded. "You always said you had no family left behind."

A slight bending of the truth, that. But they all had passed on within a few years. "Times were difficult. People starved, those not destroyed by violence. Leastways, all the folks I was acquainted with. You see …" His hands shook. Another drink would help. "Uh, a wee drink, darlin'. To the memory of those long past." He rose and went to the living room.

"Not for me, Dad," she called after him.

When he returned with a crystal glass of whiskey—at least he'd had the good sense not to show the flask or the half-full bottle—Mardell frowned. "The doctor thinks you shouldn't drink, Dad."

"Did Ernie say so? He's enjoyed a dram. Well, no matter, darlin'. 'Tis only a wee sip." He downed it quickly so as to end the discussion. "I had a daughter born there," he said quickly before the words died on his tongue. "Understand, this was long before I met your mother. My girlfriend at the time was Róisín."

"A daughter? Is she still …?"

"Listen, now. I don't think she survived. Pretty certain not. Mardell, things were not the same as here. The country was in the midst of troubles. Not much work to be had. In Dublin, where I lived, there were slums all over, hunger, sickness. I had wanted Juniper, that's what Róisín called her, to come to America with her mother. But Róisín wouldn't. I left before the baby came. Never even saw her except for one photograph."

"You weren't married?" Mardell's eyes widened. Patrick didn't want to tell her such awful things.

"We were not, but understand it wasn't possible then. We had different … you might say leanings. As you know I never claimed religion myself. I know 'tis hard to understand. You could say there were different ways of looking at things. I would have married her, but her family wouldn't hear of it."

"Did Mom know?"

"She did."

"Is Róisín still living?"

Oh, he knew she'd have questions. Patrick patted his sweating forehead with his napkin. "Róisín McGurdy died many years back."

Mardell dabbed her own napkin to her eyes. "I'm so sorry, Dad. That's very sad."

Patrick blew out a breath and gripped the table's aluminum edging with both hands. "It was so long ago. I didn't mean to upset you, darlin. I was just thinking about things, I suppose." He remembered reading a book once, he didn't recall the title, that said the dead never leave you. True, that.

Mardell offered a sympathetic smile and stuck a fork into her mashed potatoes. "Mom's passing made you reflect on all this, I suppose. It's OK, Dad. You don't need that whiskey. Just talk to me. I'm an adult. I can handle it."

"I know, darlin. You're right." He pushed his empty glass away.

He would put off telling Mardell about that mysterious letter. No reason to upset her further with things she couldn't possibly understand. This news was enough for now. And by jolly he didn't understand it all himself. "I suppose losing your mother has made me think about things. Life is fleeting."

Mardell took a swig from her glass of milk. A thought seemed to spring up and she held up a finger until she swallowed. "Dad, you say your daughter died young, so far as you know. But you don't actually know, do you?"

"I feel certain."

"Your mother too?"

"Yes, love. There was no one to tell me when it happened but she had been ill, and I was not able to discover where she had moved to. All my kin beneath the sod now."

"That's too bad, it really is." Mardell sucked on her bottom lip. What was she thinking? "But, Dad, I'd love to see where you grew up. I've got vacation time accumulated. Let's go."

"Go? You don't mean—" He'd thought about going himself, but bringing her?

"Why sure. Travel's open to Europe now. Please, Dad? This could be a healing journey for us both. Give you a chance to say goodbye, and me as well, even though I never knew them. You know how important that is because of Mom's passing."

They'd both suffered a great loss recently. Patrick's wife Veronica had not been able to conceive after Mardell was born so there was no family left now but the two of them. Veronica had passed peacefully—for her—and painfully for Patrick and Mardell. He wanted to do something for Mardell, but this seemed too much.

"I don't know, darlin. Ireland was not good to me. 'Tis far better here."

"I know it wasn't good there, but that's the point, Dad. Healing. Don't you want to find out what happened to Juniper? Put that to rest and visit my grandmother's grave?"

"No." Patrick's heart thudded so loudly he feared she'd hear. He did want to go and he did not.

"But, Dad, we need to."

He waved a hand in the air. "No, *we* don't." He snatched his glass and headed back to the living room. He'd nearly finished the bottle when he heard her come in.

"I've done the dishes and I'm going back to my apartment."

He turned toward the doorway, studying her shadowy form, the kitchen light behind her. It had grown late and he hadn't noticed. "You aren't staying?"

"No, Dad. It's time we both got back to our lives."

Mardell had stayed with him in the two weeks after Veronica's death. He needed her. "I didn't mean to sound so … bothered. Not your fault. I'm sorry. Stay, darlin."

"It's not that exactly. I can't." She took two steps into the room. "I can't help you, Dad. Don't you see? You've fallen off the wagon and you won't help yourself. I think going back to Ireland will help, but you won't do it. I don't know how to help you." She spun on her heels and marched through the kitchen and out the back door. He heard the rumble of the old Chevy.

Patrick took his glass to the kitchen and tried to wash it but a sharp pain in his lower back made him drop it, sending it shattering into the cast iron sink. If he didn't go look for Juniper, Mardell would pull away from him and she was all he had left. If he did go, Mardell would learn what a heel he was. Either way …

Before he went to bed, he dumped the rest of his whiskey down the kitchen sink.

Patrick would show Mardell the letters he'd saved, the others. Not the one that came today, not yet.

The next day he was surprised to find Mardell in the kitchen making breakfast. "I'm sorry, Dad. I wanted to tell you that, but I did mean what I said." She placed two plates of hotcakes on the table and took the chair opposite him.

"I know." Patrick sat at the table, his head aching, the food not helping. "I'm not sure it will help, but you're right. We should go and try to find out what happened to Juniper. I really would like to know."

"Oh, Dad." Mardell dropped her napkin and hurried to the other side of the table to hug him. "I'll start planning right away. You don't have to do a thing but pack."

Maybe she'd change her mind if he mentioned the young man who had her heart. "Won't you miss Leo, darlin? You two seem to have gotten close these last few years since he got back from the war."

"We're not moving to Ireland, Dad, just visiting. Besides, it was Leo who told me how beautiful Ireland is. He was over there, you know. He stayed in a small village in the north where the Americans were housed. He met some lovely people, including a woman who offered quite effective herbal treatments for sore feet, he said. When I told him you hadn't been back since you came over in 1920, he agreed that a father-daughter trip might just be the best medicine."

Mardell was serious. There'd be no dissuading her. Besides, if he didn't do this, he might go back to drinking himself into oblivion and he'd didn't want that. As bad as this was, he could not endure rock bottom. Not again. All he could hope for was that what they found there wouldn't also send him over the edge. No great options here.

"Old age makes you reflect on life," he finally said.

She nodded as though at her age she understood.

When they'd finished breakfast Mardell collected the plates and carried them to the sink. "You're not old. You've plenty of spring in your step for an overseas trip."

"Just turned fifty-six. That's old, darlin."

9

"If you say so, although I'll never think of you as old."

"Well, let's just say I've lived long enough to not want regrets." He'd become an American citizen shortly before marrying Veronica. They could obtain passports. Patrick had money in his savings and few living expenses. He could spring for a trip. There were no excuses.

"Yes. The memories might be prickly, but we'll do this together, Dad. I'll visit the travel agent in Columbus tomorrow."

"Will your boss allow you the time off?"

"Oh, fiddlesticks. If they won't let me go, I'll find another bookkeeping job."

Mardell hugged his shoulder and then returned to the dishes. "I've always wanted to go to Ireland."

"Be careful what you wish for," Patrick mumbled to himself.

LATER, as Patrick undressed for bed, he thought back over his life. He really didn't know much about his parents. His childhood had been difficult. They were dirt poor because his father was away for long periods of time, and then one day he showed up in a hospital. Patrick had been only a child then, but as he grew older, he suspected his father had beat his mother when he was at home. He drank too much. Lots of men, spineless men, had. His widowed mother had done the best she could, possessing no trade other than herbal medicine to fall back on, and not easily done in the city, His mother had come from the countryside up north but as a young woman had moved to Dublin to find work, met his father, and stayed. Patrick didn't know much about her early days. The First World War was what had brought most of the sorrow to his young life. That blasted war. Poor old Colin Reilly, his long-dead chum. From that time on Paddy, as he was called then, tumbled down a corkscrew rabbit hole that didn't stop until years later when he met Mardell's mother. If the leaders of the world back then could have found a peaceful end to their disagreements over borders and the like, he'd never have gone to war. And if marching off to fight in uniform had never been an option for Paddy, things would have turned out much differently.

IF MARDELL HAD LEARNED about Juniper some other way, Patrick wouldn't have been talked into this trip. The letter was an audible voice from the past. *I want you to come back.*

The mystery of who sent it and why kept him awake at night. He couldn't quite work out how to explain it.

"Come on, Dad. We'll be late." Mardell pointed toward a queue of passengers, men in dark suits and women with head scarves billowing.

Patrick trailed her, gripping his gray flannel cap with one hand and tugging his black overcoat closed with the other as a late spring gale blew up from the water.

A ship steward waved white-gloved hands above his head. "This way, ladies and gents. All aboard!"

Turning his gaze briefly upward, Patrick was dwarfed by the magnificent ship's smokestacks that shot toward low-hanging clouds. He clutched the chalky painted-iron railing to steady himself as they inched forward. The briny smell in the wind reminded him of his days on the Jersey shore. He'd not been east since moving with his wife in the early days of their marriage, before Mardell was born.

There were two plausible explanations for why the mysterious letter had landed in his mailbox. The message might have been written to torment him. Róisín's brother had been a bully. And there were others like him. Still, the passage of so much time should have ended all that.

The other possibility was that the letter was authentic. The idea that the daughter he'd never met was alive and after thirty years wanted to communicate her anger with him sent his mind reeling. He'd thought she was dead all these years now. Juniper had been an apparition, a long-ago fleeting mist of an idea that could never be. Then without warning that apparition materialized by way of a suggestion in a letter.

A third possibility occurred to Patrick as he and Mardell inched their way across the gangway behind what seemed to be an endless line of eager rosy-cheeked travelers. Assuming the undated letter was genuine, it might have been recently found by a third party who forwarded it. That was the most likely explanation. Patrick tapped the paper hidden safely in his breast pocket. Return addresses were not used in Ireland, unfortunately. Róisín's brother John had informed Patrick years ago of her passing—the only kind thing John McGurdy had ever done for Patrick. McGurdy could have given Patrick's address to someone else and that person forwarded it for some reason.

Patrick shrugged, as though responding to the silent debate raging in his mind. What he most wanted to know, and what Mardell was also curious about, was what had happened to Juniper.

Oh, Juniper! For however long her life had been, what she thought of Patrick could not have been good. He'd left, she knew, but she would not have known the circumstances. A lump formed in his throat. He should have gone looking sooner, but life had shielded him from past mistakes and heartaches, and most men would choose the path he had, the more palatable one. Now old age had sprung the past's regrets forward, demanding he deal with them, spurred on by booze, no doubt. Patrick took a deep breath of the briny air. *Well, one can only run for so long.* Pray God, don't let Mardell hate him after this.

Running a hand through his graying hair, Patrick acknowledged what he'd always known. *Nothing ever changes much.*

Mardell bounced on her toes next to him. "I can't wait to see Ireland, Dad! What a thrill. I mean, I know we are going to find your lost kin and see what happened to them, but let's think of all this as a grand adventure, shall we? Leo says you've never seen the color green until you've seen Ireland for yourself."

She was trying to lighten his mood. They both knew the truth. If Patrick didn't deal with this he was headed back to the gutter. Drunk and alone. Not worthy of saving. If Veronica were here, she'd know what to say to him to keep him steady.

At last, they stepped on to the ship's deck. A horn blast interrupted all conversation. Scurrying to an empty spot at the railing, they stared back at dry land. After a long train ride from Ohio to New York, they were finally about to sail toward the hostile beast of Éire. Decades of hardship, most recently the death of his beloved Veronica, had pushed away most of the painful memories that haunted Patrick when he was a younger man. The letter in his pocket stirred them up again. He'd brought along more letters he'd stored in the attic. It was time to find out what had happened to Juniper.

Mardell turned toward him, one hand pinched against the brim of her hat to keep it from sailing off with the seagulls. Patrick leaned in to be heard over the clattering of the steam engine and the chatter of passengers. "England is plenty lush, too, darlin. 'Tis all that blasted rain. After having served in the army in both England and Northern Ireland, Leo failed to tell you that."

"I'm certain Ireland's beautiful, Dad."

Patrick scoffed. Sure and it was time to go, but he couldn't make himself praise the land where he'd been born and raised. What fond memories he'd once had were trampled to bits by the Great War and the aftermath. And the losses …

"Dad, come along. We'll find the dining hall and get tea."

Patrick could no longer hide his jittering hands, so he shoved his fingers deep into his pockets. Might as well fish for loose change to tip the ship's stewards. "Don't spend this entire trip coddling your old da, Mardell. I'm grand."

Mardell sucked her lip.

"Fine, we'll get tea."

Patrick nodded, not wanting to start off the trip with an argument, although that girl did worry too much about him. He'd once fussed over his mother that way. And then stopped, focusing on his own troubles. If he could instead focus on the happy times, like the one holiday he remembered in the Dublin Mountains, he might be able to relax.

"Penny for your thoughts." Mardell smiled at Patrick after

they had waved away New York at the launch and found seats in the ship's lounge.

"I'm afraid all this is bringing up recollections, silly thoughts about the place where I grew up. Things I haven't thought about in a long time."

Mardell's face brightened. "For instance?"

"The Dublin Mountains. Took a wee look-about when I was a lad."

Patrick glanced toward a portal to the cloud-covered sky beyond. "Not been to the country outside of Dublin since I was a lad."

"We should go, then." Mardell produced a travel guide from her tote, along with her ubiquitous notebook and pencil. That gal was a planner if there ever was one. "Perhaps I can add it to our agenda after we find ... well, as time allows."

The return booking was in three weeks, but easily changed, according to the travel agent. Plenty of ships going to New York from Ireland. Loads of Irish coming to America to escape poverty, Patrick imagined. It might not take that long to discover what had happened to Juniper, the baby Patrick had never known. The sister Mardell would never meet. Then again, folks in Ireland kept mum regarding private matters. They'd have to do their own digging, which might not be easy. Easy or not was anyone's guess.

Mardell went to order tea while other passengers milled about. Patrick gazed into the crowd in the dining room and thought about the life he'd quite willingly abandoned. In less than two weeks he'd be in Ireland. What would Róisín have thought of that if she were still alive?

His hand went instinctively to his trouser pocket. No, he hadn't brought the flask. He didn't need it. He hoped he didn't.

Patrick exhaled. So much time had passed that he could barely recall the street names in his old neighborhood. This adventure, as Mardell referred to it, might resurrect some ghosts better left be. He shook his head and studied his hands in his lap. No retreat. He'd have to steel himself and greet the monster head on even if old memories barreled in like a platoon of tanks in pursuit of the Hun.

And so they did.

CHAPTER 2

P addy
August 1917, Flanders, Belgium

The rain was relentless, as though the heavens tried to dissuade the military commanders and, when they would not listen, rained all the more on the poor, wretched soldiers. Paddy had at least one buddy to watch his back. He and Colin had gone to school together. Colin understood how desperately Paddy pined for Róisín, although, thank the good Lord, he didn't speak of it now. Thoughts of that fair lass had no place in this mire.

"Advance!" came the order.

The men collectively groaned and with much grunting departed their trench, rushing as best they could with boots sucked down by mud. Paddy took a great gulp of sulfur-laced air as he scuttled forth. Being out of the trenches felt like running naked in the cold. Nothing to be done about it but to hurry on. Colin was a few steps ahead. Within the deep darkness, only the faint, shadowy form of a man in front led Paddy on his way.

An explosion to the right. "Veer left! Left!" he called.

Colin went left and tripped over barbed wire, wiggling like a hooked fish. "Paddy! Paddy, I'm hit."

"You're not, lad. The wire." Paddy shoved at the twisted line with the butt of his rifle but to no avail. Finally, by stomping on one end, Paddy was able to stabilize the winding, metal tornado long enough for Colin to free himself.

Another shell hit just in front of them, sending mud into their faces. "Stay left!" Paddy shouted as he continued on.

But Colin wasn't in front of him. Paddy whirled around, shielding his eyes from flying debris. He scrambled backward about ten feet and felt the ground for a body. *Please, God, no.*

A groan came from a spot near a blasted-out tree stump. Paddy shouted into the grimy air. "Colin Reilly? Reilly!"

When Paddy got to him Colin convulsed. Holding on to his rifle with his left hand, Paddy wrapped his right arm around Colin's waist and hauled him to his feet. The two of them moved a few steps forward toward the voice of the sergeant who was still shouting an advance. Where was the lieutenant? Dead? Paddy's throat tightened. Would this be his own last day on earth?

Colin's knees buckled.

"Come on, man. On yer feet!" Paddy half dragged his friend who walked a bit, collapsed, stood and crept forward, and then collapsed again. By the grace of God they made it to the trench where the sergeant stood waving his arms.

Another shell. This time Paddy had to dig a gasping Colin out of the mud.

"Advance!" the sergeant cried again.

"*Eejit*," someone muttered.

The sergeant, a Brit, struggled to make his voice heard. He squeaked out another command. "Stay here and be buried in bloody mud. Off with you. Go!"

That was the man's last order. A bullet landed in the sergeant's neck. The man fell hard, rolling down the revetment and collapsing on the trench board where several men lifted him.

Quite literally bloody mud.

Paddy didn't wait to discover the sergeant's fate. Latching on to Colin's shirt with strength he didn't know he had, Paddy hauled them both out and into No Man's Land. They sank behind a pile of … bodies? Shells exploded all around until a blast sent them backward. When Paddy regained his wits, he looked for Colin and spotted him marching in the wrong direction. "This way, Reilly!"

Colin did not turn back.

"Where are you going?" When Paddy reached his buddy, pleading for him to follow, Colin did not respond. His eyes were glassy and unblinking. "What's wrong with you, man? C'mon."

No answer. Paddy looked around. No one seemed to notice them as the regiment redeployed. When he tried to grab Colin as he did before, his friend resisted, seeming to have gained the strength of Samson. The Huns were up ahead, but in No Man's Land they seemed to be everywhere. They had to keep going toward the next trench, but Colin was retreating, which put him in the open. Paddy couldn't leave him. Together they moved, exposed and going the wrong way at a snail's pace. By the love of God, Colin must regain his bearings in the black labyrinth before they went too far off course. Another shell blast knocked Paddy to his knees. He didn't remember anything else after that.

Electric lights glared from the ceiling. Paddy shaded his eyes with a bandaged hand. At first he couldn't imagine where he was. Perhaps he'd died in Flanders. Mercifully, he was no longer wet or grimy.

"How are we feeling today?" A nurse stood over him, shading most of the obtrusive light.

"Hospital?"

"Indeed. A field hospital. You were injured in battle. Do you remember?"

He nodded. His throat seemed to be lined with raw wool. "Reilly?"

"There's a chap called Reilly in the next bed. Colin Reilly. That who you mean?"

Paddy tried to sit up, but the nurse urged him back down on his bed. "There will be time for reunions later. You must rest now."

Hours floated in and out, it seemed, as Paddy began to regain his strength. The nurse assured him Reilly was still alive, just moved to another ward.

The next time Paddy saw his pal Colin was at an official inquiry. Their wounds had not been too serious, but apparently the commanders thought their actions in battle had been. Paddy and Colin were accused of retreating away from the enemy and away from their post. Defection. Treason. These were foreign words to Paddy. A preposterous miscarriage of justice.

The British military commander seated in the middle of a group of men at a table in front of the accused addressed Paddy. "Private Doyle, you say Private Reilly became disoriented during battle?"

"That is correct, sir."

The counsel conferred in whispers. Then the man in the middle continued. "It is the opinion of this inquiry board that you yourself had no such disorientation. You have correctly described the battle and the commands precisely, according to the sergeant."

The junior officer in charge that night sat on the far left of the inquiry board. He had obviously survived his injury, but having fallen into the trench, he couldn't possibly have known what Paddy and Colin were doing. He was, however, one of the Brits who had no use for Dublin lads. The lieutenant who should have been in charge that night had been the wiser man. He, unfortunately, had not survived the battle.

"You did not want to leave your fellow soldier?" the man in the center asked after an elongated pause in the questioning.

"That's right, sir," Paddy answered. They'd been instructed on how to behave in battle. No man should be left behind unless absolutely necessary.

Paddy glanced to Colin who was seated to his left. Colin only stared straight ahead. He made no defense for himself. They both hid trembling hands in their laps.

"Private Reilly was the one marching away from the battle," the man said.

"Not marching, no sir. He didn't know—"

The inquisitor interrupted. "We can see what happened here, son."

"But you don't understand!" Desperation filled Paddy's voice.

The commander asked Paddy to stand. He did so, grasping his hands behind his back. "Private Patrick Doyle, the board dismisses the charges against you. You are to be assigned back to your unit immediately after you complete your next order."

Paddy let out the breath he was holding. He had not been released so he stood in place as they commanded Colin to rise. The lad tried but knocked his knees against the table and slumped back to his chair. A solider was ordered to assist. Colin trembled all the more.

"Easy, lad," Paddy whispered.

"Private Colin Reilly, the board finds you guilty of attempted desertion and cowardice. You shall face the firing squad at dawn tomorrow."

"No—" Paddy pinched his lips shut at the stern look from the commander.

It wasn't until several hours later that Paddy learned what his next assignment would be before heading back to the front. He would be Solider Number Two in the squad assigned to fire upon Private Colin Reilly.

Later, when the order had been fulfilled, Paddy hurried to the bar in the village. His commander found him there too plastered to walk back to the barracks.

DECEMBER 1919, Dublin, Ireland

After four years at war, Dublin should have been Paddy's place of resurrection and a safe harbor for his heart. Three months after returning to Dublin City as a civilian, Paddy found himself huddled under one of the arches at the vegetable market on Mary's Lane, hiding not from Germans, but from Willie McGurdy and his son John, and perhaps others who'd like to see him expelled from the city. For a moment he'd believed he was back in the trenches without his mask—one of those dreaded hallucinations. However, he soon realized his surroundings, changed as they were by revolution.

"Da, let's go home, now," John called out from near the site where Paddy had previously marched with other war veterans in a victory parade. Paddy would not be tricked. He'd learned more at war than those McGurdys could ever fathom.

War! They were calling the one he'd fought in "The Great War." The only thing great about it, other than the number of men who died, was that it was now over.

Someone called down from a tenement window above his head. "*Cogadh na Saoirse!*"

War of Liberty? Were the Irish people wanting another Great War? During his absence the Irish had revolted against the British and nearly burned down Dublin in the process. Hundreds of innocents lost their lives. Sure, unintended casualties occur in armed conflicts. Paddy could not, would not, assign blame. The McGurdys were Irish Volunteers, as were most in this neighborhood, determined to see Ireland free, independent of Britain. Certainly there'd been discontent before he'd left, but such political banter had never been of concern to Paddy or his mother. The war in Europe was meant to bring a truce as the Irish sought a common goal of driving back a European invasion. Perhaps Ireland should be free, but at what cost? The British government had been heavy-handed in its response, executing so-called rebel leaders gradually over a period of time, so as to torture the survivors, it seemed. Paddy Doyle had been away when this started. The McGurdys had seen things he hadn't, so he didn't begrudge them their fury, although they were misdirecting it at him.

While he'd been tossing grenades at the Huns. Irish discontent had swelled. Some considered the war on the continent to be a British undertaking, not an Irish one. Or perhaps a Protestant enterprise rather than a Catholic one. Paddy Doyle, who had never been the good Catholic lad his mother had wished him to be, was now British in the eyes of many just for joining up, and he'd realized none of that until he came back.

The light in the window above was extinguished, and for all he knew the occupants were coming down for him. Paddy crept to an alley closer to where the McGurdys lay in wait. They would not expect that.

He heard an argument coming from his enemies' hidey-hole. "Leave the poor dosser alone, why don't ya? He's not worth it," Willie McGurdy shouted. "Not worth the spit to say his name!"

Silent minutes followed the insult, ticking by like hours.

Finally, a sound erupted like a herd of cats rushing down an alley.

"You'll be leaving my daughter alone," Willie called out from a distance. "Do you hear me, Paddy Doyle? She'll not marry you. Go along back to the continent, why don't you? Better that than face a beatin' from our John. Do you hear me, you dosser?"

Paddy kept as mum as the Our Lady statue over in White-friar Street Church.

A rock ricocheted off a tin sign above Patrick's head. John McCurdy's parting shot mimicked machine-gun fire. Paddy had to dig his fingernails into his palms to stay in the present and not be flung back to the Flanders trenches. Only child's play, Paddy told himself, waiting until footsteps faded. After counting to ten he stood, straightening his aching back. He'd never been captured by the Huns. One thing he'd learned was how to evade the enemy. Glancing in both directions, Paddy deemed it safe to continue on home.

Not long after, two boys about ten years of age approached, kicking a can along the darkened street. They shouldn't recognize him, being barely old enough for knickers when the war began. Paddy tipped his hat in greeting.

"You're the one they're talking about. Traitor!" one yelled, tossing a rock that hit Paddy in the knee.

"Hey!" He lunged forward, hoping to drive a wee bit of the fear of God into them.

They darted through an opening in a fence and scurried into one of the waste-strewn courts where dozens of families crowded together in a single house.

"Enemy of Éire!" they shouted in their wake.

Paddy had followed orders as a soldier and in doing so betrayed a soul. These lads had no idea. Their antics were proof that his decision to leave Ireland was best.

When he'd told his mother earlier that he was emigrating, Paddy had endured her weeping as long as he could and then left to go down to the pub. He might have had too many pints true, but drowning his sorrows seemed suitable. His mother had sisters and nieces to console her. Perhaps not family by blood. He seemed to remember they were his father's relations. Didn't matter. As packed together as everyone was, they all became family just the same. Like his wartime lads billeted in France.

Those women, living in such close quarters, would all hear of his plans. Some, no doubt, would disagree with his leaving, but their opinions came from ignorance. Sure, there were some who were suspicious of Paddy's mother because of her knowledge of old-time herbal cures, her countryside ways, but the Irish had been spoon-fed on superstition. Mam would be fine, perhaps all the better without a son around who had been stamped a traitor.

In three days, Paddy would be on his way to America. He needed to see Róisín. They'd planned to meet where they'd first kissed, in Stephen's Green under the bushes not far from the Harcourt Train Station. Róisín worked as a maid nearby so that was why they met in the park. He was nearly there.

The walkway lamps shadowed the edges of the sidewalk, but the smell of her cologne was all he needed to make his way.

"What took you so long?" Her black eyelashes brushed against ivory cheeks.

"I was … detained. Sorry." He gave her his best smile. "I've got a ticket to America and enough to buy one for you."

"Don't go, Paddy. I've not changed my mind. You might change yours, though."

"No reason to."

"There might be. You've a child to think of." She touched a hand to her belly.

He took a step backward, shock from the news slapping him with frigid fingers. His right hand gripped the objects in his pocket that had sustained him during wartime. They jarred loose from their tin cigarette container. He fingered the stem of juniper, a memento from a place he'd visited during the war. He'd brought one for Róisín, too, to bind them together. He hadn't been able to afford anything finer but she hadn't minded. Dropping the stem inside his pocket, his fingers grasped beads from a blessed rosary belonging to a condemned man. Pushing them aside, Paddy retrieved the most critical object, the steamer ticket. He waved it in the air.

Róisín took it from him and rubbed her thumb across the printing. "You shouldn't have done this. We might have found a way."

"I had to." He turned his glance toward the shadowy vegetation. There was no future for Paddy in Ireland and even this news could not change that.

"Don't leave me."

"'Tis not a matter of leaving you." Tears of frustration blurred his vision. "'Tis not because of you at all. I want you to come."

She was crying too. "I want you to stay."

"Know why I was late? Your father and brother chased me with a fireplace poker. Did you tell them you're with child?"

"I did not."

Paddy's pain turned to anger. "Your da believes I'm as wicked as those who killed your cousin Kent."

"You were in the army is why. Can't blame him for hating the British. They shot our cousin. Lots of people are mad as hatters. You weren't here. You didn't see."

Oh, but he saw loads. And he was as angry as anyone. They'd been over this before. She knew the scorn he'd endured in their neighborhood.

"Da will understand in time, Paddy. Don't go."

"What do you think Ireland's future looks like? After all this? Look around. Can you not see what is right in front of our eyes? Do you have any idea? 'Tis not just me I'm talking about. War is coming. The Irish against the Irish."

"I think I do know. 'Tis not as bad as all that." Her voice mellowed. "Did you know that women got the vote, well, older women. And Countess Markievicz was elected to Parliament. These are the winds of change. Now is not the time to leave."

"Nothing's changing for me. I know when I'm not wanted. There won't be any jobs for Paddy Doyle. Don't you know, I'll never be resting my head at night in peace again. Not in Ireland." Paddy held out his arms to plead. "'Tisn't too late, Róisín. We've got three days before the ship sails. Come with me. The baby need never know the misery of being Irish."

Surprise registered in her eyes. "What did you say? Have they made you British, then?"

He grasped her arm. "Of course not. Weren't we all fighting to keep what happened to Belgium from coming over here? We drove back the Kaiser, and many a lad died doing it. Many." His hands began to shake all of a sudden. He snatched a fag from his chest pocket, lit it, and puffed, hoping to wrangle the war images back to the depths of his consciousness.

They stood for a moment in silence. Heaven help him, she was beautiful. Oh, for the loveliness of Róisín McGurdy to erase all the ugliness he'd been living with. He needed her. But not here. Somewhere in America.

Paddy blew a puff of smoke. "And what thanks do we get when we return from fighting, do you think? Called conspirators, we are. Did you hear about Michael O'Brien? Come back from the war and was seen talking to the RIC. He wasn't one of them. Didn't even want to touch a gun after France. What was he supposed to do when the constables approached him? Run away and be shot in the back? Of *course* he was talking to them. The others, those wanting a free Ireland, cut down one of their own out in the road."

She shuddered, but it was the awful truth. He lifted her chin to make her look at him. "Listen, love. There's nothing here for me. Or a child of mine. Come with me. We'll have a fresh start, so we will." She didn't believe him. He could see it in her eyes. "I don't know how to make you understand."

Anger creased her forehead. "You speak of the Irish as though we are a cursed race. You might turn your back on them over some street violence, but I won't. Who's saying there wasn't cause that night? A cause that is greater than any one person."

"You've been going to those meetings."

Róisín shrugged. "What if I have? There is a free Ireland at stake. Everyone must do their part."

Propaganda. He'd had enough of it.

She blinked. *Did* she believe what she was saying? "I will always be Irish, me and my baby." Wrapping her arms across her waist, she whispered, almost sobbing. "If as you say, the fact that the child is yours will be detriment, then he or she will be a McGurdy." She smacked a hand over her mouth as though it pained her to say it, then wiggled free from his hold and darted out from beneath the trees.

He followed, calling after her. "You don't mean that. See here. I'll go on and then send for you. You'll see."

Beyond the sanctuary of shrubbery, he trailed her through the paved street and past the silent tram lines. A motorcar rambled past. The walk home from the park would be long now that the trams had stopped. "Wait, Róisín."

"I'm grand," she called out, not looking back at him.

"I'll take care of everything. There's work in America." He punched the air as he spoke. "We'll have a flat with a garden, good food, plenty of fuel for our fire. We'll want for nothing." He needed her, and not being able to make her understand burned a hole in his head. He'd fix this. Somehow.

The door of a motorcar across the street opened and a woman with a cropped hairstyle leaned out. "Róisín, come along. We'll give you a lift home."

Róisín paused, shot Paddy a sad look, and then crawled into the darkened interior.

Paddy didn't know who Róisín's companions were, but

they'd surely overheard. The McGurdy bullies would be hunting for him at daybreak.

As Paddy traipsed along broken pavers between ramshackle buildings, dodging puddles, he reflected on how he and Róisín had ended up in this predicament.

Paddy had been back in Dublin for several weeks now. The Armistice had occurred prior to his arrival, but the war was still alive in his mind. The thought of Róisín's shining dark hair smelling of roses in bloom had kept him sane through his enlistment. Touching her had made him believe there was still good in the world. There were women of ill repute in France, but they in no way substituted for Róisín. Only she could bring true comfort. What he and Róisín had done could not have been a sin, as the nuns at their school would say. He'd done other things, vile things, that were abhorrent sins against God and humanity. But he and Róisín? Their love was nothing of the sort.

Róisín would change her mind one day. They were good for each other. They'd met at school, the Catholic education of the Doyles. Paddy had tried to impress Róisín by signing up with the Royal Dublin Fusiliers. He imagined himself a fierce Celtic warrior like those in the epic tales the teacher forced them to read. And didn't Róisín adore him when he returned to her early in September. He should have been more careful, for Róisín's sake. Still, despite roots planted deep in Irish Republican soil, this baby, his baby, could be Róisín's escape. Paddy would bring them to America as soon as he had a home in order.

America would be far away enough, he reasoned. Paddy would never see France or Belgium again. Sailing away from the bloody continent that pulsed with pain and violence, he vowed to leave his nightmares amongst the white cross–splattered fields. He'd thought Ireland would heal him. Paddy had wanted his old life back, even the distinctly mundane labor at the pier loading carts for merchants. Because now he knew its worth. But he couldn't have it. Not in Ireland. In America, perhaps.

CHAPTER 3

1 *July 1920*

To: *Paddy Doyle, New York City*

Dear Paddy,

You may wish to know that your daughter Anna was born healthy on June 2. I call her Juniper and still cling to the stem you brought me. It's the least I can do. You are her father. There are fewer Irish police now because they've been replaced by murderous auxiliary troops. We keep far away from Dublin Castle so don't worry about us. We are both well. No, we are not coming to America. The cause rages on. I've taken in sewing from the abbey and the weavers send me work too. Please do not worry about money. Baby Juniper and I are grand.

Yours,

Róisín

. . .

RÓISÍN

1920, Dublin City, Ireland

Nothing terrified Róisín McGurdy more than having a baby depend on her. She wouldn't tell Paddy that, though. As much as she had wanted him to stay, it would be better this way. Her father would have killed him if she hadn't kept her pregnancy a secret until Paddy left. She'd tried to align herself with her father's politics, almost convinced herself that there was nothing more important. And then it happened. Her father erupted in a rage when he first noticed her expanding waistline. "When I find him, I'll bate the lard out of 'im. And then you'll take care of that." He pointed a shaky finger at her.

She'd refused to do anything to harm her baby and neither would she allow someone to take her and raise her. John had backed her up, insisting that he could help.

Then, just weeks before the babe's birth, Róisín had walked in on her father molesting a neighbor girl called Noreen. The child was only six years of age. She'd looked at Róisín, pleading with her. Her sozzled father was hardly aware of Róisín kicking him and snatching the girl out of the house. Róisín had said nothing as she marched the lassie back to her home and slammed the neighbor's door shut. The memory, once repressed, now seized her anew. Before Noreen, she'd thought he no longer messed with lassies because he no longer did it to her. But Willie McGurdy was at it again.

Róisín had sobbed as she marched home to pack up her things, determined to protect her child from him. She'd been running ever since, fearful that if he ever found her, he'd take out his anger on Juniper.

Weeks after the incident with Noreen, when Róisín had been living with friends, she realized more tough decisions had to be made. The girls who had allowed her and the baby to stay on their sofa were now becoming quite radical, taking too many risks. Juniper was so tiny and innocent. An intense desire to protect her baby demanded that Róisín move on. She'd take her to Paddy's mother. If things didn't work out there, they'd go somewhere else.

CHAPTER 4

Juniper
1950, County Down, Northern Ireland

Juniper recalled but few things from her early life. Shadowy memories, crumbs of stories that did not seem to connect in any satisfying manner. She believed they were important bits that could only be valuable when pieced together, but she hadn't been able to do that. Sitting alone near a smoldering peat fire that warmed so little of her soul, she tried to cobble together her wisps of memories ...

1923, Dublin City, Ireland

A heaviness as weighty as Granny's old book lay on Juniper's chest. When the arguing started she stopped thinking about how hard it was to breathe. There was a suitcase by the door.

Juniper coughed. Granny handed her one of her special embroidered hankies.

"Leaving at once," Mammy was saying.

Juniper sank to the floor, wishing for her bed. Granny was sick, too, and she needed the bed more. She was old.

Mammy snatched Juniper up off the floor and carried her outside.

"I want to go home," Juniper cried, believing that her mother would let her stay in the flat if she understood how much it hurt to breathe in the cold air.

"Hush, now."

People rushed by, going to work maybe, or to the market. "Are we going to the market, Mammy?"

Mammy didn't answer.

Juniper buried her head in her mother's shoulder. She'd missed her while she was away. Granny said Mammy might never come back, but she did.

"'Tis raining, Mammy. I don't feel good."

"I know, sweetie. We are going to a place where you'll get medicine and clean sheets. You'll be better in no time and then you and Mammy will find our own place to live."

That sounded nice. Maybe Granny would come too. Juniper fell asleep, lured by the rhythm of her mother's new cap-toe shoes thumping on the pavement.

When Juniper awoke, four nuns in black robes were looking down at her. Juniper was sitting in church, Mammy next to her, and the group of sisters hovering overhead.

"Poor dear," one said.

"In need of a hot bath," another put in.

"I want to go home," Juniper whispered to her mother.

"I will return for her," Mammy said.

The sisters shot each other silent glances.

"Be good," Mammy said, kissing the top of Juniper's head. Mammy's voice sounded weepy.

Juniper wanted to protest, but she was sleepy. So sleepy.

1928, Dublin City, Ireland

Juniper could barely recall having a mother. She remembered she had rested her head on her mother's shoulder. Juniper had been ill. She recalled the two of them crossing Dublin streets in the rain and the sound of her mother's footsteps. But that was all she remembered of coming to the convent. Sure, her mother Róisín had come to visit from time to time, but that was not what a mother was supposed to do "An orphan," the nuns said of Juniper. "No parents to speak of." She did have Granny, who wrote her letters. Unfortunately Granny wasn't able to come get Juniper. The nuns wouldn't listen to a woman. From what she could tell, only das and granddas collected girls from this place. Female relatives were not heeded.

The sisters repeated the same story over and over in whispers, but Juniper heard. "That McGurdy woman? A harlot, she is. Dressed in clothes not proper for a woman. Thinks women have a place in politics, she does. Never married, either. That woman calls our Anna 'Juniper.' What kind of name is that for a child? Disgraceful. That lass will never amount to anything."

Juniper's mother, as it happens, was "one of those modern females who only thought of themselves." That was what the sisters said, and Juniper wondered if it could be true. If Juniper could change her surname to Doyle, like her granny, she would.

Granny wasn't able to visit, the nuns said. She was poorly. She didn't sound feeble in her letters. Granny told her about the power of herbs and the way they could heal a person. When Juniper's coughing came on, the nuns sent her to the National Botanic Gardens to work, saying fresh air would do her good. Juniper knew the real reason was so that they could collect Juniper's wages, but she hadn't really minded. Juniper had been the happiest when she'd worked at the gardens, soaking in the scent of flowers as though her skin had been thirsty for it. Even now Juniper could remember the gleam of the glass houses and the suppleness of green grass under her feet. There were a few other children who also worked in the gardens. Together they laughed and sang songs. For the first time in Juniper's life she had felt free and happy.

And then, without warning, Juniper was sent back to the nuns and confined, allowed no contact with other children, by order of her uncle, the nuns had said. Uncle who? Men were always telling women and girls what to do, and whoever this uncle was, Juniper didn't like him. He wasn't helping her and neither was her mother. And her father who, when he had been alive, must not have wanted her. Hating them freed Juniper's spirit, unburdened her from the desire for a family.

Once Juniper had been very angry. The priest had thought an early confirmation might improve her moral character, but

Juniper had wanted nothing the church insisted upon. Still didn't.

For days she had refused to eat. When made to go to mass or to sing in the choir, she kept silent. The church reeked of old candle wax and bitter incense. She missed the sweet smell of flowers and grass, almost felt starved of it.

Recently she'd held out a glimmer of hope when she overheard Róisín's voice. "I've tried everything," her mother pleaded. "I wrote to him and begged but he won't come. I've told him she's gone to the country. I had hoped to take her there myself where the air is fresher, for her lungs, but there is no more money and I have … well, I have things I must do here in Dublin. I can't explain."

Juniper stopped cleaning the water closet and stuck her head out into the hall.

"What does your father have to say about this, Miss McGurdy? Since Juniper has no legitimate father, the child's grandfather should be her proper guardian. Might he fund her care in the country?"

Legitimate? Guardian? Juniper didn't know those words. Going to the country would be lovely. Juniper hoped, prayed, they would take her out of the city to where the flowers grew.

"I'm her mother. She is my responsibility. Tell me you will not contact my father. That was what I was promised when I brought her here. My father is not to know of any of this."

Juniper did not remember a grandfather nor any other family for that matter. They said she had an uncle, but Juniper didn't know. Only this woman who seemed sad when she visited and, of course, Granny.

"You are her mother who left this child with us to be raised, isn't that so?"

"Well, I had to. You don't understand."

There was some grunting and rustling of papers in Mother Superior's office. The sound of someone coming down the hall made Juniper dip back into the tiny room with her bucket and mop. As soon as the footsteps quieted, she dared another peek. All clear. She leaned forward to listen again.

"We have complied with John McGurdy's wishes as much as possible. The special assignment to the gardens that was later revoked. The things requested are quite unusual,"

"But paid for," Róisín said. "There are circumstances."

Mother Superior grunted. "We do appreciate the financial support, Miss McGurdy, and we've done our best to follow directions, puzzling as they may be. But the child is unruly. As she grows, she will need further isolation and discipline, I fear. Now, if she had a father, our decision might be different."

"She has an uncle. Please don't do this."

"A bachelor uncle with no means and an involvement with rowdiness on the streets? Hardly acceptable. Now listen, 'tis for her own good."

Róisín again. "You wouldn't say that about him if the money hadn't slowed down."

Mother Superior. "Support is appreciated but we are at the Lord's work here. We cannot be bribed."

What was this about? Juniper held her breath.

Róisín spoke again. "She can work in a manor house in the country, one of the large estates. She could send her wages to the abbey. The asylum at St. Giles is not the answer. I … I'm about to come into some funds. Please."

The sound of chair legs scraping against the tile floor. Then Mother Superior's voice again. "We are the ones with her every day, Miss McGurdy. You must trust our judgment. We are her guardians, after all. You abandoned her here."

"Wait just a minute. I did not—"

"Call it what you like. You sent her here and not just for an education but for custodial care. We now bear all the cost of her care and therefore we shall make all the decisions regarding her welfare. That, Miss McGurdy, is precisely what you were promised when you first came."

"I suppose it was," came Róisín's soft answer.

Mother Superior's voice turned sugary. "Should the day come, when she is older, she may become a productive member of society. A wife, perhaps, but that will only happen because we sheltered her here. Protection is what you asked for, was it not?"

"You couldn't possibly understand, Mother. I don't want my child to endure what I had to at her age. I am grateful, truly." There was a pause and then Róisín spoke again. "May I say goodbye?"

Juniper popped back into the washroom and twisted the faucet handle. Sticking her mop in the bucket, she scrubbed her hands at the sink.

"Anna, stop that. Come here, child." Mother Superior stood in the doorway, fists propped on her hips.

When Juniper saw Róisín, she was surprised to find she had been crying. Róisín dropped to her knees and put her hands on Juniper's arms, looking squarely into her eyes. "One day you'll understand, my daughter. You'll have a life better than mine." She sniffed. "Listen to the sisters, now. Do what they say."

Juniper made no response.

"Promise me. You'll be good, sweetie, now won't you?"

Clearly Róisín would not leave without a promise. Juniper nodded and a moment later Róisín was gone.

Róisín

1928, Northern Ireland

Sitting on the train to Belfast, Róisín covered her face with a handkerchief. Leaving Juniper this time was the most difficult thing she'd faced thus far. She should have gone to America with Paddy but he'd moved on to a new life without her long ago. She couldn't blame him. What kind of mother gets sent to jail? He had wanted to stay away from political strife while she'd run toward it, thinking she'd find a place to belong. She blew out a breath. If only she'd been wiser in her youth. It was beyond time for her to move on as well, without him but not without her daughter, not forever.

She wished she could live in Glasgleann Cottage. Paddy's mother, Delaney, had given Róisín legal possession of the place with the understanding that Juniper was to live there. Delaney's old aunt, a woman called Bet, lived there now, but Delaney was the recognized tenant because of the 1925 Land Act in Northern Ireland. This had allowed Delaney to own the property her family had lived on for generations.

They'd gathered there to work out a plan. Róisín's brother John had come too, trying to help them sort things out. They'd believed they'd come up with a suitable plan so John had returned to Dublin. Delaney went as well, to settle affairs before moving north. And then the woman got terribly ill, according to John. Róisín sighed. It was during that time Róisín had written to her brother, something she now regretted. John had sent a telegram alerting her to her father's rage. The panic she'd felt then returned to her body now in a rush. Where could they hide? Róisín took Juniper back to the nuns while she contemplated her next move. When she returned for a visit, the nuns had other ideas for Juniper, and there was nothing Róisín could say about it, not until she had the means to support and protect them both.

Róisín couldn't risk telling Delaney where she'd hidden Juniper. If Róisín were to tell Delaney that Juniper was at St. Giles now, the woman might be forced to reveal Juniper's location—or be followed should she rally from her sickness. She felt bad about misleading the woman, but when she thought about the child Willie McGurdy had molested, Róisín knew she couldn't take chances.

Perhaps they'd been foolish to think hiding Juniper at Glasgleann would have worked. Bet still lived there, of course, but she was in her eighties. While the old lady seemed content, the place was in shambles and needed a lot of fixing up. That would take time and Róisín couldn't risk waiting. That was why she'd agreed to Juniper's transfer to St. Giles. One day Juniper could live at Glasgleann. But not today.

It was time to toughen up and do what was right, even when it caused her pain. She must do all she could for her daughter. She unfolded the letter in her lap and reread it.

Dear Miss McGurdy,

We are pleased to offer you the position of cleaner at St. Mary's. The wee cottage in the back is yours to use so long as you need it. Please report to the priest as soon as possible.

Directions were included. There was something she needed to do first, however, to secure her daughter's future.

In the satchel at her side lay the carefully wrapped ancient gold artifact she'd dug out of the bog the day she'd gotten the telegram from John. She'd never before trusted there was a God, but the discovery's timing couldn't be anything other than a divine miracle. In Belfast she would be meeting with Mr. Murphy, the same solicitor who'd helped John obtain Róisín's freedom from prison back in Dublin. He'd guide her to sell it, and hopefully provide some financial advice as well. In the north of Ireland she could invest money, hide from her father, and provide for Juniper even though her daughter would know nothing about it all.

CHAPTER 5

P atrick
14 May 1950, on the Atlantic

Mardell stood beside Patrick as they stared out at the ocean from the ship's deck. After a few moments they found shelter inside. Patrick had shown Mardell the letter where Róisín had announced Juniper's birth. They talked about it long enough to make them both sad.

"Were you in love with Róisín, Dad?"

Patrick was taken aback by the question. "Young love, I suppose. Nothing like your mother."

"Still, it must have been hard leaving her."

"Many things were difficult, but I suppose after going through the war, my heart was a bit callous. Hers, too, to be honest."

Waves beat against the ship. They listened silently for a few moments. So much time had gone by that he couldn't recall the sound of Róisín's voice. He worried it might be the same one day with Veronica.

"Tell me about when you first came to America, Dad. Was it on a ship like this?"

"It was third class, and not very pleasant. Altogether, I was happy to go."

"You started off alone. Was that hard?"

Harder than she could ever fathom. He began the story because she had asked. It was a part of his life he had been happy to leave behind.

"I wanted to get as far from France as I could. I might have gone to Australia, I suppose, but the advertisements I saw in Dublin were hawking America, so that's where I made up my mind to go." He chuckled. "Good thing I did, in the end, because I met your mother and you were born."

"Yes." Mardell smiled, looking more like Veronica every day.

Patrick glanced around the dining room. Clusters of folks enjoying coffee and tea, but nearly empty. Now was as good a time as any. So he began, careful not to muck up the conversation with too many details.

"I arrived in Manhattan, but finding a job was tough. I did all right, rooming with some others and getting work here and there. You might not know this, but immigrants, and especially it seemed to me Irish immigrants, were not looked upon fondly. 'No Irish Need Apply,' signs said. I was used to being poor and hungry, having survived the war and all. So, one day I accepted an arrand. I was to deliver lunch to a big bank up on Wall Street." Patrick sipped his coffee. A long time ago, it was. He could tell this story.

"You did your best," Mardell offered.

Until then. "'Twas how I got this scar."

She reached out and touched his face.

He put his hand over hers. "Wall Street bombing, 1920. No one knows who planted the bomb, not then, not now. Anarchists, some say. Ah, politics. Got no use for it."

"What happened?"

"I got knocked about like a lot of folks. Trouble was, unlike most of them, I had experienced bombing in the war, up close."

"Oh, Dad. You were shell shocked."

"Battle fatigue or whatever, yeah. When I found myself with the Red Cross or whoever it was come to help, I thought I was in an army hospital. I really did, for a while."

"Oh, that's awful."

"Don't pity me. It all worked out fine, didn't it? They bandaged me up." The memory caused his scar to throb.

"Was that what made you leave New York?"

"Suppose it was. Too crowded. I headed for the Jersey Shore." The real reason, of course, was that his roommates told him how much money could be made rumrunning. Two days after the bombing Paddy had shoved his extra set of clothes into a knapsack and placed his cigarette tin on top. He could still hear the sound of the rosary beads rattling inside. The sprig of juniper by this time had turned to dust. His old life had slipped away. He didn't know if he had realized it then, but Róisín was not coming.

A little over a month later Paddy had socked away nearly a hundred dollars. Both his cash and his cigarette tin of treasures were stuffed under a floorboard beneath his bed. Later he got his own rumrunning boat. He'd thought he was big stuff. He wasn't. He went on with the story.

When he'd finished, Mardell stared at him with wide green eyes. He'd told her just enough to rattle her, hitting the highlights without too much grimy detail, he hoped. Now she knew about his time in the boarding house, the blast he'd survived, the time he'd almost been arrested for transporting illegal alcohol.

"How awful. Dad, I don't blame you for taking that kind of work after that, rumrunning or whatever it was called. But it was dangerous. Thank goodness you survived it."

They went for a stroll on the deck. Patrick let the ocean breeze lift its cool fingers through his hair. "Aye, quite."

Mardell's expression fell, the look of lost innocence. Patrick hated that he caused that, but she had wanted to know. "Don't forget, darlin. You are the best of me. All these things brought me eventually to Veronica and then to you."

She nodded and squeezed his hand.

"I've got another old letter for you to read, if you're up to it."

AFTER DINNER THAT EVENING, Patrick and Mardell pored over another letter.

29 November 1920

To: Paddy Doyle, New Jersey

Dear Paddy,

You may have heard about Bloody Sunday. So many people out enjoying a match who cannot go home now. How our city has become a war zone is disgraceful. Assassins and informers are everywhere. Don't worry. We were nowhere near Croke Park as we'd had warning. I tell you that so you will know that we know how to be safe.

I'm worried about the money you sent. Don't send any more. You must not take such risks for the sake of riches. We are doing fine without it. I'm sorry, but not even a lot of money will convince me to go to America. I just can't risk it. Not at any price.

Yours,

Róisín

"She didn't want your money?" Mardell let the letter fall to the bed in Patrick's cabin where they'd gone to read more letters.

"Thought it was ill-gotten gains, I suppose. Don't forget, we were young and foolish."

Mardell nodded, staring down at the paper. "What happened then?"

"I'm not proud of a lot of it. Maybe there's something to be learned, though. Life lessons."

"I'm not judging you, Dad."

He placed a kiss on the top of her head. "Off to bed now. We'll talk more tomorrow."

She left him alone with his memories.

And he did have them. He sighed, settling back, listening to the waves outside.

It was late October of '20 when things had really started to sour. He remembered that fancy hotel he'd tried to get business from. It had almost worked. Patrick had waited in the dining room to speak to the owner, wondering how one sold bootleg liquor to Americans. How green he'd been! He chuckled at the memory.

"The evening meal will be served from six to seven o'clock. The chef has two entrées: émincé of chicken and lamb chop with bacon. I can inquire about the vegetables if you would like, sir."

"Not necessary. Thank you," Paddy had answered.

The waiter dipped his head slightly. "Shall I bring salted nuts with your coffee, sir?"

Paddy wasn't sure how much a handful of nuts would cost in a place like this. He'd only come to drum up some business with the owner. "No, thank you."

The waiter raised one brow but didn't move toward the kitchen. Paddy cleared his throat. "Just coffee and a roll. With butter." Thinking he might need to explain himself he added, "I'm waiting to see Mr. Walstad, Mr. Arthur Walstad."

"Very good, sir." At last, the waiter departed.

Now he realized salted nuts had been code for liquor. They'd brought him some anyway. Awful stuff. The scene might have been amusing if he didn't know how it had turned out.

Later, after he'd met with the club's owner, Paddy had rushed outside just before losing the contents of his stomach. What was he—a lad from the streets of Dublin—doing talking with a rich Yank about bootlegging?

After he'd thought he'd hit the jackpot, he'd received a letter from Róisín that he hadn't saved, although the last few sentences were burned in his memory: *I can't love you. Do not think of Juniper as your child. It will be easier for you that way.*

No one was a bigger eejit than him for believing he could win Róisín's affections. He had crumpled the paper into his jacket pocket and gone outside where a fire burned in a refuse barrel and tossed it in.

So had gone the dreams of his youth. Paddy was cheated in a bootleg deal and his savings stolen. The only bright spot from that period in his life had been a brief encounter with a dark-skinned man called Syd who had befriended him. After Paddy had been bamboozled, Syd paid him a visit. This was a memory to keep because someone had finally tried to help him.

Syd had retrieved a folded paper from his breast pocket and handed it to Paddy. "You know that fella from Ireland, Éamon de Valera? Been traveling the country for the cause of Irish freedom?"

"I've heard of him."

"Some of my people from down south just arrived up here in the city. They showed me this so I kept it, hoping to show it to you."

Paddy unfolded the newsprint.

Syd tapped his index finger on the paper. "Birmingham, Alabama. Worse place for de Valera to go, um-hum. Know where that is?"

"I do not." Paddy had only seen New York City and the shoreline of New Jersey.

"Deeper south than where I come from. Some of those white men ain't never gotten over Lincoln defeating them. Preaching equal rights there? Hoping for some support? Not sure if that Irish-American man, or whatever he is, got the help he was lookin' for, but I can't imagine he did down there, no sir, I can't."

Paddy peered at the article. It contained a bulleted list by a Dr. O. T. Dozier. He glanced quickly through the items. The piece accused Catholics like de Valera of outrageous things, from the Pope seeking to control American politics to the stockpiling of ammunition in church buildings. "What the devil is this?"

Syd had shrugged. Patrick now realized the man had brought a warning: *Get out while you can, because hatred of immigrants and folks like Syd is rampant.*

Syd had spiraled a finger beside his temple. "Lucky that Irish fella made it out alive."

One thing the old Paddy knew from what he'd heard about de Valera was that the man was a Harry Houdini sort. He managed to get out of jams, but Paddy hadn't been so lucky. Not back then.

Patrick still remembered Syd's final words to him. "This country gotta decide what it's gonna be, Paddy. Continue with all this hate? Or move to something more fair." He wagged his head again, a mannerism Syd repeated often. "Got a feeling America won't decide that for a long time. I mean, my people ain't been real slaves for almost sixty years. How long it gonna take?"

"I don't know, Syd. Truly I don't."

Syd chuckled again, and Paddy had watched him lumber away, passing under the gaslights. Another thing his encounter with this man had clarified for Paddy was that other ethnic groups were discriminated against in America. The former enslaved had it worse, he believed. What a peculiar brotherhood he and Syd belonged to.

Now, as Patrick switched off the cabin light, he whispered his thoughts. *I hope life treated you well, my friend.*

CHAPTER 6

J uniper

1928, St. Giles Asylum, County Monaghan, Ireland

When Juniper stepped out of the carriage, she turned away from the large building. She didn't care where she'd sleep. What delighted her was the outside. Grass, emerald green. Trees tall and majestic. And beds of flowers with sunny-yellow faces. Her mother may not have wanted her to come here, but Juniper knew this place would be better. It already smelled better.

The nun escorting her turned her shoulders until Juniper was forced to look at the home. Gazing upward, Juniper couldn't see the top of the massive white building. This new school was much larger than her old one. Sister Frances nudged her forward. "Come along, child." She tugged on Juniper's arm and the two of them approached one of the wooden doors.

"Where are the sisters?"

Juniper was shushed. She bit her lip. As they approached the threshold, Juniper could stay silent no longer. "I don't want to," she complained, firmly planting her feet on the gravel. "I want to stay out here."

Sister Frances yanked on her ear. "Doesn't matter what you want."

They marched through a hall and then entered a room where several adults wearing white coats stood together like huddled sheep.

"Sit there," a man in round spectacles said.

Juniper scooted onto a chair. No one else sat. "Where's my mother?"

A few days earlier Juniper had been with her mother and the rest of her family at Aunt Bet's cottage. They'd told her it had been a respite, whatever that meant. She had understood that it would be only for a few days and then she'd return to the abbey. No one had told her she'd be moving somewhere else until today. Juniper remembered that at the respite Uncle John and her mother had argued. He apparently was the "Uncle Who" that Mammy had spoken about to the nuns. The best part about the respite was that Granny had been there, Juniper's long-lost father's mother. Juniper didn't know the rest of those people well, her supposed family, but Granny had been around for as long as she could remember. Juniper liked Granny the best and wished to stay with Granny out in the country. The old aunt had flowers and chickens. But as Sister Frances had told her, it didn't matter what she wanted. Those adults, her family, were probably still there without Juniper, and so that old familiar cloud of anger had returned, resting over her with a heaviness that was hard to ignore.

No one answered her question. They put their heads together and made marks on papers attached to boards. Sister Frances shuffled back out the door. Juniper knew she was going to be leaving her at this place, but the woman didn't even say goodbye. People were always leaving Juniper. They must not like her.

The group of adults who now whispered about her, mentioned something about tuition. Juniper didn't know what that meant. Someone mentioned a name she recognized, John McGurdy. That could be the man called Uncle John who had been at Aunt Bet's cottage with them. Would he come get her? She glanced around but the office door had been closed and no uncle was there.

One of the men approached her. "Up with ye, Anna."

She stood and tried to make herself as tall as possible. "I am Juniper."

A slap knocked her to the floor. She looked up at the man who had hit her, more surprised than hurt.

"You will not talk unless directed to. No pet names here. You are Anna."

She didn't care what they called her, not really. The next opportunity she got she'd spit in that man's tea. She was led to a tiny room and told to stay put. They wouldn't let her go outside. There was no window in that room. Ripping a blank page from the back of the Bible they'd given her, Juniper wrote a letter to the father who would never rescue her. With her pencil she wrote "why" several times as hot, miserable tears streaked down her cheeks. When she stopped writing she felt a bit better. Stuffing the letter that could never be sent because her father no longer existed back into the Bible, Juniper made a vow. She would bide her time in this place because they let children out when they were old enough. The despicable man in the white coat had told her that. Then Juniper would live with Granny and never count on anyone else but her. *If you decide not to like someone, they can't hurt you.*

TWO WEEKS PASSED, according to the calendar pasted on the wall in the gardener's shed, and no one had come for her. She'd learned she was living in an asylum called St. Giles, where difficult children were sent. Wanting to be called the name her mother and Granny called her had earned her a slap from a worker and that was probably why she'd been considered unruly.

At least there was some time allowed outside, and Juniper treasured every moment, even if it involved loads of digging and weed-pulling for Mr. Mackenzie, the asylum's gardener. You weren't allowed to be outdoors just for leisure, but Juniper didn't mind the work. The sunny flowers still smiled at her.

It didn't take long for Juniper to accept without complaining the rough treatment the white-coated people dished out. By being agreeable, she earned her time outside to assist the gardener. Juniper would endure anything for that reward. He'd taught her that plants held special oils that you could use to soothe rough skin. Some smelled heavenly. He put them in a special stone bowl and ground them into powder. The tools were called mortar and pestle. It all seemed like a miracle to her.

The white-haired gardener's kind eyes flashed when he looked at her. No harsh words ever passed through his wrinkled lips. In fact, most times they worked without speaking. Maybe Mr. Mackenzie feared those white coats every bit as much as Juniper did.

Digging her hands into soil the color of milk-less tea helped to wipe away memories of scalding baths, freezing baths, and going to bed hungry. Juniper began to think of the plants she tended as wee fairies able to grant wishes. She made up stories that she kept to herself and tried to forget Róisín, Uncle John, Aunt Bet, her dead father, and even Granny, whom she'd thought loved her but had never come for her. That probably hadn't been Granny's fault. She couldn't help that she was old. Old people couldn't care for children. She glanced to watch Mr. Mackenzie sorting through tools. When you are old you can care for flowers but not children.

Juniper worked at forgetting the sisters at the abbey and the father she supposedly once had. Erasing all memories of the rest, those who were supposed to care for her but hadn't, emptied room for others to take their place, even if those others were creations from Juniper's imagination, fairies who lived inside the flowers and in holes in the trees.

On her thirteenth birthday one of the kinder doctors gave Juniper some ginger candies. She shared them with Mr. Mackenzie.

"You'll get out of here one day," the gardener told her, handing her a rose he'd clipped from a bush.

"Where would I go?" She drew in the yellow smell of it. She'd have to toss it away before she went inside so she drank in all its luminous smell while she could.

"There's a whole world out there, child. You'll find your place. You are too smart for this way of life. You'll find another way of getting on. Or a way will find you."

She didn't know what he meant and it didn't matter. She had her plants and that made her happy. They weren't hers really, but the plants didn't know.

Later that night she overheard some of the doctors who were working late in their offices. Juniper had been sent to empty wastepaper baskets and tidy the tea service. They must have forgotten she was there. While wiping spilled cream from the edges of a tabletop, Juniper heard her name.

"Anna McGurdy has five more years until release. See that she earns her keep. The gardens have never looked better. Anyone who doesn't know her name isn't to be told, you understand?"

Release? Juniper counted on her fingers. They'd let her go when she was eighteen. She didn't care if anyone called her by name or not. Mr. Mackenzie had been right. A way had found her.

CHAPTER 7

1 *7 April 1922*

To: *Paddy Doyle, New Jersey*

Dear Paddy,

Have you heard? A treaty was signed. Not everyone is happy about it. The way I see it, it's better to end the bloodshed but I'd never tell my father that. I've learned it's best not to argue with him. There was shouting as they debated the treaty in the Dáil. Confusion lives on the streets of Dublin like never before. I know I told you not to send money, but now I'm ever so grateful you have sent a bit to enable me to continue these sacred duties. The Cumann na mBan voted to oppose the treaty. That made my father happy.

I deliver messages and other things I won't describe here, but it's thrilling to be a part of something so vital. But please, stop asking. I cannot leave Ireland.

Truly,

Róisín

PATRICK

15 May 1950, on the Atlantic

The next day they passed the time reading and playing cards. After supper in one of the ship's lounges they spoke again about his memories of Róisín.

"That's the essence of what that letter said." Patrick wished he hadn't remembered it as well as he had.

Mardell sighed. "The way she talked about her father, do you think she might have been afraid to disagree with him politically?"

"I never thought about that, but maybe. In those days wives and daughters did what their men told them to. Not saying it was right, but that's how it was usually done. My mother was a bit independent, had to be as a single mother, I suppose. Róisín too. Old McGurdy would not have tolerated that."

Mardell crossed the room and paused at the door. "Let's go listen to the band. On the way tell me more about those early years in New Jersey."

Patrick stood, rubbing his achy knees. He could use a stroll. "Lead the way."

"What were those Irish words you mentioned again?"

"The Women's Council. When Róisín mentioned that, I remember wondering what on earth those young gals had been thinking. The mighty British military was nothing to mess with. The British government had thrown those women some crumbs. They should have taken them and let well enough alone. But some didn't. I don't think Róisín did. I've never understood how her father had so much control over her. I knew her to be self-determinate."

They climbed metal steps to the ballroom. A jazz quartet was scheduled to play.

"Did you meet any gangsters in Jersey, Dad?"

"Ha! Nothing glamorous. Not like the movies, honey. I ran into some bad fellas for sure. I was naïve, and it got me thrown in jail for a day. I was lucky, though. The false charges they tried to pin on me didn't stick."

"Golly!"

When they reached the door to the ballroom, Mardell turned to look at him. She was going to ask. He'd do his best to sanitize the past.

"What kind of charges?"

"I wandered into a KKK meeting."

"What? How does that happen?"

This was going to take some time. "Let's go in and get a table in the back."

They settled into seats as the musicians took the stage. Patrick whispered. "In the '20s the KKK was building in the north. They were anti-Catholic, anti-immigrant. If you ask me, anti-America. And it was Prohibition. There were cafes." He made a quotation mark gesture. "They were fronts for selling bootleg alcohol to the public. I thought I'd wandered into one of those joints, but I was wrong. Once I opened my mouth, and they knew I was Irish, I was in trouble. Something happened there to cause a death and they told the cops I had done it."

"Something? What?"

Patrick drew in a breath. "I think a woman miscarried a baby. I don't know, really. I wasn't part of it. They tried to pin it on me."

"How awful!"

"Indeed." As the band began to play, he nodded toward them. Time for music. The memories of that night flooded in.

1922, New Jersey

"Blasted mick!" someone cried. The odor of alcohol was missing. How had Paddy not noticed?

He smelled his own blood and spit as he was knocked to the floor. He landed on the edge of a broken coffee cup that cut him near the wound on his cheek from the Wall Street blast. His face stung as he tried to shake it off and regain his balance.

Some brute hauled him up to his feet. "We've a place for you."

Paddy tried to take a swing at him but missed. Two other men grabbed his arms and dragged him through the parted assembly. A uniformed policeman mocked him. Apparently the cops overlooked more than just rumrunning in this town.

This was what Syd had tried to warn Paddy about. A meeting of bullies and hadn't he stumbled right into it?

Someone came up from behind and flung a heavy rope around Paddy's neck, tugging until Paddy feared his neck would break. At last the man let up but the burn remained and brought Paddy to tears. Blinking, he tried to focus on what was happening and how he might escape.

Sometime later Paddy woke in a dark room. Had this been a dream? Pulling himself to a seated position, he realized he was propped in a corner, wedged in by a few wooden chairs that were weighed down by the men sitting on them. Straining his eyes, he made out cloaked forms near the front of the room. The only light came from battery-operated torches. The figures seemed to be holding the beam over papers as they read. Nothing they said made sense. Paddy's injured face throbbed. As he adjusted to the dim light, he saw the men were wearing pointy hoods. This indeed was the Klan Syd had warned about.

The chairs in front of him suddenly scooted back. A hand jerked Paddy to his feet, sending shards of needling pain to his temples. A burly blue-coated police officer lugged Paddy away from the dark room and out into the alley.

"Paddy Doyle, you're under arrest for murder."

"What? I did nothing. I was attacked."

"That's not how the witnesses described it, son. Come along."

Paddy was shoved into the back of a shiny black police truck. "But who was murdered?"

The officer placed his fat hand against Paddy's bleeding cheek and gave him a shove into the truck bed. "A baby, that's who. You've killed it, so I understand."

"That's ridiculous. I just came in here by mistake. I'm being set up."

The officer scoffed. "Did you see a dead baby in there?"

"I did."

The cop sighed. "So did I."

"Is the woman all right?"

"She went along home. Funny you being worried about that now."

Moments later Patrick felt the vehicle shift unsteadily as the officer climbed behind the wheel. The man pounded on the window between them and shouted, "Nothing worse, you coward. Got three kids of my own. You can tell it to the judge, mick, and I hope you rot in hell."

PATRICK PINCHED his eyes shut as the drummer went into a solo. A botched abortion, probably. The thugs had locked him in another room with a barely conscious woman. He'd wanted to help, but what could he do but pat the woman's hand?

TWO DAYS LATER, as Paddy sat in a jail cell wondering if he'd be sent to prison for something he didn't do, he accepted paper and pen from a visiting clergyman and wrote a letter to his mother.

22 May 1922

To: Delaney Doyle, Stirrup Lane, Dublin

Dear Mother,

Please accept my apology for not being a good son. I didn't write for so long because I was hoping to have something to tell you to make you proud. Instead, I'm writing to you from a jail cell, but I didn't do this thing they accuse me of, Mam. If I don't make it out of here alive, know that I love you and please, try to send a word to the lass Juniper. Try to make her understand, just as soon as she's old enough, that I always wanted her, that there were circumstances. Well, Mam, they are waiting for this letter and I've no more to say.

Your devoted son,

Patrick

Watching the visitor walk away with Paddy's letter made him ache as though bludgeoned by a sledgehammer. He was a failure for all his hard work. He hadn't saved Colin in Flanders. He hadn't delivered Róisín out of Dublin, and now his daughter would grow up thinking he hadn't wanted her. Paddy sprang to his feet. "Wait! Bring that back!" He would regret allowing that letter to confirm Juniper's eventual view of him as a drifter and lowlife. Paddy shook the bars on his cell with all his strength. "Come back. Do you hear me? Come back here!"

The sound of the key in the lock. For nearly his whole life no one had heard him. This was no different.

THE CROWD WAS APPLAUDING the band, jarring Patrick from his thoughts, things that he could never tell Mardell. He'd gotten out of that pinch anyway. They didn't shoot criminals without a trial in America. He'd faced the judge with no one to advocate for him and it had turned out all right. Well, eventually.

When the band finished their last number, Patrick rose to escort his daughter back to their quarters.

"About that business in New Jersey. Is that when you met Mom?"

"A few years after that. When they released me, I went back to my boarding house to discover they'd rented out my room and my belongings were gone."

"Wow. Did you get it back?"

"No chance of that. I was an alley bum for a time, I suppose you could say."

Mardell looped her arm in his. "You had a difficult time."

He sure had. Some of it had been his fault.

"May I see the rest of the letters?"

"Tomorrow. I need to go through them with you. Explain things that won't make sense."

"Oh, OK."

Before he went to bed that night, he thought about the time he'd been robbed. At the boarding house he'd found his money bag was gone, along with all his clothes. But someone, the other men, the landlady, had left the stationary box with the letters he'd saved. He also recovered the cigarette tin containing Colin's rosary and the dusty remains of the juniper twig.

An immigrant had no recourse. He'd been beaten, falsely imprisoned, robbed, and there was nothing he could do about it.

At the time he'd believed there was nothing for him in America, as there hadn't been in Ireland. His only option had been sleeping on the streets and eating at charity soup kitchens. Paddy could not change where he'd come from. He couldn't make a better life. Hope fled like an uncaged bird, but perhaps he'd never really possessed it. He'd believed then that Róisín and Juniper were a dream best forgotten.

CHAPTER 8

J uniper

1933, St. Giles, County Monaghan, Ireland

As encouraging as it was to know she was to be released one day, Juniper was hesitant to allow hope into her dreams. Her imagination kept her going. Naming the plants. Watching the birds build nests and making up conversations in a bird language only she understood.

The wild animals had families. The cats living under the gardener's shed cared for their babies. Juniper tried to pretend she didn't need a family, but she found herself thinking about them anyway, especially the mysterious father who Róisín told her had died in America.

While she was thinking about these things, the bell rang out. She had to go inside. Kicking a pebble all the way to the front door, Juniper paused, smoothed down her brown dress, and stepped carefully inside. *Make no more noise than necessary.*

After washing, she sat obediently at the long meal table with the others, keeping her hands and her gaze on her lap.

"Anna, mail."

She glanced up at the attendant who handed her an envelope bearing Granny's handwriting. Unable to hide her smile, she thanked him. They were permitted to read their mail so long as the food had not been brought out yet. Juniper opened the letter as quickly as she could.

Dearest Juniper,

She skipped over the pleasant greetings because the soup cart had come out of the kitchen. She'd read it more thoroughly later.

I didn't know your mother had told you your father died in America. He did not. When he came home from the war in Europe, he found people were cruel to him because he'd been a soldier. I received a few letters from him in America, not many, but a few, so I know he was alive at least until a couple of years ago. I've no reason to believe he's passed, darlin.

She gasped without thinking.

"Quiet!" the attendant barked.

Juniper swallowed hard and placed the letter in her lap as she continued to read through hot tears. There was little else. Just that her father wasn't dead. Her mother had lied about that. Juniper's heart began to race. She pounded her chest with her fist, trying to calm it.

The attendant was at her side. "Anna? Are you ill? Get up at once!"

Juniper sprung to her feet and ran to the toilet, crumpling the paper in her hand as she went.

He's not dead. Maybe he'll come. He might still come for me.

Another voice argued in her head. *He hasn't come all this time. He won't!*

"But he could still!" she said out loud.

"What are you on about? Who could still do what?" the girl in the next stall asked.

Juniper was dying to tell someone. "My father! He's not dead like I thought. He could still come get me. He's in America, but he could."

They met at the sink. The freckled-faced girl scowled at her. "No, he won't. Parents put us in here to get rid of us. Don't fool yourself, lass."

Hot tears streaked down Juniper's cheeks. She splashed her face with frigid water after the girl left. Juniper had to make herself presentable or they'd never let her go free.

DAYS WENT BY. Then weeks. The shock of reading that letter continued to pierce Juniper's heart. Her father was alive! She had another parent who could rescue her. Every time a motorcar pulled up in front of the asylum, she hoped he'd step out, run up the steps, and take her into his arms. The visitors were always someone else, never Paddy. Never.

Letters still arrived from Granny and once her anger dissipated, Juniper wrote back to ask why Paddy had been such an awful person. Granny's reply was to ask where she'd gotten that impression.

Only an awful person didn't want his child and now she knew he'd gone to America to get away. Granny said Paddy had moved and they'd lost touch. It might be that he'd died in America, but he had wanted her, Granny insisted. It was Róisín who kept them apart. Granny said she'd have come herself if she could. One day she hoped to be well enough. Juniper didn't blame Granny. She couldn't help being sick.

On days when Juniper wasn't feeling melancholy, she liked to suppose that the man who gave her life had been a prince misjudged. This was her story to create however she wished. She imagined Paddy Doyle to be someone like Mr. Mackenzie. On other days, though, she struggled to push away the truth. Paddy didn't care enough to return to Ireland.

The nighttime visions were another matter. She had no control over those, and while lying on a thin straw mattress on her metal bed, sleep heavy in her head, Juniper's mind led her to her uncharted lands.

One particularly disturbing dream involved a baby that died. With all the miserable groaning and wailing drifting through the halls at St. Giles and through the floor grate under her bed, it was no wonder she had this recurring dream. No baby had died at St. Giles or in the abbey she lived in previously. None that she knew of. Surely once she was released from this haunting place those dreams would cease. Granny walked the halls in Juniper's dreams, holding her hand and clicking her tongue over how sad it all was. Juniper missed Granny. That had to be the reason for that dream.

Another dream visited from time to time. Juniper clearly pictured Róisín standing in the middle of a bog with a troubled look on her face. Juniper saw herself again walking with Granny. Juniper dropped Granny's hand, racing up to the edge of the bog.

"Stay there!" Róisín shouted at her. "'Tisn't safe."

Her mother stood rigid holding a *sleán*, a tool farmers used in the soggy soil bordering St. Giles. Mr. Mackenzie had explained how they worked.

"Go on, now," Róisín called to Juniper. "Back to the wagon with you."

While her mother hadn't sounded angry, her gray eyes appeared dark as she cast her a threatening look. Róisín's voice floated over blocks of turf, gentle and cajoling. So odd it was. Juniper couldn't make sense of the disparity, not even in her dreams. Well, dreams were odd like that, but maybe this was an actual memory. Her mother had kept her father from her. She'd probably hidden other things as well.

CHAPTER 9

P atrick

16 May 1950, on the Atlantic

Patrick had taken a nap while Mardell socialized in the afternoon. Later, he found her lounging in a deck chair. "Feeling better, Dad?"

"A bit. Came down to look for the newspaper." He caught a whiff of sautéed onions. "Might it be time to eat?"

She glanced down at her wristwatch. "So it is. Shall we head to the dining hall?"

They conversed over a bountiful meal of pot roast, spuds, and brussels sprouts. Patrick picked at his roasted potatoes, remembering how much better his mother's were.

"Dad, why didn't you tell me about the years you lived in New Jersey before now?" She wrote something in her notebook. "You had a rough time and you couldn't find a decent job. There's no shame in that."

He shrugged. "Not worth talking about, other than meeting your mother. She saved me."

"Saved you from that life? How did she do that?"

"From myself, Mardell. The love of a woman, a good woman, can rescue a man, set him on the right path."

She chewed and seemed to formulate her next question.

Patrick had brought along the letters. She was eager to get through them and write down whatever clues they might contain. He didn't think she'd find much.

"Dad, why wouldn't Róisín take the money you wanted to send her for Juniper? She accepted some after first refusing, and after that it seems she didn't want money. I don't understand. She had a child to take care of."

Patrick drew in a deep breath and set his fork and knife down next to his white china plate. "Aye, she took a bit at first, but then later she didn't think my earnings had been obtained properly." He made a little mocking motion with his head. "Sure and she may have been right by the time Prohibition hit."

Mardell nodded.

"I left Ireland around Christmas and arrived just after the New Year. I didn't know much about things, seeing I was just off the boat. Many tough years followed, as I've told ya. Once the stock market collapsed, and jobs were even tougher to find than before, Prohibition provided opportunities. I was no Al Capone, you understand, but folks still wanted their liquor. I worked hard. Just didn't know I shouldn't trust some men." He waved a hand dismissively. "It ended up all right. For everyone. There is nothing to learn there. All in the past." He shook his head. "She wouldn't come, Mardell."

"Róisín?"

"Aye, she wouldn't do it." He felt his facial muscles tighten. "Her kin, they told her lies about me. Suppose that wee lass grew up believing them. And then … well, you've read about it. No sense in rehashing it, lass." He laid his napkin on the table.

"That's all right. We can talk about it some other time." She looked sorely disappointed. Patrick had never talked about his past because it was nothing to be proud of.

He raked a hand in the air. "All bygones." Except it wasn't. Not with them about to be nosing around in Dublin. "Oh, all right. I'll tell you something more, but 'tis not a pretty picture. Just the same, we're off looking for my long-lost daughter, and since you're here with me, you should know how it happened that I did not get to see her, ever." He told her about how Syd had tried to warn him about the Klan. "I told you earlier I was hauled off to jail? I was falsely accused of killing a baby."

She gasped.

"The charges couldn't stick because I hadn't done anything. But that's how those thugs operated in those days. If they didn't like you, and they didn't like fellas fresh off the boat like me, they tried to get you locked up for something." Patrick reached for his water glass and took a big gulp. Then blew out a breath. "So, I'd been accused and word got around, and I suppose that whole business could have given the McGurdys more reason to despise me. My mother could have told Róisín about it. It was a mistake to write to my mother about those things."

Patrick proceeded to tell Mardell how his rumrunning days had led to some tough luck. "After that I lacked a place to rest my head for a while, like I told you before. But then I met your mother and got myself all straightened out."

Mardell dabbed a handkerchief at her eyes. He probably should not have told her just how down and out he'd been. He'd made her feel sorry for him. "There now, darlin. 'Twas so long ago it hardly matters now."

"Dad, of course it matters. You came to America and had all your dreams shattered."

"Not all. I met your mother. I had you. You two made my life worthwhile." He reached for his daughter's hand and squeezed it. He wanted her to know how much he meant that.

Mardell smiled and then twisted her lips, thinking. "Why do you suspect Juniper did not survive, Dad?"

"Well, you'll see what was said about her." He handed her the bundle of letters. "The lassie wasn't of a strong constitution, and conditions were harsh in Ireland." He patted Mardell's hand. "But we'll find out her story and we'll visit my mother's grave proper, like a son should."

He wished his daughter would turn her focus away from him and to her young man instead. "Tell me about Leo, Mardell. Did he talk to you about the war? No one would have guessed when the Great War ended that we'd be fighting the Germans again so soon."

"Only a bit. Like you and your war, Dad."

Patrick understood. "Well, let's talk about what he said all the same."

"You're changing the subject."

He winked at her. "Suppose I am."

Mardell drew in a deep breath. "He said there was a little confusion at first. He was sent here and there. Did ... this and that. Apparently, the Minnesota guardsmen needed a few more fellas in their unit. He was lent out, I guess you could say."

"So he spent time near Belfast. Is that right?"

"Yes, I believe so."

"Well, he didn't get to Dublin, I don't suppose. Are you wanting to see some of the places he saw?"

"I would love to go to Giant's Causeway, but only if we have time." Mardell flipped through her travel guide as they finished lunch. "He told me about a woman he'd met."

"You mentioned that. Something about sore feet?"

"She was a bit eccentric. Had a beautiful garden and made some ointments that helped him. He encountered her when he was stationed at the headquarters of the 8th USAAF Composite Command."

"Where was that?"

"Northern Ireland. A village called Moira. If we could manage it, it would be a favor to bring her Leo's greetings. He said she gave him something that cured the blisters on his feet. He'd been quite miserable and was expected to patrol on foot for twelve hours straight. This woman did for him what the army medic could not. He was grateful and feels he owes her more than the six pence he gave her at the time. He said he was low on money then and always meant to go back but he couldn't because he got shipped out. He would have written her and sent money but he couldn't remember her full name or her address. Time passed and then when I mentioned Ireland, he remembered."

"Do this for Leo, you say? As a favor?"

"It would be a kindness."

Patrick liked the lad, and he knew Leo was fond of Mardell. "Well, why not? We're like Hercule Poirot from *Murder on the Orient Express*, on a mission to solve mysteries!"

"That's us, although no murders, hopefully."

"I agree. To Moira! Wherever that is."

Patrick had never been to the Causeway, and he was sure looking for Juniper would only bring dead ends, so they could find the time. "We should have brought Leo with us."

Mardell sighed. "Dad, stop trying to marry me off. Leo and I are not that serious."

"You're right. About him not coming this time. He's too busy starting up his mechanic business."

She glanced over the stack of letters. Patrick wanted Mardell to be happy, like he and her mother had been. Veronica Green Doyle. Now there was a woman with a good heart. Patrick hoped Mardell would grow to be like her. He hoped she'd settle down, take care of a family if that was what she wanted. He didn't even care if she wanted to work at a career so long as she was happy and stayed away from politics.

When Mardell was just seventeen years old, she'd penned a letter that was published in the *Columbus Chronicle*. A contemptuous editorial piece speaking out against Ohio's senator Robert Taft who had gotten a law passed restricting the nation's servicemen from receiving books with political content. Like the Nazis had done, she'd argued. Her work in the libraries had compelled her to write it, he supposed. Patrick didn't understand it all. He was just terrified she'd get herself in too far, like Róisín. Nothing had come of it, other than the fact that this campaign against the senator had ultimately succeeded, but Patrick wanted her to learn to be cautious. The wee "adventure" they were now on might show Mardell what being assertive in government affairs could cost a woman, specifically Róisín McGurdy. What it cost her family.

A coughing fit sent Patrick reaching for his water.

"They have a doctor on board," Mardell said, patting him on the back. "We should pay him a visit."

"Nah. I have the syrup Ernie gave me. I'll be grand."

Mardell wrinkled her button nose. "Well, Dr. Nelson's cure is not helping, it seems. He's your friend, and it's not good for your doctor to also be your buddy."

"Why not?"

"Because, Dad. A buddy doesn't want to irritate you. He's too nice. You need to take care of yourself, and he won't tell you that."

"You worry too much. Besides, what he gave me does help at night. I'll take it when I get back to the cabin. Makes me too sleepy during the day, darlin." He shook his head at his daughter's reprimanding look. "My mother had some remedies, let me tell you. Perhaps we'll find something similar on the oul' sod." He winked. "And don't be so hard on good old Ernie. He's taking in our mail and making sure the place is safe and sound. A good friend and a good doc."

Mardell sighed and poured more tea. "Maybe so. About Leo. I'm not ready to marry yet, Dad. You know I want to clerk for Don Ebright."

"Who?"

"The gubernatorial candidate? He's the State Treasurer now."

"Oh, right, right."

"And I'm hoping to finish college."

"That woman dean at Ohio University. Voight, I believe her name is. She's put ideas into your head."

"No, she hasn't. But what's wrong with a woman having a career?"

"Nothing, depending on what it is. We'll see if this trip changes your mind." When she heard how politics dominated Róisín's life, she might think twice.

"I don't see why it should."

Patrick dropped a sugar cube into his tea. "Right."

Mardell consulted her notebook. "The letter dated the seventeenth of April, 1922. I think she hints that she supported the treaty with England, but her father did not."

"To be truthful, darlin, I didn't take sides when it came to the Irish Civil War. Neutral, I was, like de Valera during the last war."

Mardell fingered one of the letters. Patrick turned it toward him. When he read the date, he remembered what it contained. "Ah, a brush off, 'twas. Róisín had her mission in life, I suppose. Go on. Read that and then think again about getting involved in politics, darlin."

11 December 1922

To: Paddy Doyle, New Jersey

Dear Paddy,

You were right about one thing, life has not been easy since you left. Many shot in the streets. Do you remember that lad from school, the one with the flaming red hair who teased me endlessly? I know you never cared for him. Diarmaid he was called. He was shot for having a weapon, and he had none. His poor mother. I remember now that you warned me about that. I didn't understand back then.

You may not believe it, but news of what's happening in America has traveled here. Gangsters in New York City and Chicago. You are not far from it, I should think.

We pray for you, Paddy. Wee Juniper, too, on her knees at church, although she doesn't really understand. John thinks it's best that she believe you've died. I'm sorry to say it, but I also think it's best and I will tell just when she's old enough. I do tell her about you, though. How brave and handsome her father was.

Before you ask again, no, we can't come to America. There are reasons, things I cannot explain. I expect life is no better there, despite all the talk about streets of gold. You made a choice. So have I.

Yours,

Róisín

Mardell sighed. "Oh, how sad that she told Juniper you'd died. What things couldn't she explain, do you think?"

"I'm not sure, darlin. Quite possible that was just an excuse, an attempt to push me away. She got involved in things. Loads of women in Dublin did."

"And you think what I want to do is like that? Dad, people are not being shot in the streets in Ohio. There's no civil war going on."

"Aye, but things do happen. Women begin to think they must play a role instead of looking out for their families. That kind of thinking probably cost Juniper her life, put them into deeper poverty without any support. Disease grows in places where folks can't find a job."

"I'm sorry, Dad, I really am. But I'm not going to neglect anyone just because I'm working on a gubernatorial race. You and me? We've got each other. And whoever I decide to marry will support my choices." She shrugged. "Who's worrying too much now?"

Patrick had been correct that Mardell couldn't conceive of how things were in Ireland. Maybe after they arrived more would make sense. As much sense as could be had, that is.

Mardell wrote in her notebook and then looked up at him. "The other letters aren't reassuring. That poor child. If we find her, I'm going to tell her that her mother made the wrong choice. Being raised by you would have been far better."

Juniper, if she were still alive, might not agree. He examined the next letter in the stack and then handed it back to her. "Perhaps what Róisín couldn't explain was this. Some kind of spy, she was."

2 January 1923

To: Paddy Doyle, New Jersey

From: John McGurdy, Dublin, Ireland

Dear Paddy,

I thought you should know that my sister Róisín has been arrested, wrongly I assure you. Many women have been branded as militant, but Róisín should not be among them. She is currently in

Kilmainham Gaol, but I don't expect her to be there long. She, along with some on hunger strike, will be sent to a workhouse. Rest assured I will see that she is released.

Had you any worry about the child, she is in the care of your mother temporarily. Róisín, the chancer that she is, insisted rather than leaving her with our da. I'm not sure that was wise. Your mother, Delaney, is not well. Lung fever is the current plague around here. Pray and hope for the best, boyo.

Thought you should know.

John McGurdy

Mardell gasped. "Did that say *arrested*? Both Róisín and her brother had nearly illegible handwriting. Both practically identical in that respect."

"That is what it says. Schooling was not so good when we were growing up."

"So she went to jail. How awful."

"I told you 'twas not a pleasant time, especially in Dublin." He flicked his fingers toward the stack of letters. "Go on. She got out all right."

"And your mother? Delaney? How sad that she was so sick."

"Poverty in Ireland was not widely talked about in America. Wee farms not able to sustain families, workers laid off from factories in the cities. 'Twas not the Great Hunger of the nineteenth century, but many desperate people just the same. My mother could not have fared well, I'm afraid. And Juniper probably got sick then as well."

Patrick remembered that he'd written his mother after that, and that was likely the last letter of his she'd read because the ones he'd tried to send later had been returned. He'd begged her forgiveness, asked that she tell Juniper he had not abandoned her, and sent what money he could. He'd gotten one more letter from her, and Mardell had it now.

2 February 1923

To: Patrick Doyle, New Jersey

From: Delaney Doyle

Dear Son,

I was delighted to get your letter. Do not worry about us or what your daughter may think of you. I've only spoken your praises. I have been ill, but time will heal me and I hope to get back to work next week.

Do not judge Róisín too harshly, son. She is doing what she feels is right. Something is amiss with that girl. I'm not sure what it is, but something is driving her to join forces with those women, not the Women's Council, but others. I sense that it goes beyond duty to country. We may never know. What I can tell you is she was arrested not for violence, but for couriering dispatches. Please, take care of yourself. And write more often.

Your loving mother

"Women's Council?" Mardell flipped back through the stack of letters. "She mentioned that in Irish, I think."

"Ah, the *Cumann na mBan*. I believe she *was* a part of it, though. My mother must have been wrong about that."

Mardell stared out a porthole toward the white capped water. "My grandmother sounds like a wonderful woman."

"She was."

"What kind of work did she do?"

"She was a healer. Knew all about plants and herbs. Folks who couldn't afford a doctor came to her."

"That's so interesting. I wish I had known her."

"More's the pity you'll never meet."

"You're sure she's passed on?"

He nodded. "In that kind of misery barely anyone survives to old age."

CHAPTER 10

8 *July 1923*

To: Paddy Doyle, New Jersey

From: Róisín McGurdy, Dublin

Dear Paddy,

I know your mother wrote to you. I am fine and reunited with my child. My imprisonment is proof that there is still work to be done to make people understand. Had our child been a boy, life would be different. I must protect her, Paddy.

Surely you heard about the ambush that killed Michael Collins last year. Weeks later an end to the war was declared. Some things are ended but skirmishes still rise up. Those without political undertones as well.

I have learned so much. I know how to keep safe, when to go out and when to stay home, and who I should avoid. I intend to elude arrest. I cannot tell you how humiliating and painful the treatment is in there. Even so, life outside of the jail is barely better for women and harsh for a wee lass. I know you think John and my da were part of the killings in Dublin during the civil war. There was a time I would have argued with you, but I don't know anymore. Perhaps the fear of them keeps enemies from our door. Juniper and I have sought solace in the church.

Many of the girls have turned against the church. While the priest does not support our efforts, I'm of the firm belief that we need the church's assistance, covertly. For example, the nuns look after my daughter so that I may continue my work, even while they don't know what it is I'm doing.

I've heard it said many times, and it's very true, it is. The British government's gift to Ireland has been workhouses, prisons, and lunatic asylums. We must reject those things as we build our own government, but not in the manner some wish.

I must tell you of Juniper, though, and your mother. I returned from my unjust confinement to find them both extremely ill. Juniper will recover with the help of the nuns now that she's away from your mother's foolish folklore herbal concoctions. Like I say. We are grand. Knocked down a bit, but grand.

Start a new life, Paddy. The past is past.

Yours,

Róisín

P.S. If you need to contact me, do so in care of my brother John.

16 May 1950, on the Atlantic

Mardell rubbed her temples. "Were you surprised by any of this?"

"I thought perhaps I didn't know Róisín as well I thought I did. For some reason she got involved in some dangerous stuff."

"Did you answer her?"

"I didn't see the need. My mother was dying, Juniper thought I was dead. I feel like the dead, darlin. I'm ready for my bed."

He reached for the remaining unread letters. Mardell put her hand over his. "Do you have to take them?"

He gathered them up. "Better that we read them together." He stood. "Got your notebook?"

She picked it up along with her purse. "Yes, get some rest, Dad. And take your prescription. Your cough sounds bad."

When Patrick got into bed, he felt thankful that he had shelter. He'd not thought about how good a bed felt in a long time. But now, he had his awful memories to remind him to be grateful.

PADDY

1923, Jersey Shore

Now that winter had set in it was too cold to huddle up near the shore. The steam grates on the sidewalks in the city provided some heat.

On a quiet street late at night, Paddy found a bit of refuge. Digging through a trash barrel, he found unsoiled newspaper to blanket himself. Inside another bundle he discovered a bit of fish and chips and ate it. Tears coursed down his cheeks with each bite as he wondered what his mother would think of him like this.

Wiping his fingers on the seat of his pants, he settled into a dark corner and drifted off to sleep.

"You can't sleep here!"

Paddy jolted awake. A young man shoved rubbish into a bin. Paddy scrambled to his feet. "Sorry. Good night to you."

"Irish trash," the fellow mumbled as he stomped back inside the building.

Gathering his paper blanket, Paddy wandered to the next street and found another suitable place to lie down. His dreams took him to the center of Dublin City where he lived with his widowed mother. They walked hand in hand down a cobblestone street. He could hear his mother crying. "Don't worry, Mam. I'll find work. I'll take care of us."

She stopped and knelt beside him. "You will get your education, Paddy. I will do the working."

They strolled on. He noticed she carried a suitcase. In his dream-washed consciousness, Paddy realized they were on their way to live with cousins. This was the beginning of hunger, of cold, of having nothing. She'd tried, doing what she knew, brewing up remedies for the sick and balms for the injured. Paddy joined the army in part to help save her from poverty. Not out of a sense of duty or a desire to keep Europe free from the Kaiser, as he had long ago convinced himself. He had done it to escape destitution.

When Paddy woke, the sky at the end of the street gleamed with a rosy hue. Shuffling to his feet and tossing away the newspaper, he thought about his dream. He was living in poverty again, this time in the Land of Opportunity. He remembered that his father wasn't quite the man young Paddy had thought he was. He worked it out later that Da had often drank away his earnings. Somehow, while Da was still alive, Paddy's mother had made up for that. If only Paddy had been more like his mother and less like his da.

A bit of a broken bottle amidst the alley's rubble caught his eye. He picked it up, cutting the tip of his index finger. Crimson blood bubbled and then pooled along the edges of his fingernail. He stared at it thoughtfully. Life was fragile, painful. The rewards were short-lived. This sharpness could end it.

Paddy leveled the cold glass against his neck. He'd been a soldier. He knew how to do this quickly. The world didn't want him. Why should he stick around?

Dropping his arm, Paddy stared again at the bit of glass in his hand. It had come from a gin bottle and the label was still visible, festooned with juniper berries, from which gin was made.

Juniper.

The image blurred through his tears. Paddy *had* done something worthwhile. He'd produced another human being. He might not ever see her, but she was on earth because of the role he'd played in giving her life. Paddy pressed the glass again to his neck. His part in that was done. The lassie thought him dead anyway.

The tears coursed down his cheeks and dampened his collar. He couldn't do it. Not because he was a coward, but because of Juniper. Should she ever find out, by some miracle, Paddy didn't want to prove John McGurdy's assessment of him correct by bleeding to death in a godforsaken alley. Paddy did not deserve the reputation McGurdy attributed to him. Living on the streets, eating from trash bins? Aye, Paddy Doyle deserved that for trusting those he should not. He'd lost the instincts war had once embedded in him. One thing remained, though, something he could not name. Pride? Stubbornness? An Irish temper? Whatever it was, Paddy would live with it, miserable though he might be.

The shard dropped to his feet and he kicked it away.

PADDY

1924, Jersey Shore

"That's an ugly scar on your cheek, mate."

Paddy shoved back the chair he was sitting on and raised his fists.

"Whoa, now. Don't take offense, Paddy." Max, the daytime worker at the Salvation Army, urged Paddy to back down. "Joseph is new here. He didn't know you don't like to talk."

Paddy sighed and went back to eating the mushy scrambled eggs on his plate.

Joseph whispered. "I got my own scars. Tell you about 'em, I would, if you want to know."

"I don't."

But later, as the men prepared for sleep in the basement area where the Salvation Army housed homeless, penniless men, Paddy had a change of heart. "If I hadn't walked into that hall in '22, my life would be different."

Joseph chuckled. "Many's a man ruined themselves on the devil's drink."

"I drank too much in those days, but that's not what did it."

Joseph seemed sincerely interested, and Paddy hadn't talked about it in so long he suddenly felt as though the story would burn a hole through his middle if he didn't unload it. "I was a small-time rumrunner, you see. Worked for myself, made good money."

"Many's done that, I reckon. Don't see a problem with it myself." Joseph shifted on his cot and turned his back. He might think that was the end of Paddy's story.

"I was played for the eejit I suppose I am. I think it was because I am Irish."

"Always someone at fault," Joseph said. "Mine was a woman." He sighed, then pointed a gloved finger at Paddy. "Gave you that, did he?"

Absentmindedly, Paddy stroked the stubble on his face in the spot where the bottom of a mug had cut him two years earlier. The scar encompassed the earlier one he'd gotten in the Wall Street bombing, making the disfigurement double in size. Though no longer clearly visible, Paddy sensed the burns from the rope as well. Memories seared into his soul.

"I asked for a Jameson. There was a brawl. In Ireland there are Catholic drinks and Protestant ones. A man knows what brand belongs in certain pubs. This was a bit of the same, I suppose."

"That so?" Joseph chuckled. "Never known a Catholic and a Protestant who wouldn't share a bottle if it was offered."

Paddy shook his head. "This is America, for God's sake. It should not matter." Paddy reminded himself that it was a bad idea to condemn one side until you were sure who you were talking to.

Joseph grinned. He had missing teeth and unwashed hair. Badly in need of a shave too. Did Paddy look that awful? "It happens," the man offered.

"Don't suppose some hooligans need a reason to beat a man, but these fellas knew me, you understand. Knew I had a bit of dough as well, you see."

"Ah," said Joseph. "That's not good."

"Indeed not. When I woke the next morning face down in the alley, I found my room key was missing out of my pocket, as was my wallet. Bloodied and not in my right mind, I lost it all before it was said and done." Talking like this was lifting his spirits. Wouldn't do any harm to unload his story to a bum. "Ah, I worked a bit after that but I was on a downward slide. No possessions save for a few sentimental items." He paused and drew in a deep breath that tightened his chest. "No country either, and no Róisín." Paddy tweaked the story, sure, but that was the sum of it. "Suppose my own mother must have thought me dead. I don't know." He'd not received any letters in the last year because the postman who brought mail to the boarding house got reassigned. Before that he'd kept Paddy's mail until he saw him on the street.

Paddy scratched a patch on his head while he thought about that. There'd be no one to write to him anyway.

Max had been passing something out to the men on the cots. When he came near, Paddy saw he had a pile of woolen socks. "Much obliged," he said, reaching for a pair.

"I never heard that story before, Paddy," Max said. "We could help you write to your mother."

"Thank you, no." Paddy didn't want his mother to know how

far he'd fallen in America. If she were still living, she'd be disgraced.

Max shrugged. "Well, as you like, then. Come by on Thursday, why don't you. We can set you up with some work on the docks."

Max said the same thing every time Paddy came in for shelter. The charity worker wouldn't bother if he knew the whole miserable tale. Max hadn't heard Paddy tell Joseph that he'd been a rumrunner. Paddy steered clear of the docks because if he recognized any of his old roommates he'd probably knock the lights out them.

"What happened after that?" Joseph asked.

"Plenty. I had to do something for my bread, you know."

"I beg. Down by the river. Pays well some days." Joseph pointed to his right side. "Bum leg from the war. You fight in the war, Paddy?"

"I wasn't here then," he answered, hoping that would end that.

"Well," Joseph continued, "go on. The quiet here can make a man go off his nut. Tell me the story."

"I am a pug, out on the streets," Paddy said.

"A boxer? No kidding. You any good?"

"Not very. Too skinny. But it pays when I can find the work."

"Ain't that something," Joseph said.

"Not really. Fellas want a rube to make them look good. A human punching bag."

"A young lady's bringing breakfast in the morning, boys," Max called out to the group. "Fried eggs, bacon, fruit, toast."

A collective sigh of longing rose from the group.

"Get yourselves up and clean before she comes at seven."

"Breakfast? Since when?" Paddy asked. All they normally got was a donut and a cup of joe, for which he was grateful. Sure, they'd had scrambled eggs from time to time, but a full breakfast was unheard of.

"Started last week by a young man from a charity organization," Max answered. "While you were in the city. This time we've a nice girl with a big heart coming over." Max glared at the lumps of men, most too tired or plastered to pay heed. "Behave as gentlemen." He turned down the light and took his place behind a desk in an adjacent office.

Paddy appreciated the shelter most nights. Other times he wondered if any of it was worth it. What was he doing on this side of the grave with no purpose? At least in the war he'd had a job to do. When he'd had money and the opportunity to make more, he'd had a chance with Róisín. But no more. America didn't want immigrants.

"Hey," Joseph whispered. "When ya gonna get your revenge on whoever did that to your face?"

Revenge? The voice of Paddy's Catholic nun schoolteacher reverberated in his mind. "Revenge is the Lord's," Paddy said, rolling over to face the wall.

Other voices from the past haunted him that night.

Old man McGurdy: "Go along back to England, why don't you?"

The school lads on the street in Dublin: "Traitor!"

Róisín: "Don't go, Paddy." Her words on paper. "You weren't here, Paddy."

"Advance!" came the order.

"Paddy! Paddy, I'm hit."

Commander: "Stay here and be buried in bloody mud. Off with you. Go!"

"You shall face the firing squad at dawn tomorrow."

Spectemur agendo. Let us be judged by our deeds.

17 MAY 1950, on the Atlantic

Lying on his bed now on a ship in the middle of the ocean, Paddy was determined to keep these memories to himself. He was ashamed of who he had been back then. All Mardell needed to know about that chapter of his life was how her mother had made all the difference.

When Mardell joined him for breakfast, he insisted on speaking about Veronica rather than the lowest point of his life.

His daughter nodded. "All right. I know she was a social worker or charity worker. Did you meet her in a shelter?"

"That's right. In fact, I met her at the front door. She was wearing a houndstooth skirt and a matching jacket with a wide collar, soft curls under a black cap, and a red lipstick smile."

Mardell chuckled. "That's a rather complete memory."

"An image I'll never forget. She was loaded down with paper sacks and I helped her carry them in." He must have looked like the street bum he was, and he remembered thinking he'd better clean himself up if he had any chance of her noticing him. And yet, she *had* noticed him. She was kind and caring, unlike most of the Americans that he'd met so far.

Mardell ordered eggs and Patrick asked for oatmeal before they continued talking.

"You were smitten," Mardell said.

"Oh, I surely was. You see," he glanced at the letters he'd placed on the table, "Róisín had told me to move on, hadn't she? It was time. Your mother introduced herself and when I did the same, I used my proper name Patrick. Decided to leave the old Paddy behind and become a better version of myself. For her."

"I'm glad I know Patrick," Mardell said, sipping tea from a white cup.

I am too, darlin.

Patrick remembered that the evening after he'd had breakfast with Veronica at the shelter he'd lost all interest in putting himself up for a beating as a pugilist.

Mardell arranged a napkin in her lap when a waiter brought over a tray of food. "So it was at that point you and Mom became an item?"

"These things take time, darlin, as you are always telling me with Leo."

She nodded as she bit a toast triangle.

"I encountered a lad on the streets who needed some help." Again, he couldn't tell the whole story. Mardell shouldn't hear these things.

But the scene came back to him vividly.

PADDY

1924, Jersey Shore

After he'd left the fella who arranged fights, he noticed another guy scuffling with a young boy. "What's going on there?" Paddy had demanded.

"Mind yer own business," the lug said.

"You all right, son?"

The wee lad's eyes were glassy. He didn't seem to be able to focus on the question.

"Get lost," the man holding the boy said. "He's mine."

"What's wrong with him?"

The man swung at Paddy. Little did this lout know he was messing with a seasoned fighter. Paddy landed a good punch between the man's eyes, sending him backward until he flattened against a brick wall. With blood dripping down his face, the man charged forward like a bull. Paddy was ready and ducked, grabbing the man around his waist. Shoving both of them back toward the wall, Paddy pounded him again and again until the man gave up and dropped into a crumpled heap by the trash bins where he belonged.

Paddy lifted the boy, light as feather, and made for the closest police call station. The cop there directed him to the station house.

"Keep breathing," Paddy said to the bundle in his arms. Why was no one helping him?

"I've got a hurt child here," he called when he barged through the door.

Several uniformed officers strolled through the hall, glancing up and then back down at papers they held. Paddy rushed up to the desk. "Do you hear? This lad needs help. A man over on First Avenue was harassing him and he's not very alert, this one. I snatched him and came as fast as I could."

The man at the desk glanced up over his spectacles. "I see. Set him down over there." He pointed to a row of six wooden chairs lining an adjacent corridor.

Paddy placed the boy on one and sat in the chair next to him, cradling the lad's limp head against his chest. The kid breathed but still didn't respond.

"You don't have to wait," the officer at the desk said.

"What?"

"A matron will be over. She'll take him to the women's ward and in the morning he'll be right as rain and back to …" he grunted. "Back to whatever it is he does."

A boy prostitute, probably. And no one cared. "It's not right," Paddy protested. "I'll take him to a boys' home, an orphanage. Surely there's one around here somewhere."

"Nah. You brought him here. We will deal with it. Move along, chum."

"Now hold on." Paddy tossed out every argument he could think of and was threatened with a charge of disturbing the peace, ludicrous because they were in the least peaceful place in town that time of night. Then he heard someone calling his name.

"Patrick Doyle! Whatever is going on here?" Veronica rushed from the doorway to join him at the desk.

"You shouldn't see this, miss." Paddy tried to position himself to block her view of the drugged boy.

"I've seen my share, I assure you." She turned to the man at the desk. "Officer Laney?"

"Miss Green, this fella here is a do-gooder, but we got no time for this. Perhaps you could …" He flipped his head to the side as though wishing to whisk them out the door.

"Let's sit over here a moment, Patrick." Veronica led him to the chairs just as a portly woman in uniform carried the boy away. "Tell me what happened."

Paddy explained it all. "Why won't they help? Is he Catholic, maybe?"

"Don't you worry. That's why I'm here. I'm an advocate for the downtrodden. I'll make sure he ends up somewhere safe. But I must say, you were quite brave to snatch him out of that dangerous situation. Good on you!"

Paddy's cheeks warmed.

"Now, do you have a place to shower up or are you headed back to the shelter? I can give you train fare."

Paddy hated that he was just another charity case to her. He would fix that as soon as possible. He stood. "Thank you, no. I'll be off then." There had to be a decent job somewhere. He'd bum a razor off Max at the shelter. He'd finally found a reason to improve himself.

~

SOMETIME LATER PADDY ladled syrupy fruit cocktail into a small bowl and handed it to a man waiting in line in the shelter's kitchen. Veronica stood next to him and handed out napkins. "Would you like to have coffee with me at the diner when we're done here?"

Veronica smiled. "Of course I would."

Over coffee, she had asked him about his story.

He couldn't lie to this woman and hope to keep her in his life. She was goodness itself and would see right through the usual malarkey he fed others about his coming to America. He had started with the war, told the story about Colin Reilly without too many harrowing details, and when he got to Róisín, tears had flowed down Veronica's face. He'd given her just enough of the picture.

Veronica had reached for his arm then. He'd never forget what she said next. "I am so sorry that happened, Patrick. Fear makes people cling to bad choices, and perhaps that's why your girlfriend remained with her family despite the violence happening all around her."

No one had ever before said they were sorry for his troubles.

"You are not to blame," she continued. "You did the best you could. I knew you had a virtuous heart when I saw you in the police station that night with that poor boy. Makes me angry so many people in your life refused to understand your intentions. You tried to help your army comrade in the Great War. You wanted to help your girlfriend out of a difficult situation, even after she rejected you. You took to rumrunning for her. Who hasn't made bad choices at some time or another? The difference is why we did those things and whether or not we regret our mistakes. You, Patrick Doyle, are not a selfish man in the least."

That was the moment he knew he wanted to marry Veronica Green.

17 MAY 1950, on the Atlantic

"You're smiling, Dad. Thinking about Mom?"

Patrick swallowed his last bit of oatmeal and gave his daughter a wink.

"As you know, your mother had grown up in Ohio. She'd come to the East Coast as part of her church's mission project and then stayed on for a few years. But she wanted to go back to Ohio and I had no reason to stay back east. She agreed to marry me, despite all my flaws."

Mardell smiled.

CHAPTER 11

R óisín
1938, Causeway Coast, Northern Ireland

Over the years her waste bin filled daily with half-written letters to Paddy. Ultimately Róisín had given up. It had been years since her last letter. Earlier she'd feared the guerilla violence popping up in Dublin. The bombings had been mostly of government buildings and meant to upset the rule of law and intimidate officials, but she hadn't understood that then. She never should have blathered on about those things to Paddy. She and Juniper had found assistance from the church and her child had been safely tucked away for a decade. Nothing Róisín came up with over the last ten years had allowed her to remove Juniper from hiding. Old man McGurdy and his thugs were still around Dublin and news traveled. She couldn't risk anyone finding out where she was.

But now the most tragic of circumstances brought an opportunity, a new scheme. Her brother John was dead. Róisín had a plan to convince her father and his wretched associates that she was the one who had died in the attack that killed her dear brother John. Willie McGurdy wouldn't know the difference. No one would.

It happened in Dublin. She'd arranged to meet her brother under cover. He had signed some papers for St. Giles. She'd taken an envelope from him and stepped outside just as a bomb went off. She might never learn if John had been targeted or if the blast was meant for someone else, the owner of the warehouse, perhaps. Róisín was the only other person in the building, the only one who had seen John's body. Poor John was instantly burned beyond recognition. She'd left quickly, anonymously phoned the police, stating that Róisín McGurdy had been killed. From now on she would continue to pretend she was John through letters, practicing until no one could note a difference in the signature. With the help of her trusted solicitor, she could do this. She'd already arranged for the body to be shipped to the churchyard near Aunt Bet's place. That had been a harrowing venture, but she'd managed it. Faking her death was the best way to keep her and Juniper safe. After all, John had already been acting in her behalf, obtaining favors for Juniper that the nuns would only grant because a male family member insisted.

Rubbing a polishing cloth along the back of the pew inside the church where she was employed, Róisín steeled her resolve. She might have needed Paddy when Juniper was young. Juniper had not adjusted well to the asylum in the beginning. Róisín had asked for help from afar but because Paddy had previously offered to help and Róisín had rejected it, he'd refused. There was only one last thing Paddy might do for their daughter. He had made her a promise before he went to America: If their child ever wanted her father, ever asked for him, he'd come back to help her. But for no other reason. He'd been insistent, and she knew he was true to his word. She hadn't insisted back then because if Paddy Doyle got involved he'd mess things up. Róisín had kept their daughter safe so she reserved this promise as a kind of insurance policy, even though she was not likely to be able to use it. Juniper thought her father and now her mother were dead.

She glanced up to see the priest enter the church. He'd be preparing for a meeting with the church maintenance committee. She'd tarried too long. Gathering her cleaning supplies, she ducked out the door. It was time for her to telephone the solicitor anyway for their monthly chat about her investments. Her solicitor referred to her as a very wealthy woman. Ha! A wealthy woman scrubbing church floors in a wee village. This wealth, as he called it, was for Juniper alone and, God willing, her daughter would never know where it came from, because knowing that might lead back to Wille McGurdy.

CHAPTER 12

P atrick
17 May 1950, on the Atlantic

"Oh, Dad. I'm so happy to know how Mom healed you. I wish you'd told me this long ago."

Patrick dabbed at his damp eyes. "I've been called Patrick ever since I met your mother. 'Twas the name of my resurrection, like Jacob being called Israel. 'Thy name shall be called no more Jacob, but Israel: for thou hast striven with God and with men, and hast prevailed.'"

"That's beautiful, Dad. I didn't know you knew any Bible stories."

He knew a lot more than she realized. "Your mother often told me that I'd prevailed." He swallowed hard. She was no longer here, his anchor.

Mardell patted his arm and reached for a biscuit from a plate a waiter had placed on their table. They'd been sitting there so long past breakfast the staff probably thought they'd might as well eat something. "You have overcome so much, just like Mom said. I always wondered why there was only one wedding photo and Mom wore a plain skirt and blouse instead of a wedding dress, but that does sound like Mom, now that I think about it. She'd didn't like what she called attention getting."

"She surely did not."

Mardell continued to munch on what Americans called cookies. Patrick had never gotten used to the term. To him they'd always be biscuits. His daughter sighed contentedly. "I'm proud of you, Dad. Your mother, my Granny, would be proud too."

"I'm not so sure." He grinned at her. "But it does my heart good to hear you say so, darlin." He coughed again and quickly swigged some tea.

Mardell shuffled the pile of old letters. "You sound as though that's the end of the story but there are more letters dated after you married Mom." She consulted her notes. "You married in February of '26."

"That's right. And a week before Christmas that year you were born."

Patrick had fond memories of that St. Valentine's Day when he and Veronica had stepped out the door of St. Edward's Episcopal Church in the small town of Golden, Ohio, as a married couple. The only sad bit was that his mother hadn't been there. He'd tried to contact her, but his letter came back addressee unknown. Instead, he'd written John McGurdy, just so someone knew where he was if Juniper ever needed him. Paddy had a new life now as Patrick—with his bride.

CHAPTER 13

J uniper
1938, County Monaghan, Ireland

Juniper opened the letter from her mother's brother with apprehension. She'd rarely heard from him. The asylum had stopped opening her mail recently because, as one of the workers secretly told her, John McGurdy would not send any more money if they continued to do so.

1 May 1938

Dear Juniper,

As you will soon be released, I've made arrangements for you. A purse will soon be delivered with some money. I've enclosed directions.

I'm sorry to tell you that your mother passed away this morning. She was hunted down by thugs due to her past activity. Not the civil war, child, as that violence occurred long ago. This was related to her work as a courier fifteen years ago. Something occurred, she may have taken something they wanted back, I'm not sure.

Powerful people were out for revenge and now they have it. But for that reason, it's important you do not tell anyone your true name. Your mother shielded you all these years from people who would hurt you if they could.

There will be no funeral, but it wouldn't be safe for you to attend if there was one. I have had her buried without a marker in St. Finian's churchyard near old Aunt Bet's cottage. Second row from the south entrance, fifth plot, should you want to visit. Just don't tell anyone why you're there. I'm sure this sounds odd but trust me. I have your best interest at heart.

The money should get you started at Old Aunt Bet's place. It's been empty since she passed years ago. You'll be safe there. I will be in touch once you arrive, but as you'll be there alone, I repeat: do not tell anyone you are a McGurdy.

Sincerely,

John McGurdy

Her mother had been murdered? Juniper's head swam, her heart raced. She would have no problem not claiming the McGurdy name, but she wanted to know what had happened.

During her kitchen duty, which included cleaning up the staff areas, Juniper collected all the discarded newspapers to read later in her room. Poring over them for hours, she finally found out what had happened to Róisín. She tore out the article and stuffed it into her traveling bag, then shoved it under her cot. The words seemed to leap into her thoughts despite her effort to cover them up.

Member of Cumann na mBan.

Ambushed.

Crushed by falling timbers.

The paper was from a republican stronghold. Her mother's name had been listed with several others who died over the last few years. A type of memorial, it seemed.

A few days later Juniper was called into the superintendent's office.

"What is your earliest, most unpleasant memory?" The man crossed his legs at the knee, adjusted his long white coat over them, and nodded toward Juniper.

She didn't like memories and told him so.

He huffed. "I am trying to help you, Anna. Now try to recall."

Inhaling deeply, Juniper closed her eyes, willing her mind to produce words rather than images. "My mother leaving me at the abbey."

"And why did she take you there?"

"I cannot pretend to know her mind, Dr. Callahan." He wasn't a doctor but preferred to be addressed that way.

He stood. She would not cower. Not any longer. She was no longer a child. "I can tell you what she told me."

"Go on, please." He wandered toward the window and stared out at the verdant garden, insinuating that her memories were not that important to him even though he'd asked.

"I was quite young, but I believe she said something about needing redemption. I don't know if she meant me or herself, but she was right."

He spun on his heels, tapping a pencil to his temple. "About?"

He really wasn't paying attention. She sputtered her lips but he didn't seem to notice. "Needing redemption."

"Indeed. Do you feel you attained it at the abbey or perhaps during your time here at St. Giles?"

Redemption was not the work of men. But if she said anything of the sort, she feared she might not be released. "I do. Both places. I am a new woman, thanks to all of you."

He smiled. Flattery had done its job. The man sat at his shiny desk and scratched a fountain pen across some papers. "Your guardian, your mother's brother? He has been most persuasive in recommending your release. Your character over the last few years has been exemplary. Therefore, I'm signing the papers."

Juniper released a tight breath and bit her lip to hide her emotions. Even though she remembered that she was supposed to be released at the proper time, she dared not believe it. There were old women at St. Giles who could not remember living anywhere else. Juniper had behaved perfectly to avoid the harshest punishments. They'd terrified her as a child, and she'd witnessed the mistreatment of other girls. What she hadn't seen was talked about in whispers among the inmates. Self-preservation had been her aim. Keep your head down and do what you were told. Many times she wanted to strike back, to shout that she was a human being, worthy of kindness. She'd bitten it all back so as not to delay her release. Whatever Uncle John had done in her behalf, she was glad for. His influence and her self-control had brought her to this moment.

"Your release will be effective tomorrow morning. I hear you'll be going to a house willed to your family by your aunt."

"An old aunt, aye." She knew the place because Uncle John had given her directions in his letter. But she also had faint recollections of the cottage from muddled childhood memories. Was Aunt Bet her mother's family? Perhaps not. It seemed to her Granny and Bet were family because Granny had been at the cottage with Róisín and her brother John. Why Uncle John would send her there Juniper didn't know, but surely Granny had something to do with it. She couldn't wait to ask Granny to come.

"Your mother will live with you then?" The doctor's question pierced through her pondering.

Róisín was dead, but obviously this man had yet to be told. Uncle John's letter had arrived unopened so they didn't know. Best to keep it that way in case the doctor changed his mind.

"I suppose my mother always will be by my side, Doctor." She meant it figuratively because her mother was gone, but he wouldn't realize that.

"Good, good. I'm pleased for you, Anna." He was not one of the doctors who had tended to her psyche, nor attempted to. Callahan was a director or administrator of some sort. He didn't know her at all. Only one person in the world truly knew her, and that had not been her mother. Her Granny, her father's mother, had written to her ever since Juniper was old enough to read. They'd corresponded for years. John had probably kept Granny from visiting, but now that Juniper was released she could send for her grandmother. They hadn't been together earlier because Granny couldn't take care of Juniper. But now Juniper could take care of Granny.

"Thank you." She stood and accepted the man's hand.

"All the best, Anna."

She smiled. A sarcastic reply came to mind, but she swallowed it, as she'd learned to do, and left to pack.

5 May 1938

Dear Granny,

Róisín is dead. Her brother wrote to tell me. If credit is due her, it is because she was loyal to a cause. Perhaps no one can enact two roles with efficiency, mother and activist. I am sorry to say those convictions led to her demise.

I have information of my own to share. St. Giles has let me go. I will be living at Glasgleann Cottage in County Down. Do you know it? Old Aunt Bet's place. You may write to me there, but I'd prefer you come in person. Granny, I'll be alone. Please consider moving in. I want us to be together and I can care for you.

Yours,

Juniper

She was not afraid to be alone, but she hoped her letter would convince Granny to come. Juniper placed her jumper and underclothes in the suitcase that had once held the clothes of a young child. Fastening the latches, she decided to leave behind the Bible the nuns had given her. If Granny had her own copy that was what they'd keep on the mantel. The words were sacred, not the binding. She had memorized enough, she thought, to sustain her. Holding the Bible as she sat on her bed, she flipped through the pages. She'd hidden a few notes inside over the years, poems of angst, a letter her father would never see. Perhaps they would offer the next girl who stayed here some solace. Juniper didn't need those things any longer. She could now begin to write new chapters for her life. Flinging the book to the mattress, Juniper left the asylum and stepped out into the sunshine.

"I'm going to town," the gardener shouted to her.

She'd always liked Mr. Mackenzie because he enjoyed plants as much as she did. Hopefully the outsiders she was about to meet would be as kind as this placid man.

"You're welcome to come along," he said. "The train depot is a short walk from the shops."

"Thank you." She tossed her bag into the wagon bed and climbed in after it.

When she got to the train she'd banished all the ugly memories.

When they arrived in the village, Juniper accepted Mr. Mackenzie's hand as she climbed out. Then she opened her pocketbook. "I've a bit of money my ... my family sent me."

The man's face reddened. "There will be none of that, Anna. I was coming to town anyway. Off with you and make a good life for yourself. Didn't I tell you this day would come?"

She smiled. "You did. On my thirteenth birthday as it happens."

He held up a hand. "Well now, there'll be happier birthdays ahead." He tugged a burlap bag from beneath his seat. "Take this. You'll make some lovely things with all you've learned about plants."

Juniper recognized the familiar weight and shape of the bag. "Oh, the mortar and pestle. Are you quite sure you want to give it to me?"

He dipped his chin to his chest. "You'll make better use of it than I, Miss Anna."

She kissed his cheek and then hurried toward the train. She didn't know what things cost but there were quite a lot of notes in her bag. She at least had the means to get to where she was going with extra to set up a household. The staff at St. Giles believed the purse had been left by her mother along with directions to the cottage. The truth was Uncle John had left her the money out of guilt, she supposed. Who allowed their niece to live under such conditions for this long?

The man behind the ticket window asked for the train fare. Fumbling with the notes in her purse, Juniper gave up and shoved a handful at him. He huffed, counted out a few, and then returned the rest to her along with a paper ticket.

"Put that away, honey," an old woman in line behind her said. "Wouldn't want you to get robbed."

Embarrassed, Juniper nodded and walked to a bench, gripping the purse against her chest. She'd learn. She had to.

Moments later the train arrived. Relieved, Juniper boarded, found a seat, and produced the ticket when asked. She'd done this without too much help. St. Giles was behind her.

As the world outside the train window merged into a green blur, the images Juniper wished away came forth anyway. She wiped a tear. She hadn't felt loved by her mother, and yet her death made her sad. Perhaps it was the way she had died. No one deserved such treatment. Juniper would pay tribute at Róisín's grave and then make her way to Aunt Bet's cottage. It was the proper thing to do.

CHAPTER 14

P atrick
17 May 1950, on the Atlantic

Patrick and Mardell had spent the day playing board games and watching others play cards. She had all the letters now, but thankfully she'd allowed Patrick a bit of a break from questions. Now that they were at dinner, though, she'd want to revisit the topic of his life in Ireland.

"Dad, there's a letter from Róisín a couple of years after the last one we talked about. I haven't read it yet, but it's here in my bag. I declare these letters are nearly indecipherable. I thought you might help me understand the writing."

He nodded. "Tell you what. Let's talk about that tomorrow. I'm off for a dose of that syrup and then my bed. But mind you, all that's good in my life began in '26." He winked and she kissed him goodnight.

What would Mardell think of him when she read the last letter from Róisín? He'd been obstinate in his youth, but he'd done what he'd thought best at the time. Young Paddy made mistakes. It was what he did. When he saw how his daughter looked at him at supper, he wondered if perhaps he'd committed another faux pas by not burning that letter.

And that other letter? The one recently postmarked from Dublin? It still sat in his suitcase. He didn't want to believe Juniper had sent it, although it did seem to be written by her. What it said, he did not wish Mardell to see. His American daughter believed their trip to be a simple fact-finding venture and perhaps a reunion with a few distant cousins when in fact it called for Patrick's comeuppance.

The next morning at breakfast Patrick could tell from Mardell's face that she'd deciphered Róisín's last letter.

23 July 1928

To: Paddy Doyle, Golden, Ohio

From: Róisín McGurdy, Dublin, Ireland

Dear Paddy,

I understand that you have a new family now and a new home, and I do not wish to interfere. However, I am compelled to write to you as you are Juniper's father.

There was some concern at the church after Juniper's first communion. I argued that she needed at least two more years before her communion, but Father Moore would not hear of it. Juniper is tall for her age, and very bright. Father said she was at the age of reason and no delay should be made unless my father thought differently. So I agreed to it. I couldn't have my father intervene. He's a horrible man, worse than you even thought.

Juniper rebelled against everything. Mass, choir, the Christmas pageant. I insisted that she show respect to the nuns who helped me raise her. She refuses. She is so young to be behaving so. I have done all I can and as her father you have the right to know about her.

In your absence I have had to make the best decisions I could. Juniper has no big brother, as I had. If you'd like to come over, you might make a difference in her life. I would like that very much. Surely your new wife will approve of a temporary absence to see to your daughter. You can speak to Juniper. Set her straight. At least write, Paddy. I know I said not to, but I was wrong. Juniper feels abandoned. You told me you'd come if Juniper asked you to, but that can't happen. She still thinks you're dead, and I won't tell her otherwise unless you decide to make contact. I will spare her feelings.

Juniper will soon live in the country where her lungs will have better air. It's a fine asylum up north, very good for Juniper and her difficulties and I'm sure she will get better in time. I learned of your address when you wrote to my brother and told him your whereabouts. I did not think you truly wanted to hear from us again. That's why I have not corresponded until now.

Write to us in care of John McGurdy in Dublin.

Yours,

Róisín

Mardell frowned, her blue eyes watery.

"Perhaps it was ill-advised to give you that letter, honey." Patrick's heart thumped wildly in his chest. "Your mother never saw it."

"Dad, why? Why did you not go back for Juniper after you got that letter?"

Patrick shook his head, thinking about the letter he was keeping from her. Juniper had asked for him to come even though she'd thought he was dead. Guilt was a terrible thing to live with, but he had believed until recently that he'd made the correct decision, painful as it was. "You know, Mardell, you cannot judge in the present actions taken in the past. We are not the same people we were back then. A measure of knowledge comes with age and experience." *And also regret.*

She patted his arm. "I believe that is true, but what were you thinking then?"

Patrick sighed and patted the pocket of his flannel shirt where he kept a pack of Black Jack chewing gum and some mints wrapped in crunchy cellophane. "The girl thought I was dead. Róisín was only seeking more money from me and doing what she could to shame me. She knew I wasn't coming to Ireland. And writing to that scum, John? I wasn't about to do that again. Didn't trust him, and I still believe I was right not to. Besides, Róisín never wanted my help before. She'd made it clear she didn't want me involved. She would never have told the child about me even if I had written. At least this way the lass thought her old da left unwillingly in a coffin." He'd believed that once, but now, with that cursed letter? The mints weren't enough. He needed a wee dram. Maybe later when his daughter wasn't around.

"So you think Róisín lied about Juniper being troubled?"

"Can't say if she did or not. What I believed was that disrupting that child further could bring no peace. And I didn't want to upset the lives of the people I loved in America. I told your mother Róisín had stopped writing and she could see it was true. Róisín never wrote again after that." Patrick patted his chest again and reached into his pocket for a peppermint. "Think of me what you will. That was the younger man called Paddy, and for better or worse, 'tis what happened and I cannot change it."

Mardell stirred her coffee with a spoon. "I can't judge you, Dad. I wasn't in your shoes. I do know the father who raised me was a swell humdinger."

Odd lingo the youth today used. "You made it easy, darlin."

Mardell wrinkled her nose. "I still don't understand why you didn't tell me years ago, Dad."

"I'm sorry." *The other letter.* He would need to show it to her, but when the time was right. Not while she was still reeling from this one. "I had wanted it to stay buried in the past. However, your mother's passing made me consider how short my own time on Earth will be. You should know this story. I know it's a sad one, but about your family, though all the characters in this tale are dead now. All but me."

"But we don't know for certain that everyone's passed," Mardell insisted.

He patted his pocket of gum. "I feel it deep down. Hear me out. Juniper was sent to an asylum. Her health was fragile. We will look for the lass if for no other reason but to find out what happened to her. For you."

Mardell shook her head. Placing a hand to her side-swept curl where a bobby pin had dislodged, she let out a long slow breath. "No, Dad. I believe this trip is really for you."

They sat in silence for a moment. Had he been wrong not to respond to Róisín's last letter? He might never know.

"Just one left," Mardell said.

"Indeed. The letter from John."

Mardell read it aloud, squinting at the paper and asking for clarification when she found a word she couldn't untangle.

3 May 1938

To: Paddy Doyle, Golden, Ohio

From: John McGurdy, Dublin, Ireland

Dear Paddy,

It is with sorrow that I inform you of the passing of Róisín. There was a fire. She passed two days ago and was buried today. I thought you would like to know. I've had no word from your mother so I did not know how to reach her. She was terrible sick the last we knew. I suppose you will tell her if she still lives.

With regret,

John McGurdy

"You see, Mardell. No mention of Juniper. And with what he said about my mother, it's clear she's passed as well."

"Mom didn't ask you to look for them when you got this? Don't tell me you kept this one from her as well."

"I did not. She read it. Your mother understood me, Mardell, in a way no one ever had and ever will again." He coughed as the scent of the peppermint lifted through his sinuses. "Listen, darlin, I know you'd like to have more family. I'm very sorry your mother and I couldn't have more children. But you won't find what you're looking for in Ireland. Make your own family. Get married and have lots of children. Leo is a fine man."

She shook her head. "Not me we are talking about, but you."

"Here now." He pointed to her pocketbook. "Take a look at that guide and plan our wee holiday, won't you?"

Mardell gripped her purse but didn't open it. "Ireland's a beautiful place, but the guidebook will not tell me what I most want to know."

"Don't suppose it can," Patrick admitted.

"I want to know the people. Our roots are here, even if we are Americans."

Patrick studied his daughter's beautiful face, his child who was here right now. They should not spend all their time looking for a ghost. "I expect you'll meet a few folks. The Irish are all right, save for a few."

She smiled.

"But then when we return, what about Leo? Don't you like him?"

"Of course I do, Dad."

He sighed. "Then don't lose him. He needs a wife, his own business, children. After a war, those are the things a soldier wants and needs." He thought of Colin. Poor dead Colin. The rosary in Patrick's trouser pocket lay there like an iron weight.

"Later, Dad, if it's to be."

"Modern women," he mumbled, making her laugh. How could he possibly make her understand? He wished for his daughter not to struggle as he had. Perhaps the only way for her to appreciate that she needed to grasp the best of life right now while she could was for her to learn his story. Patrick wished for an uneventful trip, although his heart told him this would not be that.

CHAPTER 15

R óisín
1938, Causeway Coast, Northern Ireland

She'd written a lie but it was best that everyone, including Paddy, believe she was dead. Using the guise of being John, she was able to keep track of Juniper and send her money. Her poor dead brother would have wanted her to do whatever she needed to. He alone knew how evil their father was. Besides, Paddy's silence had made it known that he was done with her and their child. Róisín didn't owe Paddy the truth.

She did, however, owe Juniper the truth, and now that she was old enough, Róisín needed a new plan, a way to explain without causing too much pain. Not now, though. Juniper was finally going to be released from St. Giles. That was enough to deal with.

Pouring tea into her cup, Róisín breathed in the welcome fragrance. How often she'd wished for someone other than the local rector to share her table. Once, while out walking, she'd noticed some folks watching her. Holding a hand to her chest now, she felt her pulse rising as it had then. It had only been an American couple on holiday seeking directions to the pub. She'd not been discovered, unlike that day in Belfast, the reason she conversed with her solicitor only by mail or telephone now.

Sitting down at her kitchen table, she remembered the terror she'd felt when she'd stopped at a newsstand in Belfast, planning to pick up a magazine to read on the train. A ruckus rang out from across the street. At the entrance of the Royal Hippodrome theater a group of men shouted and pointed in her direction. As they came toward her, she recognized one of the men. He worked for her father. She tried to run, clutching her tote of legal papers. The man caught up with her and pinned her against a red phone box. "We've got our eyes on you, Róisín McGurdy," he snarled. "Got orders to squeeze you a bit should you talk about … private family matters. You and that bonny lass of yours. I'd enjoy that." He'd pressed a hand into her blouse, fondling her breast with the butt of a pistol. She couldn't breathe, even now smelling the stale tobacco odor coming from the box and the stink of the man's sweaty flat cap as it pressed into her face. She wouldn't let anyone touch her child like that, no matter what she had to do.

When the thug let her go, she'd run into a shop and spent way too much money on a new emerald green coat with a matching hat that adequately covered her hair. Róisín McGurdy had never worn anything so colorful and expensive, a fitting disguise. They knew she was alive! Her mind raced. They didn't know where she lived, though.

She'd lingered in the shop, counting to a hundred before sneaking out the employees' exit, vowing never to leave her concealed wee village until she was sure she wouldn't be followed.

CHAPTER 16

J uniper

1938, County Monaghan, Ireland

"Headed home, my dear?"

The elderly gentleman seated across from her smiled. He had been asleep when she boarded.

"I am."

"To your sweetheart, perhaps?"

His words bit right through her. Why did women have no identity unless connected to a man? It was as though all the years of holding back her tongue came crashing forth. "I've no need of a sweetheart." That was rude. She was about to apologize when he interrupted.

"One of those, are you?" He vacated the seat and wandered down the aisle in a huff.

What did that mean? An insult? She supposed she deserved it. Her first conversation with a stranger since leaving the asylum and she'd failed miserably. A couple of schoolboys in short pants stared at her and whispered behind their hands.

A young woman about Juniper's age took the old man's seat. "I know what you are saying, there." She bobbed her head up and down. "Divorce is illegal under de Valera's constitution, as you know."

Juniper did not know. Hadn't even wondered.

"Because of the church, so it is, but I had hoped the Free State would be more progressive." She shrugged. "That's why I'll never marry." She stuck out her hand. "Shelagh Lucey."

Juniper was not prepared to make friends so soon. She had hoped to observe life for a while before stepping into it. "Nice to meet you," she said, intentionally not offering her name.

"And what would you be called?"

Juniper blew out a breath. "Anna." She was used to the name, even though in her own head she was Juniper. She supposed it would always be that way.

The girl tilted her head, waiting for more. "Anna … ?"

John had warned her. Juniper had no reason to doubt him but hadn't thought this through. She glanced at a tea advertisement on the wall by the window. Nambarrie's, established 1860. "Barry. Anna Barry." Reinventing herself. Granny would understand.

"Nice to meet you, Anna Barry. May I call you Anna? You may call me by my Christian name."

"Certainly."

"I'm going home after visiting cousins in Armagh. You?"

Nosey lass. Juniper had thought about opening a shop so she'd have to get used to small talk. "I'm going to be living between Lisburn and Moira. Do you know it?"

"Ah, we'd be neighbors then. My home is just beyond Kircassock House."

Juniper's puzzlement must have shown on her face.

"The manor house, you know?"

"Sorry, no. I've been away in the south, lived in Dublin for a time." No need to tell anyone she'd come from the asylum in County Monaghan. "I'm planning to open a shop."

Shelagh rubbed her hands together. A crucifix bounced at her neck as she moved. "I will be your first customer." Shelagh, a Catholic who believed in divorce. What a new world Juniper was finding herself in.

Amused by the lass's forwardness, Juniper said, "You don't even know what I'm selling."

"Tell me now, won't you?"

"Herbs, tea, a few sundries." She'd need to get some of that Nambarrie tea too. "I expect it will take a few weeks to get set up."

"Say, trade has opened up because of the Ango-Irish Agreements. Read about it in the papers." Shelagh shrugged. "I like to keep up with things. Will you be getting in some goods we haven't seen around here, Anna? Most folks don't have the luxury, if you call it that, to travel into Belfast, and even when we do, we can't always find what we'd like."

"Oh, I'm not sure." Juniper had no idea what country folk wanted. She hadn't been in any shops. She just knew what things people needed, whether they understood that they needed them or not. "Soaps, lotions, throat syrups, digestion aids, all homemade."

"No stockings? Magazines?"

"Nothing like that, I'm afraid. At least not to start."

"Well, I'll tell my mother about your shop."

"Thank you."

The girl moved on when they approached the next stop.

Juniper collected a notebook and pencil and wrote down the items she thought she'd sell. She'd spent as much time in the abbey gardens as she could and was allowed to continue the practice when they'd sent her to St. Giles. Mr. Mackenzie taught her which plants grew the best and how to use the mortar and pestle to grind herbs and seeds into oils that could be used for different purposes. She'd been a good student. She needed seeds to start planting her medicinal gardens but for now she'd forage. Granny would help. Though she'd lived most of her life in Dublin City, Granny still surprisingly knew a lot about herbs. She'd given Juniper written instructions for some tinctures to try.

Juniper got off at the next stop and approached a railway worker. "I'm in search of Glasgleann Cottage. My aunt Elizabeth Campbell used to live there before she died. We called her Aunt Bet."

The man grumbled, stroking his brush-like mustache. "About a mile north up the road. Don't know what a young one like you would want with that dump. No one's lived there for nearly a decade."

Of course it was vacant. The directions to the cottage had mentioned a need for repairs. When she was a child, her mother had taken her there for a holiday to visit their old aunt. She was sure Granny had been there. Uncle John too. The adults had argued fiercely. Looking back on it now, Juniper realized they'd quarreled about her. Uncle John insisted Juniper stay in the north and far away from someone. She didn't know who. Or maybe it had been her mother insisting. She didn't know. These gaps in her memory were troubling. So much duplicity. Juniper felt loved, she felt neglected. Someone cherished her, someone scorned her. If her worthiness resided somewhere in the middle, perhaps there was a chance she could succeed.

Racking her brain for what Uncle John had meant about shielding her from someone, Juniper assumed he referred to some political insurgent wanting to murder the McGurdys. Whoever it was that had ambushed her mother, apparently. Because Aunt Bet had married a man named Campbell, Juniper could avoid mentioning the McGurdys or even the Doyles to anyone she might meet there.

Juniper tried to recall the cottage and what it had looked like, but she simply could not remember. The holiday at what was called Glasgleann Cottage hadn't lasted more than a couple of nights because Róisín had whisked Juniper away. There'd been a pattern of drawing close and pushing away. So much so that Juniper had thought of her mother as a sort of Father Christmas, someone who only visited once a year bringing toys and peppermint sticks.

The first thing Juniper must do now was write to Granny and convince her to come. Whatever state Granny's health was in, it would be better for her to be cared for by kin. Juniper had paper and could get some stamps and figure out how to mail a letter straightaway.

The stranger before her seemed to be waiting for her to say something. Juniper cleared her throat. "That's the place I need to get to. Thank you for your help."

"Might get a spot of tea before you go on." He pointed to a building with a wooden sign out front. It read, *Ellen's Café*. Tea would be delightful.

Juniper dipped her chin and hurried toward the door painted a cheery yellow shade.

"Not from around here, are ye?" a woman stacking biscuit tins at a counter asked when Juniper entered.

The single room contained two square tables, each with four chairs. Juniper and the woman were the only ones inside.

"Aye, I'm new here."

"Well, you are very welcome, so you are. I usually have customers in on the four o'clock. Don't get many before that, but you're in luck. Water's hot and I've got a few warm scones with sultanas and jam. How does that sound?"

"Absolutely heavenly." Juniper paid the woman with one banknote, received some coins back, and then sat to wait for her tea to steep, studying the sky outside the lone window. She didn't know what she'd find at Aunt Bet's cottage, so she dared not tarry. It needed at least a sweeping, she imagined. Taking a bite of the pastry, Juniper was delighted by the flavor. "These are wonderful!"

"Glad you like it. Nothing fancy."

Sure it was. Porridge and soda bread were the closest things St. Giles had to this, and those couldn't compare. She'd need to learn to cook like this. "May I purchase a few tea bags to take with me?"

"You may indeed."

"May I ask, are they Nambarrie's?"

The woman appeared pleased with Juniper's question. "Indeed. The best from Belfast."

"Thank you."

After tea, but before finding the cottage, Juniper would look for the grave. Uncle John's instructions had briefly mentioned the name of the churchyard where her mother was buried, saying it wasn't far from the cottage. An unmarked site that was far from where Róisín had lived most of her life. Whatever his reasons were for interring his sister there, he'd done it and Juniper would visit. Once. No one would wonder about it, especially without an identifying marker.

"Excuse me," she said to the café worker. "Are you familiar with a church called ..." She took the letter from her pocketbook to find the name. "St. Finian's?"

The woman nodded. "A ruin, 'tis. A quarter mile down the road that way and you'll find a country lane leading right to it. Fond of ancient ruins, are ye? Don't get many tourists around here."

"Just curious and I thought I'd take a look. There's a burial ground there?"

"There is."

"Thank you."

Later, when Juniper opened a low iron gate to let herself into the churchyard, its squeaking caused her heart to thump. From grief or fear?

The place was a bit overgrown and the gravestones still standing stooped as though passing centuries weighed heavily on them. Second row, one, two, three, four, five. Yes, the ground was soft here and recently disturbed. *Oh, Mam. Why were you so reckless? Why was your heart so cold?*

On top of the dirt she placed a yew stem she'd snagged from a nearby tree, the best she could do. A juniper branch would have been better, but she'd never seen one. Mr. Mackenzie had told her they were not easily found in County Monaghan, at least not near the gardens he tended. He'd also said her parents had not likely found the bush in Dublin either, which was where she'd been born. The reason she'd been called Juniper was another detail no one had shared with her. Juniper's troubled childhood, the loneliness, more doctors than she could count, the sisters at the abbey who treated her as though she were less than the soil under their shoes … all behind her now. A new name. A clean slate.

CHAPTER 17

P atrick
18 May 1950, on the Atlantic

After they'd finished eating a steward approached the break-fast table. "Ship to shore call for you, Miss Doyle. From a Mr. Leo Walsh. I'll escort you to the telephone."

"Oh, good heavens," Mardell said, rising from her chair. "What that must have cost him."

Several minutes later Mardell met Patrick in the corridor outside their cabin.

"Not an emergency I hope."

"No, Dad, not at all."

"What then?"

"Seems he forgot to tell me some things."

That he loves you? That he wants to marry you?

"I told him we would be looking for Juniper in Dublin. I mentioned that we may take a trip up to Northern Ireland. Do you think they may have taken Juniper up there? I mean, they moved her to the country, the letter said."

Patrick willed himself not to cough again and hoped Mardell didn't notice and fuss over him. "Six northeastern counties are not in the Republic, my dear. Well north of Dublin, where the border lies, is part of the Crown. Róisín would never have moved there."

"I realize that Juniper's mother was an active insurgent and anti-British."

Paddy grabbed her arm and tugged to the side of the corridor as a group of men sauntered past. "Pipe down, Mardell. You don't know what you're talking about."

Eyes wide, she studied the backs of the men until they rounded a corner and disappeared from sight. "Help me understand, Dad."

Patrick's chest ached. *How to explain this?* "Those who wanted to see Ireland independent don't see themselves as insurgents. They believe they are true and rightful inhabitants of Ireland and the British are the interlopers. I'm not saying that view is right or wrong, but I will say this." He leaned in to whisper. "When I lived in Ireland there were those who despised a native-born son just for fighting in the first war. For all I know, nothing's changed. We mustn't speak of it over there or even on this ship."

She nodded, tight-lipped.

They continued their stroll as though walking through a minefield. "So what else did your lad say?"

"I told him maybe, if things worked out, we might be able to go to Moira for him, and he said he couldn't remember the woman's name who healed him. But I assured him we'd ask around if we are able to go north."

Patrick scoffed at the notion. Snooping around wouldn't be tolerated. He didn't want to meet the barrel of some old soldier's rifle. "I hope you told him to wire us if he remembers. It would make things much easier."

Mardell gave him a smirk.

Later, over a dinner of Salisbury steak and boiled potatoes, Mardell urged Patrick to continue his story about the early days of his marriage to her mother. Patrick was pleased to discover that talking about Veronica now came easier. He found relating stories about her oddly comforting.

"She loved that old apple tree," he said.

"Is that why you sit under that tree in our yard so often, Dad? Because it was your special spot?"

"Indeed, Mardell. Reminds me of those days, the best of my life."

Mardell sniffed and dabbed a tissue to the corner of one eye. Patrick changed the topic to the possibility of a gathering storm at sea, then the type of currency used in Ireland, and finally they discussed how many woolen stockings they'd packed. Patrick studied his daughter's face. She was grieving, too, and he felt ashamed he hadn't tried harder to comfort her.

Later Patrick took Mardell's arm in his as they strolled the deck. "Your mother loved our plot of land and so do I." He patted her arm. "I don't mind talking about your mother if you don't. We must remember the happy times."

She agreed. "So, Mom was a social reformer and you needed delivering from the poor house, you say?"

"Something like that. She saved me, she did. Always looking out for the downtrodden, your mother. After we moved to Ohio, she continued by knitting mittens for orphans and visiting the sick."

"With the church."

"That's how it's done in Ohio. A good woman, your mother."

"I know. I hope talking about this hasn't upset you."

Patrick shuffled his feet as another cough overtook him. Clearing his throat, he answered. "As I said, we must keep her memory alive."

Mardell sighed and paused to scribble in her notebook, perhaps to distract herself from crying. Veronica had left a great void.

"Maybe I should be buried one day under that tree."

"Dad! Stop talking like that."

Patrick chuckled. "She wanted to be buried in the cemetery like most folks, so we granted her that wish. I suppose I should be there, too, but that apple tree seems like a better spot to spend eternity."

CHAPTER 18

Juniper
1938, County Down, Northern Ireland

Less than an hour after visiting the graveyard, Juniper allowed her aching feet to pause at the top of a rise in the road. At the bottom of the hill a roofless stone cottage seemed to wheeze against the breezes. Vines crept up the walls and only one of the two windows she could see had panes. Glasgleann Cottage looked like a burned-out famine house, those the police destroyed in the 1840s so tenant farmers with potato-blighted fields would not return. She'd learned of that practice from a girl at St. Giles who said that had happened to her grandparents and others like them. And here she was going into a dilapidated building rather than running from it. With a heavy sigh, she trudged on. There was no place else to go.

A postman on a bicycle approached from behind, ringing a tinny bell. "Good day, miss." He dismounted, obviously intent on having a chat. "You're new here, so you are." It wasn't a question. "Name's Evans, Toby Evans. Suppose everyone should know the postman, don't you think?" He chuckled as though he'd told a joke.

Smiling, Juniper introduced herself as Anna Barry, remembering to use the name she'd decided upon. She inquired about posting her letter to Granny.

"I can take care of that. No more than two pennies for your average letter."

"Thank you." She turned toward the cottage.

"You think you'll live there, do you?"

"I shall. I have the paperwork." A paper that seemed to indicate ownership had been in the pocketbook. It had her mother's name on it but since she was now dead Juniper doubted that mattered. She wondered if she'd need to show it to him to get her mail. She'd been instructed not to divulge her surname.

He chuckled. "No matter if you do. No one else will have it. Sometimes when a house is abandoned, squatters move in. But not there." He cleared his throat. "Are you all right, there? Anyone with you?"

"Uh, soon. I'm to get started."

He glanced at her small suitcase. "Be needing some tools, I expect. I'll come 'round tomorrow with a few things."

Surprised, she nearly forgot to thank him. "So kind of you, Postman Evans!" she shouted after him.

He waved an arm over his head and pedaled away.

After several minutes of pushing and shoving, the cottage door finally inched open. The dampness made her sneeze.

There was a small room up front, a kind of shelter from the wind coming in the door. That could work for her shop. She didn't need much room. Behind an opening in the wall, large enough for a door should she decide to put one in, lay the main room of the cottage: a hearth, a dresser for dishes, one table pushed up against a window that looked out on a garden of brambles. Another door led to a cold room for storage. Maybe one day she could make that a separate bedroom. With some ticking she could assemble a straw mattress. She'd learned how at St. Giles. Glasgleann certainly had possibilities.

A cabinet near the hearth housed a broom. Getting to work, she cleared dried leaves, clumps of wet weeds and grass, and more cobwebs than Mr. Mackenzie's shed had ever seen. She even scared up a nest of mice. This cottage, such as it was, belonged to her, according to her uncle. Not even weariness from all the walking she'd done that day could deter her from tidying up her inherited property.

Pausing, after taking in the space, Juniper decided she'd done enough for now, but there was one sobering problem. No roof would make for a disagreeable night. She'd spotted a pile of lumber near an abandoned cow shed on the property and carted a few planks to the house. With the sky darkening, Juniper struggled to lift a few boards across the top of the stone walls until she had a wee covered area. *Good enough for tonight.*

Finding a flint stone and two stubby candles in the cottage's mildewy dresser, she was successful in bringing some light into the cottage. After that she labored to get a bit of a fire burning in the hearth. A bed on the dirt floor felt luxurious because she was completely free. Knackered beyond belief, Juniper soon drifted off to sleep.

When morning dew dripped between the boards and landed on her nose, Juniper rose to assess her surroundings by daylight. She hurried outside to relieve herself. She'd figure the toilet part out later. Back inside a kettle hung near the now-cold fireplace. She scrambled to find some dry sticks to restart a flame. This time the work would be easier because she'd had a bit of luck: dry matches on the mantel. With a small blaze glowing, she collected the kettle, pulled on her Wellington boots, and headed through the door to ferret out the spring that must be in the brambles somewhere. There was no well she could see, but since folks once lived in the cottage, there had to be a source of water nearby.

Juniper was just emerging with a pail of water when she heard Toby's whistle. "Come with a sickle and a shovel," he said, smiling. "I'd stay to help, but of course I've got the mail. Do you think you can manage?"

"I shall. Thank you so much, Mr. ..."

"Toby will do, Miss Barry. I hear you'll be opening a shop."

"Where did you—?"

"See if you can get some sweets, won't you? When you're ready?"

"Well, I'm not sure how long it will be. I'm a long way from being ready." She accepted the tools and leaned them against the cottage wall. "This is very kind of you."

He dipped his chin. "Right. Well, in due time." Toby straddled his bicycle and waved in the direction of the large sycamore at the north end of her house. "The ghost tree ... or was. See that you don't disturb it, so. The people around here won't come near your place if you bother it. Don't trim it, and try to make sure no one has to get close to it to walk in. A fence or something. That should do it, so it will."

"Ghost? You mean haunted?"

Toby smacked his lips. "Not haunted exactly. Not unless the spirits are released, and thus far no one believes they have been. A priest bottled them all up and trapped them in the tree." He rubbed his chin. "Suppose that was ten years going on now, so."

"Why would he do that? I mean, if it were even possible."

"Oh, talk is a young lass was murdered here long before any of us were born. Now, don't believe it myself, but you know how people blather on. The priest, Father Joseph Barr, gone to his great reward now, of course. Father Barr put an end to the high tales by capturing those evil spirits and confining them to that tree, so they say."

Juniper blew out a breath and mumbled under her breath. "So that's why there were no squatters."

"What's that?" Toby asked.

"Oh, nothing." When someone got an idea about a curse or some supernatural occurrence, it was better to go along than try to convince them otherwise. She'd been shunned at St. Giles when she questioned the fairy faith of the girls, and that had been among children. How much worse would it be with adults? No, she needed customers. "I will take great care with the tree, Toby. Thank you kindly for telling me."

"Makes for some fine craic, doesn't it, so?"

"May I ask you something?"

"You may, of course."

"This area, is it Catholic?"

He chuckled. "From Dublin, are ye?"

"Well, yes." He must know that lass she'd met on the train. "You mentioned the priest. I only want to know the people I will be serving at my shop, to respect their religion. Doesn't matter to me otherwise." Juniper didn't care how someone practiced their faith, but she had lived only among Catholics. There were many Protestants in Northern Ireland, so the papers said. That was probably why her mother didn't stay, she supposed.

"Will your shop be a Catholic shop or a Protestant one?"

The question surprised her. "Oh, it will be for everyone."

He nodded as though she'd given the right answer. "We've a small parish. You probably saw the church on your way in. The Church of Ireland is further down the hill and a wee bit to the east. Not many people altogether, though. Fitting that they can all come shop here. Don't know if the others feel the same way about the tree—'tis not talked about amongst Protestants—but I imagine they do. Legends being what they are." He smiled. "In that case, those folks might stay away from here just because of what the Catholics believe about that tree. If that is the situation, nothing can be done about it, so it can't. Best to respect that tree and not touch it."

Confusing. "Would you mind letting folks know all are welcome? I mean, as the postman you probably know everyone." And he would likely tell everyone about her anyway.

Toby straightened his shoulders. "I imagine I do." He winked. "I'll do my best." He tipped his hat, placed the letter she'd given him for Granny in his knapsack along with the coins for the stamps, and shoved off down the road.

She moved closer to the sycamore. Its branches stretched out near where the roof should be but could probably be avoided. If she marked off the area around the trunk by building up a stacked stone barrier and then planting some wood anemone in front of that … no, too late for blooms. She'd find something else to bring in a wee bit of sunshine and good thoughts.

Juniper made her way back to the spring, taking account of the vegetation growing in the vicinity. The days were wetter than in the winter, and the temperatures warmer, enabling more plants to bloom. *Let's see.* A bit of yellow caught her eye and she moved toward it. A vast carpet blanketed the side of a wee hill. Ah, creeping buttercup. A few cuts of the shovel and there was enough of the plant to brighten things up front.

By the time the postman returned the next day, Juniper had tidied the front of the cottage.

"Very nice, Miss Barry. Very nice indeed." He raised his brows as he inspected the barrier she'd made. "That should do the trick."

"Thank you for loaning me the tools. Would you like some tea? I'm afraid I don't have a table, but I have cups and some Nambarrie tea I purchased from the café at the depot."

"Delighted, Miss Barry."

She cringed. How long before people realized she named herself after a box of black tea? Should she ask him to call her Anna and drop the formalities? She was just getting used to it herself. And besides, was that how it was done? Living so long in institutions meant she hadn't learned things other people seemed to know instinctively. Hopefully Granny would come straightaway when she received the letter. Juniper needed her.

"I'll send a man down for the roof, Miss Barry. And I've brought you some milk and eggs to keep you until you get some animals yourself."

"Oh, I'm afraid I've not enough money for a roof." At least she didn't think so.

"No need. 'Twas all taken care of, so it was."

Uncle John. Where was the man getting all this money? "Did a man called John pay for it, then?"

"I don't know the details, Miss Barry. I just know 'tis paid up. Maybe by those coming to join you? You'll be needing a roof, so you will."

She didn't want to sound ungrateful. She did intend to pay her uncle back, though. "Of course. Thank you for letting me know."

He handed her a cloth bundle that smelled of currants and cinnamon. "A gift from herself, Mrs. Evans."

"How kind."

Toby's gaze took in her makeshift attempt to cover part of the house in boards. "The gardening, aye, that's fine. The roof's been sorted. Now, a latrine?"

She hadn't planned well. There was so much to think about. "Do you suppose, Postman Toby, these men coming to put on the roof, might they be willing to barter for their labor? I know you said it's been handled, but I'd like to pay what I can myself. I know how to make soap, lotions, even a few medicinal items."

"If you brew only cosmetic items, I would say there aren't any men who would take such a barter." He winked at her.

She felt her face betray her disappointment and turned her head.

"But their wives might," he added.

Wives. Of course! She faced him. "With a promise for a pair of silk stockings just as soon as I can procure some goods?"

"That'll do it, for the younger lasses. I'd work on your roof myself if it weren't for the mail but then my wife has no use for fancy silk stockings, so she doesn't."

Juniper couldn't help but wonder if Toby's wife would agree. "You've been very kind already. Please thank Mrs. Evans for the scones."

He blushed as though the compliment was too much to bear.

"Wait, I've money for the eggs and milk."

"No, please. 'Tis a welcoming gift between neighbors."

"How lovely." She would return the kindness just as soon as she got settled so as not to owe anyone.

After he left, she grabbed the borrowed shovel and stomped off to the spot behind the empty cow barn she'd chosen for the latrine. It seemed one had been there at one time and it shouldn't be hard to reestablish it.

When Juniper returned to the house, a dead mouse lay on the doorstep. She shoved it aside with the shovel. After washing up, she opened the door, preparing to return to her work and found four more dead rodents. *A schoolboy antic?*

She glanced around. "Hello? Anyone here?"

A boy dropped down from the branches of an oak and scrambled away. "You haven't scared me!" she shouted after him. "Come back for tea if you'd like."

The next day the postman arrived with two muscular men and a wagon of slate and lumber for the roof. Juniper could not imagine how expensive that must be. If only she had proper carpenter skills. There were so many things she would need to depend on others for. Too many things.

"Wouldn't turf be less expensive?" she called to them.

One of them shrugged but gave no other reply.

"I've got to go into town for a wee bit," she said.

More shrugs.

Juniper ambled a few miles down the road, and then passed through a pasture where she greeted a couple of lads and a dog tending a few sheep. Following Toby's instructions, she found another wee path, and continued on, taking in the landscape. A few neat, whitewashed cottages stood beside the path. As Juniper passed by, she did not notice anyone around. Finally, she found the heart of the village.

The shops Toby told her about were lined up in a row. A greengrocer, a sundry shop, and a pub where Toby said the post was delivered. You could drop off mail and buy stamps.

Nervously, Juniper moved about the grocer's shop, picking up potatoes, turnips, and some tinned meats.

"Good day to you, lass," a man wearing a white apron said as he continued stacking a display of apples. "Passing through, are you?"

"I just moved into Glasgleann Cottage."

He stood and held out a golden apple. "Glasgleann, is it?"

She nodded.

"Go on lassie, a gift."

"Thank you." She placed the fruit in her basket with the other items. "I would like to purchase these things."

"Certainly." The man moved to stand behind a counter.

She lifted her basket and set it in front of him.

He flattened his hand against his chest. "Terrence Boyd." He motioned toward the door. "Boyd's Fresh Fruits and Vegetables."

She'd seen the sign. "Nice to meet you."

"You're opening a shop, I hear." He licked the tip of a pencil and began writing figures on a pad of paper.

"You heard?"

He shrugged. "Too bad there's no place in the village for your shop. But I suppose if you offer out-of-the-ordinary items out there, you may do all right for yourself."

Was that encouragement? "My name is Anna Barry. Mr. Boyd, I'm afraid I'm not good with numbers. I need to learn how you do ... what you are doing there." She inclined her chin toward the paper. She'd learned basic mathematic skills, but barely. Her teachers had said she hadn't paid attention.

Lifting his head to look at her, the grocer winked. "I'd be happy to show you, Miss Barry. Why don't you stop by tomorrow afternoon?"

"Thank you kindly." Juniper handed him a note and accepted

the coins he placed in her hand, slipping them into a pocket inside her bag.

Back at the cottage, the laborers worked without speaking, so Juniper went about her own business of boiling herbs and smashing shells into powder with the mortar and pestle from Mr. Mackenzie.

The men brought their own lunch in a large hamper and ate in the wagon. Juniper skinned a rabbit she had caught. One meal a day would have to suffice for now. They ate in silence, something Juniper was used to in the sanatorium. The lack of conversation wouldn't help folks to get to know her but perhaps these men were just quiet types.

Juniper didn't mind being alone, but their sidestepping grew blatantly obvious with each passing day. The tree caused the trouble, she supposed. They had avoided touching it while putting on the roof.

The routine continued for many days. Roof-building was an arduous business. During that time she'd managed to ascertain the names of the primary workers, if not their apprentices who came and went, including a young boy Juniper thought might be the culprit leaving the dead mice on the step. James Sullivan and Mick Lucey were the two main workers. Mick was Shelagh's brother, the lass she'd met on the train. Juniper would owe those families a year's worth of soaps and stockings at least. Juniper had only worn wool stockings herself, but the girls at St. Giles had blathered on about silk being so glamorous that she figured that type of hosiery would be most desirable and perhaps bring people to her door, as Shelagh had hinted.

But first things first. Juniper purchased two goats from a woman who lived in the lane that led to the village, a Mrs.

Mulligan who, like the roofers, shared little conversation. There had been goats and sheep at St. Giles. Mr. Mackenzie showed her how to milk a goat. Most of the milk was sent off to a farmer who returned with cheese for the cooks to use. But Mr. Mackenzie always kept a bucket back to combine with the lye he made. She was fascinated by the process and couldn't wait to make her own soap. Fresh goat's milk would also be a good addition to her diet.

Juniper went about her business and did not seek out her neighbors again after purchasing the goats. Perhaps when Granny arrived they could go visiting together. How slow the post was! She could hardly wait to see Granny.

Late one afternoon, glancing up from her labors, she caught James staring at her. He nodded toward Mick, who was on the roof. They had worked efficiently all day as though they longed to complete their task and remove themselves from her company as soon as possible.

The day was warm. "You'll be getting a wee bit thirsty in this heat. Help yourselves to the spring out back," she called up to them. "You'll find cups and ladles out there."

"Thank you," was all they said.

Before the men left for the day one mumbled something about finishing up in the morning. Thankfully she'd prepared by ordering a few packages of silk stockings using the allowance from Uncle John. The stockings had just arrived in the post from Belfast, imported from London.

Juniper tried to interrupt the men as they readied to leave. They didn't answer so she called out, "Oh, Mr. Sullivan and Mr. Lucey, I'll have baskets for your relatives ready by the time you finish. Thank you so—"

The rumble of their wagon cut her off. Rude, that was. Haunted tree or no.

The next day was Sunday. Juniper hadn't expected the men to come at all, but they arrived at first light. Two reed baskets filled with goat's milk soap and bouquets of flowers she'd picked the previous evening from the meadow near the spring sat ready at her front door. Juniper tucked in one package of stockings each. These hampers should make a fine first payment.

The roof would be a glorious comfort after sleeping in the damp cottage. Humming a tune in the Irish language she'd learned from Mr. Mackenzie, Juniper gave the baskets a final check while breathing in the floral bouquets and the earthy smell of the new lumber above her head. Stepping outside with a basket on each arm, she startled at the sound of horse hooves. They were leaving without the baskets. Juniper called after them. "Wait!"

Mick shouted back. "No time, Miss Barry. We'll be late for mass. Expect you will be too if you don't hurry."

Well, if that was what they believed, why hadn't they offered her a lift? She'd just have to pay a visit to those families tomorrow. Juniper had no wish to darken a church doorway.

MONDAY MORNING WHEN TOBY ARRIVED, Juniper asked him where the men's families lived. "I've their baskets of soap and flowers and stockings. The men left yesterday without them."

The postman massaged the back of his neck. "Came before mass to finish the roof, did they? Well, I'll deliver those for you, Miss Barry. No trouble at all."

"I'd like to do it."

He frowned. "Hear me out now, lass." He rubbed his chin. "If James and Mick were working on the Sabbath, 'tis because they were spooked and wanted to finish the job straightaway. Now, don't you mind them. Will take a bit for the folks to come 'round to you and this here ..." He cleared his throat. "Your shop and all. They must get to know you first. Give 'em some time. Mary and Ellie will be right glad to get your gift, though, I'm certain. Shelagh too. Right glad."

"That's fine, then. Do make it clear 'tis a partial payment, won't you?"

When the postman was far down the road on his bicycle, a basket swinging from each handle, Juniper sat on the flat stone in her garden where she'd served Toby tea when they'd first met. The place looked suitable now, didn't it? Why had those men stared at her so strangely while she worked? It was as though their grannies had never used a mortar and pestle or chewed on sticks of wild bark. Juniper had been there only a short while and already she was an outcast. Hot tears formed at the corners of her eyes, stirring up righteous anger. She was a shopkeeper. They'd appreciate her for that. She'd just have to figure out how to get more stockings and a few magazines.

CHAPTER 19

P atrick
24 May 1950, Ireland

They arrived at the port in Cobh on a delightfully warm day. "I thought you said the sun never shines in Ireland, Dad." Mardell winked at him as they collected their luggage.

"Like this weather, do you?" a fellow passenger with a brogue said as he waited to collect his own belongings. "Just wait a moment, lass. Rain, clouds, winds, and bright sun, all in one day. That's Ireland!"

Mardell laughed. "Thank you for the warning." She then took Patrick's arm. "We best purchase an umbrella, then."

As they strolled along the streets, Mardell gasped. "Ah, look at that cathedral! Have you ever seen such a thing?"

"I left from Cobh, Mardell. Called Queenstown then. But aye, 'tis a wonder." They paused to gaze upward from the seaport. The houses and rooftops resembled a fairy-tale illustration. Truthfully, Patrick had paid little attention to his surroundings when he left thirty years ago. Who knew if he would have noticed anything this time either if it weren't for his keen daughter. So much like her mother. They both delighted in such simple things.

Perhaps his years away made him a common tourist now. Cobh was nowhere the size of Dublin and it smelled fresher, he admitted.

"Let's get some tea and biscuits," he told Mardell. "We need a rest, wouldn't you say?"

"Sure, Dad."

She didn't seem nearly as fatigued as he felt. Ah, to be young.

They sat in a café sipping dark tea.

"Strong stuff," Mardell exclaimed, setting her white teacup back on its saucer.

"Have some milk, darlin. 'Tis the only way to drink Irish tea."

She smiled and reached for the miniature cream pitcher on the table between them. "I've a lot to learn about Ireland."

"Here is something I bet those guidebooks don't tell you."

She arched her perfectly penciled brows.

"Here near Queenstown, as it was called then, during the war … uh, I mean the war I was in, a cruise liner much like the one we were on was torpedoed by a German submarine. The Americans had been warned by Germany but when the ship departed New York, no one took the threat seriously. Many lives were lost, although the townspeople here did the best they could to rescue survivors using just their ordinary fishing boats. That was 1915, I believe."

"That's terrible." She frowned and swirled her tea with a spoon. "There is so much tragedy in Ireland's history, isn't there?"

"I suppose there is in all the world. You are right, though. The Irish have endured a lot. That's why I wanted ... well, I don't regret going to America." There were things he regretted all right, but if he hadn't gone, hadn't suffered through what he had, he would not have his beautiful Mardell.

She sighed and gazed around at the other faces in the café. "It's a beautiful country, though. I'm sure there is much to like here. I want to see some high crosses and medieval castles. Hey, maybe we can find some live bands. You know, fiddles and tin whistles." She winked. "Maybe even follow a rainbow and catch a leprechaun."

Patrick shook his head. "You never can tell."

They found a hotel to spend the night before beginning the search for Juniper in Dublin. Patrick was weary, perhaps more from dreading the return to his hometown than from the transatlantic travel.

CHAPTER 20

J uniper

1938, County Down, Northern Ireland

Two months after opening her shop, Juniper realized making a livable income at Glasgleann would be more difficult than she'd imagined. She'd hoped to set aside something and work toward paying back the money her uncle had given her when she left St. Giles, but so far she'd saved nothing. He didn't seem to mind. The few correspondences she'd had with the man since arriving at the cottage had always intimated that Juniper didn't have to repay him. But she wished not to be under obligation.

Juniper did sell silk stockings, when she could get them, but the locals would not browse her homemade items, preferring to grab the most coveted goods, pay for them, and be on their way as quickly as possible. No one by the name of Sullivan or Lucey had dropped by. She couldn't say she was surprised, given their beliefs about her sycamore tree, but she was grateful for the quality work they had done on her roof.

The local parish priest had stopped in one day. That had been a disaster. He'd asked about her lotions and tinctures, wrinkled his long nose when he sniffed them. She'd tried to explain the benefits of her wares, but he never met her eyes. Instead he'd mumbled the words "utter tosh" and then invited her to mass. She'd given him a polite smile but said nothing.

In previous weeks while traveling to Belfast to obtain goods, Juniper had made note of the items people on the train with her were seeking during their shopping jaunts. Through observation as she passed by their farms and by questioning the postman, Juniper learned which items were difficult to find, and those were the items she ordered from Belfast and London to sell in her shop.

Sure, soap and lotions could be made by anyone, and folks might mend their tattered clothing rather than buying cloth or purchasing new, but there were other items like matches, nails, tools, and cookery items, that Juniper stocked. The only other shop in town, the one run by that man Boyd, Juniper hadn't visited since finding out he wouldn't teach her how to figure sums without employing roving hands. He'd gotten his due, however. A month ago lightning had struck his roof and the shop had burned to the ground. He'd gone off to Galway to live, Toby said. Fate had made her the only shop offering tools now. She pondered adding vegetables but as of now she grew only what she could eat.

"These are hungry times," the postman had told her. "Folks don't have much money."

"Well, I'm here to meet a need. I'll find a way," she'd told him.

Juniper sold wild rabbit she'd caught in traps and fish from her stream she preserved with salt for those who couldn't spare the time to hunt for themselves. Simple fare but it sustained her and kept hunger from her doorstep. She offered the meat at a price low enough that even the poorest families could afford it when food stores ran low and barns were nearly empty. She traded more often than not for honey, potatoes, whatever was available. Juniper even offered blocks of turf for a fair price so they could make their tea over a fire. Heaven knew many ran out of fuel before they could sell their livestock at market and needed it desperately.

Skinny, wide-eyed beggars sat on the stoops of both churches. Despite her wish to help them, most didn't come to Glasgleann Cottage unless they desperately needed a folk cure. That was what they called her medicine. She was happy to assist, but she couldn't eke out a living selling cures. The bills she still had in the purse that Uncle John had sent to St. Giles got her through.

Juniper might not be able to help the proud poor, or anyone as superstitious as the Sullivans or Luceys, much to her regret. But why did some folks wait until after harvest and then travel all the way to Belfast for items she carried right there in her shop?

And at long last, Toby delivered a letter from Granny. "Good to hear from your people," he said. Since the greengrocer shop had burned, Toby delivered mail to the door.

As eager as she was to read it, Juniper needed to first question the postman, her only source of village information.

Toby wasn't one to tolerate moments of silence. As she stared at the letter, he pointed to the sky. "'Tis a soft day indeed, Miss Barry."

"Oh, please come in, won't you? Tea kettle's hot."

He looked down at the threshold to her cottage. "No mice today, I see." He gave her a toothy grin.

"Did you know about that?"

"Oh, the lads. Don't mind them. Out here in this tall grass you're sure to have pests anyway. That's why I've brought you something." He lifted a furry bundle from his knapsack.

"A kitten!"

"Ah, so 'tis. We've a litter in our barn, so I brought you one. My daughter called him Michael, but you can name him as you like. A gift."

"I think that's a fine name. Thank you, Toby. And thank your daughter as well."

She brought the cat inside and let him loose to explore while she led the postman past the front room where her goods were displayed on shelves and in baskets and through to the rear kitchen. The room was brightened by the best feature of the house. She'd managed to clean and restore the framing around the wide window, and often admired the view from the homemade table she placed in front of it. She lit an oil lamp and placed the letter facedown as the two sat and sipped tea.

"Mighty kind of you, Miss Barry. Ready, so I was, for some refreshment." The postman took a bite of one of her lemon and spring mint biscuits. "Right good. And no one makes a better cuppa," he said, giving her a wink. "You won't be telling Mrs. Evans?"

"Our secret." She smiled at the thought of having at least one friend. "Won't you call me Anna, Postman Toby? I consider you a friend."

"Sure and that's fine, Anna." He popped the last of the pastry into his mouth and washed it down with tea. When she offered more, he declined. "I must be on my way."

"Please, may I ask your advice?" The sparkle in Toby's eyes told her he could not resist giving a say to whatever she asked. "The local people, they seem reluctant to spend time in my shop. Might you know why? I mean, I've tidied up the ground around the tree and no one has to brush past it to get inside."

He pointed to his empty teacup. "May I?"

"Please do."

Pouring more for them both, Toby cleared his throat. "Folks around here are a bit buttoned-down, you see. Cling to the old ways, they do. Your habits are not what they are used to."

"I don't understand. I produce my lotions and soaps according to the old ways." She stressed the word *old*. But she knew what he meant. "I may not go to mass, but I'm not wicked."

"Oh, no, my dear. Certainly, not. Folks are thinking you've some magical abilities about ya, and they've yet to construe if 'tis for good or malice. You came here unexpected, so you did, and moved into a derelict cottage, which you've improved mightily I must say." He drew in a deep breath, the shoulders of his jacket lifting. He relaxed and locked eyes with her. "Understand that this was an afflicted place, some folks believed, as I told ya before. There was a woman here before you, and she grew things and brewed things, like you."

"Indeed. Aunt Bet. Did people avoid her as well?"

"I'm afraid so. They did come to her wake, so they did. They respected her but there's that legend about the tree, and all. Some things never change." He rubbed his chin. "And, with you brewing and cooking up concoctions now, foraging for food in the honey-and-locust-manner of John the Baptist."

"What? People don't hunt and forage?"

"People farm and fish. Oh, and there's the speaking the Irish … well, 'twill take them a bit of time to get used to it, that's all." He cocked his head and reached for another biscuit.

"I learned a few songs from an old gardener, is all."

He nodded.

Juniper passed him the blue and pink flowered luncheon plate that held four more. She'd bought the plate at a charity shop in Belfast last week. Then she sighed, swallowed tea, and leaned back in her chair. "I mean no one harm nor trouble. I have no other home. I've got to make a go of it here."

Toby tapped an index finger to his temple. "Why not use this to your advantage?"

"What do you mean?"

"A woman of mystery, aren't ya now?"

"Mystery? I think not," she scoffed.

"Now, hear me out. Play the part. Folks are drawn to the … shall we say fanciful, mythical, unknown but greatly imagined? In the proper manner, I'm saying."

They shared a laugh. There was nothing mysterious about what Juniper was doing. Even so, she began to ponder how she might encourage that perception. Trying to fit in hadn't worked, so why not? One thing that came to mind was her discovery of snowdrops past their blooming, cultivated roses growing with wild abandon, and a sizable patch of soil tangled with herbs. These things weren't typically found at abandoned places, but Aunt Bet had grown quite a lot, as Toby said, and the earth hadn't forgotten. Glasgleann Cottage could produce rather quickly with only a little effort. Folks might think she grew a mature garden from seed in just a few months, like Jack and the Beanstalk. They'd believe the fairies worked alongside her, now, wouldn't they?

"That's it," Toby said after she told him what she was thinking.

She sighed. "Oh, I don't know. Do you really think that if I act like some sort of herbal magician, people will be intrigued and come out here?"

"Not that you use herbs. Sure, the poor do the same, as they couldn't afford a doctor even if there was one. You're an herbal healer from unknown parts, though. An enchantress of the garden. Sure, and they'll believe it. They want to already. They will be drawn to your cottage like flies on honey."

"They've stayed away so far."

"That's because they couldn't figure you out. Once they know what shelf they can put you on, so to speak, and see you as I do, they'll come."

Juniper stared in the direction of her crowded store shelves. "I'll try anything."

"Grand. I'll be off now. Thank you for your hospitality, Miss … ur, Anna." He tipped his hat before leaving.

Juniper returned to the letter and examined it quickly, hoping to find confirmation that Granny was coming.

At the bottom she noted *"your kind offer."* Juniper sighed, believing it to be a refusal. Then she saw the rest.

I shall arrive in late September. I will send a telegram when I'm on my way. I only have the one trunk, but it will be heavy so please send a man with a cart to the station.

Granny was coming soon!

FOR THE NEXT FEW WEEKS, to occupy her mind as she eagerly awaited Granny, Juniper put the plan in motion. Leaving dressed rabbits on the doorsteps of poor families when they were out working in the fields, wearing the black cloak St. Giles had allowed her to keep, doing whatever she could to give off an aura of mystique.

Once on the road as she passed one of the lads she thought may have been involved with the dead mice caper, she heard him say to his friend, "Has powerful magic, so she does."

It was working!

A few weeks later just as the sun rose, Juniper awoke to banging on her door. "Miss Barry! Wake up! Please!"

Pulling on her blue robe, Juniper scrambled to the door. A young woman cradling a wheezing baby stood on her stoop. "Come in straight away!"

"I didn't know what else to do," the woman said, her eyes shadowed. "The doctor is in Belfast and won't return until tomorrow. My Declan won't sleep nor suckle. I … I supposed you had something, some potion or herbs. Might you, Miss Barry? He's terrible sick, so he is."

Juniper instructed the woman to lay the child on her bed. Placing a hand on his face, Juniper breathed a sigh. No fever. A good sign. The child's nose was raw from running mucus, but his eyes were as clear as a lake in daylight. This was a common cold. "Your first babe, your Declan?"

"He is."

Juniper nodded and left to search her cupboards for eucalyptus. Retrieving a pestle, she ground the leaves and then mixed them with a bit of lard. "Rub this on his chest twice a day. Do not let him lie flat for a few days. He'll sleep better on your chest or propped up on pillows. He'll be well very soon, I promise."

Another voice came from the direction of the front door. "Aye, and I have some brooklime poultice that may help as well."

A stooped woman wearing a dark blue shawl smiled at her. "Granny?"

"Who else would I be?"

Juniper rushed to the woman. "When did you arrive? I would have come to the train to meet you."

Granny shook her head and began to dig into the basket on her arm. "'Twas quite early. I found my way and you got your sleep." She turned to the young mother, holding out a green glass jar she'd produced from her bag. "Let my granddaughter scoop some of this into a jar for you, lass. Your wee one will be better in no time."

Gleefully Juniper tended to the task, wondering how long Granny had been observing her.

"Miss Barry, madam, thank you both ever so much!" The visitor and her child left a small sack of potatoes as payment and hurried out into the misty morning.

Juniper hugged her grandmother. "'Tis been too long, Granny."

Granny wept as they embraced. "I wanted to come for you, but for some time I didn't know where you were. I was overjoyed to get your address and write. I was not able to travel before now, my dear."

"But here you are!" Juniper hugged her again.

"I thought you'd come here eventually," Granny said. She glanced around. "I like it. Been years since I was here but there's no doubt you've improved the place."

Juniper led her grandmother to the cushioned chair. "You grew up here?"

"Not in this house, but near here. Ah, a lifetime ago."

"I remember I came here with you and my mother. To visit Aunt Bet, I suppose. And you knew my mother would send me here when I was released?"

Granny frowned. "You were here with us for a short visit, and, aye, that was the plan."

"I'll make tea and we will catch up, Granny. Oh, your trunk."

"I met a friendly postman who said he'd have a man deliver it this afternoon."

"That would be Toby. You'll like him."

"Uh, Miss Barry? Why did that woman call you that? The postman, too, when I said I was going to Glasgleann Cottage."

"My way of making a fresh start. You don't object, I hope."

"No reason to. I'll still be your Granny Doyle."

"Miss Barry or Anna, I'm called. Let me show you what I've done to the cottage so far."

After taking a look around, Granny nodded and pointed to the room where Juniper's handmade bed was.

"Yes, please rest, Granny. I'll unpack for you." Never had Juniper been so happy. She had a friend now, a confidant, and the one person who could answer her many questions about her past.

"I want to show you something first." Granny wiggled a thick, ancient-looking book from her sack and placed it on the bed.

"Your Bible, is it, Granny?"

"Not the kind you mean."

"I recall you having a big, old book. Don't remember anything about it, though."

Granny carried the book back to the kitchen hearth and sat in the chair. The effort seemed to leave her winded. Drawing in a shallow breath, Granny opened the book on her lap. "This here is an old text. Perhaps a century or more has passed since its printing. Given to me by my grandmother. Filled with cures older than the pages, 'tis. And now it shall be yours, darlin."

"Mine?" Juniper took the book from her grandmother's outstretched arms and examined it. Yellowed pages displayed botanical drawings and lists of plants and preparations and what they were good for. "This is a valuable book, Granny. I've learned a bit from the abbey gardens and from a gardener at the asylum, Mr. Mackenzie. You sent me a few recipes in your letters. I understand how plants can heal. But I had no idea you had a whole book of plant wisdom."

"My eyes are too old to read it now." She gave a dismissive wave of her arm. "And I know what's in it all the same." She tapped her temple. "Locked away up here. This book is to be passed down in the family and finally I am able to fulfill my duty and give it to you." Granny waggled an arthritic finger. "Hard to keep a book like that safe in Dublin. The old ways … well, they are not appreciated there as they should be. Modern folks with their doctors now." She clicked her tongue. "Healers are what's needed, child. Someone must carry on the work of nature before 'tis all forgotten." Granny poked a finger toward the cottage door. "And won't that child's mother appreciate it and tell others." She chuckled. "We will be busy here, the two of us."

"Busy sounds grand." Juniper laid the book down and returned to pour boiling water over dried leaves and a bit of mint. Then she set the steeping teapot on the kitchen table while they talked.

"You think so? Well, consider it, dear lass. Folks here may like having a healer or two in their community, but there's a cost. You must decide if 'tis too dear."

"A cost? Folks here are beginning to think I'm something special because of it." The scent of the tea created an aroma that made her think of the home she'd always dreamed of. If there was a cost, Juniper would willingly pay it.

"Listen, child. We'll be outsiders. They think you special, aye, but you'll not be included in their craic, not invited to their music sessions at the public house, not paid visits at teatime.

I am an old woman. What do I care? But you are young, my dear."

Juniper huffed and scooted a teacup closer to the pot. "I'm already an outcast, Granny. You'll see. I always have been. But now that has given me a certain appeal when it comes to medicinal cures."

Granny left the chair and came to the table. She wrapped her hand around Juniper's wrist. Her fingers were bent and leathery. *Age is a thief,* Juniper thought. *If only time would slow a wee bit.* Juniper had been denied freedom for far too long and missed spending time with her grandmother.

"You should be prepared if you think a healer's life's for you," Granny said. "Sure, folks know how to use some plants to help wounds and digestion, but you'll know much more than they do because of this book, and they'll be suspicious of you."

"Granny, please sit."

Lowering herself slowly onto the kitchen chair, Granny let out a breath.

Juniper poured the tea. "I've never even been to a public house." The truth was, she hadn't been anywhere much. Just traveling to Belfast to make purchases and occasionally walking to the village center. "I don't care about those things. I've never been included before and don't care to be."

Granny puckered her lips as though she didn't believe her. "That's because you were excluded by way of the places where they put you, wrongly. Don't know any better."

"Believe me. I don't care. Especially since you're here now." Juniper nodded to a plate of biscuits. "From a tin. I'll bake something better in the morning."

Granny thanked her but returned her hands to her lap. "You were quite young. Don't suppose you remember much about your time living with me."

"I know that you wrote me. That meant everything. No one else sent letters, save for some from Uncle John and those were more instructions than anything else." Her father hadn't written either, but she didn't want to mention that and upset Granny. "I remember images. Just a bit. And I knew you loved me, Granny. That kept me going."

Granny stared past Juniper as she spoke. "The last letter I got from your father was troubling." It was as though she'd read her thoughts. "I shared it with Róisín, but I should not have, because her brother read it and wasn't he the one to shoot arrows into your father's reputation given half a chance."

"That must have been hard for you, Granny. My da being your only child. Why did he leave, Granny? Why did he leave us and never come back?"

Granny smiled and stared at the bottles on the shelf behind Juniper. "I knew you'd have questions. Ask all you have on your mind. I suppose Paddy believed he had no choice. No one would hire him in Dublin."

"Why not?"

Granny whispered. "The war, my dear, the First World War."

"Oh, aye. And then in America. My mother claimed he died."

"She should not have told you that. She thought it would be easier for you to accept, I suppose, and Paddy agreed, once he understood Róisín would not emigrate."

"I wish we could ask them."

"So do I, dear lass."

Juniper rubbed a finger along the rim of her teacup. "You haven't written him? I mean, there must have been an address on the letter he sent."

"Oh, aye, but the letter came back, addressee unknown."

"I'm sorry."

Granny sighed. "Nothing to be done about it but pray. I do plenty."

Juniper nodded and sipped her tea. "I'm glad you didn't lie to me, though."

"I couldn't. I know it may have been against Paddy's wishes, but I thought you should know the truth. As much I know."

Granny gazed into a dark corner of the room. "I cannot blame my son for not writing to me more. The folks in our lane didn't care for Paddy being a soldier in the British army."

"Even your cousins?"

"Distant relations. They took us in out of obligation but never thought of us as true kin."

"So they didn't like him joining up, but what other army was there back then? Ireland was not a free state yet."

"Ah, the timing of it all. Not his fault but they thought him a traitor just the same." She stared directly at Juniper. "He was not."

"Of course not." *Just a traitor to his child.*

Granny bit her bottom lip. "And me? They feared me as he was growing up, and he was surely ashamed."

"What? Who would fear you? They must have been daft."

Granny chuckled and sipped her tea. "No matter that I lived in Dublin for decades and married a Dubliner. I was still an outsider with a northern lilt to my speech, so I was."

"I'm sure my da wasn't ashamed of you, Granny. How could he be? Róisín perhaps, but not you."

"He loved the lass, but that was long ago." Granny put a hand over her mouth. "I should not speak ill of the dead."

"You may speak any way you'd like about my mother, Granny. 'Tis just us now."

Granny chuckled. "Us and the spirits." She tapped her knuckles on the wooden table. "But don't you see? I was a healer in the old ways and folks didn't know what to think of me. It will be the same for you, dear."

Granny got to her feet and shuffled over to retrieve the book. "I did nothing unusual, nothing supernatural. 'Tis all in here." She held it to her chest like treasure. "Spider webs bind bleeding wounds, comfrey root eases painful muscles, wild garlic soothes a cough." She gently placed the book on the table. "But no matter. Folks believe there's dark magic because they choose to believe it. I'm a proper Christian, but they don't care. They'll avoid you until such a time as when they're ailing and then they will come, usually under the cloak of darkness so the neighbors won't see. Fear, my dear. Fear drives folks to act not only unmannerly but sometimes with violence. If we could rid the world of fear most every scourge would vanish with it."

Granny left the book and plopped down on the kitchen chair with a sigh. Cradling her cup in shaky hands, Granny sipped and then drew in a long breath. "The thing about fear, though, is it burrows down deep inside." She wiggled a finger over her heart. "Folks can't cut it away, so they strike out against others as though doing so might force fear to the surface and plunge it out, like a deep-seated splinter." She shook her head sadly. "Doesn't work that way, though. Might burn down your cottage if they take a notion. To ward off evil, they'll tell themselves."

"Oh, Granny. Did something like that happen to you?"

Granny clicked her tongue and waved her fingers in front of her face. "Plenty of ill will. Never harmed me, but it was enough to make me think twice. After I put out a fire on the steps of our flat one day, I came with you and Róisín to Aunt Bet's cottage. John McGurdy joined us soon after."

"Why didn't you stay here, Granny, if Dublin was so bad?"

Granny let out a slow breath. "I had hoped to. I grew too ill to return. They took you away, child. I had no say in it. Even Aunt Bet didn't know where your mother and her brother had gone, but there was word saying they found a good place for you and they had meetings to attend back in Dublin. Talk was your mother had been arrested at one of those meetings, the kind the British government didn't approve of. I waited. I wrote to Aunt Bet, but she never learned anything more. I didn't find out where they'd sent you until a few years later when John forwarded a letter you wrote me from that hospital. By this time old Aunt Bet had passed away. I was the one who owned the cottage so I put it in Róisín's name, for you. We'd all agreed."

"Don't worry. 'Tis all in the past. Your letters were sunshine to my soul." Juniper reached out and gripped her grandmother's hand. "Tell me, Granny, how did you get interested in herbal cures?"

"I've had that book for quite some time, as I told you. My grandmother passed it down to me. How I came to live in

Dublin was I had gone there to find work. Not much opportunity around here and my parents needed my help. I met your grandfather there and decided to stay, thinking life would be better in Dublin. I was wrong but all past now."

"What do you mean?"

"Paddy's father was a drinker, half cut most the time. While Paddy was still a boy your grandfather was killed, God rest his soul, in an accident at the factory where he worked. Turned up hammered at the job, I expect. I had no family left up north, just Aunt Bet who was not able to help, so needing to support us, I turned to that book and my knowledge of nature's medicines to earn my living. It was all I knew, and I had a young son to feed. Perhaps it would have been better if I had gone to work in the factory if they'd had me. My occupation made us outcasts, which is hard on a young one. Sure, they believed in fairies and unexplained happenings. They were happy to pay me for my herbal treatments, but I was never accepted as one of them, and neither was Paddy. And when you were lost to me as well ..." Granny cleared her throat and sipped more tea.

"I understand, Granny. I would never blame you for what happened. My parents, aye, but not you."

Granny ignored the negative comment about her son, but Juniper needed to watch what she said. Her father was due some criticism, but Granny didn't need to hear about it.

"I made inquiries after I found out where you were, but the hospital administrators would not allow me to visit. I offered to raise you myself but was told that would not be permitted."

"'Twas my mother who sent me away."

"And her brother. The McGurdy men did not like Paddy. They made light of my work with plants. They didn't want me to be an influence on you. So I kept the book a secret. Until now. They can't keep us apart any longer."

"That's right."

"You must proceed with caution. There are plenty of folks who fear what they don't understand. I was an outsider in Dublin and you are one up here."

Juniper nodded and pushed the tray of sweets toward Granny. "The only evil I know of dwells inside the hearts of those working in the abbey and asylums."

Granny's cheeks reddened. "Were you harmed, dear?"

"I learned to keep quiet and I got along all right. They let me help the gardener."

Granny finally took a biscuit. "Ah, you mentioned that. 'Tis in your nature, I expect."

This was true, but Juniper would not tell her grandmother everything about that time. No need to relive some of the torture like the freezing then scalding baths they'd forced her into. To calm her down, they'd said. Those who feared Granny should visit the asylum and compare her gentle ways to that.

"You seemed to like the abbey, as I recall from your letters. You were young then, but I could tell you appreciated it there."

"I enjoyed the time they allowed me to work in the gardens. My rebellious nature only came about because they had moved me. My mother didn't want me."

"I don't know, child. She and John were deeply involved in some kind of business, all right. God only knows what."

Time to change the subject. "I don't go to mass anymore, Granny. I suppose I'm pleased to make my own choices these days. But if you'd like to go, we'll ask Toby about it."

Granny wrinkled her brow. "I'm sure the Catholics here are suitable folks, darlin. You must not scorn the church over a few rotten apples."

"I'll keep that in mind."

"Oh, my dear, what your mother put you through because of her narrow-mindedness. I'm at fault too. I should have tried harder. Can you ever forgive us?"

"You? No need. You couldn't do anything about it, Granny. You had your own health to consider. Besides, 'tis all behind me." Juniper hugged her grandmother. "We are together. That is all I care about. We will do good, you and me. I don't care a bit about being excluded from gatherings."

Juniper led her grandmother away from the kitchen table and back to the chair by the fire. Then she sat on the rug at her feet. The warm silence soothed her. Later she'd ask her questions. There were more things about her past she wanted to understand. To whom did all the voices in her head belong?

Granny napped while Juniper tidied up the dishes. A knock at the front door meant the trunk had arrived. Juniper was surprised she didn't recognize the man.

"Just arrived. Looking for work," he said as he set the trunk down inside the shop.

"I'm afraid I've none for you. Check the farm off the road just to the north. Can you do farm labor?"

"Sure. Thanks." He glanced down at the name written on the trunk. "Doyle?"

"My Granny. We appreciate it." Juniper handed him a few coins and he tipped his hat as he left.

After Granny woke from her nap, they discussed a few plants Juniper was curious about in the book. Then Juniper asked if she minded some more questions.

"I'm as comfortable here in this cottage as can be. What's on your mind, darlin?"

Juniper straightened her back. The room still held the scent of mint, which helped clear her mind. She told Granny about her recurring dream involving the cottage and something about a baby. While they were both in the dream, Juniper could not make sense of it. "Do you know what it all means, Granny?"

The older woman paled. "I held you that night as your mother and uncle read the lies about my son. They believed them. 'Twas published in a wee newspaper in the States and found its way to us. Rosemary O'Toole lived in the same building as the McGurdys. Her nephew, I believe, sailed to America at the same time as my Paddy. Suppose that's how it came to find us, something O'Toole had mailed home." Granny's brow creased. "Paddy wrote to me, explaining that he was innocent, and of course he was. He didn't want you to believe those things."

"Me? He mentioned me?"

"Aye, love. He knew the McGurdys would spoil your mind

against him. I didn't know, until later, that they'd told you he'd died. Otherwise I'd have told you sooner."

Juniper tried to breathe deeply but a rock seemed wedged in her chest, impeding every inhale. Spoil her mind? He couldn't hide the fact that he'd left her behind, could he?

Granny clicked her tongue. "I would not have thought you'd remember that night, but it has apparently been seared into your memory. Oh, my dear. What you have had to endure." Granny's weeping brought Juniper to her side.

"Please, Granny, don't cry. I didn't mean to upset you. We don't have to talk about this."

Granny cleared her throat. "It seems we do. God has given you these memories and we must try to find out why."

Juniper had never thought of her dreams as some kind of message. If Granny thought it was, so be it. She patted her grandmother's hand.

Granny licked her lips. "Róisín sent Paddy letters after that and she may have received one or two back, but shortly thereafter the letters stopped. I only got two. Paddy sounded despondent. He did want you to know, my sweet, that he loved you."

It didn't seem likely. "He never met me."

Granny shook her head. "As if that matters. Things just never worked out for you to be together."

Juniper smiled. "I am glad to hear you say so, Granny. Thank you." If Juniper had believed this years ago, if she believed it today, what would be different? Nothing. She hoped her father had loved her, but there was no way to know now. She'd grown comfortable with not forgiving him.

Granny's smile reached her eyes. "I have had the great honor of delivering that message at last." She kissed the top of Juniper's head. "Curses to John McGurdy for keeping us apart."

Juniper chuckled. Finally, someone on her side. Unlike Róisín, Juniper did not believe country came before family. She hugged Granny again but the uneasiness would not go away. "They spoke of a baby, Granny. What baby? Not me, as I don't believe I was harmed before I was sent away."

"'Twas a baby in America the newspaper spoke of. Paddy had nothing to do with whatever happened to the poor child." Granny made the sign of the cross. "Paddy denied it in his letter. But what happened to him after that, I don't know." Tears welled in her eyes again. "My Paddy, oh, my poor son." Granny held a handkerchief to her cheek. "He knew only trials his whole life. As the sun's coming up tomorrow 'tis sure that he did not kill any child. And I pray to the good Lord he did not pay for it." She sobbed and then wiped her tears while Juniper tried to console her. Granny showed her a medal she kept in the pocket of her skirt. "St. Jude, the patron saint of desperate causes." She kissed the medal before tucking it away. "I do not know if my son lives today, but you, his daughter, should understand that he was a good man with a gentle, kind heart."

Juniper once wrote him a letter, a scathing letter. Something about how he must not have wanted her. She couldn't remember all she'd written. She'd left it behind in the Bible in the asylum. She'd hadn't known he was alive then. If she could have sent it, or perhaps another that was less impertinent, would he have come? She'd never know.

CHAPTER 21

P atrick
1950, Dublin

After boarding the morning train in Cobh traveling east, Mardell continued her habit of snapping photographs through the windows. Patrick napped until they pulled into the station.

Dublin was not as he had left it. Scads more cars and bicycles crowded the roads now. Far more advertising signs were plastered to building fronts and double-decker buses had replaced the trams. New apartment buildings stood straight and glittering in the afternoon light, a modern enterprise replacing tenements. But more than all that, the place had a different feel. Thirty years. Of course the city would have changed. The whole country had, for that matter. This was now the Republic of Ireland.

Later, with Mardell on his arm, they made their way from their hotel to Stephen's Green.

"This is lovely, Dad. Right in the middle of the city."

"Old, quite old, this park." He couldn't remember where he'd rendezvoused with Róisín all those years ago. Somewhere nearby.

"Look at the swans! I've never seen one before." Mardell approached the edge of the pond as though the birds could be petted. "Such graceful long necks and pure white feathers."

He'd not seen one since leaving Ireland and hadn't even thought about that. No swans on the Jersey shore and only ducks in Ohio, save for the occasional goose and pheasant.

"Did you come here often?" Mardell put her hands on her cheeks and twirled around. "I can just imagine a young Paddy skimming rocks off the water."

He grumbled. "No time for that, lass. We were more concerned about putting food in our bellies. Survival." He was glad her childhood had been better.

Mardell took his arm as they walked through to the other side of the park. "Oh, Dad. I'm sure you had some fun as a child, besides that time in the Dublin Mountains."

Clouds encroached on the sun and Patrick opened the black umbrella he'd purchased when they first arrived. "I don't remember this place fondly, Mardell. Just how things were."

When they emerged from the trees they took a left onto Grafton Street. Mardell continued marveling at everything— the buildings, the lampposts, the bicycles. To hear her talk they'd arrived on the moon. When they rounded a corner Mardell halted in her steps. "Look! The famous Davy Byrne's. Shall we go in?"

"Might as well. I could do with a pint."

"Bloom ate a cheese sandwich and drank a glass of burgundy there."

He huffed. "That's only in a book, Mardell."

"I know James Joyce made up Leopold Bloom, but not the pub. Here it is. I can't wait to see it. I secretly added it to my list, you know." She winked.

"Nothing wrong with a bit of cheer. Let's go."

They found an empty circular table and Mardell sat on a round stool, gazing up at the lavish bar. Overhead, huge fixtures, also round in shape, were embedded into the ceiling. "Been in here before, Dad?"

"I have not. Hope the beer's good."

She shushed him.

Patrick approached the barman, ordered a pint for him, red wine for her, and two gorgonzola sandwiches. Mardell wasn't the only one who had read Joyce. After paying, he asked the barman for directions, using the details included in the old letter from his mother. "Take the bus over there," he recommended. "Twenty-minute trip, I'd say. North of the Liffey, she is."

Delighted with the lunch, Mardell continued eyeing the room. "I can't wait to tell Leo we came here."

"He's read Joyce, has he?"

"Of course. We both read quite a lot. He said books kept him going through the war."

Well, the two of them shared an interest. That was good.

Patrick was pleased she kept bringing him up. There was a flame.

When they finished, he stood. "Shall we go to the bus?"

Eyes wide, she agreed.

"Juniper wasn't living at this address when Róisín died," he told Mardell as they bounced along on the bus.

"We have to start somewhere, Dad. Hopefully someone on Stirrup Lane knows where she went. Your cousins might still be there."

Patrick shrugged. He didn't want to inquire. Folks didn't do that. Patrick didn't do that, not since getting his face kicked in back in New Jersey.

"Come on, Dad, chin up. This is our great adventure. 'A man of genius makes no mistakes. His errors are volitional and are the portals of discovery.'"

"Joyce again?"

She nodded.

"You should read something else."

Mardell was still behaving like a tourist, aiming her Brownie out the bus window in a somewhat futile attempt to take photographs. "We'll get you some postcards, darlin."

She giggled.

When they crossed Mary's Lane, memories flooded in. He gripped the back of the seat in front of him until his knuckles turned white. No one knew him now. Nothing would happen. *Calm down, man!*

Patrick pulled the cord and stood. "Let's go." He paused before exiting the bus. "Where do we catch the return to the city center, kind man?" he asked the driver. Content with the answer, they strode out into a decrepit neighborhood as though stepping back in time.

These buildings were at least as old as Paddy's grandfather would be if he were still living. A brisk wind stood a good chance of knocking them down. Wee lads scurried along barefoot, just as Patrick had once done. The sleeves of their coats and hems of their trousers exposed pale skin. A Dublin lad never had clothes that fit. Couldn't afford them.

No motorcars traversed down the streets in this neighborhood, only a few hand carts and the occasional horse. When they turned on to Stirrup, Patrick felt as though he had stepped back into his young adulthood. Nothing had changed on those streets in thirty years except possibly the names of the people who resided behind the closed doors and boarded up windows.

"What are you here for?" A lad approached them sneering, his face covered in chimney dust. It was a fair question. Outsiders would not be commonplace.

"Looking for someone," Patrick replied, holding tight to his daughter lest her pocketbook be snatched. "Might ye know the surname Doyle?"

The boy wrinkled his nose. "My old auntie's a Doyle. What's it to you?"

Patrick slipped the lad a coin. "I'm a Doyle as well. Looking for my relations."

The boy dipped his chin and motioned for them to follow. They entered a doorway, climbed a set of shaky stairs, and then paused as the lad pounded on a splintered door. "Auntie Delia, someone called Doyle to see ye." He scurried back down the stairs before the knock was answered.

Mardell's wide glance made Patrick wish he'd left her at Davy Byrne's and come alone.

"What's that?" a voice called from the other side of the door.

"Patrick Doyle, missus. Delaney Doyle's son. Might you know what's become of her?"

The door flung open revealing a thick-waisted, white-browed woman wearing a colorless scarf on her head. "Wee Paddy Doyle, is it? Gone to America and now come home?" She pulled him into an embrace before he had a chance to step back. "You don't remember me, do ye? I'm your father's cousin's wife Delia. I do recognize those handsome eyes of yours. 'Tis himself for sure." She slapped him hard on the back. "Come in, you."

They followed her inside the single room flat. Directly across from the door stood a sofa scattered with newspapers. Two tidy quilted beds hugged the walls, and in the center sat two upholstered chairs with a radio between them. In one of them sat a man, smoking a pipe. Tattered lace curtains fluttered against an open window.

"Old Mike, look who's here," the woman said, turning to the man who had not risen to greet them. "Your cousin from America! This is my son," she explained to Patrick.

Patrick dipped his head in greeting and Old Mike did the same.

Delia Doyle tapped Paddy's shoulders until he and Mardell reluctantly pushed aside the newsprint and sat down on the stained sofa. The one called Mike glared at them as though horns grew from the top of their heads. A teakettle whistled on a cooker in the corner.

Old Mike didn't know him. Patrick didn't know Old Mike. Or Cousin Delia. He couldn't recall Delia's husband's name. His father had had lots of cousins, none of whom had ever paid him any heed. None offered to help Patrick or his mother other than housing them in the slums out of obligation after his father died. This was a foreign place to him, an impoverished place. It was humbling to realize how much better he'd had it in America. Paddy would have become another Old Mike if he had stayed, hiding in a hole like this and drinking away his meager wages. Yes, Patrick had done better.

Delia handed them two teacups that they balanced on their laps.

"Very kind," Mardell said. "Thank you."

There was no sugar and no milk.

"My mother, madam. Do you know what happened to her? Has she passed on?"

Delia pulled her neck back like a chicken. "I should think you'd know, you being her only son."

"I don't."

Mardell stared at him, silently begging to leave. Patrick stood. "My apologies for bothering you. We'll be going." He took Mardell's cup and placed both of theirs on a rickety table next to Old Mike's chair.

"I heard she moved in with her granddaughter, but that was a long time ago," Delia said.

"That I did know," Patrick said, moving toward the door.

"Anna, wasn't that the girl's name?" She directed the question to Old Mike. "Not what they called her though." The old woman seemed to search the floorboards for her memory.

"Doesn't matter. They are both gone now," Patrick said, reaching for the door latch.

Delia's answer came in a high pitch. "That's right. Gone to County Down. To Delaney's kin's place. They called it Glasgleann Cottage. May have been for a time, not forever, seems like. Don't know for certain." The woman shrugged her thin shoulders. "Don't know why anyone would go there. We've got all we need right here in the city. Who wants to go back to herding sheep?" She clicked her tongue.

"There was good reason." Old Mike spoke for the first time. "That old McGurdy. Favored the young lassies, that scum did. Not when they reached womanhood, you understand. Just the wee ones. Róisín had to get that girl away from him. She was called Juniper."

Mardell gasped and brought a hand to her mouth.

Delia attempted to snap her gnarly fingers. "That's it! Juniper. Have you ever heard such a name?" The old woman hadn't seemed to have heard the rest.

Patrick turned toward Old Mike. "That John, you say?"

"McGurdy himself. John was the son. No trouble with the younger that I ever heard."

Thoughts swirled in Patrick's mind. Had Róisín's father molested her? Had there been signs he hadn't seen? Time blurred so many things—but he'd never imagined *this*. "Did Old Man McGurdy hurt wee Juniper?" he asked through clenched teeth.

Old Mike shrugged. "Things are not spoke of, you know. I just tell you what I believe to be true. Because you're kin, right."

Patrick squeezed his hat between his fingers. "Much appreciated."

Old Mike sighed. "The two of them got out of Dublin at least along with that sick old lady. That was your mother, so it was?"

Patrick nodded.

"Mam was right. Don't believe that first trip was to be permanent. Maybe to scope the place out like. Whether they returned, I cannot say."

"A tumbled down old famine cottage, I hear 'twas," Delia put in. "Who'd want to go there?" She held up a finger as though reminded of something. "Róisín McGurdy did come back, before she was killed in a fire. Read about it in the papers. Never saw Cousin Delaney again, though."

Patrick and Mardell exchanged glances.

"Delaney had the coughing, but not the lass."

This woman obviously loved gossip. All the better.

"She was crushed when a ceiling fell on her. That's what they say," Delia said.

Patrick wondered if this very ceiling might do the same to them.

"And Juniper?" Mardell asked. "Was she in the accident as well?"

Delia jiggled her chin. "I heard that before she died Róisín committed the child to a hospital for the mind." The woman tapped a gnarled finger to her forehead. "You see, that girl never got over her father leaving her. Never." She did not look directly at Patrick while speaking. Perhaps she'd forgotten or had never known he was Juniper's father. "And Cousin Delaney? As I said I never saw her again, but there are those who say she came back to Dublin City when the child went to hospital. Or maybe Del never did go north with them. Can't remember." Delia smiled sheepishly. "I forget some things. I do know Delaney dealt in potions. Some say she was a witch." Delia smacked her lips. "I never believed that. I thought she'd died and that's the real reason I never saw her again. You say you don't know, Paddy?"

"I've no word," Patrick said.

Mardell piped up. "County Down, you say? Are you sure, Cousin Delia?"

"Course I'm sure, girl. Think I've lost my mind, do ye?"

"Oh, no, ma'am."

Mike gave them a quick nod to confirm it was County Down.

Patrick dipped his chin and then turned toward the door. "We won't bother you any longer."

"Wait. What have you brought from America? Surely you've got something for your kin. A watch perhaps? Or a vase? Beautiful things in America, so I hear." Delia narrowed her gaze. "You gave that messenger lad something, I should think. What have you brought me?"

Patrick wanted to give her a piece of his mind for being so cheeky, but Old Mike was bigger and younger than he was. And at least Mike had been helpful. Patrick took off his tie tack, an inexpensive trinket he'd gotten at Woolworth's in

Columbus. "For you." He placed it on the small table by the door and then reconsidered and added a few Irish pounds. They hurried out the door.

As Mardell and Patrick made their way to the bus stop, Mardell chittered excitedly. "County Down. That's where Moira is, Dad."

If his mother and Róisín had gone to the north, it was to ride out the war and that was long ago. He doubted Róisín would have remained there. Still, there was the puzzling business about her father. "We'll head to the library next and look up city directories. When we find the first year where my mother does not show up, we'll know to look in the cemetery. She'll be buried in the parish churchyard." He shrugged. "Might find Juniper as well."

Mardell sighed and quickened her steps to catch up with him. "Delaney said, in one of the letters, that something was amiss with Róisín. Do you think the problem with her father, Juniper's grandfather, might be what she was referring to?"

"I don't know." Patrick felt unsure about everything now. Had his daughter actually gone mad because of his absence? The asylum may not have been for her lungs as he'd always thought but for her mind. Had the knowledge that he was not dead after all brought her world crashing down and caused her to write the letter he now carried in his pocket?

Patrick stared at the rooftops as they walked, desperately wanting to make sense of all this without Mardell coming to the conclusion that he was a heel, a man without honor.

More thoughts swirled in his mind. Róisín's death may not have come from natural causes. Who should he believe? That old Doyle relative and her son who seemed to take pleasure in his guilt, or John McGurdy?

CHAPTER 22

R óisín

1939, Causeway Coast, Northern Ireland

Outside the phone box two boys kicked a ball. Róisín turned away from their glances as she thought about her solicitor's suggestion. "If this goes wrong I'm holding you personally responsible."

She heard his intake of air. "Listen, I've got children of my own. I know this has been hard for you. I think this is best."

She noticed the lads had gone. She studied a robin as it hopped along the road.

"Are you there?" Mr. Murphy asked.

"I am. May I think about it and call you back tomorrow?"

He cleared his throat. "Miss McGurdy, if the threat from your father is as serious as you believe—"

"You know it is, Murphy. Have you forgotten what I looked like when I was in jail?"

"Of course I haven't."

She glanced at her hands, now calloused from scrubbing and cleaning the church, but otherwise fine. Back then both hands were black and blue from being stomped on. She'd been fortunate her fingers hadn't been broken. Before the police came for her, old man McGurdy had unleashed his wrath, claiming the smuggling money had been stolen from him. She couldn't surrender it, though. She'd needed that money to get free, and it didn't belong to him anyway. Her father had her rounded up with other women and thrown into Kilmainham Gaol. Poor John had helped her then, getting Mr. Murphy to assist. She'd left there shaken and frightened. With John's help she'd written to Paddy and said she was fine. But John could no longer help, God rest his soul.

"I can't contact my daughter?"

"Not if you value your life and that of your daughter's. He's been to visit me in Belfast."

"My father?"

"Aye. I put him off track, told him I'd had correspondence from you postmarked Dublin. Listen. He was in the company of men who ... well, let's just say they are well known to the Royal Ulster Constabulary."

"He'll be back." Her voice cracked.

"Therefore, you cannot risk communicating with Juniper."

But John could. No one knew he'd died.

"I still need to know if she's all right."

"Don't worry. Remember the guy I sent around not long after Juniper moved to the cottage?"

"Right. The fella learned that Delaney was with Juniper because he'd delivered her trunk."

"That's right. I know a couple nearby. They rent rooms. The woman is quite the gossip. I'll be able to check on Juniper through her."

Róisín exhaled. That and letters supposedly from John would have to do.

CHAPTER 23

J uniper
1939, County Down, Northern Ireland

Granny and Juniper worked well together. Shoppers came
and dropped money on her counters. They purchased her
salves for colicky babies, sought after her dried herbal teas,
purchased all the sweets and stockings she had managed to
import, came looking for tools and other miscellaneous
items. In recent weeks they had nearly cleaned her out of
goat milk lotions.

Granny added to the tinctures, expanding the variety of
ailments Juniper was able to treat. There was so much
wisdom in that old book, enabling them to help loads of
folks. Some had come to trust Juniper and her grandmother
even more than the doctor, something that Granny claimed
would never have happened in Dublin. Granny loved being
back in the county of her birth.

Of course, Juniper never outwardly claimed that her
mixtures possessed mystical healing capabilities. The things

she made were remedies from nature. Even so, the perception that she and Granny practiced fairy magic persisted.

Juniper was an actor in a play, a character in a novel. Mr. Mackenzie's Irish-language songs sounded foreign to her customers' ears. Most did not have the Irish and only heard it when traveling to Galway or Kerry or other areas where it was spoken. "One must never lose the soul of the land, Juniper," she remembered the gardener saying. "No matter how much Anglo-English is pushed upon us."

Juniper loved Irish Gaelic for its musical depths of meaning. She spoke it freely to the plants she tended, both in St. Giles's gardens and now here on her own plot of land, not in whispers but in loud orations for the benefit of eavesdroppers. Granny did too, although when she spoke the old tongue it seemed to flow from a place of sincerity. Juniper hadn't realized Granny knew Irish. She was full of surprises. They had much in common. Folks seemed to marvel at the tunes, stopping by to sit and listen to her sing *Eamonn an Chnoic*. These northerners, especially the Protestants, had no idea the song was political, written about a nobleman who had lost his lands in the Cromwell conquest. "Ned of the Hill," as it was titled in English. While Juniper could not remember all of it, she knew enough of this old-style ballad to lend credence to her reputation.

Time passed. Glasgleann Cottage embraced her as the seasons chased each other with a rhythm that at last gave life meaning. Summer brought bounty and long days followed by starlit nights. Autumn chased summer away with falling leaves and cozy fires. Winter pushed off autumn with brisk winds and occasional blankets of snow tucking in Juniper's herbs and flowers for a long rest. And then finally spring slipped in and brought newborn sheep, blooming flowers, and the promise of a bountiful summer to come. Juniper was home and she hadn't needed Róisín or Paddy or anyone but Granny to find it.

June 1943, County Down, Northern Ireland

The war brought unease to Juniper's previously quiet existence. People were on edge, especially during the Blitz, when Germany bombed Belfast. The train stopped taking shoppers to the city, and once again supplies were difficult to obtain. Most of what Juniper and Granny sold consisted of cough syrup and salves for sore muscles. Without magazines and stockings to sell, the shop saw few customers save for old Martin Healy, the fellow with prominent facial features. The size of his nose and ears made him memorable and had prompted Granny to write a ditty about him once. The man could not live without a supply of boiled sweets, which Juniper was happy to provide.

Now that the Americans were involved, hope was renewed that the war might end soon. Churchill and Roosevelt had meetings and just recently the Germans surrendered North Africa.

It wasn't until the Americans arrived that soldiers in uniform lingered in her shop. Some of the neighborhood lads had gone off to war and sometimes she'd see one waiting for a bus or strolling the lane with a lass, but they had soon been shipped off. Seeing the Americans made the war feel closer, even if their presence brought a sense of security.

The Americans began stopping in to see what was available to purchase. Some bought soaps and lotions to send home to loved ones. A few others preferred her goat cheese and scones.

"Not happy there's a war on, but we certainly can use the Americans' coins. Better they spend it here than on pints and cigarettes," Granny told her as they packaged chunks of rosemary-scented soap.

"I expect they do both," Juniper told her,

They glanced up as the bell on the door announced another arrival. "Good afternoon," Juniper greeted. "You are very welcome. What can I help you with?"

A rosy-cheeked American GI limped through the door.

"Oh, my. Let me help you." Granny held the door open while Juniper guided the man to a chair.

"Many thanks," he said. "I'm Corporal Walsh. I heard you might have some salve or something to help my feet."

"Let's have a look," Granny said, pointing at his boots.

When he pulled off his stockings, he groaned.

"I see the problem," Juniper said, examining red boils on the man's heels. "That looks painful."

"Hospital didn't give me anything that helped. Said to bandage up and tough it out. But I'm on my feet for twelve hours straight. Thought I'd check in case you've got something here."

"Good thing you did," Granny said. "This is my granddaughter. She can help you. I'm off to the chicken coop. You're welcome to some eggs, if you'd like," she offered. "Just boiled a dozen."

He tugged a wallet out of his pocket. "I'll take two and some of those scones you've got on the counter." He counted out the money while Juniper collected some ointment. "Oh, I'm afraid I don't have much."

"Pay whatever you can. 'Tis my pleasure to help those who are helping us," Juniper said. "Wash well and apply this comfrey salve twice a day. I've only got a wee bit left. Take this and I'll mix up some more and send it to the hospital. Is that where you're staying?"

"I was, but I'm better except for my feet. I'm staying with a family in town for a couple of days while I'm awaiting orders. The Sullivans. Know them?"

"I do. I'll send something over with the postman tomorrow. And don't worry about payment." She picked up the cash he pushed across the table toward her. "This will suffice."

FEBRUARY 1950, County Down, Northern Ireland

When Juniper finished dressing for the day, she checked on Granny. Still asleep. Holding the book of cures in her lap, Juniper smiled to herself. In the beginning she'd known only basic things, and even now what she understood about nature's cures was but a thimble-full compared to what Granny knew. The woman had the entire contents of this massive book stored in her memory. Or at least she had before the latest sickness hit.

Primrose? Juniper bit her lip, realizing that she should have remembered and tried it long ago. She'd used the fleshy leaves before to ease an old man's aching joints. That was why she had collected it.

Rising from her chair to begin steeping the plant for Granny, Juniper thought about all those years ago when she'd started her shop or tried to. Closing her eyes, she imagined it now.

Oh, those lads and their pranks. If they'd thought Juniper was a wee bit looney, they believed she with Granny brought twice the crazy.

Juniper rubbed her cat's head as he showed appreciation for the meal she'd put out for him. "And to make matters worse, you had to be a black cat. Why couldn't you have been *Pangur Bán*, eh?" She rubbed his head and chuckled. She hadn't meant he annoyed her. Quite the opposite.

That ancient poem about a monk's cat chasing mice had been written about a white cat. If Michael had been more fair, perhaps the prevailing superstition would have been entirely different. She'd never forget that awful day when Michael used up one of the proverbial nine lives cats were supposed to possess.

A storm was raging, and Juniper hadn't seen Michael the cat for some time.

"They hide," Granny said. "Animals know when fierce weather is coming."

They both donned scarves and headed outside to search, calling the cat's name.

"Shh," Granny said as they stood near the turf pile.

Juniper peeled her scarf away from her ears and stood still. The wind howled, stirring the hem of her skirt. "I don't—"

Granny held up a hand. "There is always a pause. Wait for the wind to collect a breath."

Sure enough the wind stopped for just a moment and the wee sound of a cat's cry led them to the turf pile.

"Michael, have you gotten yourself stuck in there?" Juniper began to shift the bricks from side to side as she dug through. A mewing sound grew louder. Soon she could see two round green eyes staring back at her. "Foolish, cat. Come out now."

A guttural wail made her gasp. "What's wrong?" When she lifted another peat brick, she saw why he hadn't moved. His fur was plastered to one of the bricks. Something sticky had glued him there. "Granny, what's on him?"

Juniper's grandmother moved closer, clicking her tongue. "Oh, for pity's sake. Tar, the stuff they use to waterproof boats, child. What devil has done this to our poor Michael? Get a basket. If we try to pick him up he'll sink those white blades of teeth into our hands. A blanket too."

Juniper ran back to the house, sobbing as the wind resumed screaming in her ears. The boys' mischief must stop. Scooping up one of the baskets she used to gather herbs and the blanket from the cat's bed, she rushed back outside.

Granny wrapped the blanket over her hand and tugged the cat, still attached to a brick, into the basket. Then they rushed back to the house.

"Goose fat, bacon grease, whatever you've got, lass."

Juniper retrieved a jar from the cold-room attached to the kitchen, the wails of the cat pounding in her ears. They lathered the cat in the grease until he pulled free and sprang from their grasp. He darted all over the cottage, pausing momentarily to lick lard from his coat.

"We could give him a bath," Granny said, hands on hips. "Or let him do it himself."

Juniper laughed. "At the moment I don't think he'll give us a choice. Later for sure or he'll stink up the house."

Juniper and Granny scrubbed their hands and gathered up the soiled blanket and cloths for the washing. Granny moved to the soft chair. "What an adventure that was."

"One that must never happen again, Granny. We've got to do something to keep those troublesome children away."

"Ah, so we must. I've an idea. Come sit, child. The cat will tire himself out soon and you can see to him then."

Juniper sat on the rug at her grandmother's feet while Michael curled up in a corner, furiously working his pink tongue over his fur.

"I remember old Aunt Bet telling a story about a churchyard in Rostrevor." Granny stared into the gathering darkness. "Old Bet told a lot of stories, and I remember this one well. Bet was a pet name, as is Juniper." She winked.

Juniper smiled. "This is about your idea to stop the pranks?" Granny's mind sometimes wandered.

She nodded, running her fingers along her sleeve as though gathering up the memories. "There are some ruins in Kilbroney graveyard. Aunt Bet said there used to be an ancient tree there, among others, of course, but this partic- ular one held a secret no one knew about until a storm knocked it down."

"What kind of secret?" Juniper knew trees were sacred to the ancient people, and many folks revered them today, choosing to plow around them rather than remove them from their farm fields. Like the sycamore outside the cottage that had to be set apart and not touched. She appreciated trees for the myriad healing powers certain species could provide.

"St. Bronagh was a follower of St. Patrick. This was her church. So much history, sacred history, lives on. And *yet*"—

216

she held up one hand to emphasize her point—"there was belief in the fairy faith that prevailed, as there is regarding that tree here at our wee cottage."

So she'd brought it around. Juniper hoped there would be a valid point, something to help put an end to the boys' tormenting. "I'll make tea."

"Thank you. Much needed. As I was saying, old Aunt Bet said that for many generations after the saint's death a bell could be heard in the churchyard, yet no bell was ever found. There simply was no bell, but the sound could not be denied. The people wondered, what could be the purpose of this sound? A warning for seafarers on Carlingford Lough? A call to worship? Some said it was the work of fairies, banshees even, and the very thought struck fear into the hearts of even the most vigorous men."

Juniper lifted the kettle over the fire. "Tall tales, that."

"Oh, but it wasn't, you see. The sound was real, all right. They all heard it, all the ancestors now in their graves dating way back to the ancient saint."

"So they heard something that couldn't be explained." Juniper was finding it increasingly necessary to remind her grandmother to come back to the original conversation.

"Not at that time, but 'twas explained along about the year of 1839, when Aunt Bet's older siblings were alive."

"What happened in 1839?"

"Ah, terrible weather. I remember my grandmother talking about it. It was wicked fierce all across the island. Such things are not soon forgotten. That winter there was a great deal of snow, and not just in the mountains, I'm saying. All over. Deep snow. And then a warm wind, brutal, bringing a harbinger of change from Satan himself. *Nollaig na mBan*, was the day, which made it all the worst. Little Christmas."

"Satan?"

"Ah, what I am saying is that it was horrid. People died in that storm. About a hundred people, if I remember correctly."

"What did this have to do with the bell sound, Granny?"

She smiled. "Everything. You see, those terrible winds knocked down a very ancient tree. And what was discovered inside that split tree, do you suppose?"

"A bell?"

"Indeed so. The old kind that a saint would have walked with. Must have been hung when the tree was a mere seedling and then forgotten. The tree grew up around it, concealing the wee bell from view, but it was still loose enough to allow the breezes to move it. As that tree got taller, no one could see it."

Juniper chuckled as she collected china cups for their tea. "What a funny tale, Granny."

"So, you see how a mysterious bell held the folks in fear for a very long time. What if we rigged up our own hidden bell?"

"I don't want to scare away shoppers, Granny, just those unkind lads."

Granny rubbed her chin. "We'll keep it up only at night."

"Oh, I don't know, Granny. Nothing we've tried so far has worked. I don't think these pranksters can be spooked."

"Why not try?"

Juniper gave up. "Sure, why not."

In the following days the plan took form. They hid a bell in the sycamore tree and tied a string to it, weaving it across the doorstep and tying it to a nail at the base of the front window. The bell was light so that the slightest movement would ring it. Every morning Juniper pulled back the string and hid it behind the tree. In the evening she put it back. Juniper had her doubts that such a wee sound would make a difference but it humored Granny.

"Oh, it will work if the idea has first been planted in their minds." Granny composed a verse that Juniper painted on a sign and attached to the wall next to the door at a young child's eye level.

"Thought of this because of that Martin Healy," Granny said.

"The old man who comes in for sweets? The fella with the bulbous nose?"

"That's him. Told me the tree put a terrible fright into him when he was young."

Beware the sound of the bell

The curses it will tell

It cannot be seen

No matter how keen

And your nose and ears will swell.

Juniper covered the sign in the daytime with a towel so that shoppers wouldn't ask about it. They kept Michael inside at night, much to his displeasure. And sure as the rising of the dawn, the mischievous lads returned. The sounds of their whispering woke Juniper and she silently roused her grandmother. They huddled together inside the front door and listened.

"What's that say?" a voice asked.

Another lad read the verse. "What bell?"

"Shh," someone said. And sure enough, they unknowingly tripped the hidden bell and ran hither and thither down the road.

Juniper laughed so hard her sides hurt.

As luck would have it, Mr. Healy was in the store the next morning and so were two of the lads with their mother. Juniper and Granny locked eyes and then Granny approached the old man.

"Mr. Healy, didn't you tell me a story about that big old tree out front? What happened again?"

Martin Healy loved to weave a tale. "Aye, let me tell you, my mam warned me away. Said my granddad used to climb it when he was a lad and there's spirits locked in there. I doubted it, but being a curious lad, I visited alone and got the fright of my life. They're there, I tell you. I heard 'em screaming like a banshee."

At just the right moment Martin shoved his hanky to his face and blew his nose loudly. The two boys stared at him and hid behind their mother's skirts. Juniper had to run out the back door to hide her laughter.

Ah, poor Michael. He did recover although some spots on his fur were never the same. Juniper never would have come up with the bell scheme on her own and the prank was one of the fond memories she would call on when Granny's breathing problems flared up again and they needed a distraction. This was one of those times.

The primrose was ready. Juniper added it to some broth and warmed the soup in a saucepan. Granny began to stir. "Let me help you, Gran."

Granny grunted her thanks and Juniper fetched the bedpan. When she had the woman cleaned up and dressed, she fetched the primrose concoction and explained what it was.

"You've learned well, my dear. A proper heir to the healing arts. Aunt Bet would be proud."

"She did make herbal cures, then. Toby mentioned it when I first came."

"Oh, indeed. We had some wonderful conversations the short time I was here. She had marvelous gardens all around her house. Took better care of them than she did her shelter."

That explained the plants Juniper had uncovered and worked to bring back to life.

"Oh, that woman had a lot of stories. If only I could remember them." Granny tapped a gnarled finger to her temple. If only Juniper had something to say to make it all better.

An hour later Granny was asleep again, seemingly content.

Juniper returned to her thoughts. She knew that Granny was her only relative, the only person in her life who deeply cared about her. And yet, there seemed to have been someone else, so her child's heart told her. Someone besides Mr. Mackenzie. *Someone else had cared.* Perhaps someone at the abbey or a priest, she wasn't sure. Juniper clung to the thought like a life preserver.

Granny grunted in her sleep and then called out Paddy's name. She'd been doing that a lot lately.

"You're all right," Juniper whispered. Then she took up the song Granny sometimes mumbled in her waking hours.

So she bid farewell to Eireann.

And next morning at the dawn,

That poor broken-hearted mother,

Bid farewell to Noreen Bawn.

It was a sad song about immigration, and it surely reminded Granny of her son. In the song, Noreen died from tuberculosis. Was that what Granny had? Juniper went back to the book and tried to find the answer.

CHAPTER 24

P atrick
1950, County Antrim, Northern Ireland

On the train from Dublin to Belfast, Mardell pulled out her notebook. "I'm sorry the directories in Dublin were of no help, Dad."

"Not sure why I thought it would help. She was living with kin. She'd not be listed anywhere."

"At least the parish had no record of either of them. That keeps hope alive."

"That's not to say we won't find their graves up here, darlin."

Mardell worried her lip. "Have you wondered what might have happened to Juniper based on what else was happening in the country at the time, Dad? Other than the poverty, I mean."

"I'm not sure I can tell you what was happening while she

was growing up. I had quite a few things demanding my attention in America."

"Oh, well, you knew what Róisín told you. There was a civil war right after Juniper was born. You knew that."

"True enough. It kept Róisín from coming over, I should think."

"But later?"

Patrick stared out the train window at the green landscape. What had he forgotten and what had he never known? "The Great Depression. Hard on us all."

"Since they went north, what was it like there, I wonder? And in an institution?" Mardell smacked her lips in a pitying expression. She continued writing notes as she spoke. "That poor girl. What would the treatment have been like? How long was she there? If she did perish there, what from? Róisín said the air would help her lungs. I wonder if she had TB?"

"All questions we don't have answers for, Mardell." Patrick folded his arms across his chest. "We have to consider that my father's cousin's wife might not be telling the truth."

"Why would she lie?" Mardell scribbled large question marks in her notebook and then tapped the tip of her pencil on the paper.

"Not sure. Could be she's just fabricating an interesting tale." He shrugged. "Maybe she wants me to feel guilty for immigrating." He had the letter convicting him. That was enough without his distant kin contributing to his guilt.

Mardell's shoulders rose and fell with a great sigh. "Well, we have to start somewhere, rabbit trails or not. Let's find out the names of institutions and ask to see a list of past patients."

Patrick laughed. "If we could even get an appointment with an administrator or a doctor, he'd not tell us anything, Mardell."

"We'll convince them."

"We won't. We'll start with past issues of newspapers in the library."

"Fine. We've got a plan. Now, in case we are able to interview folks that might have known Delaney or Róisín, give me a description of each."

A waste of time. The Irish were not as intrusive as Americans and they wouldn't respond well to outsiders. However, giving Mardell something to concentrate on might earn him a few minutes of peace. He needed a nap, since his cough had been causing him to lose sleep, and now he had a new malady, a slight pain in his side.

"Róisín, when I knew her, was a petite woman with gray eyes, rather dark hair, darker than mine."

"Would you say she was my height? I'm five-four."

"No, indeed. A wee one. If I had to guess I'd say no more than five feet tall."

"All right. And Delaney?"

"Auburn hair, green eyes."

"How tall was Delaney?"

"Oh, Mardell. I don't know. I never thought of her as short. Average for a woman, I suppose."

Mardell scribbled something down as she talked. "All right. Probably about my height." She gave Patrick a scrutinizing look.

"What?"

"I was just imaging what Juniper might have looked like. She had a short mother and tall father. Dark hair probably, although sometimes a child will take after a grandparent instead, which means she could ..."

"There was a photograph, although she was very small when it was taken."

"A photograph? Where? Why didn't you show me?"

"It came with that letter, the one where Róisín said Juniper needed me to ... well, the one where she accused me of abandoning her." Patrick gritted his teeth, remembering the way he'd felt when he'd first read it. Angry. Betrayed.

"Where is it now?"

"I don't know. It must have gotten separated and lost over the years."

"How?"

"Don't look at me that way. I did not throw it out. I remember it though. I believe she did have dark hair. Resembled her mother as much as I could tell from a photograph. And like I said, she was a just a wee one."

"All right."

They rode along in silence for a few moments. Patrick rested his eyes until his daughter's voice jolted him.

"So you found us a hotel?"

"I did. The concierge in Dublin helped by ringing up and obtaining a booking. We'll have to stay in Belfast. Not much outside of there."

"Then we'll rent a car?"

"Bus, I suppose. Maybe train. There's likely some way to get to Moira, since the American soldiers were there during the war, but I doubt there will be a taxi. Maybe a donkey cart for hire."

She giggled but he was serious. All one had to do was look out the train window now to see that they'd landed in a sparsely populated area. Time stood still in those parts.

After a brief snooze the announcement came that they had arrived in Belfast City. Patrick and Mardell shuffled along with the others until they were out the door. "I'll get the luggage. Wait here," Patrick told her.

Again, Mardell stared wide-eyed at everything around her and scrambled to snatch her Brownie from its case. Soon they were walking on the sidewalks of Northern Ireland's capital city.

Patrick had never been to Belfast. Bustling, like Dublin. Red and white electric trams shared the streets with motorcars and horse carts. The city was a seaport where ships were built. The country might be overall rural, but most of what they'd seen so far, aside from the train ride, was industrial and commercial. Mardell would be in for a shock later. All they'd see after leaving the city would be small farms and pastures of sheep and cattle. Like Cousin Delia had said, who wanted to go back to herding sheep? While Patrick was growing up, everyone he knew said the same. Nothing up north.

When Mardell agreed to put away her box camera, they continued to their hotel and were welcomed by a pleasant desk clerk. Noting the American lilt to Mardell's speech, the clerk smiled. "Welcome to one of the world's best cities. *The Titanic* was built here, you know."

Mardell frowned.

"Come on," the fellow said. "She was fine and dandy when she left here, a spectacular achievement for the day. It was afterwards, so it was, that all the trouble came. After she was out of Irish hands."

Mardell seemed enchanted by the clerk's jovial air. The Irish could be charming, no question.

As Mardell settled into her room, Patrick examined the contents of his wallet while sipping black beer at the hotel bar. They'd only be able to stay two nights with the budget he worked out, but when they moved on to the village they'd be grand, seeing as they'd find accommodations cheaper. There'd be a farmwife who'd put them up for a fraction of what the hotel charged, he supposed. As poor as the people in Northern Ireland were, they'd be glad for the extra income.

He felt calmer now, more relaxed than he'd been when they first arrived. Likely because they were away from Dublin, where most of his bad memories lay. Patrick struck up a conversation with the lad on the stool to his right.

"America, you say? My brother Peter is in America. What part? Maybe you know him."

"Ohio."

Patrick's response was met with a blank stare. He chuckled and nibbled on the soda bread and creamy butter the barman brought. Patrick would have had the same reaction as this lad if someone had mentioned Ohio to him before he'd gone there.

"Is that in Oregon?"

"'Tis not, my man. Ohio is more, uh, well, towards the center. Oregon is on the west coast."

"Ah, I see. Iowa, is it?"

"I've come looking for some kin," Patrick said, giving up on the geography lesson.

The young man, who'd said his name was Paddy and stated that if he didn't know, Paddy was short for Patrick, leaned forward on the bar and cradled his glass of dark stout between his two large hands. "They say everyone's related to someone in Ireland. That's something, aye?"

"I suppose. I'm off to a library to see what information I can find."

"Oh, you don't want that," the man said, shaking his head sharply. "My misses? She's an archivist, so she is. You'll be wanting the Public Records Office, and lucky you, man, 'tis here in Belfast."

"I'm not sure what that is."

"Well, you know how down in Dublin they bombed the records office? Was a horrible fire."

"The Four Courts?"

"The same. Was in '22. Don't suppose you were there then?"

"I was not. But we are in Belfast, aye?" Patrick was beginning to wonder if this Paddy had had too much to drink.

The lad held up a finger as if ready to make a point. Then he wrinkled his brow, sipped from his glass, and then smacked his lips. "Well, the next year, or maybe the year after that, they opened a records office here. An archive, 'tis. My wife works there, and she says from the beginning there was work to recover or replicate, so to speak, records lost in Dublin. Of course, they've got records from the north, too, so I'd say go there. Might save you some time."

"Thank you for the tip. Where is this place?"

"Started out at Murray Street."

Patrick wrote the name on a paper bar napkin.

"No, no. Not there. Now they are at Royal Courts of Justice in Chichester Street. If you ring over there, ask for Mrs. Mary O'Connor. That's herself. She'll help you, so she will."

"Thank you kindly."

Later as Patrick readied for bed, anxiety stirred in his gut. He was going to find out what had happened to Juniper, he felt sure, and hopefully also his mother. Grief washed over him. Veronica was the great loss in his life and the most recent. Colin's death had battered him to the core, something he'd never gotten over. And here he was, willingly putting himself in the path of grief's great encompassing inferno. He had no choice but to pray it would be a cleansing fire. Thankfully he'd ordered a whisky to take to his room and Mardell was already tucked into her own room.

The next morning Patrick woke groggy, not sure how many drinks he'd actually had. He thought about his father. Had he drunk to cover up something, like Patrick was doing? Patrick promised himself he'd stop before it ruined his life like it had his father's. Over a breakfast of beans and toast, Patrick told Mardell about the advice the fellow at the bar had given him.

"Well, let's find Chichester Street, then, as soon as we're done here."

Patrick sipped on his tea, willing his head to stop aching. "You know, this could prove to be the end of our journey."

"Well, if it is, we'll enjoy touring." She reached for his hand across the table. "Thanks for bringing me, Dad. I know it was hard for you."

Patrick felt his heart race. In that moment he saw Veronica in Mardell's face, sensed her charity in Mardell's words, and realized that his wife's goodness was not truly lost but lived on in the daughter she left behind. A great comfort, that was.

An hour later Patrick and Mardell entered the building that housed the Public Records Office. They were introduced to a stately looking woman wearing a navy-blue suit and chunky, black heels. Her hair was pulled back tightly, and a pair of cat's-eye spectacles hung from a beaded chain around her neck. After explaining what they were looking for, the woman donned her spectacles. "Let me see. Well, we have the welfare system now, of course, but earlier there was the poor law and we have records. In addition, there are maps you might want to consult. And valuations that might tell you who the cottage belonged to."

Mardell spoke in a reserved tone. "We are also wondering about asylums. Are there records for those?"

"There are and we do have many of them, but I'm afraid they are not open to the public."

Patrick huffed. "Why do you have them if no one can look at them?"

231

The woman wrinkled her nose. "They can be examined by officials of the institutions or by those who have a right to see them."

Might as well come out with it. "I am the father of the girl we're looking for. Does that give me the right?"

"That depends on if your name is in the record."

He handed her his American passport to prove who he was. "But I was born in Dublin," he attempted to explain.

She glanced at it and handed it back. "If you'd like me to check, Mr. Doyle, please write down all the pertinent information on this form." She turned, collected a sheet of paper from a file on top of a desk, and then handed it to him.

Patrick must have given her a puzzled look because she softened her tone. "Just sit here at this table, and I'll bring you some documents to look through after you fill that out."

"Arc you sure?" Mardell asked. "We don't want to impose. I mean if you're busy with something else."

"Not all at. I am happy to assist where I can." With the completed form in hand, the clerk marched down a corridor.

Patrick leaned in to whisper to his daughter. "If she's not busy? What would we do if she was? We don't know the first thing about records or where to look."

"Of course we don't. I think we'd be better off asking around."

"This is not Ohio, Mardell. That doesn't work here."

"It might. You haven't lived in Ireland in decades."

Several minutes later the woman returned with a cart full of ledgers. "These may help with some of your questions. I'm afraid you may not see the asylum records, Mr. Doyle."

Mardell stood. "You didn't find her name?"

"I did indeed find an Anna J. McGurdy but you are not listed as guardian, Mr. Doyle."

Sure he wasn't. A lame idea to think the McGurdys had named him at all.

The woman pointed a pencil in Patrick's direction. "That doesn't mean they are closed to you, however. Not if you get permission from the asylum. I suggest calling in there and seeing what they will share." She handed back the form they'd filled out. Something was scrawled at the bottom. *St. Giles Hospital Asylum, County Monaghan, released 1938.*

Stunned, Patrick could not find his voice. Mardell thanked the woman.

"Just leave these ledgers on the table when you're through and I'll be back later to collect them."

Mardell placed the form inside her notebook and gave Patrick a look that said her idea would be required after all. They'd have to go asking questions.

Patrick massaged his temples and attempted to clear his throat without bringing on a coughing fit. His hands trembled. How to calm his nerves?

Mardell whispered. "So we know she was in this hospital and that she's not there now. She did not die there. We know when she left. I think the clerk just did us a favor. I don't think she was supposed to write the release date. See, Dad, some people here are kind." Mardell consulted her notebook. "After you got that letter in 1928 would have been the timeframe. She was in the asylum sometime between then and 1938."

Patrick had to admit he hadn't expected to get that much help. Perhaps the presence of his American daughter was easing the way. "And we know she at least made it to age eighteen," he added. Maybe she *had* written that letter. It could be that old, *older* likely, judging by the childlike handwriting. And if that was what she truly thought of him she probably didn't want to be found. Still, he had to know, perhaps approach her unnoticed, just find out, not make contact. His head swam with all the possibilities.

Mardell tittered. "Since Juniper was released, she probably survived."

"We don't know that. It's been twelve years."

"Even so, it's a distinct possibility."

Yes, it was. It would be easier to leave it be, assume that what the unexpected letter said was true, but wasn't that what he'd done all those years ago by not keeping in touch? If they did find her, and she said she never wanted to see him again, at least that would close this chapter of his life. He should prepare Mardell for that outcome. "Darlin, we don't know how she feels about me. She may still believe I'm dead. This could be a horrible shock. We will need to be careful."

"We'll find someone, a clergyman perhaps, to break the news to her and see if she's open to meeting us. There is a solution without being too pushy, I'm sure. But, Dad, we're almost there. This is so exciting. We are going to find out what happened to the family you left here."

Left behind. Abandoned. Patrick hadn't meant that to be the result of his leaving. The constant dry tickle in his throat squirreled its way up to his larynx again. "I'll be back. I'm going to look for a drinking fountain and then get a wee bit of fresh air. I'm an old man who gets stiff with all this sitting."

"Sure, Dad. Take your time. I'll keep searching."

When he returned Mardell nearly bounced off her chair. "It took some time and some help from the staff here, but I believe I found the cottage. Glasgleann Cottage. It was owned by the Doyles as recently as 1945."

"Doyles? Which Doyle?"

"Doesn't say."

"We don't know if they are related, then," Patrick said.

"But Dad, the old woman in Dublin said they went there. It has to be your family. And Juniper could have gone there in 1938. We know where it is!"

"No recent records?"

Mardell checked her notebook. "All I can tell is there is no record of it being sold."

The clerk overheard. "There is a street directory you might find useful, to see if the cottage still exists."

"Oh, yes, please, thank you," Mardell said.

"Not here. Head over to the library." She gave them directions.

The hours they'd spent researching wore on Patrick. "Mind if I wait back at the hotel, darlin?"

"Not at all. You rest. I'll be along shortly."

Patrick's coughing grew worse when he got back to the hotel, so he turned on the hot water tap in the bathroom and breathed in the moist air. When he was a kid his mother had rubbed an ointment on his chest. He toweled off and then telephoned down to the front desk.

"Might there be a pharmacy, I mean chemist, that delivers, please?" he asked the voice on the other end.

An hour later he had some menthol drops and aspirin and settled down for a good nap. Not as effective as his mother's old cures, he thought. What he would give for some of that today.

CHAPTER 25

J uniper
February 1950, Glasgleann Cottage, County Down,
Northern Ireland

Granny snored softly, the primrose having done its soothing
work. Aunt Bet sounded like a delightful woman. Granny
was the best. What had happened to Juniper's parents to turn
them into people who could not raise their own child?

Pulling on her wellies, Juniper prepared to tend her plants.
The smell of damp earth was as good a medicine as anything
she could concoct. Michael trailed after, crisscrossing as
though someone might snag him if he took a more linear
path. A robin nosed the edges of her turnip field while other
birds called to him from a perch in the oaks separating her
property from a neighboring farm where cattle and sheep
grazed lazily in the green grass. Just as when she was a girl,
the earth soothed and reminded her that sorrows lasted only
a moment. The sun always reappeared.

Shoving a spade into the dark soil, Juniper worked to cultivate an area for transplanting parsley. She had no trouble finding locations for the herbs that preferred cooler conditions. It was the sun-loving rosemary, thyme, and marjoram that needed transplanting the most. The tree cover had increased quite a bit since Aunt Bet first planted them.

Dragging her spade, Juniper trudged up a slight incline that was blanketed with wild daises. She loved the untouched beauty of the spot, but the herbs needed it more. She'd try to disturb only a corner. Driving her tool into the ground, she found resistance. Ah, rocks. She'd been spoiled by previously only working cultivated beds. Wiping her brow, she set to work.

A few hours later she wearily returned to the cottage to make tea. When she entered, memories flooded in again. Juniper hadn't thought about those early years as intently as she had been lately. Perhaps rewinding the tape of her life story might help her manage today's challenges.

Reliving her memories while she tidied the cottage, Juniper served Granny tea, mended a few stockings, and dusted her shop shelves. Reflecting on her time at Glasgleann, Juniper knew the fresh start had been good even if it had come with a bit of trouble.

That night both she and Granny slept little. Juniper had helped Granny to the toilet, rubbed the woman's aching back, hummed a few tunes. Eventually they both slept until the cock woke Juniper.

Glancing around at the silhouettes the furniture cast in the early morning light, Juniper contemplated beginnings and endings, each one bringing its own unknown shadow. An ending approached, one she dreaded. Who would she be in a world without Granny?

A knock on the door did not rouse Granny. Juniper grabbed her cloak and went to answer it.

"Good morning!" Toby stood at attention, a letter in his hand.

"Surely it is, since you have not brought me bills." She invited him in.

"Where's your grandmother, Anna?"

"She had a difficult night. She's still asleep in the back room. Would you like a spot of tea?"

"Thank you, no. Just had some with the Sullivans. I wanted to come straight away because I thought you'd want this correspondence." He glanced shyly to the floor. "I believe 'tis from your John McGurdy, so 'tis."

Juniper accepted the letter. "Toby, before I came, might you have met my Uncle John?"

"I have not had the pleasure."

"The priest, I mean the one who was here years back. Do you think he might know my uncle?"

"I suppose he might have. I hope nothing is amiss." He turned toward his bicycle.

"Oh, no. Not at all. Thank you."

He tipped his hat. "Give your grandmother my best wishes."

"I shall." Juniper shut the door and looked at the envelope with the terrible penmanship. She sat at the table and opened it. A few banknotes fell out. Where was he getting all this money? And why did he keep sending to it her? He was a bachelor, but even without a family of his own, he surely had something else to do with all his money.

The paper gave off a slight scent. She lifted it to her face. Perfume? Well, if John had a girlfriend these payments might be coming to an end after all.

Juniper placed a tray with tea and a round loaf of barmbrack on the floor near Granny's bed. Granny enjoyed sultanas and black currants and would hopefully rouse to the aroma. Pulling a chair up beside the bed, she gathered Michael onto her lap. "Ah, what a time I had getting used to it all here when I first came, Michael."

An innocent time it was before Juniper fully understood that no one was as they appeared, and she would always be an outsider. That fresh shopkeeper, Mr. Boyd, the lads who had pestered her and her cat, and all the others. They were acquaintances she sometimes had to do business with, but otherwise they kept their distance. Unlike St. Giles and the abbey where the residents were disciplined and kept in line, no one told these people how to treat their neighbors. Granny had urged Juniper to be kind above all else and sometimes in order to do that, Juniper found it best to keep the others no closer than necessary. Was she lonely? Maybe.

Juniper rose from the chair beside Granny's bed and shooed Michael away from the bread. Placing one hand at the small of her back, she stretched and rubbed her neck with the other. "If you hadn't come, Granny, I might never have learned how to count money. Old Mr. Boyd wasn't the kindly old gentleman I had taken him for. I was ignorant of more than just figuring sums. I wonder what his wife thought of his pinching and handling the young lassies visiting his shop. I never went back after he accosted me. And with all the vegetables and apples the people brought us in payment for their cures, I hadn't needed to. Was probably a jealous husband who burned down his shop and kicked him off to Galway."

Juniper had never told Granny any of that before. Such a humiliating story wasn't fit repeating but on forlorn days the mind tended to unwind the happenings of the past.

"Out with you." She urged Michael through the back door. "Do your part and keep the mice away, laddie."

Granny opened her eyes. "Out with who?"

"The cat, Granny. Will you take some tea?"

Juniper helped her eat, see to necessities, and then settle back. She read Emily Dickinson aloud.

Hope is the thing with feathers that perches in the soul—and sings the tunes without the words—and never stops at all.

Never stops? Those words seemed ill placed in this moment, but Juniper had never known Emily Dickinson to be wrong before.

Granny slept until noon, shuffling out to the chair by the fire when she woke. She flipped through the pages of her treasured book, making notes in the margins with a stubby pencil. They passed the hours by quizzing each other on what ailments called for which cures as Juniper filled the herb jars and hung what she'd picked earlier from the rafters to dry.

Soon the sun set on another day.

In the morning, Juniper lit the stove for tea. Glancing up at the ceiling, she was satisfied with the number of herbs she was drying. She thought about Uncle John. She'd been naïve when it came to that man.

"Did I ever tell you the story of how this roof was built?" she asked the dozing woman on the bed.

Granny stirred and opened her eyes. "Tell me," she whispered.

CHAPTER 26

Patrick
May 1950, Moira, County Down, Northern Ireland

Patrick carried their two suitcases and followed his daughter, who in turned trailed a woman named Ellie Sullivan.

"Don't get many visitors from the States," the woman said.

Ellie was perhaps ten years older than Patrick, wore a long dress topped with a plain white apron. Her hair was pure alabaster, tied up in a bun. Her substantial ebony shoes plodded along as they mounted limestone steps leading into her house.

"Very kind of you to accommodate us, Mrs. Sullivan," Mardell said.

"My pleasure, love. There are two rooms at the top of the stairs. The loo is shared downstairs."

Patrick was delighted with the rent she had required and the fact that they could leave their booking open ended.

The woman invited them to examine their accommodations unaccompanied, shunning the stairs herself, claiming lame knees. "My daughter-in-law tends to those rooms. She'll be back midweek to see to your linens and towels," she called up the stairs. "Full breakfast is at seven. We are up early on this farm, so we are. Will that suit?"

"Indeed it will," Patrick replied.

Roosters woke Patrick just after five, reminding him of home, although the sun rose later in Ohio that time of year. Peeking through the lace curtains, he observed a couple of men approaching the barn. He pondered offering to help, but the ache in his chest and the twitch in his side convinced him to stay put, warm in his bed and out of the chilly, damp air.

At 6:45 there was a knock at his door. "Dad? Are you up?"

"I am indeed." He'd risen minutes earlier, washed and dressed. He met Mardell in the hall.

Rosy-cheeked and wearing a smart skirt and blazer, Mardell was proof that good looks were for the young. She tapped the toe of her cream-colored pump. "So, now that you've slept on it, what do you think we should we do first? The hospital or look for the cottage?"

"Hospital. We might find all we need to know there. And 'tis very possible someone else is occupying the cottage these days."

Breakfast was served in a sunny room painted yellow so that even on dark days it would be cheery, or so said the hostess.

"Eggs, black pudding, beans, and tomatoes. Of course, toast, butter, and jam. Will that do?" Mrs. Sullivan asked, folding her hands across her middle.

Patrick stared at the purple flower in a vase at the center of the white tablecloth. "Thank you," he said, although he wasn't especially hungry.

"Tea?" the woman asked.

Both Patrick and Mardell thanked her again as she poured steaming black liquid from a white ceramic pot. The smell was rich and warming. Like home. Once the teacups were filled, Mrs. Sullivan blanketed the pot with a flowered tea cozy, sending Patrick's thoughts back to his mother. He hadn't written her when he should have. Now that she was certainly in her grave, could he be forgiven? He'd ask where the purple flowers came from so that he might bring some to Delaney Doyle's resting place, should they discover that she died close by Juniper and not in Dublin. His mother would have been with her granddaughter if she possibly could have been, he believed.

After they'd eaten Mardell interrupted the hostess before she could disappear again into the kitchen. "Mrs. Sullivan, pardon me. We need to get to County Monaghan today. Might you tell us how to accomplish that?"

"Indeed, my man can take you over to the train, but that can't happen today."

"Oh?" Mardell sat straighter in her chair.

"There's a cattle market in Moira today. No one will be going out. Only coming in. At least not until tea time. Would you care to wait?"

"A cattle market?" Patrick glanced out the window. Several men drove livestock toward the road as they spoke.

Ellie Sullivan nodded. "That's right."

Patrick cleared his throat and tried to ignore the pinch in his side. "If we can't go until late in the day, we might as well wait until tomorrow."

"I suppose you're right," Mardell agreed.

Patrick set his teacup down on the saucer. "Is there a telephone we can use? I will need to call the steamship office to rearrange our travel." He chided himself for not doing that while they were in Belfast, but truly until they learned about the owner of that old cottage he hadn't thought they'd stay longer.

"Oh, there is. If you go up to the post office. It's just down the road. You can't miss it. You can even pick up some picture postcards there to send home. Most are of ships in Belfast but it might interest you." She bobbed her head.

Mardell patted his hand. "I'll go, Dad."

Mrs. Sullivan pressed her hands together. "Why don't you relax for the day? You've done a lot of traveling, so you have. We've pleasant grounds for walking. My James can deliver you to the train first thing in the morning."

"Thank you," Mardell said.

"I'll get more tea." The woman took the teapot back into the kitchen.

"Things move a bit slowly out here," Patrick said. "We'll need to adjust to Irish time. Let's make the best of it and add on another week. I could do with a wee bit of rest anyway." He didn't think they'd need many days but he needed to gather some strength. The stress of the trip was taking a toll. Or maybe he was procrastinating, but either way they needed more time.

Mardell beamed. "After I make the call I'll take a stroll around the farm. You rest, Dad. Mrs. Sullivan said the grounds are lovely and I haven't seen much of it yet."

"Fine idea."

"I'll bring some tea to your room later. Maybe one of those swell scones I smell baking as well."

Patrick stood and winked at his daughter. "That's grand altogether. Now, Mardell, remember what I told you. Be cautious about asking folks questions about our Juniper."

"Dad, I will not promise I won't talk to people. You know how I don't know a stranger."

"Aye, but—"

"Don't worry." She stood, gave him a hug, and whispered in his ear. "I promise I will not reveal anything specific or ask about war, all right?"

"That will do. Just mind your p's and q's."

Patrick shuffled off to the stairs leading to their rooms. The flight seemed longer and harder to climb than before. He really did need a lie-down. Once he reached the top of the stairs he regretted not having stopped in at the john. Descending again, he contemplated his symptoms. The cough wasn't much of a bother anymore. Having to visit the toilet so frequently was. And this blasted toilet was a fair distance from his bed. No bedpans, either.

When he returned to his room his thoughts again migrated to his mother. He remembered a time when he was a boy and a man paid a visit. At the time Patrick had thought he was an old man. Now he realized the fellow was probably about the age Patrick was now and complaining of the same thing that ailed Patrick. His mother had given the man some dried leaves and later the fellow stopped them in the vegetable market to exclaim how well he'd recovered.

"Well, if it hadn't worked," she'd said, "I'd have sent you to County Fermanagh for dirt from Father McGirr's grave."

Patrick hadn't known then what she meant by that, still didn't, but the cure *had* worked and he wished he had some of that stuff now. If only Patrick could remember more about Delaney's cures—there had been blood in the toilet.

CHAPTER 27

J uniper

February 1950, Glasgleann Cottage, County Down, Northern Ireland

Granny rallied a bit and took some soup. Relief flooded Juniper like a breath of spring air. "Would you like some bread, Granny? Perhaps some goat cheese?"

"Thank you, no."

"Well, happy you enjoyed the soup." When Juniper had emptied the chamber pot that morning she noted a few crimson drops. Later she'd consult the book of cures.

Granny pointed to a shelf. "You dried the leaves of mayflower. 'Tis there on the shelf?"

"That's right."

"I need that, lass. Brew some up."

"All right. But why do you need it, Granny? Shall I have a look at the cures first?"

"No need." Granny's voice sounded gravelly.

Juniper poured spring water into a cup and handed it to her.

Granny sipped and cleared her throat. "Acute catarrhal cystitis. You can look it up if you want, but you saw the chamber pot, I suppose. Nothing to worry about, lass, that a wee spot of mayflower won't take care of."

After Juniper made the tea, she left Granny sitting by the hearth with a steaming mug and went to fetch more water. The air smelled of moss and leaf mold. But spring was coming. It was St. Brigid's Day, after all. The path to the well was spongy, prompting Juniper to keep to the edges to avoid the mud. She kicked up a bit of leaf litter and noticed some snowdrops underneath. Smiling, she knelt to pick a tiny blossom. The milky white bell shape reminded her of the first day she'd found them growing by the well. It had been late for blooms, but she had known what they were and was elated. That discovery led her to pull back layers of leaves and moss in several places around the property. The condition of the soil told her the patch of ground around the cottage had been cultivated before. Now, of course, she knew that Aunt Bet had been an expert gardener when she lived there. But at the time all Juniper thought about was bringing back a garden that had lain dormant. She'd known that would be much easier than starting from scratch.

Juniper smiled to herself. That revelation had come on the same day she'd realized her shop needed something more than just magazines and silk stockings. And it was also the day she had learned Granny was on her way.

CHAPTER 28

P atrick

May 1950, County Down, Northern Ireland

Patrick was hungry by the time Mardell arrived with tea. "Got any sandwiches with that, darlin?"

She turned up the flame on the oil lamp beside the door. "I do, although I had to cross my heart and promise Mrs. Sullivan we'd thoroughly clean up after ourselves."

Patrick popped one into his mouth. "These wee cheese sandwiches are the best. You cannot beat Ireland for its dairy foods. Not even the Amish Millers back home make cheese this good."

Mardell poured the tea as they sat at a small round table near the window in Patrick's room. "You're in a good mood, Dad. Feeling better?"

"I am." It was only a small mistruth. "Any trouble changing the tickets?"

"No. I wired the difference and we're all set."

"I'll pay you back when we get home. Take your walk, did you?"

Mardell's eyes rounded as she spoke. "It was exhilarating. This farm is not much bigger than ours but it's incredible what they do with it. There is a vegetable garden, hayfields, a barn with two horses, pastures for pigs, a large field just for a handful of cattle who seem quite happy with all that green grass to eat. I declare, they smiled at me."

Patrick chuckled. Only his whimsical daughter would think such a thing.

She continued after dabbing her mouth with a linen napkin. "The Sullivans own sheep that graze openly among the neighbor's and there's a flock of chickens scattered about. Their neighbor helps collect all the sheep in the evening, driving them to the appropriate barns. They say we can watch from a footpath near the road."

Patrick chewed thoughtfully. After taking a swig of his tea, he said, "I expect they have to do all that and more, Mardell, despite the small size of their holding. No factories nearby. Folks have to live off their land. I expect Mrs. Sullivan takes in boarders to afford the things the farm doesn't produce."

"I image you're right. You've done quite well for us in Ohio, Dad. So many people all over the world, I've read, are struggling with poverty. The war's been over for a few years now. Let's do hope things improve soon."

It did his heart good to hear her appreciation of his hard work. "Well, now, I'm glad you had yourself a good stroll."

After tea they went downstairs to sit by the fire and read. The Sullivans busied themselves elsewhere in the house.

Mardell studied her tour book. Patrick didn't have a book, so he perused Mrs. Sullivan's bookshelves. One title on the shelf caught his eye. A paperback he thought Mardell had read before. This copy had an unusual shape, longer than it was tall. Mardell's book at home might not resemble the shape of this one, but he recognized the title. "Look here, darlin. *A Tree Grows in Brooklyn* by Betty Smith."

She glanced up. "I read that some time ago. I'm surprised it would show up here. I'm glad it has, though. More folks should read it. May I have a look?"

He handed it to her.

"How interesting. Dad, remember during the war there was that women's group at home that worked with the librarian in a national effort to bring books to the troops?"

"I do recall that."

"This seems to be one of those books." She gave it back to him.

Mrs. Sullivan entered the lounge carrying a tea set on a tray. "Ah, I've read that one myself, so I have. Most of us around here have a relative or two who went to America and probably lived a life like Johnny and Katie in that novel."

Mardell bobbed her head. "Is that what interested you about this? I believe Johnny's parents came from Ireland. I've always been fascinated to learn why people buy the books they buy."

Mrs. Sullivan huffed. "Don't buy these books. They are left here by visitors like yourselves." The woman motioned for the book and Patrick handed it to her. "See this?" She tapped a spot on the cover. "Armed Services Edition. Left here by an American G.I."

"Yes, that's what I was thinking," Mardell said. "I'm happy they left you a good one. Did you enjoy it, Mrs. Sullivan?"

"Oh, I did indeed. You are very welcome to borrow it if you'd like or any of the others."

Mardell leaned her head to one side. "I wonder if Leo read this, Dad. We talked about these books distributed to servicemen. He was very interested in our efforts since at the time the Germans were burning books."

"Terrible business, that," Patrick put in.

Ellie Sullivan cocked her head. "Leo, you say?"

"That's Mardell's beau back home," Patrick told her. "The young man was stationed in these parts during the last war."

Ellie handed the book back to Mardell. "Ah, he may have been the one who left it. What was his full name?"

"Leo Walsh. Might you have met him?" Mardell asked, nodding her head as though encouraging a positive answer.

"Soldiers weren't billeted in farmhouses," Patrick scolded. At least not American soldiers.

The woman's face brightened. "Ach, sure he did not live here, but I believe I did meet him, love. A long time ago, but I do recall. Oh, that's jammy, isn't it? Lucky, I mean. To think after all these years Americans from his home came back here."

Mardell twisted her neck in such a way that Patrick figured she was having trouble with the accent. "So you think you did meet him, Mrs. Sullivan?"

"He must have been that fella who stayed here one night before going back to his barracks. Tall, blue eyes, wavy hair the color of beach sand? Quite attractive as I remember."

"That sounds like Leo," Mardell said.

"How is our man Leo? Recovered from his boils, I hope. My, my, that was a while ago, but I do remember he had trouble with his feet."

Patrick stifled a moan and returned to his chair. At least Mardell hadn't balked when he referred to Leo as her beau.

Mardell and the hostess sat close together on wooden chairs. "Leo loved your country, Mrs. Sullivan. He said the folks here were very kind."

The old woman blushed. Any small compliment seemed to delight her to no end. Despite Patrick's warning, Mardell was about to ask. He could see it in her expression. Well, perhaps it *was* time to fulfill their promise to the lad.

"He mentioned one woman he'd like us to visit while we are here," Mardell said. "Perhaps you know her."

"What's she called, love?"

Mardell bit her lip. "I'm afraid he couldn't remember her name. His blisters, uh, boils, as you said? Leo visited her for a treatment that cured him. Was that you?"

"Heavens, no. That would be Miss Barry. Lives a mile or so from the command center."

"Can you direct us there?"

"I can. Now, more tea, dear?"

CHAPTER 29

J uniper

April 1950, Glasgleann Cottage, County Down, Northern Ireland

After Easter passed, Granny seemed better. The infection in her kidneys cleared up and so did the woman's foggy mind. Spring seemed to cheer her. If only the coming of winter were not inevitable. As frail as Granny was, she might not survive another cold season. For now, though, the fish were spawning, the sheep were lambing, and the days grew longer, hinting at hope renewed.

In mid-April, after a delightful day when Granny had been more like her old self than she'd been for many weeks, Juniper counted her blessings as she settled in to sleep. A treasure of a day it had been. Granny had eaten well, praising the flavor of the mutton stew. She spoke fondly, without a touch of melancholy, of her long-lost son, Juniper's father. And lastly, Granny had kissed Juniper goodnight and not flashed her a sad look. All in all, a spectacular day, the kind of day that if you never got another you could at least say you'd had the best.

The next morning Juniper left Granny sleeping and stepped outside wrapped in her familiar old black cloak. The frigid air seeped through the material, reminding her it was time to replace it.

She encountered Toby on the road. "Where are you off to this fine day?" he asked.

"Up the road to get new chicks. Stop in and see if Granny's awake, would you? I left scones on the table, and you're very welcome."

"Quite kind." He tipped his hat. "Oh, and I do have a fat letter for you." He handed her an envelope.

"This is not like my uncle. He's been a man of few words."

Toby straddled his bicycle. "I hope 'tis a wee bit of good news, then."

Juniper stared at the weighty letter. How long would it take her to decipher all this? He obviously never learned proper penmanship. She dropped it into her basket, wondering what they could possibly have to converse about.

When she returned from her errand, Juniper discovered Granny in the kitchen.

"You're up. How are you, Granny?"

"Right as rain. The postman and I had a bit of refreshment. Did you get the chicks?"

"I did indeed. Those Garritys are doing quite well for themselves over there."

"They are, are they? That's nice. They likely have quality poultry, then. I will visit the chicks in a bit."

"If you're not up to it, Granny, I'll bring them in here."

She shook her head and tied her gray locks up in a headscarf. "Toby said you've a letter from your uncle."

"Right. He gave it to me on the road. I almost forgot it was in my basket."

Placing the thick letter on the table, Juniper paused to gaze out the window. "The chicks are enjoying the sunshine."

Granny took a peek outside, smiling, then watched as Juniper opened the letter. "What's it say, darlin? My eyes are bad."

Juniper shook her head. "No matter if you had perfect vision, Granny. He's a terrible writer, that one." She pulled the pages out. "Doesn't seem to be any bank notes this time. He probably won't send any more. Smells of perfume so I bet he's got a woman, that one."

Granny chuckled. "Too old for that, I'd say."

"Men are never too old." Juniper unfolded the paper. What she saw was confusing at first, so many words and only a few meant anything to her. She studied it until understanding dawned. Some authority in Belfast had compiled this and Uncle John had only addressed the outside.

"Granny, these are legal papers." She shuffled through the stack, but there was no personal note of explanation. "He's giving me ownership of Glasgleann Cottage, the surrounding gardens up to the stream that separates me from the next farm, and the bogland. I never knew the cottage and garden

259

hadn't belonged to me. I thought it belonged to you. You mentioned that once."

"Well, of course he should sign it over to you, but I thought it transferred long ago. When you were of legal age your mother was meant to give it to you. I didn't know if I'd survive my illness so I gave it to your mother, trusting she'd give it to you." Granny took the papers and looked them over. A few moments later she puffed out a breath. "Your mother, it seems, never took possession until recently. So I did still own it until she did that. She paid the taxes, though. It's all in here. A bit late, but perhaps there was a spot of trouble because your mother passed. Fitting it's done now, though." She tapped a gnarled finger to her forehead. "But … bogland? Quigley's bog?"

Juniper studied the paper Granny handed to her. "Seems so."

"I didn't realize that was part of this property," Granny said.

Juniper shrugged. "Does explain, though, why the Quigleys supply us in turf for the fire. They were probably hoping we'd never find out." Splaying the papers across the table, Juniper leaned back in her chair and crossed her arms over her chest.

Granny's forehead wrinkled. "Wants payment, does he?"

"No." Juniper tapped a finger on one of the pages. "It says he relinquishes his claim to the land and cottage forever, effective immediately."

"Like I said, he better. This place was my family's, not theirs. With all you've been through, you deserve this. Rightly yours."

"And yours, Granny."

"You are the future, my dear. And, don't you know, you are the one who has restored the cottage and gardens. When you wrote to say you were coming here and that your mother had died, I thought it was passed to you then. Apparently John got it. At least he did the right thing in the end."

Juniper gathered up the papers. "I should have had the courage long ago to speak to John face-to-face and ask what in the world he is doing. Now's the time."

CHAPTER 30

P atrick

May 1950, County Down, Northern Ireland

Before retiring for the night, Patrick knelt in front of his bed. His knees ached and a sharp, sporadic pain in his lower back made the effort difficult, but there was something about coming back to Ireland that compelled him to consider his mother and what she would want for him. Confession was good for the soul. Sure, others had done him wrong, but he could do nothing about that. He could, however, ask for forgiveness for thinking Juniper would be better off without him. Because of that letter he now knew he'd been wrong and selfish to think that way. And the truth was what he'd have to live with, as the letter suggested. He needed to find a way to accept that. This was a start.

With trembling hands folded, Patrick rested his chin on his knuckles and began to pray for the departed souls whose absence had left a hole in his heart. He prayed for God to forgive him for not keeping Colin Reilly focused on the battlefield. He prayed that Colin would forgive him for surviving the war. With tears clogging his throat, he whispered what he most regretted about that. *Please forgive me for not protesting loud enough the unjust sentence Colin received.*

Rising unsteadily, Patrick retrieved Colin's rosary and then went back to his genuflect position. He raised the beads above his head and whispered at the ceiling. *I've brought it back home, Colin. God rest your soul.*

He prayed for Veronica's soul and for Mardell, who was now motherless. *Give me strength to be the parent she needs.*

He wanted to pray for the departed souls of his first daughter and for his mother, but he could not find the words. Perhaps they had been two strong women who truly did not need his prayers. Guilt flooded over him when he thought of those he'd left behind in Ireland. He pleaded for God to forgive him, although this felt selfish somehow.

A jabbing pain in his side and the urge to get to the toilet again made him wonder if asking for healing would be selfish as well. No time to contemplate. He rose as swiftly as he was able and lumbered down the stairs. After relieving himself he paused to glance in at the room where they'd sat earlier. The book he'd pulled from the shelf still lay on a table beside Mrs. Sullivan's chair. Patrick picked it up and carried it upstairs.

The urgency to visit the bathroom woke Patrick so frequently that he decided to stay up reading *A Tree Grows in Brooklyn.* Sometime before dawn he read the scene where the children were visiting a medical clinic for vaccinations. The doctor had made a disparaging remark to the nurse about the children's poverty and then there was a statement that so moved Patrick he kept his bookmark on that page to refer to it later.

At breakfast he recited it to his daughter: "A person who pulls himself up from a low environment via the bootstrap route has two choices."

"What's that, Dad?" Mardell buttered a slice of toast.

"From that novel, the one about Brooklyn."

"I'm afraid I don't remember that part. What were the two choices?"

Mrs. Sullivan entered the conversation when she brought in the teapot. "If I may say, I do remember it quite well."

Patrick smiled up at her. Ah, the Irish, the people who all must pull themselves up in this world. "Please," he said.

"The two choices are to forget about it or to remember it."

Mardell muttered. "Of course. Is there more to it?"

Patrick coughed lightly into his napkin. That malady was easing up, God be praised. The damp Irish air out in the country was good for his lungs, just as Róisín had said it would be for Juniper.

"More than meets the eye, dear." The hostess brought over a pot of jam from a vacant table. "If you remember your struggles you can rise above them. Isn't that what the book said, Mr. Doyle?"

"You are correct, madam. Rise above and never forget to have compassion for ..." He snatched up the paperback he'd placed in his lap. "Let me see. Oh, here, '... keep compassion and understanding in his heart for those he has left behind him in the cruel upclimb.'"

Mardell sighed. "Mrs. Smith has such a way with words, doesn't she?"

"She has a way that the average Joe can understand," Patrick agreed. *Or the average Paddy.*

Mrs. Sullivan turned toward the kitchen door. "I imagine that's why so many American servicemen read that book. Your eggs will be ready shortly."

"All these years I've worked hard to forget where I came from and what I suffered with," Patrick said. "I've learned something, Mardell. Even an old coot like me can discover something new."

His daughter smiled.

"Now I understand I *must* remember, for the sake of those left behind. I didn't want to remember, but that's not good. There is a purpose in having memories."

Mardell reached for his arm, her eyes watering. "The power of words is in the ideas they plant in hearts and minds. That's a universal truth and what we were hoping would happen when we worked to send books to our servicemen—hope, compassion, understanding. All the things the Nazis tried to block. I'm so pleased you enjoyed this book. It seems we're on more than just a simple adventure after all."

Patrick could find no response. He might be too late to affect those he'd left behind when he got on that ship in 1920, but it was not too late to be a father for Mardell. She was going to see quite soon that her father was fallible as they walked through this "simple adventure." She'd learn that he'd made some bad choices and those decisions had ultimately hurt a child that hadn't even been born yet when he left. A line from a Greek tragedy he'd read so long ago in school floated to the surface of his thoughts: *Men shall learn wisdom, by affliction schooled.*

Patrick could not deny that his afflictions had worked to educate him. But by some miracle he hoped Mardell would also see her father as he was now, with a heart bursting and filled with compassion. Patrick straightened his posture as best he could and set his sights on what could be done right now. "Let's take care of our promise to Leo today by visiting that herbal healer woman as soon as we get back from that hospital."

"Sure, Dad. So long as you're up to it."

He'd have to be.

Mrs. Sullivan appeared again carrying two china plates with eggs and rashers. The smell of grilled meat set Patrick's mouth watering. Nothing like a hearty Irish breakfast.

Setting the plates on the table, the hostess cleared her throat. "Wanting to see Miss Barry, are you? She has a shop, so she does. Don't go there myself, but others say she brews old-fashioned medicines, folk cures that have supposedly helped some." She cackled sarcastically. "Away with the fairies, that one, if you ask me." She puffed out a breath. "Many folks seem to appreciate her wares, though. If you've a mind to try it, who's to stop ye?"

Patrick shifted on his chair. "So you think she's away in the head?"

"I do indeed."

Patrick turned to Mardell. "Folks thought that of my mother in her day, but she was as sane as you and I." He glanced up at the surprised expression on the face of their hostess. "Just the same, we've a mind to visit. What else can you tell us about this woman?"

Ellie Sullivan jiggled her head as she spoke. "That old broken-down cottage? Folks believed it was haunted even before she came, so they did. An old lady lived there years ago. When she died it was empty and began to fall apart. Suppose Miss Barry deserves credit for tidying it up again. She arrived several years ago and fixed it up pretty as you please, planted flowers all around." Mrs. Sullivan crossed her arms over her chest. "You can't put silk on a goat and get anything besides a goat, so they say. That's why I'm not inclined to go there. She makes potions, lotions, that sort of thing, and I've no use for it."

Patrick laid his napkin across his lap. "That so? I wonder if she has anything like what my own mother used to make."

Mrs. Sullivan seemed surprised. Irish folks were superstitious and fearful. They'd always been so around his mother. He ignored her. "Right, Mardell. We surely will stop in to say hello."

"Suit yourselves. If you're still wanting to get to the hospital you mentioned yesterday, my James can take you to the train in an hour. You must know, however, the place is no longer a hospital. St. Giles is a school now."

"Thank you, Mrs. Sullivan," Mardell said. "They may have hospital records still. You've been very helpful and this smells divine."

Ellie blushed, dipped her chin, and then returned to the kitchen.

Mardell leaned over her steaming plate of eggs. "Fussy one, isn't she?"

"Oh, she just doesn't care for that Miss Barry. That's all right. I want to see if the woman might have some of the same ointments my mother used. I'd like to take some back with us, for aches and pains as they come up, you understand. And we've to keep the promise to Leo anyway. Sounds likely this is his healer. St. Giles first because you're probably right about them housing old records. Like the woman in the records office in Belfast hinted at. Worth taking a look."

Mr. Sullivan transported them to the train where they embarked on a mission to find the old hospital where Juniper once lived. As they chugged away from the station, Patrick thought about the daughter he'd only seen in one black-and-white photograph that he'd since lost. The memory of that image became seared into his mind after he received the letter. Left alone to fend for herself up here in the green north of Ireland. Róisín wrote that she loved plants and nature, like Patrick's mother. He and Róisín gave her a fitting name it seemed. Juniper. A rare and beautiful plant, at least in Dublin. Patrick hoped the girl had inherited some of his mother's strength. She wouldn't have gotten what she needed to survive in one of Ireland's asylums from either of her parents, and she *had* survived, hadn't she? Dismissed from there twelve years ago. He hoped they'd find out.

THE FORMER HOSPITAL, now a boarding school, was a massive stone building with white doors and shutters. Patrick and Mardell stood on a gravel drive staring upward.

"It's like one of those European manor houses I've read about. Where do we go in?" Mardell asked.

A trio of boys darted past them and through one of the doors. "That's a clue," Patrick said, urging her forward.

Once inside they stared down a long corridor of shiny wood flooring. The boys scampered down another corridor.

"May I help you?" a male voice asked.

The sound came from one of the open doorways. They moved toward it. Inside a tawny-haired fellow sat behind a desk. "Are you lost?" he asked.

Mardell stepped inside the room. "Is there an office?"

The man tipped his head to one side. "We don't have any openings at the school at present."

"Oh, no, no," Mardell said, extending her hand to him.

The fellow took it as she introduced herself.

"This is my father, Patrick Doyle. We were wondering if perhaps you have an archive of records from the time when St. Giles was a hospital."

"I'm Stuart McCabe. I'm afraid that's before my tenure here. I suggest you see Dr. Callahan. He's our headmaster and also a medical doctor. As old as the stones, so they say." He chuckled at his own joke. "I'll show you over."

They followed the fellow through a maze of hallways until he paused at one door and knocked.

"Enter." Dr. Callahan rose from a chair behind a desk as they walked in.

"Dr. Callahan, Mr. Doyle, Miss Doyle. From the States, they are," the lad offered before leaving.

"What can I do for you?"

"I'm originally from Dublin, sir," Patrick corrected. He surprised himself by speaking up and revealing his lilt. "We are looking for information on a child called Juniper. She was released here in 1938."

"Ah." The doctor motioned for them to sit on ebony leather chairs while he returned to his position on the opposite side of the desk. "That certainly is an unusual name. I was on staff here until the hospital closed down in '40. The war years. We could not sustain it and it was a time when medical changes were being made, expectations of new treatments were being advanced, and ... well, we closed up because we could not comply. I expect you are wanting to look at some records?"

"Yes, please," Mardell said as she bounced her pocketbook on her lap.

The man shook his gray head. "That is not possible."

"You don't understand," Mardell said.

Patrick held up a hand. "Please, Mardell."

She bit her lip.

"I should have a legal right to see them. I am Juniper's father."

"Mr. Doyle. I would have remembered a name like Juniper. And, you see, my memory is all we have to depend upon. The records were destroyed when the hospital closed."

A likely fabrication. Very convenient. "Give me the paper, Mardell."

She opened her bag and handed him the note from the records office. "See here, Dr. Callahan?" Patrick laid it in front of the man. "Says here she was released from St. Giles."

The man perched wire-framed spectacles on his nose and peered at the document. "Anna McGurdy, is it?"

Patrick nodded and then remembered. "Her legal name. I should have said so."

Dr. Callahan took off his spectacles. If he wondered why Juniper's last name was not Doyle, he didn't mention it.

"Well, I can confirm that she was here. No idea where's she gone, but just last month I found a letter she'd written. We'd been cleaning out an old dormitory we're renovating for classrooms. I found the note in a discarded Bible in one of the rooms. The Bible had her name written in it so I posted the letter to her guardian." He cleared his throat. "That was not you, Mr. Doyle."

Patrick's heart beat an unsteady rhythm at the mention of the letter. "Her uncle John McGurdy."

"I believe that's correct. Perhaps he can help you." The doctor opened a drawer and drew out a sheet of paper and wrote with a pencil while consulting a diary on top of his desk. Then he handed the paper to Patrick. "The address of his solicitor. Mr. McGurdy made all correspondence through this office in Belfast."

Patrick studied the paper. "Belfast? Does McGurdy live in Belfast now?"

"I can't say," the doctor added. "That's all I know."

Twelve years, records destroyed, and he knew McGurdy's contact still? The Irish never gave it to you straight, but Patrick had to admit this was more information than he'd expected to get.

Mardell sat up straighter in her chair. "Do you recall what the letter contained, Dr. Callahan?"

He frowned at her.

"I just thought it might hold clues. We'd really like to find her. You see, my father has never met—"

"Mardell, please!" Patrick gave his daughter a firm look and then turned to the doctor. "You've no idea where she went? We know she did not go back to Dublin where her uncle lived."

"Well, as I said. Ask her uncle." He nodded toward the address in Patrick's hand.

"I doubt that'll help. So many years have passed. Juniper is a grown woman now. We don't intend any harm. Only want to know she's all right. Like my daughter here was about to say, I never even met the child."

"You seem like fine folks to me." The doctor rubbed his chin and turned to gaze out the window behind his chair. Then he turned around. "Wait a moment. I may have remembered something else. The girl was quiet and reserved. Never caused much trouble after the normal period of adjustment they all go through. The unobtrusive patients don't tend to stay in one's memory. But there was something unique about this one. Her mother owned a cottage, I believe. Inherited, I think. I recall asking about that before I signed her release. Wouldn't want to send a previously committed patient out unsupervised."

Patrick glanced at Mardell who was smiling and nodding her head. "County Down, was it?"

"I believe it was. I do apologize that I don't remember more."

"So she left here and went there?" Mardell asked. She seemed to be itching to scribble the information in her notebook. No need. They would not forget this.

The doctor shrugged. "'Tis likely. So long ago, you understand."

Patrick stood and held out his hand. The doctor rose and shook it before they turned to leave. At the doorway, Patrick paused. "Mardell, you go along and I'll meet you outside. I'm off to find the men's room."

She rolled her eyes. She'd likely noticed his frequent need for the toilet, but this was not one of those times. "All right, Dad. There's a bench out front. I'll wait there."

When she was gone, Patrick waved away the doctor's attempt to give him directions to the toilet. "The letter you found. Might this be it?" He pulled the envelope from his jacket pocket.

Putting his spectacles back on, the doctor removed the letter and unfolded it. "Yes, this is it. How extraordinary. So the uncle must have forwarded it to you?"

"It would seem so."

The doctor gave Patrick a sad look and handed it back. "I can see why you are anxious to find her. I pray you'll be successful, Mr. Doyle. I wish I could do more to help."

"You've no word of her after 1938?"

"None, I'm afraid. The uncle was quite insistent the girl's whereabouts be kept private while she was here. We honor our families' requests for discretion. There is a certain ... uh, stigma for some, so a request like that is not uncommon. What they do when they leave us is no longer our concern

274

but believe me when I tell you that I know nothing about Anna McGurdy after she left us. That's the truth."

"Thank you." Patrick stood in the doorway and then turned around. "You are certain you sent this to John McGurdy? Through that solicitor in Belfast?"

"Right. John McGurdy was Anna's guardian and paid for her care."

"He paid?"

"That's right. He must be a wealthy man. Juniper was here for many years and was granted some privileges."

"Privileges? What kind of privileges?"

Dr. Callahan drew in a breath and pulled his fingers through his hair. "Life skills that extra money could provide for. Gardening, I believe 'twas in her case. That's how things were done back then. Like I said, Mr. McGurdy must have had considerable funds."

Patrick sputtered. "Not when I knew him."

Patrick moved unhurriedly down the corridor, wondering what Juniper's life there had been like. She had not been the difficult child Róisín had claimed she was, according to this doctor's account. Why put her in an institution? If Juniper did not happen to be at the cottage presently, hopefully the neighbors would know where she'd gone. He'd have to put on his best Dublin charm to convince them to talk and right now he was not feeling up to it. First he needed to find that woman with the country herbs to fix him up.

CHAPTER 31

J uniper

May 1950, Glasgleann Cottage, County Down, Northern Ireland

Thinking about the letter she'd written her father so long ago made Juniper's heart weep for that young girl without a father. She'd needed him then to look out for her, to save her from the scalding bath treatments. She no longer needed him. She felt only pity. Granny thought highly of her son. Plenty of other Irish went away to America and were never heard from again. That was the reason many families held a wake before their loved ones left. It was a kind of death, even if letters did come later. Folks knew it was likely they'd never see their loved ones again. Some did come back for visits if they'd done well for themselves in America, but since there was never any guarantee, a wake was appropriate. They hadn't been able to have one for Paddy Doyle, but it would have been fitting and helpful for Granny.

Writing down her frustrations and worries had helped young Juniper. She should have burned that letter, though. When she'd left the county asylum, she'd forgotten about it, focusing her thoughts on her mother's death at the time. Juniper pinched her lips and she realized that lately she'd been doing a lot of reflecting. There was no good to come of it.

It wasn't as though Juniper spent all her waking hours thinking about the family she never had. Most times she was content with how things were. It was just in the last few weeks that dreams disturbed her sleep. Who Paddy Doyle was or might have been and what his reasons were for leaving continued to trouble her.

"Come here, Michael." That fool cat had climbed up the sycamore. "That's all we need, someone noticing my black cat is up in the cursed tree." She wished she'd never given in to the assumptions made about her. Granny's warnings when she'd first come to Glasgleann Cottage echoed in her mind. There *had* been a cost, and despite Juniper wishing it didn't matter, it did. She was growing forlorn. If she didn't have Granny …

With summer coming and the garden bursting with possibilities, hope that Granny would fully recover arrived with the warm breezes.

"Nearly the feast of St. Kevin," Granny had told her. "Don't suppose the folks around here observe that, seeing as he's a patron saint of Dublin, but just the same, that's the day to bless the woods and the blackbirds. St. Kevin had a blackbird come and nest in his outstretched hands one day as he knelt praying. Because the bird had laid eggs in the saint's palms, Kevin dared not move lest he destroy the nest. Therefore, he stayed in that position until the baby birds hatched and flew away. Such was his devotion."

It was good for Granny to have a date to look forward to because just as quickly as hope settled in, it swept out the door again. When Juniper was a girl, she'd thought Granny was old. Now she truly was. "My time must come soon," she'd said. "I cannot keep my hands outstretched much longer. 'Tis time you, my baby bird, flew off to your own adventures."

Granny would at least see the saint's feast day in early June, Juniper believed.

Granny groaned from her bed. Juniper went to her and placed her hand on Granny's forehead. "You've a fever, Granny." She glanced around the cottage. There were plenty of potions for fevers. Juniper had just handed out some earlier in the day to the Comber woman who had a houseful of offspring. Lifting her oil lamp, she examined her shelves. Yes, here it was, meadowsweet.

There was still enough left.

Mixing the meadowsweet into a mug of hot water for Granny, Juniper hoped her grandmother would be alert enough to advise her. "Granny," she whispered. "Won't you try to sit up and take some tea?"

Granny grumbled and turned on her side to look at her over her shoulder. "What kind of tea?"

"I've made you some meadowsweet."

Granny scooted upward and Juniper boosted her with a pillow.

"Thank you, darlin'. 'Twill do me well."

Several minutes later, Juniper told her about the Combers' illness. "The two older boys, Mrs. Comber told me."

"That should help them," Granny agreed.

Juniper sighed. "Oh, poor Mrs. Comber in that crowded household."

Someone knocked at the door. Nighttime calls were frequent. The needs were not always emergencies. Folks visiting late did so because they did not want to be seen. Being awakened to dispense her cures wasn't ideal but she'd come to accept it.

Opening the door, Juniper found a young girl with a heavy blanket wrapped around her shoulders, carrying a lantern. "Miss Barry, I'm Mary Comber. I've come to tell ya that after that terrible potion you gave my mam, my wee brother Sean died. If I were you, I would leave here before the men in the village arrive to burn your place to the ground. You seem like a nice lady. Come to warn ya, I have." She spit on the threshold before rushing off into the night, leaving Juniper stunned.

Back inside, Granny sat up on the edge of the bed and slipped her toes into her house shoes. "How old was their Sean? Did they suppose to give a baby this tea?"

"It was ginseng. Sean was ... perhaps two."

Granny waved her blanketed arm. "Should not be given to a young child. I'm sure you did not give it for the baby."

"I did not. Mrs. Comber said it was the *older* children who were sick." Juniper searched her memory. "I gave her the appropriate dosage for a twelve-year-old. I told her she herself could take the same, but she never said anything about the younger ones being ill."

"Well, there you have it. Those Combers must be a lot of eejits."

"Granny, what have I done?" Juniper flung herself at Granny's feet.

"Listen to me now. You've done nothing. Whatever they did is on them." Granny narrowed her eyes. "Should not have killed the child in any case. One dose. Whatever he was ill with must have already progressed before they came to see you, darlin'." Moving stiffly, she stood and glanced out the window. "The truth won't matter. They'll blame us. Say we cursed them. Pack a bag and we'll wait out the night in the church. The Protestant one is closest, aye? Down the hill and across the lane by the standing stone? You know, the one in the corner of the bull pasture."

"I know where 'tis. Must we, Granny? You could rest here, and I'll keep watch by the window. Michael too."

"We should go, child. I've seen what an angry mob can do."

If the folks were madder than Mary, who had spit on Juniper's doorstep, Granny was probably right. Glancing out the back window, Juniper spied four or five wee sparks of light dancing on the horizon. "I think I see torches. Sure and the whole town wouldn't be coming."

"Sure and they might. I can walk just grand, love. Slow, but we've not far to go. By morning we'll sort what's what."

Juniper tugged Granny's traveling bag from underneath the bed and shoved in a change of clothing for each of them. As she tossed in the day's leftover bread and some cheese, she thought about the grieving family. "Should I check on the Combers, Granny? Might be others ill. I could bring them something to settle their stomachs."

"If the stars all aligned, I'd agree. But they never will for the healer. To the church now, darlin."

Juniper had tried to argue with Granny. The woman wasn't well enough to be traipsing around the countryside. In the end her protests gained nothing, so they made their way to the church and crept inside. Exhausted, Juniper extinguished their battery torch and soon they both fell asleep on a pew.

"BLESS MY SOUL!"

The voice of the startled clergyman woke Juniper. "I'm sorry, Father." She scrambled about collecting their things as morning sun streamed through colored glass on the windows.

As the man in a black suit moved toward them, his darkened figure nearly disappeared against the dim interior of the sanctuary. It was a sanctuary, wasn't it?

"Do not apologize, ladies. This is God's house. Are you in distress? How may I help?"

Granny sat up and adjusted her scarf. "There has been a misunderstanding. I am Delaney Doyle and this is my granddaughter, Juniper."

Juniper held out her hand. "Miss Anna Barry. That's what folks call me."

Granny proceeded to explain. "So you see," Granny concluded, "my granddaughter is not to blame for this child's untimely death. And I do hope you'll forgive us for not making your acquaintance sooner."

"I see. Oh, no need to apologize. I am new here. You are always welcome. The church is a place to come in times of trouble."

The rector was not much older than Juniper. She'd never seen him before, although she'd heard there was a new minister.

Smoothing a hand through his coal-black hair, he bent forward and stared at the altar thoughtfully. "You are likely correct, Mrs. Doyle. The family won't see it your way. A fierce bit superstitious, so they are." He turned to Juniper. "Just arrived last week. Haven't met all the families yet, but I have visited the Combers." He cocked his head to one side. "You are the young lady who's set up a shop, aren't you? I've heard about you."

Of course they'd talked about her. Juniper could only imagine what they'd told him. "That's right. I only aim to help people, Father."

"Please, Canon Duffy, or just Mr. Duffy. I am not a Catholic priest, Miss Barry."

"My apologies."

The rector shook his head. "I expect you'd both do with some tea. Come with me to the rectory next door. Have you been here before?"

Juniper rarely ventured off their piece of land except for occasional trips to the markets, train rides to Belfast, and her recent visit to the Garrity place for chicks. "I'm afraid not."

His crestfallen expression made her wish she hadn't admitted that.

"Well, please come. Mrs. Haggerty tends to my washing and she's in the rectory now. She'll be most pleased to have company."

On the way over Granny whispered in Juniper's ear. "He's very handsome."

"Hush, Granny!" The tea would do well to settle Granny's tongue.

When they stepped inside, the small house smelled of freshly baked bread. A curly-headed woman wearing a turquoise apron scurried to the door. "Ah, come right in ladies. You are very welcome, so you are."

Canon Duffy nodded toward them. "Mrs. Haggerty, may I present Mrs. Doyle and Miss Barry."

The woman gripped both of their hands at once. "Quite delighted to have company. Canon Duffy hardly touches my scones and eating so many myself is not good for my waistline."

The clergyman smiled. "I do eat them. Just not by the boatload. She makes the best scones in the county. You won't be disappointed."

Granny made the sign of the cross as soon as the man had blessed their food. Juniper glanced at their host's face as she poured tea but did not see the expression of surprise she expected from him or Mrs. Haggerty. The villagers she'd met did not seem to cross religious lines, but perhaps Juniper had misjudged them. Oh, the things Granny stirred up in Juniper's mind. Her entire life she'd never been as curious about the church as she was becoming now.

Meeting clergy. Dreaming about her childhood. Wondering about her father. Worrying about Granny. The last several weeks had brought a thunderstorm of thoughts she wasn't prepared for.

Canon Duffy delicately explained to Mrs. Haggerty what had brought them to the church.

The woman clicked her tongue as she bustled around the kitchen. "That Comber family. 'Tis a tragedy, to be sure, but to blame it on someone who had tried to help them is a pity and just not right at all. So many children and hardly looked after, so they're not." She nodded to the rector. "Going to set this right, are you?"

Juniper deposited her teacup on its matching saucer, splashing a bit of the liquid in the process. "Please, no. I mean, we did not come here to impose, Canon Duffy. We only planned to wait until morning when we could better address the situation. I ... you see, I am the one they sought help from, and I must try to make things right." Juniper blinked back the emotion in her voice. "I will do what I can for them, if they'll allow me."

Mr. Duffy smothered his scone in butter as he spoke. "You did the right thing in coming here, Miss Barry. The Combers are members of my congregation. As their minister I must pay a visit to the family. I expect they'd come for me shortly anyway. Why don't we go together? First we will check on your cottage, though I doubt they'd truly do any harm. Then we'll go from there to the Comber place. They have a farm about a mile to the south of your cottage."

"You are very kind," Granny put in as she reached for more jam.

"You've gotten acquainted with the area quite well in your short tenure," Juniper said. Was that too forward?

"I made as many visits as I could in my first week. I apologize for not stopping by your place but you were on my list."

"We didn't expect you, Canon Duffy. You should not apologize," Granny said.

"Kind of you to say, but you will find that I extend greetings to everyone, whether they are in my flock or not."

Juniper wasn't sure what he meant. Maybe he was referring to them being Catholic.

Later, as they returned home, Juniper was pleased to discover that Glasgleann Cottage was undisturbed. However, moving closer to the door she saw that a note had been nailed to it. Words were scrawled in black coal dust. Ripping it down, she handed it to Granny and then unlatched the door.

"Banshee, Hag, Witch?" Granny exclaimed, lumbering in after her. "Horrid notions and it seems they can't make up their minds what to call us." She tapped a finger to her chin. "They may think we've disturbed the fairies that live in the tree!"

The rector stood in the doorway, hat in his hands. "Try not to judge them too harshly. They shouldn't have done that but they do tend to be fearful. Perhaps you better wait here while I go see to this."

Juniper spun on her heels. "Do you know about this tree, Canon Duffy? Folks think 'tis cursed, along with my cat by way of the color of his fur. I will go. I must."

"Please. Allow me to smooth things over first."

Juniper tied another knot in her scarf as she spoke to Granny. "You have a lie-down. We won't be long. Bolt the door when we've gone." She turned to the man still standing in the threshold. "If I don't go, they will accuse me of worse. I will explain that I only sent them with herbs, nothing to cause death and obviously nothing that could have prevented that baby's death. 'Tis hard to accuse someone of evil misdeeds to their face." She sounded more confident than she felt. But this was the only home she had. For far too long she had put up with accusations and rude stares.

Granny plopped down on a chair at the kitchen table. "Leave no dark corners unlit, darlin. There's no profit in permitting folks to believe we use fairy magic for our cures."

"Granny!" Juniper was horrified she'd speak this way in front of the clergyman even though she had to admit she was right.

Granny pointed a finger. "As I told you when I first came here, there is no blackness in the cures we make, nothing magical nor mysterious. 'Tis botany, for heaven's sake. Folks will think what they want, but 'tis all practical, old folklore medicine our ancestors used before us." She grunted. "Not many of us would be here today if they hadn't discovered those remedies. Better to show folks these treatments are normal and not harmful or in any way evil."

"I think she's right," Canon Duffy said. "Show them you are just a lovely young woman who wants to help people."

Juniper's face heated at the compliment.

The rector traveled by bicycle. While Juniper had watched Toby ride, she'd never been on one before. Now she was sitting on the contraption and had no control over it. "Slow down," she pleaded. "I'm going to fall off."

"Grip the seat or the back of my belt. You'll be grand. How is it you've never ridden on a bicycle before, Miss Barry?"

With one hand clutching the man's shirt and the other holding onto her head scarf, Juniper shouted into the wind. "Never had the opportunity." He asked too many questions and she was having trouble deflecting them all.

He turned sharply to the left, forcing Juniper to grab onto his waist as they went raking down the lane. "We're almost there. Just a wee bit down this road and then off to the right."

She would not have referred to this cow path as a road. The rector deftly dodged water-logged hollows as he kept his legs pumping the pedals with incredible might. Her backside began to ache. Hopefully there'd be a farm wagon around to hitch a lift with on the way back. Or perhaps a donkey. Anything moving at a more reasonable pace.

Moments later they turned down a lane where a house appeared up ahead. As they got closer Juniper saw the place was badly in need of whitewashing. Someone was hanging laundry on one side of the building and someone else was slopping hogs on the other. Several children raced around a single apple tree in the front garden. They waved their arms as the bicycle approached.

"Canon Duffy," a boy shouted. "We're going to build a bonfire for the harvest. Have you come to help?" He frowned at Juniper.

The rector whispered to her. "They won't be honoring a saint when they do that or asking for God's blessing. Pagan ritual." He waved at the lad. "I see you're feeling better, Tommy. Where's your mam?"

A skinny girl of about twelve who had been hanging laundry answered. "Taken to her bed, Canon Duffy. Our wee Sean died last night."

"I'm very sorry, Annie. May I go in?"

Like her brother, Annie frowned at Juniper.

"I've brought a visitor. I hope you don't mind."

The girl didn't answer but led the way into the house. It was cold inside. They dipped their heads to dodge more laundry hanging from ropes stretched across the room.

"Mrs. Comber?" Canon Duffy called, as they passed a table strewn with soiled dishes.

"Here," a quiet voice said from within a back room.

"I'm sorry for your trouble," the rector said, standing in the doorway.

Juniper kept close behind him, wondering what they'd done with the boy's body. She shivered from the cold or perhaps the pervading sorrow in the house. She waited outside the room while Canon Duffy went to the woman's bedside.

Mrs. Comber sobbed while the rector recited a prayer.

"My mam will be back soon and finish preparing his body," Mrs. Comber managed to say. "He's in the cold room now, my dear poor babe."

The sound of the front door slamming made Juniper jump.

"What are *you* doing here?"

Juniper turned to find Mary Comber glaring at her.

"I've come to help. To see if I can—"

"Get out! You being here is stirring up the spirits." The girl's face turned crimson.

The rector rushed out of the room. "Mary Comber, what's come over you?"

The girl slumped to the floor and covered her face with her hands. "I told mam to give him that potion. He died because I made her give it to him. I thought it would help." Mary turned her face upward. Her features were distorted in pain. "And you're the one who made the stuff!"

Juniper wanted to run out. There was nothing she could she say to change their minds. But the horrible pain on the girl's face made her feel more compassion than fear. She had to try to help. She spoke softly. "Sean's illness, Mary. Does anyone else have it?"

"Donny. He's out back right now. Can't get off the toilet, he says. Annie, his twin, she's been poorly as well, but she's better today. Will Donny die too?"

Juniper hurried outside. A tall, lanky lad emerged from the outhouse, face like a ghost. "Donny, I'd like to help if I can."

The lad grimaced. "Fever's gone. Stomach's a wee bit improved now. Granny's brewed the heather tea."

"Ah, good." Granny Comber used something without Juniper's help it seemed.

He moved to an outdoor pump and splashed water on his face. "Who are you?"

"Anna Barry."

"Oh, the one with the shop. Sorry about all those mice we left at your door when I was a laddie."

She laughed. "Quite all right. I am also a healer. Will you allow me to take a look at you?" She inched toward him and held out her hand. He seemed amenable so she placed her palm on his forehead. Cool. Good. "Have you no heat in your cottage, Donny?"

He shrugged. "Tommy should have seen to it while I was sick, but he's a stubborn lad."

"Come, let's get you inside. I'll find that tea and get a fire started."

"My mam. She's bad off since my wee brother died. Is that why you're here?"

"The rector is inside with her now. Let's make sure you're all right. Anyone else ill?"

"Just me, I suppose. Annie says she's better now. Poor Sean hurt himself last week, so he did. Cut himself bad on some rubble he was climbing on." Emotion caught in Donny's voice. "Always playing make believe, that one. Got a fever a few days later. I don't think that's catching."

"Don't suppose so." She had obviously found the most cooperative Comber. Juniper led him inside while enduring dagger stares from his older sister. Working to build a fire from what little wood she found by the hearth, Juniper turned to the younger Comber boy. "Tommy, be a dear and go out for something we can burn." She hadn't seen a peat stack but hopefully they had something dry stockpiled. The cold teapot smelled of mint and she could see heather bits inside. Granny Comber's tea. Juniper filled it at the indoor pump. Taking a pouch from her pocket, she sprinkled in some of her own heather.

"That fairy magic?" asked Donny's twin who had been doing laundry.

"There is no such thing," Juniper shot back. "I gave your mother some herbs, that's all. Sometimes they help. But sometimes they don't. 'Twas nothing to cause harm, though."

"I heard you take primrose inside your house," Annie said as she unpinned some of the laundry hanging from the rafters. "Bad luck, that is."

The rector finished speaking to Mrs. Comber and joined them in the main room. "Listening to gossip now, are you, Annie? You should know better."

Annie stared at the rector. "Are you saying that's not bad luck, then? My granny says 'tis."

The rector bent down to the girl's height and placed his hands on his knees. "When something happens, folks sometimes attribute it to luck, good or bad. I believe our Good Shepherd leads us through, and something as simple as what plants we bring in and what ones we don't has no affect."

The girl huffed and returned to her work. "So you say."

Juniper whispered, "Oh, the cheek of that girl."

Canon Duffy whispered back. "The upbringing, 'tis. Don't blame her. She's still a child."

Juniper could defend herself. "Annie, the primrose you mentioned? I use it to make a poultice for aching joints. And it works quite well. Better to risk a wee bit of bad luck than to disregard something that can offer great relief. Your granny was by last week for some."

The rector sat on a bench near the table. "Miss Barry makes a good point, so she does." He turned to Donny, who huddled on the floor in a blanket. "How are you keeping, lad?"

"I'm all right. Our poor Sean though."

"Aye, your mother told me." The rector looked directly at Mary, who had said nothing, biting her lip. "Got an infection from that bad cut, so he did. God rest his soul and may God our Father bring you all comfort." The rector motioned to Juniper. "How kind that Miss Barry made you a fire and is preparing tea. When I come back I'll bring you all some of Mrs. Haggerty's scones."

Tommy came in with an armful of sticks just in time to overhear. "Oh, Canon Duffy! Will you truly?"

"I will indeed." He retrieved the hat he'd left on the table and stood. "I expect the children can take up from here, Miss Barry. Their grandmother will return shortly. We should be off." He turned toward the children. "I will be back soon, but one of you fetch me straightaway if you or your mother need anything."

Juniper said goodbye, and the two of them returned to the bicycle. "Since there is no emergency, Mr. Duffy, might you slow down a bit on the way home?"

"Sure and I will. 'Tis uphill."

When they reached Glasgleann Cottage he politely refused her invitation to rest before heading home. "I have an early day tomorrow and need to be getting on. I'm glad things are smoothed over. I'm sure with time the people of this village will come to admire you, Miss Barry."

They'd already had plenty of time to make up their minds about her, but she supposed the light could be kindled now. Minds could be changed. Next to Postman Toby, this was the kindest man she'd met since moving to Glasgleann Cottage twelve years ago. It had probably been wrong to shelter herself away for so long.

"I would say I hope to see you in services on Sunday, but you'll be at the Catholic church. Well, until we meet again, Miss Barry, God bless!"

He pedaled off before she could say she was not Catholic. She could forgive him for that assumption. She had been raised Catholic, after all. She wasn't sure what to call herself now. A flame of curiosity sparked in her mind and for the first time she found she wanted to go to church. It was probably wrong to go because she liked the rector. Probably. Lifting her head to gaze at the stars just beginning to reveal themselves, Juniper drew in a breath, relieved to have shown that she hadn't caused the boy's death. She would collect some flowers and send them over to the Combers with Toby just as soon as she could. Or maybe even deliver them herself. Turf too. They needed that. She'd tell the Quigley lads to deliver some. It was her bog now, after all.

Inside, she found Granny awake, lying still on her bed, eyes wide. "Oh, are you feeling worse? I'm so sorry we went out to the church last night for no good reason."

Granny gave her a weak smile. "Oh, there was a reason, darlin. There was for certain. How is that family? Are they over blaming you?"

"I think so. One of the girls is angry, but she aimed her temper at me to keep from blaming herself. She wasn't at fault, though."

"Oh? What happened, love?"

"It was no one's fault. Seems the poor lad had cut open his leg and it got infected. Pity they didn't come for help for that. Mrs. Comber never mentioned his wound to me. I would have gone to tend to him if they'd asked." But of course they wouldn't have asked. She'd been hiding behind the label of fairy healer. "He died from his injuries."

Granny weakly crossed her chest and sighed. "I shall pray for them. How is the mother?"

"I didn't speak directly to her, but the rector did. She is full of sorrow."

"Indeed. 'Tis painful to lose a child."

"I think the rector helped. The grandmother was out while we were there, but she will return to help care for the children."

Granny nodded. "Good, good. Now we should talk about my own transition."

"Your what?"

"I'm soon to meet my Maker, love." She tutted at Juniper's objections. "Come now, child, we know death will visit us all one day. I want you to be prepared."

"Oh, Granny. Is there not something in that book we can use to make you better?"

"There is a limit to all things human, darlin. In the morning I want you to fetch the priest." Granny had been to mass many times since moving in with Juniper, alone, when she was able to do the walking or when Toby and Mrs. Evans picked her up in their pony cart.

"I will."

"That's grand, dear."

"Granny, what about that rector? He was just here. I'm sure I could catch up to him."

"The priest, darlin. That man seemed like a decent man of God, and you should go to his church one day. But I want the priest. You will do this for me?"

"Of course." Juniper had known this was coming but hoped it would not happen so soon.

CHAPTER 32

P atrick

May 1950, County Down, Northern Ireland

"My James can take you over there," Mrs. Sullivan offered. "He'll be in from the barn shortly. Many years ago he put a fine roof on that old place. A man down in Dublin paid him to do it. Don't think around here there's any other with so fine a roof as that."

"I'm not sure why you want to start there," Mardell said, helping Patrick on with his coat.

"Let's just say this reminds me of my mother. A way to honor her memory."

He could tell she didn't understand, but he had no other way to explain. He could go to a doctor, sure, but something told him a natural cure was in order for what ailed him. He felt in his pockets. The old rosary and the letter were still there. "We'll pay Mr. Sullivan," Patrick said, removing his wallet.

"Oh, no need. 'Tis not far, that shop."

"For the petrol," Patrick said, removing a few notes.

"You may take that up with James," Mrs. Sullivan said.

Mardell slipped on her own coat. "May we pick anything up for you, Mrs. Sullivan? At the shop?"

"Miss Barry's shop? Can't think what. Unless ... unless she's got some of that lavender soap. A bar of that would be nice, if 'tis no trouble."

"No trouble at all," Patrick said, glad he'd be able to repay the inconvenience in some fashion even if it was surprising, since the woman had disparaged the shopkeeper earlier.

Mr. Sullivan had a rusty old truck. They slid into the front seat as they'd done when he took them to the train. Patrick had been glad then he'd not have to soil the only clean pair of trousers he had left by riding in the straw in the back. His farm back in Ohio was really just a plot of land with chickens in the midst of cornfields farmed by others. His occupation had been in a factory so he'd no experience riding in a farm truck.

"We'll make the best of this time by inquiring about Juniper and Delaney," Mardell said. "They had to have lived around here somewhere."

"We never heard of anyone called Juniper nor any McGurdys, around here," James Sullivan said. His wife had said the same earlier. "No luck at St. Giles?"

"Not really," Mardell answered, and then grunted when Patrick elbowed her side.

"I'm sure the man's not interested in all that, Mardell. He's kind enough to give us a lift. Let's not burden him further."

"No bother," James said. "This Miss Barry, she's an odd bird, though. Lives beside a fairy tree, so she does. Some folks say that very tree harbors spirits, souls of the dead who have not yet passed on. The fairy folk trapped them there, so they did. Take care not to step near it."

Mardell gasped. "I'm not sure—"

Patrick interrupted her. "Thank you kindly for the warning," he said. Either the man believed in fairies or he was taking the opportunity to rattle a couple of Yanks. Mardell didn't understand.

James dropped them at the door of a quaint house with a tidy garden of flowers out front. A carved sign hanging on a post near the door read, *Barry's Sundries.*

"Be back within the hour." James drove off quickly.

"He put the roof on this place. Imagine him being so spooked," Mardell said.

"A wee bit of fun at our expense. That's the Irish, Mardell."

She gave him a tight-lipped smile and then turned toward the shop. "How adorable. Shall we knock? It's a business, I suppose, but it looks more like a residence."

Patrick nodded, noticing the sorrel growing at the side of the house. Memories of gathering the plant swirled in his mind. They'd gone to the countryside so his mother could gather what she needed to make things to sell in Dublin. He remembered sorrel just as he saw it now, tall with wee red flowers. He hadn't known anyone else who appreciated that plant the way his mother had and here it was cultivated rather than pulled up and burned as a weed.

They waited but no one answered.

"Hello?" Mardell called, knocking again.

Nothing. Patrick nosed around the garden. Thyme grew in front of rose bushes that were just beginning to show pink in the tip of the buds. A few paces away a dense patch of rhubarb waved giant leaves in the wind. The smell of wild onions stirred the air. Behind the cottage he heard chickens. Taking a peek, he noted a path leading into a meadow of wildflowers. He recognized columbine, a flower in his youth he'd called granny bonnet. Aware that he'd been wandering uninvited, he returned to the front where Mardell stood peering in through the lace-covered window. "I don't think anyone is home, Dad."

A large boulder in the yard beckoned them to sit and contemplate their options.

"My mother would have loved living in a place like this where she could step out the door and pick all the flowers and herbs she wanted." The chime of a bicycle bell made them to look up.

"Hello, there!" A man wearing a blue suit and an official looking cap approached on a bicycle from the direction of the road. He steered up to the boulder and dismounted. "Come to shop, have you?" A sack of white envelopes was strapped to the bike. The postman, it seemed.

"We have," Patrick answered. "Seems no one's at home."

"They are not for certain." He nodded toward the mail sack. "Came to slip mail under the door. Miss Barry gets quite a lot of invoices in the mail these days. Not like when she first came. Back then she made more of what she sold. But folks today, you know, they want whatever commodities they couldn't get during the war, and Miss Barry does her best to procure them. I do her the favor of bringing her mail her so she doesn't have to go into town."

Interesting, but where was she? "Does she still sell home remedies? That's what I'm after," Patrick said.

The postman continued to blather. "Oh, for certain. Pity she's not at home at the moment. I took Miss Barry and her grandmother to see the priest. Her grandmother, you see, she was ailing but rallied enough to make the trip. I conveyed them there in my horse cart just a few hours ago." He chuckled, pointing again to the bundle of mail. "Got a wee bit behind in my work."

Mardell stood. "Do you know when they'll return?"

"I can't say, I'm afraid. I'll will check when I'm done with work. Miss Barry's grandmother is still not well, sad to say. Come all the way from America, have you?"

"We have indeed," Patrick answered. "We'll have to wait for our lift to return and take us back to our rooms. Suppose he's on some errands."

The postman gave him a quizzical look. "Don't hear many Americans talk that way."

"I'm originally from Dublin."

"Ah, I see. Welcome home."

Mardell answered. "Thank you. My father was hoping for one of Miss Barry's homemade cures, though."

"Well, like I said. Don't know how long they'll be. But seeing as I'm the postman, I know where everyone lives. Might you be staying with the Sullivans?"

"We are."

"Nice folks." He stuck the mail under the cottage door and then mounted his bicycle. "I'll be off now. Lovely to have met you."

"A moment," Patrick said. "You know everyone around here?"

"I believe I do,"

"Might you have heard of a Miss McGurdy? We called her Juniper. She might not be in these parts now, but she would have been around 1938."

The postman twisted his lips, thinking. "I'm afraid not."

"Are you sure? She gardened quite a bit, we are told. Maybe like this woman."

"Sorry, no one here by that name. Good day to you both."

"Would you tell Miss Barry we are sorry to hear about her grandmother and hope she recovers soon?" Mardell asked. "I am Mardell Doyle and this is my father, Patrick Doyle."

Patrick exhaled loudly. "She won't care who we are, Mardell." He turned to the postman. "We won't bother you any longer. Thank you for your kindness."

CHAPTER 33

J uniper
May 1950, County Down, Northern Ireland

The church was small but contained all the liturgical elements Juniper was familiar with. She sat in a pew and studied the single stained-glass window with its depiction of the crucified Christ. Granny had been in the confessional for a long time. Juniper's legs were beginning to ache from sitting so long on the wooden bench with her feet tucked under. She stood and was about to go outside to wait when she heard the confessional door open.

Hurrying to Granny's side, she helped her step out and whispered. "Was this really necessary, Granny? The priest would have come to the cottage."

"I wanted to see God's house again, darlin. There is a peace here. Do you feel it?"

Juniper nodded, without understanding. The robed priest rounded the back of the confessional to join them. With a warm expression, he put a hand on Granny's shoulder. "Bless you, Delaney. I will come to the cottage to check on you this evening."

Granny spoke weakly, her strength from earlier waning. "Thank you, Father Barr."

Juniper helped her Granny move toward the door. "You should know, if you don't already, Father, that there is a certain tree on my property that people think is cursed. No one from the Catholic church ventures out there unless they are desperate for one of my herbs."

"My apologies I have not come sooner, Miss Barry. I should have, especially when Delaney took so ill."

A priest had come by once, she remembered. This was not the same the man, thankfully. That one had been as nosey as everyone else and balked at her natural cures. He had not come again.

Granny sighed, her breath sounding shallow. "Oh, don't worry about that, Father Barr. My dear granddaughter … well, she was not expecting you."

Granny was too honest. Juniper tried not to look at the man, to save him some embarrassment. Or to save herself. Funny how his name sounded familiar. Hadn't Toby mentioned him when they'd first met? Yes. Father Barr had caused folks to not want to visit her due to that ridiculous tale about a tree. "Father Barr, wasn't it you who bottled up evil spirits, so they say, and put them in my tree?"

He chuckled. "My, no. That happened a very long time ago."

So he *did* know about it.

"My uncle Father Joseph Barr is who you are thinking of. I am Father Timothy Barr. He did perform that rite, to appease folks at the time, you understand. He blessed the tree and the house. If anyone still believes there could be any evil there after all that, they are greatly mistaken."

"I'm glad to hear you say that." Juniper put her hand on the door to push it open for Granny.

Father Barr held up his palm. "Please wait for Toby to escort you home. I don't believe he'll be on his mail route too much longer. He only delivers to a few homes. You are welcome to wait inside."

"You are very kind." Juniper meant that. After her experience in the abbey and then in the asylum, she was fairly surprised to discover two genuinely pleasant clergymen in the village. Both new arrivals, it seemed. Fortunes were turning just as Granny was declining.

A short time later Toby arrived and led them outside. Granny paused at the threshold, and then turned back and bowed her head. After a few moments she allowed them to lead her to the cart bed cushioned with a mound of Mrs. Evans's quilts. "You have both made me very happy by bringing me here," she said, leaning against Juniper and closing her eyes.

After tucking Granny into bed, Juniper collected some things for the postman. "These flowers, can you give them to the Comber family tomorrow? If it's not too much trouble, that is. I would bring them myself but I don't want to leave Granny."

"I would be happy to."

"And these are for you and your family." She handed him a wooden box of soaps. "I'll be sending the Quigley boys over to the Combers with a load of turf for them. I wish I could do more."

"You have done a great deal, Anna, just by coming here. You and your grandmother have done such good."

"I do try. I wish I could have helped the Combers."

They said goodbye and shut the door.

Toby called out to her. "Forgot something, Miss Barry."

She opened the door. "What's that?"

"Some folks were here earlier from America. They were hoping to buy some things."

"Oh, well that's delightful. I hope they come back."

"I expect they will. Said to give you their well wishes for your grandmother."

"How very kind. Thanks for letting me know, Toby, but like I said, I'm really tired."

"Said their names were Mardell and Patrick Doyle."

Juniper felt as though a jolt of frigid air had slapped her in the face. "Patrick Doyle? From America? Are you sure?"

"That's what they said, so they did. And come to think of it, they were looking for someone named McGurdy. I told them no one lived in the area with that name, but isn't that the name of the uncle who writes to you?"

She gripped one of his hands. "This is important. Are you absolutely sure that was the man's name?"

"I'm the postman. I don't forget names."

"No, of course you don't. Did the man say he knew me?"

"I don't believe so. Said he heard you had some folk cures he was interested in."

"American, they were?"

"Well, the young lady. The gentleman said he was originally from Dublin."

Juniper's knees went weak. "If you see them again, would you please ask them to stop in? Tell them they must." Her heart told her not to welcome him, not to open up that hurt, but her head said she had to. Closing the chapter on her childhood would be best. And Granny. Oh, Granny. She'd be overjoyed.

"I surely will. Said they were boarding at the Sullivans. I'll convey that message. Mrs. Evans will drop in tomorrow and bring you some soup. All right, then?"

"Thank you. That's quite kind." Juniper shook after closing the door. She wanted to tell her grandmother what she suspected, but Granny was already snoring.

CHAPTER 34

P atrick

May 1950, County Down, Northern Ireland

"We have the cottage we are looking for on this map," Mardell said, spreading the paper on the breakfast table.

Patrick drew in a deep breath. "She's not here, Mardell. You heard that fella."

Mrs. Sullivan set bowls of oatmeal in front of them.

"Now don't give me that look, darlin. There's nothing to be done."

Mardell didn't answer as she studied the map, chewing on a toast triangle.

Patrick excused himself to visit the toilet. Again. He thought they should go back to see if that woman with the herbs had returned before they tried to find that cottage. And truth be told, he was dreading finding the cottage and facing up to the fact that he had been a heel in his younger years. They would not find Juniper and Mardell would be sorely disappointed.

When he returned, Mardell stared at him, her breakfast forgotten. "What's wrong, darlin?"

"We were at Glasgleann Cottage yesterday."

"We were?"

"Yes. The herbal healer lives there, Miss Barry."

"Well, isn't that something. We'll have to see if she knows what's happened to Juniper and my mother. Even if the postman didn't know, she might, having moved into the cottage where Juniper once lived."

James Sullivan walked through the kitchen door as they were talking. "Miss Barry won't be at the shop today, Mr. Doyle. There's been some trouble, I'm afraid. An inquiry is being conducted."

CHAPTER 35

J uniper
May 1950, County Down, Northern Ireland

"You have to let me go, Constable. My Granny is dying!"
Juniper sobbed uncontrollably. This could not be happening.
Not now.

"First things first, Miss Barry."

"What does that mean? You are robbing me of precious time."

"No need to worry. Mrs. Evans is sitting with your Granny."

"I should be there. She needs her family and I'm all she's got."

The man rubbed his ridiculous sideburns. "Should have
thought of that before you went around handing out
dangerous concoctions. You're not a doctor."

"I never claimed to be and they are not dangerous."

"We will determine that through our investigation, to be
sure."

Juniper thought the Comber family understood after she and the rector had visited. "I want to see Canon Duffy or Father Barr. Either one. Immediately!"

"Is that so? What are you, Miss Barry? Make up your mind. Catholic or Protestant?"

She didn't want to take sides. Especially not in her predicament. "Please, just see who is available."

"I am."

Juniper glanced up to see the rector standing in the doorway of the office. She almost said something idiotic like he was a sight for sore eyes. Mr. Duffy took the chair vacated by the constable who moved to another desk.

"I'll be right over here if you need me, Canon Duffy," the constable said. "But you might want to know, she was asking for Father Barr just a moment ago."

This time she did not hold her tongue. "Troublemaker. I asked for either."

The rector turned his bright blue eyes toward her. "I'm so sorry you're here, Miss Barry. I just came from seeing your grandmother. She's resting comfortably. Mrs. Evans is there."

"I'm so grateful. Thank you for coming to tell me."

"Of course. Now, we will work to get you out of here. I've had a word with Mrs. Comber. She's grieving terribly, but I believe she understands you are not to blame. 'Tis that Mary causing all the trouble, but we'll set it right."

Juniper could breathe again. "When may I leave, then?"

He glanced toward the constable. "I'll see about that too. I'm sure as soon as we can get a statement from Mrs. Comber, they'll let you go. The problem is, as I said, she's in a terrible state."

"I can imagine. Losing her young son like that."

"You are grieving too." He put his hand on her forearm. Warm and comforting. He removed it before she was ready. He stood. "I'll have a word before I go. See what I can do. Then I will send for Father Barr. I expect, being of that faith, you'll want his counsel."

She didn't know what to say. She didn't want him to leave, and yet, she needed him to. "Thank you."

When Mr. Duffy left Juniper realized the warmth that he had brought with him was gone too. The room felt icy and dismal. She shivered. *Oh, Granny, please hold on.*

Hours passed. A window near the ceiling let in waning light. The constable appeared with a tray of food. He placed it on a narrow table. "Go on now. There won't be anything else." He shuffled out to his desk.

She glanced at the tray and then spun away from the table. Her turning stomach wouldn't allow her to look at the mushy peas and spuds for long. What was taking so long? She prayed Mrs. Comber hadn't changed her mind about making a statement.

Returning to the table, Juniper poured a cup of tea and then returned to the chair she'd shoved under the window. With shaking hands, she sipped on the lukewarm beverage. She had no one to blame but herself. She'd made a mistake. Even if it hadn't been a fatal one, it was still careless. The penalty seemed too harsh, though. Right that very minute Granny was breathing some of the last breaths she'd ever take and Juniper could not be with her.

Sighing, she glanced up at the fading light, wondering if she should move far away from Moira once Granny was gone. Here at least she had a few friends. Toby and his wife. The two clergymen. Canon Duffy had brought kindness to this primal, wearisome jail. Juniper felt drawn to that, whatever it was. If he could convince the Combers that she was not the crazy outsider most of the village seemed to think she was, there might be a chance for her to stay on, perhaps even get to know the rector a bit better.

A clean slate, something she always seemed to be seeking.

Another hour passed. She turned her thoughts to her father. Had he really come looking for her? For Granny? *Oh, Granny, stay strong!*

"Good evening, Miss Barry." Father Barr approached, a rosary dangling from his fingers. Deep in thought, she hadn't noticed the door opening but now saw the constable securing it closed against the wind.

Juniper stood. "Thank you for coming to see me, Father Barr, but I'd much prefer you go to my grandmother instead."

"I will do that. First, is there anything I can do for you?"

Juniper studied the beads he held. He wanted to pray with her or take confession perhaps. She needed something else. "Yes, please, Father. Someone came to see me at my shop today when I was away. I think it might have been the father I never met and my grandmother's only son." Drawing in a breath, Juniper told him the entire story. Perhaps this was confession after all.

"Oh, I see, Miss Barry. You were just a child. What happened was not your fault. No one can blame you for wanting a fresh start with a new name."

"I've not been truthful, about who I was. I'm sorry. I wonder, though. You may have heard that when I came my cottage was in ruins. My uncle paid for a new roof."

"I did hear that. The funds helped out the families of the men who worked on it."

"I wonder. Have you met John McGurdy? Has he been to town?"

The priest shook his head.

"Please, Father, I'm Juniper McGurdy. I don't want to deny who I am anymore. Juniper is my second name."

"Very well, Juniper it shall be. Thank you for telling me." He looked a bit put off by the fact that she'd used an alias. He was kind not to say so.

"The visitors are likely staying with the Sullivans, I hear."

"Very well. I'll pop over and inquire before I see your grandmother."

"Thank you, Father."

"Of course. Is there anything else I can do?"

She nodded. Biting her tongue, she placed a hand on what felt like a growing hole inside her chest. "If they don't let me out of here soon, would you prepare Granny? I'm afraid the shock of seeing her long-lost son will be too much for her in her weakened state. I mean, if you find him at the Sullivans and he agrees to come back."

"I promise I will find out and counsel her if he intends to visit. I will stay with her until you return home. I'm sure they won't keep you here too long." The priest sent a scornful look toward the jailer.

"You are most kind."

"I'm employed in the Lord's work."

He blessed her before leaving. The sun had set. Hours slipped by like sand in an hourglass.

CHAPTER 36

P atrick

May 1950, County Down, Northern Ireland

Hours after dinner and several games of cribbage, Patrick contemplated going to bed before James Sullivan entered the dining room wearing his muddy wellies. "She's down at the jail, our Miss Barry, while the inquiry is conducted."

"Off with you," Ellie scolded, leading him back into the kitchen.

"An inquiry about what?" Patrick shouted toward their retreating backs.

Mardell poured tea into Patrick's cup. "Perhaps whatever this is about will be resolved by tomorrow."

Not many things ever got resolved in Ireland. The ache in Patrick's ribs twisted and he could not hold back a groan.

"You're not well, Dad. Why don't you go up to your bed? I'll check on you in a bit."

"Mardell, we may never find Juniper. I'm at peace with that. Are you?"

She folded the cribbage board and gathered up the playing cards. "I am not sure if I am, but I'll have to be." Mardell paused, placing the cards down on the table. "Dad, you're pale. Please go rest."

"I will, but promise me you'll ask around, about the herbal woman and about our Juniper if the opportunity arises. I know I told you not to, but we can't stay much longer and … well, my heart tells me I must do what I can to find out what's become of her."

Mardell hesitated.

Patrick took her hand. "Darlin, can you forgive me for these secrets? I was wrong to keep them from you."

Mardell didn't answer.

"I understand if you think I was wrong. A bad person."

"Dad, I only know the man you've been since I was born. That's who you are to me. Who you were, the younger you, I don't know that man at all. There's nothing left of him in the man I know. There is nothing to forgive."

He hugged her, choked with tears.

She nodded when they pulled apart. "I'll see if Mr. Sullivan knows anything else after he's shed his dirty boots. Leave the light on for me."

Patrick swallowed hard. He felt terrible but worse than that was a sense of urgency pounding at his heart, crueler than any physical discomfort. He kissed his daughter and leaned to whisper in her ear. "Don't delay. Find out what you can."

"I will."

Alone in his room, Patrick swallowed a couple of aspirin and tried to rub away his pain. Mardell thought he'd go to sleep, but that was impossible. The only position that lessened his discomfort a bit was standing so he leaned against the window in his room. Peering over the roof of the first floor, he could see the gravel driveway below. The wee shadow of a horse-drawn buggy appeared, a lantern light swinging from one corner. He watched as the visitor disembarked. Moments later he heard footsteps and voices downstairs.

"Father Barr," Mrs. Sullivan was saying. "What a pleasant surprise."

A great shuffling of feet.

Odd time for a priest to visit. Was someone ill? Not likely. There was only Mr. and Mrs. Sullivan in the house along with Mardell and himself and everyone seemed dandy.

Glancing out the window again, Patrick noticed that the rig still stood at the door. No one had come out to put the horse in the barn. A brief visit then.

Voices rose through the floorboards, but he couldn't pick out the conversation, nor did he care to. Mardell would ask questions on his behalf. A priest would know everyone in the parish. When she came to check on him later, he'd ask for a hot water bottle for his aching side.

The sound of footsteps rushing up the stairs made him turn toward the bedroom door. Mardell burst into the room. "The herbal woman living in Glasgleann Cottage is Juniper!"

CHAPTER 37

Juniper
May 1950, County Down, Northern Ireland

They had taken her to a cell with a bed, but Juniper would not sleep. She hadn't heard anything else from the rector or the priest. Poor Mrs. Evans was probably dozing in the upholstered chair back in Juniper's cottage, waiting for her to return.

Juniper would stay awake, keep a vigil. She thought of Canon Duffy. If he were here, he'd take her hand, bow his head, and pray. She believed that was what one did while keeping vigil. *Please, Granny, wait for me. And your son.*

When Juniper was younger, the nuns tried to teach her to pray. They smacked her hands for not focusing, jarring the beads of her rosary until they cut into the flesh of her palms. They didn't seem to understand that hadn't helped. Even now her fingers throbbed thinking of it.

Muffled voices floated down the hall. Hearing the sounds escalate didn't help her concentrate either. Whatever God expected, she wanted to comply. For Granny. *Please!*

The voices came closer.

"You cannot refuse a clergyman, Constable."

The rector! She stood, rubbing her hands together against the crippling cold.

He appeared, carrying her black cloak across one arm and something wrapped in brown paper in the opposite hand. Flashing a smile, he arched his brows at her as the constable unlocked the gate to let him in.

"I … uh, I am surprised to see you. Has something happened?"

"May I?" He pointed to the lone chair. "Your grandmother is all right, Miss Barry."

"Please." She sat on the edge of her cot.

"I've come from your cottage. She is resting easily."

Juniper felt her shoulders relax. "Considerate of you to let me know."

"And Maggie Evans has been busying herself in your kitchen." He lifted the package. "Currant scones."

Tears came.

"Oh, now. 'Tis all right, so it is." He sat next to her and put an arm around her shoulders.

Juniper sobbed harder, all tension spilling out.

He handed her his handkerchief.

Inhaling deeply, she regained her composure. "I have never known kindness like this from anyone other than Granny."

He returned to the chair to unwrap the scones. "Well, that's very unChristian. It would seem I have a bit of work to do in this community."

"Oh, don't blame them, other than maybe that Mary Comber."

He gave her a slim smile. "That's the way, Miss Barry. Stand up for yourself. You'll be out of here soon."

"'Tis hard."

"Aye, 'tis hard, but that young lass will be here in the morning to set things right. I've made sure of it."

Her chest ached. All that compassion he showed her and she had not been truthful. "I am not Anna Barry."

The rector bobbed his head. "You did tell me people call you that. Your name, what your grandmother calls you, is Juniper, that right?"

"That's right and there is loads more I would like to tell you, Canon Duffy."

He did not look surprised. Wrapping a scone in a bit of paper he'd torn from the package, he handed it to her. "I will stay as long as you'd like. I'm an excellent listener, so I am."

After explaining her situation, and the way Uncle John had been supporting her, she told him about the legal papers granting her ownership of her property. "Will that be taken from me?" She stared down at the half-eaten scone in her lap, worry turning her stomach.

"Why should it?" He began tidying up by sweeping crumbs from his lap and the chair back into the sack.

"I'm in here. I'm a woman. They might even send me back to St. Giles for what I've done."

He bent his head low to catch her gaze. "That would never happen. I would not allow it."

Setting the scone aside, she stood, rubbing her aching fingers. "Why are you being so compassionate, Canon Duffy? You hardly know me and I'm not a member of your church."

He appeared deflated. "I'm aggrieved that you would think that of me, Anna. I'm here for all."

She blew out a breath. "Juniper. But thank you."

"Sorry. That will take time to get used to." He glanced to the wall and shook his head. "This is not about my feelings or who's a member and who isn't." He sat up straighter in the chair. "Now, we will get you released in the morning. I'll be bringing Mary Comber here myself and make sure she gives a proper account to the constable. Then I'll take you home straightaway."

He sounded so confident.

"Thank you. I am in your debt."

He stood as the constable returned. "Try to rest until I return."

She looked at him through tear-clouded eyes. "I will be praying for Granny."

He smiled. "I shall keep both of you in my prayers."

When he left, the feeling of emptiness she'd experienced the last time returned. The man brought something to her that she could not comprehend.

The next morning Juniper awoke, surprised to find that she had indeed slept and felt a bit rested despite a lumpy mattress that reeked of body odor. She used the chamber pot discreetly beneath her skirts, a practice she had gotten good at from years of being institutionalized. The constable called out to announce his presence before clambering down the hall. There didn't seem to be anyone else locked up.

"I'm decent," she called back.

He approached carrying a white ceramic pitcher. "Freshen up. The rector will be here shortly. I've nothing for you for breakfast but if need be I'll come up with something."

"How thoughtful." She watched him enter and set the pitcher of water on the floor near the cot.

After he left, she splashed the cold water on her face, rubbed her teeth with her finger, and then used her damp fingers to smooth her hair.

Not long after, she heard people talking but no one came her way. Juniper pressed against the bars and strained to listen. The rector was talking to someone other than the constable. Mary Comber, she assumed.

"Go on, then. You must admit the truth so that our Miss Barry may go home to her ill grandmother. You know the pain of someone dying, lass. Think of that."

"Has she thought of us?" the cheeky lass said loud enough to be overheard.

"She is very sorry for your loss, Mary, but you know quite

well she was not responsible. Making her pay will not bring your wee brother back, so it won't."

Silence followed by a door opening and closing. Footsteps. Two shadowy figures moved down the corridor. Juniper was going home.

CHAPTER 38

P atrick
May 1950, County Down, Northern Ireland

Patrick and Mardell had talked long into the night after the priest brought the news that Juniper was alive and well and knew that he was there. Patrick could not bring himself to mention the letter. Soon though.

Mardell sat cross-legged on his bed wearing flowered pajamas, looking much the way she had when she was a child. She had just come back from her room, saying she needed to show him something. Her notebook lay open in front of her. "I've been going over all those letters, Dad, and I've drawn some conclusions about Juniper's mother. Maybe we should talk about these things before we meet Juniper."

"What have you got, darlin?"

"Looking at the earliest letters, Róisín said things like, 'We keep far away,' and 'We're nowhere near the violence.' I thought it odd that she kept saying that and yet, she seemed to know what was going on."

"Well, folks talk. She was probably repeating rumors."

Mardell tapped a finger on her notes. "I don't think so. Hear me out."

She was a smart one, his daughter. He'd listen.

"Like I said earlier, I think she was in favor of the treaty and on the side of Michael Collins, at least in the beginning."

"Aye, Collins, the leader for Irish independence."

"That's right. Her father, however, was not in that camp. She repeatedly refused to come to America, and I wonder if she was afraid to come."

"Lots of folks are leery of ocean travel."

"Maybe." She flipped back to a previous page of notes. "Remember what your cousin in Dublin said, about Róisín's father?"

"I was surprised by that. She gave me no clue that there was trouble at home."

"And they were on opposite sides of the fighting. I wonder if she might have been one of those abused women. There was a gal like that who came into the library. No one could convince her to leave her home no matter how bad it got. The only reason we knew about it was because she came in wearing a lot of makeup, trying to hide bruises. It's a psychological problem, I think. They just cannot see the truth of their situation."

"If that's true about Róisín, I'm greatly sorry to hear it. 'Twas for the good, then, that Juniper was living apart from all that."

"Ah, and maybe that's why she was. Róisín wanted to shield her."

"Possibly."

Mardell drew in a breath. "There are a few other things I think we can deduce."

"Go on."

"In her brother's letter he said Róisín was arrested but she ..." Mardell studied her notebook until her eyes paused on one page. "Yes. He said Róisín should not have been among the women arrested."

"Well, of course he'd say that, darlin. She was his sister."

"But maybe there was another reason. She was not in the Women's Council, your mother said. You assumed she was. Maybe everyone assumed she was, and that's why she was rounded up with the rest."

An image of long ago came to his mind. Leaving Róisín after meeting in Stephen's Green. She'd gotten into a motorcar with some women. "An act, you think? A deception to fool her father?"

"It could have been. You thought she was a spy."

He nodded.

"And then much later when Róisín said the priest did not support their efforts, I wondered about that. The efforts she spoke of, could that have been the treaty?"

"It may have been. The way I understand it even the Catholic

Church was not in agreement when it came down to each individual priest."

Mardell bent low over her book, brows creased. "Dad, she mentions the treaty debate and the Dáil. What's that?"

"The parliament at the time. The place where these kinds of debates happened."

"But Róisín kept insisting they were far away from the turmoil. I think they were not. She seems to know a lot."

"The lady doth protest too much?"

"Yes. She was trying to convince you and everyone else probably that she was uninformed."

"Ah, well, what she knew and didn't know doesn't matter."

"It might have mattered for her daughter."

IN THE MORNING they resumed their conversation at the breakfast table. Unfortunately, Mrs. Sullivan insisted on joining in. "I always knew that girl had secrets, so I did. I could tell the moment she came here something wasn't right about her. She never mentioned she'd been at a county asylum, so she didn't."

Patrick was about to put the woman in her place when someone knocked on the front door. Ellie Sullivan huffed and marched off to see to the visitor.

"We must expect this kind of thing," Patrick told his daughter. "This is how 'tis here. And if they find out I'm a veteran of the Great War, I expect they'll throw us out."

"Now why would they do that, Dad? Perhaps they were against it, but that was so long ago, and there's been another war since, one that affected the people around here quite a bit. I would think that would be more on their minds now."

"Keep mum," he warned.

"All right. I'll not be saying anything at all."

He fingered Colin's beads in his pocket. *Pray for us sinners now and at the hour of our death.*

A man followed Mrs. Sullivan into the room. Well-dressed, walking with a straight gait, he held himself with an aristocratic air.

"A visitor to see you, Mr. Doyle."

The man extended his hand. "I'm Percival Murphy, solicitor. Might we have a word in private, Mr. Doyle?"

"What's this about?" Patrick stood and wiped his hand on his napkin before accepting the man's greeting.

"It's about your daughter Juniper. I have some news about her family." He turned to Mrs. Sullivan who hovered like a summer dragonfly.

"Is there a lounge where we may speak privately?" Patrick asked her.

"Of course."

"This is my daughter Mardell. She's come with me from America to find Juniper."

Mr. Murphy held out his hand to her. "Delighted." He turned back to Patrick. "Just the two of us, please."

"It's all right, Dad," Mardell said.

Patrick followed Mrs. Sullivan and Mr. Murphy into the front room. When Ellie closed the pocket doors behind them they moved to wingback chairs facing each other.

This is what happens when you spread the word around about what you're doing. Patrick should have kept to his original plan and insisted Mardell keep quiet.

"I know I have no legal right to information on my daughter, Mr. Murphy. We don't mean any harm. Just want to know she's all right."

"I understand, Mr. Doyle. I am not here to accuse you of anything."

Patrick relaxed the tension in his shoulders.

"Róisín McGurdy had once believed you'd never come back to Ireland, Mr. Doyle."

"I expect she would be surprised, if she were still alive."

"She is very much alive."

Patrick leaned forward in his chair. "What do you mean? Her brother sent me a letter some twelve years ago informing me of her demise."

"That letter, Mr. Doyle, along with one I believe you recently received, were sent by Juniper's mother. I am her representative."

"What in heaven's name is this?" Patrick balled his fingers into fists. "I should have known I'd be played for the fool. Was this some kind of trick to get me into the country? Does she expect me to provide support? After all these years? For heaven's sake the lass is an adult."

Mr. Murphy retrieved a silver cigarette case from his breast pocket and offered one to Patrick. He waved a dismissive hand. The solicitor lit his cigarette and then leaned back in his chair. "No trick and no request for money nor financial support, Mr. Doyle."

"Then what? Why have you come?"

"Róisín's daughter believes, as you did, that her mother passed away in 1938. There were circumstances necessitating that deception."

"Big ideas, that one. It led her to abandon our daughter to a county asylum, I believe."

"I do not agree with that summation; however, she did indeed enroll her at St. Giles, and pay for it."

"Her brother paid for it. The administrator there told me that himself."

"That was the perception, certainly."

"Look, Mr. Murphy. I have a chance to meet my daughter for the first time. She knows I'm here. I've no time nor patience for namby-pamby blather. Get to the matter, if there's one at all. Obviously Róisín wants nothing to do with either of us. If she's sent you to tell me to stay away from Juniper, I won't."

Mr. Murphy blew out a puff of smoke. "If that was what she wanted, she would not have forwarded that old letter from Juniper, would she?"

"Then, pray tell, what does she want?"

"Discretion. Your word that none of what you and your daughter, the young woman who traveled with you, learn will be revealed to anyone."

"If she's in that much trouble, why come here and tell me she's alive? Shouldn't she want to stay hidden?"

"Fair question. My client wishes to reconnect with her daughter."

"Now? After all this time? The Irish Civil War ended long ago."

"As you can imagine, this is a complicated matter. Let me just say that the timing of Ireland's leaving the Commonwealth, just last year, gave Miss McGurdy a bit more freedom. That and the passing of her father, which just occurred a few months ago."

"Her father, is it? Had her wrapped around his wee finger. It took his death for her to come at last to our Juniper. What kind of mother is that?"

"One who wished to shield her daughter."

"Well, she did not want my help years ago."

"She was hoping you'd come now, smooth the waters, invite some healing to occur between the three of you. That's why she forwarded that letter."

"Did Róisín write it?"

"She did not. It was sent to her, uh, rather to John McGurdy, by someone at St. Giles. They found it while cleaning out a neglected room at the hospital."

That was what the administrator had told Patrick. His head swam. What was Róisín up to?

"My client saw the letter as an opportunity to convince you at last to come see your daughter. And here you are!"

"She could have written me directly."

"As I said, it was complicated. I'm sure she'll explain in time."

Patrick did not like being manipulated. Even so, hadn't his own heart been telling him the time had come? "I don't see why Róisín would care about me. If she wants to connect with her daughter, she doesn't need me."

Mr. Murphy cleared his throat. "The letter, sir, would seem to indicate that she does need you."

"Perhaps. Juniper had been abandoned by her mother. Whatever regret I felt, having read it, should belong also to Róisín."

"Agreed. Róisín McGurdy has supported Juniper over the years, posing as her brother. Her brother John was the one who died in 1938. The deception was created—I tell you this in all confidence—because her life was threatened."

"By whom?" Patrick said, standing.

"She and your daughter are fine, but that's due to the precautions she's taken over all these years. She will explain because she wants to speak to you before you see Juniper."

Patrick cocked his head to one side, his old instincts for trouble on high alert. "Two questions." He returned to his seat.

The gentlemen brushed a hand across the lapel of his suit coat as though dust might have fallen from the ceiling. His clothes, his mannerisms, even his speech pointed to affluence. "I am happy to answer your questions, sir."

"How did you find me? And how was Róisín McGurdy able to pay you? I imagine a solicitor of your standing commands a high fee."

The man didn't seem rattled. "We were expecting you at some point, Mr. Doyle. And the Sullivans are the only folks in this part of the county who lend rooms. Words gets around when visitors show up in this part of the country, especially Americans."

The Sullivans! It wouldn't have mattered if Mardell asked questions or not. Ellie and her husband were as good as a bullhorn in this tiny village.

"And as to your other question, I'm afraid that is confidential."

Patrick groaned inside. He'd been so sure earlier when he'd been on his knees at his bedside that he needed an atonement of sorts. Róisín calling the shots, as she always had, was not what he'd had in mind.

Mr. Murphy stood, preparing to leave just as Mrs. Sullivan knocked and entered with a tea tray. "Thank you, kindly, but I must be on my way. Are you coming with me, Mr. Doyle?"

"To a secret location? I'll have no part of it." He realized it didn't matter anymore if Mrs. Sullivan overheard. "Don't I know how a veteran of the Great War is treated around here, Mr. Murphy. I must be certain I can bring my daughter Mardell safely back home to Ohio."

"No one wishes you harm, Mr. Doyle. No secret location. She is waiting in the car outside."

CHAPTER 39

J uniper

May 1950, County Down, Northern Ireland

Juniper rode on the back of the rector's bicycle, biting her lip and continuing to pray for Granny to hold on to life for just a bit longer. A sudden jolt brought them up short.

"What happened?" she asked as they both got off.

The rector examined the front tire. "A puncture, I'm afraid. We'll have to walk the rest of the way." He leaned the bicycle against a stone wall. "I'll come back for it later."

She fought tears as they marched forward past the lane leading to the Comber place and then around a bend. A light mist whisked just above the ground. She stared at clumps of lamb's lettuce growing along the edge of a field. "They should have picked that a month ago before the leaves got tough."

"Picked what?" He stopped and looked around.

"Lamb's lettuce. Most folks call it a weed, and more's the pity if they're hungry and could have eaten it. Lovely in a salad or steamed a bit."

"That? Right there?" He pointed.

"Aye."

He laughed as they continued on. "I must tell Mrs. Haggerty. Miss Barry, there is so much folks could learn from you. Would you teach me about the plants? I have a wee garden behind my house and I've been meaning to till it up, so I have."

Juniper smiled. "Of course."

The rector tipped his hat at a man passing by driving a donkey cart. "You know, if you mingled more, they might not be as suspicious. If you brought a salad of lamb's lettuce, for example, to one of my parish's suppers, the people would be amazed by your ingenuity."

"You think so?"

"I do." He pointed off into the distance. "Look, I see the top of Garrity's new barn. We'll be at your place straight away."

If God had answered her prayers, she'd know soon.

Once they entered the lane to Glasgleann Cottage, Juniper ran ahead. Toby's horse cart was parked outside the door. Rushing inside, she found Toby's wife knitting by the fire.

"Oh, Miss Barry, you're home." She tossed aside her work and hugged her warmly. "Your grandmother finished her breakfast and is napping."

"Thank you so much, Mrs. Evans. You must be eager to get home."

"Oh, I can stay awhile if you like." She glanced behind Juniper. "Canon Duffy. Would you like tea? I was just about to make some and I've some rashers left from breakfast."

The rector set his hat on the shop counter. "That would be lovely. Thank you. That is if Miss … if Juniper does not mind."

"Not at all. Excuse me." Juniper paused before entering the bedroom. "Mrs. Evans, has Father Barr been to see my grandmother?"

"He has. Left about an hour ago. Sorry you missed him, love."

Michael darted through the bedroom door when Juniper opened it. He jumped up on the bed and snuggled down at Granny's feet. Granny opened her eyes. "Oh, my sweet lass."

Juniper hurried to her side and kissed her wrinkled cheek. "I'm home now. Is there anything I get for you?"

Granny puffed out a breath. "I think not. That Evans woman has done nothing but cook and bake since you've been gone. Fed me well."

"Oh, that's wonderful. How are you feeling?"

"I've been better, but I cannot complain, love. I suppose you know the Father has been to see me. And your father …"

"Aye. I sent Father Barr because I wanted you to learn about it before Paddy arrived, in case I wasn't here."

"My Paddy." Her eyes watered. "I'm quite surprised."

Granny scooted up a bit and Juniper placed a pillow behind her back. "Good?"

"Aye, thank you. I suppose you are to meet your father at last.

God's miracles are beyond my imagining. How do you feel about this, Juniper?"

She had spent so much time worrying about Granny that she'd pushed the idea of a pending reunion to the back of her mind. Juniper removed her cloak and hung it in the wardrobe. "I am well pleased that you will see your Paddy, Granny. I know how much you've missed him."

"Hear me, child. Let the past be the past. You are young. Too young to harbor ill will. You have a family. A sister, too, I hear."

"A sister? I hadn't thought about that." Juniper felt shaky. She hadn't eaten. This was all happening too fast.

"Mardell, the Father said."

"That's right. Toby told me her name earlier. I didn't know who she was, though. I thought maybe a wife."

"Father Barr says Paddy married in America and had a daughter, but now he's widowed."

"Oh, I'm sorry." He'd made a family when he already had one. How was this to be all right? Juniper snatched a scone from the tabletop and then returned to Granny. As she ate, she tried to put some order to her scrambled thoughts.

Juniper had a sister who had also lost her mother. She'd had a father, though. How might that have made this woman different, and indeed she must be very different, American and all.

Trying not to think of that, she blurted out the first thing that came to mind. "I wonder where they came up with that name, Mardell."

Granny reached for the hairbrush on the bedside table. Juniper helped Granny groom.

"Unusual, isn't it? Almost as extraordinary as Juniper," Granny said.

"We shall ask him when he visits." And a lot more besides.

Granny squeezed Juniper's hand. "God has blessed us, and especially you, love. You have a family."

Granny might not be speaking this way if she knew what Juniper had written down before she left St. Giles, what she still harbored in her heart somewhat. She'd wanted him to come, to answer her questions. Now that it was about to happen, she almost wished he'd stay away.

"My blue dress." Granny said, pointing.

Juniper helped her dress in her best clothes and tied a green and blue scarf around her thinning hair. "You look beautiful." Juniper could imagine Delaney Doyle as a younger woman with dark red hair and smooth alabaster skin. When Granny went to heaven, maybe she'd be that young woman again, bright eyed and full of energy. Juniper had never wanted to ask spiritual questions, but perhaps now Canon Duffy … "Granny, do you mind if I go speak to the rector? He brought me home and he's having tea."

"Go along, child. I smell the rashers. I suppose you must be famished."

Juniper paused at the door. Turning around she saw Granny close her eyes. "Rest now, Granny." Just getting dressed had exhausted her. "Come on, Michael," she whispered to the black cat who bounded off the bed and darted out the door.

Juniper sat in the kitchen with Mrs. Evans and Canon Duffy, Michael weaving around her legs.

"Tells me he's been transporting you all over on the back of his bicycle," Toby's wife said as she poured tea.

"He has. I appreciate it, though I cannot say he's the best driver," Juniper teased.

"I will speak to Toby about finding you a pony and cart, Miss Barry. You need it bringing in all those goods," the rector said.

"Oh, that's very kind. I'm not sure I can afford it, though."

The man smiled, his face lighting with an idea. "I've been thinking of getting one myself. What if we split the cost of it and I'll come by and pick it up when I need to use it for parish business?"

"That's a lovely idea," Mrs. Evans put in.

"Oh, well, it would be convenient." Juniper glanced at the closed bedroom door. "Shall we consider it later?"

"Surely," he said, taking a sip of the Nambarrie tea.

There were many things she'd like to talk to him about. Would Granny live forever in a new place after she left her earthly body? Would Juniper see her again? And, more disturbing at the moment, would Juniper be required to forgive her father in order for God to love her? Forgiveness would be proper, but she wasn't sure she could manage it.

CHAPTER 40

P atrick

May 1950, County Down, Northern Ireland

"I'd rather not speak to her." Patrick left Mr. Murphy and Mrs. Sullivan in the lounge and sought out Mardell.

Rushing her outside, he answered her protests. "Róisín never died."

"What? That's what he came here to tell you?"

They went around to the back of the house to avoid encountering the car where he said Róisín waited. "I'm sure James Sullivan is in the barn and he'll take us to Glasgleann Cottage."

"Dad, wait." Mardell stopped, her pocketbook balanced on one arm. "I've forgotten the notebook. I won't be a minute." She darted back into the house.

He called after her. "Mardell, leave it!"

She disappeared inside.

Patrick paced along a hedgerow. *Hurry up!*

"Are ya avoiding me, Paddy Doyle?"

Róisín stood at the corner of the house. She had one of those upstyled hairdos and despite the heavy black raincoat she wore, she was as poised and lovely as he remembered her.

He nodded. "Róisín. 'Tis been a long time."

"I'll say it has indeed."

"Why didn't you write me, Róisín? You knew where I was. Why try to trick me to get me here? Sure, we're not children now."

Her cheeks reddened. "'Twas for your own good, Paddy. I would be happy to explain if you wouldn't run away from me." She took a silver case from her pocket and stuck a fag into her mouth.

"Sorry I don't have a light. Haven't smoked in ages."

She blinked her impossibly long, black eyelashes. Then suddenly her bravado seemed to vanish. She looked past him. He turned around.

"Uh, Mardell. This is Róisín McGurdy. Róisín, this is my daughter, Mardell."

Róisín licked her lips and shoved her unlit cigarette into her pocket. She kissed Mardell on each cheek. Patrick had never seen Mardell look so stunned.

"Uh, nice to meet you," Mardell sputtered.

"I understand your mother passed away recently," Róisín said. "My condolences."

"Thank you." Mardell stared at him.

"We have to go," he said, taking his daughter by the elbow.

"Sure, take off again, Paddy," Róisín called after them. "Only this time I could have told you why I wouldn't go to America. I couldn't then but I can now."

"Dad," Mardell whispered.

Patrick stopped, drew in a deep breath, feeling a pounding rising in his temples. It would be a pack of excuses but might as well get it over with. Mardell would never let him hear the last of it if he didn't. He turned around. "All right, Róisín. What have ye got to say?"

"Please." She pointed toward the driveway. "Let's sit in the car. There won't be any eavesdroppers that way."

They approached a shiny, dark blue Ford. A man, the driver presumably, was wiping one circular headlight with a white cloth while conversing with Mr. Murphy. The two men looked up as they approached.

"Give us ten minutes," Róisín commanded.

The two men wandered down the drive, lighting up smokes as they paced.

The car's chrome trim glimmered despite the dull day, ill-suited here among carts and wagons. The locals could be forgiven for assuming Princess Elizabeth and the Duke of Edinburgh had returned to Ulster to take tea with the Sullivans.

Patrick noted two farmhands gawking at them from a field gate. What rumors would swirl now about the visiting Americans?

Róisín opened the back door and scooted inside. Mardell went next and then Patrick after her. He considered leaving the door open for a quick escape, but a mist had begun to fall and sitting in the damp was not appealing, especially with the ache in his back that revisited him as soon as he sat.

As the car door thumped shut, the air inside felt pea soup heavy. Mardell worried her hands in her lap, stuck in the middle of the tension.

"We can't stay long," Patrick said, realizing he'd be trading one uneasy meeting for another, but longing for some fresh air.

Róisín cleared her throat. "Thank you for coming, Patrick. I know that letter must not have been easy to read."

She would have to start with the letter, the one Mardell did not know about. The idea that Róisín would be the one to make him expose this to his daughter infuriated him. He gripped the door handle.

"No, wait," Róisín said. "I'll make this brief. If I can. Where to start?"

"Start with your refusal to come to America. Isn't that what you said you'd explain?" he asked.

"Right. My father. 'Tis complicated."

Mardell opened her mouth. Patrick stopped her by gripping her gloved hand. "We heard things. He wasn't kind. I'm sorry I didn't know. You might have told me then, Róisín."

"I wanted to but doing so would have been selfish. He chased you on the streets. You told me that yourself."

"Ah, so. A bit of mischief."

"It might not have been. He was an angry, jealous man." Her voice cracked.

"He despised me for my war service."

Róisín shook her head, her salt and pepper locks falling free from loosened pins. "He despised you for loving me."

Mardell gasped. Patrick patted her knee in warning.

Róisín let out a shaky breath. "And he had a brotherhood of sorts to help him."

"The IRA?" Mardell asked.

Patrick knew his clever daughter would work out whatever Róisín said and get to the bottom of it. She would not have waited in the house if Patrick had asked her to. She wanted to be part of this search, so here she was.

"At first it was the IRA, or some part of it," Róisín answered. "You see, Paddy, Ireland's independence was the means for him, when it suited him. I spent many years trying to be on the other side of the conflict, but things kept shifting. He smuggled, took money from folks and didn't always deliver. That's why we were on the run so much."

"That must have been terrible for you, especially with a child," Mardell said, steering the conversation.

Patrick thought about the letters she'd written, fresh in his mind since Mardell had been reading them and asking him questions. Róisín did sound in the beginning as though she was trying to avoid the violence. But then she knew things about the Dáil, and such. She was heavily involved, perhaps more so as the civil war spanned out across Ireland.

"Why didn't you move away from your father and John, Róisín? Stay at your aunt's house?" Patrick asked.

"Don't judge John harshly. He … well, he tried his best to

protect me and Juniper. My father was …" She cleared her throat.

"You don't have to explain," Mardell said. "We've heard things. I'm so sorry."

Róisín took a deep breath and continued. "I intended to get away. Paddy, your mother came with us and signed over the cottage so that we could secure Juniper's care. And then I noticed someone following me after a visit to Mr. Murphy's office in Belfast. It seems my father was associated with some nefarious men. They'd have murdered me, after they followed me to Juniper." She grunted. "Complicated business, but it had something to do with money. I won't go into it all, but I will say that I stayed away from Juniper and cared for her under the guise of being my brother."

Patrick swore an old Irish curse. "This is not going to be a quick bit of craic, Róisín, is it?"

"I'm trying. There are decades to explain."

"Explain how you took care of our daughter," he said.

"The bog. I found a bit of treasure, it seems. I saw it as divine intervention. A means to pay for what she needed. At the time the laws were loose and quite vague."

"Did my mother know about this unexpected find?"

"No. She'd returned to Dublin by that time. I needed money to hide from my father, so with Mr. Murphy's help, he's a well-connected solicitor I highly respect, I sold the torque and few other items to collectors from the States. I promise you, I kept no proceeds for myself, Paddy."

Patrick let out a breath. "Ah, well and good. Why take Juniper to an asylum?"

"I asked for you to come, as you might remember."

Mardell mediated. "We can't change that. Please, Miss McGurdy, tell us what happened. We want to understand."

"Thank you, dear. That is my wish as well, as much as can be understood." Róisín shifted on the leather seat and rolled down her window a crack. "My father tracked me down in Belfast, as I mentioned. Before that, John had been successful deflecting him and his ruffians."

"You were a grown woman. Why cower to him, Róisín?" Patrick was running out of patience.

"I had thought my father's perverseness ended with me. When Juniper was a baby, I discovered otherwise. Not her, but with a neighbor girl. I know I should have told you, Paddy, but I was in a difficult spot because of something that happened earlier. I had a lot of money from some Americans that I was meant to deliver to a contact. Alcohol was illegal in America back then and businessmen came over here to buy Irish whiskey. They paid three and four times the price. The cause for a free Ireland needed the money for guns and ammunition. That's why they got involved in providing the liquor."

Mardell shot him a look. He nodded to indicate that he understood the irony. Both he and Róisín had been involved with Prohibition on opposite shores. The greed of mankind.

Róisín swallowed hard, as though the memories were hard to extract from her throat. "My contact, the men I picked up the money from, were caught in an ambush and all perished." Taking a cigarette from her pocket, she twisted it between jittery fingers. "I saw it happen. I had just gotten the satchel of money and was walking away. A group of men passed me, one apologizing as he bumped into me. I was terrified they'd figure out what I had in that bag. They moved on and I turned around to make sure they weren't going to follow me. As I stood on the footpath just a few yards away, some men in tweed hats and long coats knocked on the door. When it unbolted, they opened fire, stepped over the poor man's body, and then fired several more times inside the house. I turned away and made my way to the train, deciding right then I was finished with the business. The only problem was I still had the bag of money those men had given me and couldn't deliver it knowing they'd probably shoot me too. My father knew it was me who had gone on the job. He might have figured the assassins had gotten the cash, but word spread like wildfire and he learned I'd come into some wealth. He didn't know it was because of the bog discovery and wouldn't have believed it anyway. He was ... brutal in his response to me."

Mardell blew out a breath. "How awful."

Róisín nodded. "'Twas all chaos. I didn't know what to do, so I hid with the money until I found John. Knowing my father would not rest until he tracked me down, John worked out a plan for me with Mr. Murphy's help. The solicitor had previously worked out some legal problems for some of the women prisoners, me included, and John knew he was discreet. I wanted Juniper to be safe and I was afraid to keep her with me. The money provided a way to keep her well taken care of."

"If I'd only known," Patrick said, staring out the fogged-up window.

"I couldn't tell you. It all happened in the middle of the Rising. You've heard of that, I suppose."

"We have," Patrick said. "Destroyed a lot of records. Thought it might have prevented us from finding Juniper. Why didn't you just tell me where she was, Róisín?"

"I didn't know if you'd come. I reasoned that you wouldn't, truth be told. I didn't want to break her heart again."

Mardell spoke. "Like she said, Dad, mistakes were made all around. We have the opportunity now to make things right." She turned to Róisín. "Have you any word of Dad's mother, Delaney? What happened to her after she left Glasgleann Cottage?"

Róisín turned her gaze to Patrick. "I know she had been ill. She went back to her old home in Dublin. Did you inquire there?"

"She's not there," Patrick said. "We will try to find where she's buried."

Róisín nodded. "John's plan included faking my death. He even reported to the papers as though I'd been a loyal part of the rebels my father supported. We were both ambushed. No one knew it was John who had died, except for Mr. Murphy. In the churchyard we registered the grave as though I was buried there, using John's newspaper article as proof." Tears rolled down Róisín's pale cheeks.

"I'm grateful your brother at least took care to keep Juniper safe."

Róisín sniffed. "I am too, Paddy."

Mardell handed her tissues from her purse. "So you wrote the letters that were supposed to have been from John."

"I did." She shrugged her shoulders. "Don't know if I fooled anyone, but Mr. Murphy thought they'd suffice."

"Do you no longer fear those who were trying to find you?" Mardell asked. "It's been so long now."

Róisín laughed sarcastically. "Ireland never forgets. But time can be the victor. My father is dead now. Éire is now the Republic of Ireland and has left the Commonwealth. There is nothing to fight over now."

"I would not be so sure of that." Patrick thought about the tensions he'd observed here on their visit. How long would it take for time to become the supreme victor?

"Well, in my situation, anyway. I want to explain all this to Juniper, to tell her I'm sorry. When St. Giles sent that letter, I wondered if I could ever make her understand. I hoped you might, Paddy."

Every mention of his old name felt wrong. He was not who he was back then. Neither was she. He retrieved Colin's rosary from his pocket. War was not only a bloody, physical act, it was also an assault on the mind, one that obeyed no peace treaty.

Mardell stared at Róisín. "What letter from St. Giles?"

"This one." Patrick tugged the paper from his chest pocket.

CHAPTER 41

J uniper

May 1950, County Down, Northern Ireland

Mrs. Evans left after showing Juniper the bread she had baked. Juniper thought she might weep on the woman's shoulder.

"I am off to see a man about a pony cart. Do you mind if I stop in after?" Canon Duffy asked.

"That would be lovely. Tell me what I'll owe you for my half."

Juniper returned to Granny's bedside. The comfort of home permitted her to wander back through the fields of her memory again.

A dead baby.

Something about the bog.

Uncle John was too generous.

Juniper had more questions for her mother than her father, questions that could never be answered. What would she talk to her father about? Surely the Sullivans would be bringing Paddy and his daughter by, and when they came, what should she say?

Why didn't you come get me?

Why did you have another daughter to take my place?

Why did you wait so long and cause your mother so much grief?

Michael appeared in the window, peering down at her. Juniper rose from her stool. "All right. I'll join you."

Outside, she plunged her fingers into the dark soil, relishing the cool, calming feeling gardening provided. Planting, watching things grow, harvesting, and creating substances that could bring healing. These were the things that gave her life meaning. She loved her grandmother, cherished their long talks, but it had been the garden that had sustained her through all the lonely years.

Turning her face upward to watch billowing, cotton clouds sail in the bright blue ocean sky, Juniper felt not alone, but in complete harmony with something outside of herself. *Oh, God, if you're there, teach me how to manage meeting Paddy Doyle.*

She continued weeding for a while, then checked on Granny. Content that she was still comfortable in her bed, Juniper returned to her work. When she returned to make tea, she noticed a visitor approaching. Walking to the end of her lane to gaze up the road, she saw the rector driving a pony cart.

"Look at you!" she exclaimed, rushing out to pet the pony's russet mane.

"Like it?" The rector jumped from the cart and tugged at his clerical collar.

"I do like it. How much do I owe you?"

"Let's wait on that. I'll keep the pony and rig in the barn at my home until we get one built for you. Since I'll have the most use of it at the start, you delay paying for now. All right?"

"Well, I suppose. If 'tis not too much trouble."

"Not at all. But anytime you need it, I mean anytime, just let me know."

"Lovely. Would you like some tea?"

"Indeed I would. I'll get some water from the spring for the pony, wash up, and be there shortly."

She handed him the tea towel she had been holding. "What's the pony's name?"

"I'll let you choose."

The kettle was not quite ready when he returned. While she set out plates, Canon Duffy went to Granny to pray over her and read from the Psalms.

"I suppose I should have a Bible," she said to him when he returned to the table.

He set his black book on the table. Perfect match for the clothes he always wore, the uniform of a holy man.

Juniper patted the Bible. "I had one, of course, but I left it at St. Giles. Thought it a wee bit of bad luck to bring it along."

He chuckled and then tried to wave away his amusement.

"Forgive me. I've heard the Holy Scriptures referred to in many ways, but never as bad luck."

"Oh, that's not what I meant." She offered him some sugar, hoping the availability of the rationed substance would distract him.

He tapped his fingers on the Bible's leather cover as it sat next to his teacup. "I would be happy to acquire one for you, Juniper." He had gotten used to using her name already. "I would give you this one, but I have notes written inside that I need for Sunday morning."

"I wouldn't dream of taking yours. I'll pick one up the next time I'm in Belfast."

"No need. We have some at the church." He finished a slice of bread, grinning. "The most delectable treat I've ever tasted."

She poured more tea. "Apples. When there isn't much sugar you save it for the tea and sweeten with something the earth provides."

He bobbed his head. "Ah, indeed. God gives us what we need, he does. All the time, every time."

Juniper thought about the garden and what her plants needed: sunshine, rain, dark earth, deliverance from weeds. Simple, vital elements. If she were a plant, she'd have what she needed here at Glasgleann. Glancing at her new friend, enjoying how much pleasure he was taking in the few things she offered for tea, an overwhelming need to be by this man's side surprised her. Suddenly he was the only one she wanted to spill out her feelings to. She told him her father, a man she'd never met, would most likely be coming by soon.

"I wrote him a letter once," she confessed. "Not posted. I suppose writing down my hurt feelings helped a bit."

"I cannot pretend to understand how that felt, Juniper. But I do have a few thoughts on what might help now, if you'd allow me."

"Please." She felt herself smiling and hoped she didn't appear to be flirting. His caring expression and the way he presented himself as not stuffy, but wise beyond his age, told her even if she had been coy, he would not condemn her.

"You and your father have lived separate lives, had your own experiences. We cannot go back in time and undo what's been done. You'll want to know why he left. My advice is to allow him to tell you what he wants to tell you before asking any questions. You may be surprised to hear his side of things."

"I hope so. I imagined all kinds of reasons why he left once I found out from Granny that he had not died."

Canon Duffy sighed, leaning back in his chair. "Most men I've met would not even tell you they'd fought in that war. Some won't talk about the latest war either. I believe in talking. That's my business, so it is."

Had he winked at her? She hid her surprise behind her teacup.

"I was a chaplain in the war."

"You were? Here or in France? England?"

"Mostly in France. Many a young lad I prayed with, and many I prayed over. Life is short, no time for regrets."

He *was* wise.

"You might think about writing another letter now. You don't have to give it to him, but I've found that writing helps me sort out my thoughts. I kept a journal during the war, and I still scribble in it from time to time."

"I believe I will. 'Twill give me something to do. Waiting around for him to show up is almost as bad as sitting in jail."

He got to his feet. "I'll leave you to it. Thank you for the tea." He leaned over and gave her quick kiss on the cheek.

Her face warm, she followed him to the door where the pony waited just outside. Michael arrived and sat at attention on the stoop. "Would you like to come back for a bite? I've got a chicken to stew."

"I would be delighted."

Juniper glanced at the pony. "Let's call her Patience. She's good at waiting, now, isn't she?"

"All right, Patience," he said, clicking his tongue. "I think my pony's a Quaker." This time she was sure she saw him wink. "We'll be off. God bless."

Juniper watched him leave, at a much slower pace than he took with the bicycle, thankfully. Patience the pony might be a grand influence on the young clergyman.

After he disappeared down the lane, she noticed a gleam of something reflecting the sun. Against the far corner of the cottage, right behind the fuchsias, stood the rector's old bicycle. Juniper crossed her arms and stared at it, amused. He'd taped a paper sign to the handlebars.

For leisurely trips.

CHAPTER 42

P atrick

May 1950, County Down, Northern Ireland

"Here it is, Mardell." Patrick handed her the letter. "This is the reason I hesitated to come and yet knew I must." He watched Róisín, but the woman did not return his glance, so he addressed his daughter instead. "Juniper's mother still knows me after all these years. When you read this, you won't blame me for wanting to toss it away, erase it from my life. Róisín knew Patrick Doyle wouldn't do that because he keeps his promises." He wanted to aim a blow at Róisín, send the message that she hadn't kept hers. But maybe she had.

The letter sat in Mardell's lap unopened. "Promises? What do you mean?"

"I told Róisín so very long ago that if Juniper herself ever asked for me, I would come. Even though I first thought the lass had passed, I just had to come because of this."

Mardell slowly unfolded the letter. Patrick reread it over her shoulder as tears streaked down his cheeks. He heard Róisín sniffling as well.

To my Da, whoever you were,

I know you will not get this unless angels carry it to heaven. If that's where you got to go. You left me. I want you to come back and say why. Why did you go away, Da? Won't you tell me? You are angry, maybe, because I am not a boy? Did you not want me because I'm ugly? Too dirty? Too sick? Too poor? I wish you'd come back but you won't because you didn't want me. I wanted you, though.

I want you to come back.

A.J.M.

"Oh, how sad. She must have been a child when she wrote this, judging by the rudimentary penmanship." Mardell refolded the letter and handed it back. "You didn't want to show me this."

Patrick glared at Róisín, who turned away.

"I'm not proud of it. I deserve the things she said."

"I deserve them too," Róisín added.

Mardell sighed. "I wish you had shown it to me, but I understand why you were hesitant to."

Patrick stuffed the letter back into his jacket.

"She doesn't know all you went through, Dad, and that you didn't plan to leave her. I'm sure she doesn't feel this way any longer. She's a grown woman."

"Whether she does or not, we will find out. She asked me to

come. Here I am. That was my promise, Róisín. I don't owe you any more than that."

Róisín still would not look at him. "I wasn't the one who told her you were alive. That was your mother."

"Well, I'm pleased that she at least had Delaney Doyle in her life," he shot back. "For as long as she did."

Róisín opened her car door. "Perhaps 'tis better Juniper's mother stays dead. For everyone's sake." She placed one foot outside the door.

"No, wait," Mardell said. "I have something I'd like to say."

Róisín looked at her. "What is it? I think everything's been said."

"Where are you living?" Mardell asked.

"I have a wee house Mr. Murphy secured for me near Giant's Causeway. It's provided with my job at the church there and I have all I need. All the rest goes to Juniper and her care."

Mardell pivoted to look at Patrick. "No one is living a perfect life. Why not end all the pretension? Show all the cards, so to speak."

Patrick raised both hands. "I have nothing to hide. I went to America to earn a living. I got mixed up in bad deals and ended up homeless for a time. I found myself again and married and had a wonderful daughter. I was wrong not to come when you asked, Róisín. But I'm here. I'll try to make right whatever I can."

Róisín sighed, shoulders drooping. "I will not hide anything either. Ask me anything."

"This is your car?" he asked.

"Heavens, no. It belongs to Mr. Murphy."

"Why is he helping you like this?"

"He was close with John. 'Tis a kind of allegiance. And he gets a percentage of the interest in my bank account."

"Figures," Patrick huffed. "Whatever your reasons for making the choices you've made, I'm no better, not fit to judge. Give us directions to your place. We will meet Juniper, share that with her, and she can decide if she'd like to see you."

"Fair enough." This time Róisín looked him in the eye, giving him a somber expression he recognized, as though the years had melted away and they were two young kids again standing under lamplight in Stephen's Green. "Thank you for coming, Paddy. And for being a man of your word. I was wrong to keep her from you. From others, aye, I had to. But I do regret—"

"No time for that," he said, opening the door on his side. "Regret only serves to slow us down. Enough time wasted already."

"Do you blame me, Paddy? I mean, can you at least forgive me?"

Surprised by how easily it came out, he said, "Aye, Róisín. I hold no bitterness in my heart. Like I said, I made wrong choices, too, on my side of the pond." He swallowed hard, knowing what he must say and trying desperately to force the words from his throat. Tapping his fingers on the black leather seat, he said, "And I ask your forgiveness as well."

She nodded and he and Mardell scooted out of the back seat and rushed off to find James Sullivan.

"Maybe Mr. Murphy would take us over there," Mardell suggested.

"I didn't want to be in Murphy's car for a moment longer, Mardell. I was suffocating as it was."

"I'm proud of you, Dad. You took the high road."

Get this over with, he silently pleaded to God on high.

The drive over was bumpy but otherwise silent. Patrick's insides tightened. He'd failed many people over his lifetime. Juniper's request in that old letter, asking him to come, might not have been in earnest. She may have changed her mind over the years. She might be bitter and he couldn't blame her. At least he knew the priest had prepared her for his visit.

"Whatever happens, Dad, it will be OK." Mardell leaned her head against his shoulder.

The day's sunshine had given way to clouds and then showers. The road turned muddy, but the Sullivans' truck handled it adequately. When they turned down the short lane to Glasgleann Cottage, a black cat darted across the truck's path.

"The healer's cat, that one," James said. "Don't want to say 'tis bad luck, but ..."

Rain, black cats, sharp pains in his lower back. Patrick longed to get back to his bed. His own bed in Ohio. The conversation with Róisín had been draining and what he faced now would be even harder. However, he had promises to keep.

"Will ye be wanting me to return soon?" James asked. "Got the animals to tend, so I do."

Patrick hadn't thought of that. If the rain didn't let up, a long walk back might do him in for good. He didn't have to answer because James kept talking.

"Look there. Seems Canon Duffy is at the shop. He's got a new cart, so he does. I suppose he'd deliver ye back to the house if you ask him."

"Aye, thank you," Patrick said, exiting the truck and then helping his daughter out. He grinned at the man. "Seems we've a bit of good luck after all."

James only shrugged and took off, his truck smelling of exhaust fumes.

"He should get that checked," Patrick said. They turned toward the cottage. Lace curtains at the window fluttered. Patrick swallowed hard as the door latch clicked.

JUNIPER

Juniper had served Granny broth about an hour before the rector returned.

"Is it all right if I go in? I read to her a bit before and she didn't seem to mind." He nodded toward the bedroom door with Bible in hand.

"Certainly. While Granny's Catholic, she never objects to anyone's religion."

He sat with Granny, reading aloud from the Bible while Juniper prepared the meal. The sound of a truck's motor sent her to the window. James Sullivan. *He never visits the shop except to bring visitors.* "They're here!"

Juniper glanced at herself in the mirror by the door. She was presentable, of course, because she'd expected Canon Duffy for supper. It was better this way, with a houseful of people. She flung the front door open.

Mr. Sullivan tipped his hat and she waved before he took off in a cloud of smoke. Standing before her were her father and her sister, she presumed. They stood stiffly. "Please, come in." Juniper stepped back into the house.

They inched past her and then she shut the door, nearly nipping Michael's tail in the process. Juniper held out her hand. "Mr. Doyle, I assume?"

"I am Patrick Doyle and this is my daughter Mardell."

My daughter. How strange that sounded.

"Nice to meet you," the young woman said, taking Juniper's hand. "You knew we were coming? Father Barr told you?" She had thick, tawny hair and a pleasant smile, probably only a few years younger than Juniper, although they looked nothing alike.

"He did indeed." Juniper glanced at Paddy, who did not look at all as she had imagined. Juniper shared his dark hair and straight posture but otherwise there was nothing she recognized. She had thought his features would be hard, his body stout and muscular like a cross between Humphrey Bogart and John Wayne. But of course, her father wasn't American, just lived there. Even his voice gave away his Irishness.

"I wasn't sure if we'd be welcome," he said, barely meeting her gaze.

"You are very welcome indeed. The rector has come for supper. There is plenty for all of us. Please, sit down at the table." She wasn't used to having guests. They were still cloaked. "Uh, hand me your coats, if you will."

They removed their overcoats and she laid them on the shop counter, motioning toward the table. "Sit, please."

"This is so nice of you," her sister said. "We don't want to intrude." She began to sit but paused when she noticed her father hadn't moved.

"Juniper, you must be wondering—" Paddy began.

"First, sit. The tea is ready if you'd like to pour. I need to check on ... Excuse me, please."

She rushed into the bedroom and shut the door behind her. "They are here," she whispered.

"You mean your father? I thought maybe you had customers." Canon Duffy rose from his chair.

"'Tis them. Thank you for suggesting I write a letter. I think I can better speak to him now that I have."

"Then what are you doing in here?" he asked.

She rubbed her hands together. "I don't know." She turned to Granny who was sleeping. "She has to know. She's waited for many years to see her son again."

"You go along and talk with your father. I'll stay with her. I'm sure she'll rouse after a short nap. For now, go along and have your chat."

She mouthed the words *thank you*, almost afraid to speak.

"A moment." He collected his Bible from the nightstand and flipped some pages. "Think on this, from 2 Corinthians 2:15: 'For we are unto God a sweet savour of Christ.' It means we carry a fragrance, we who believe. Carry that fragrance like honeysuckle so that your relations will see not you, but God who made you." He shrugged. "That's the pep talk I give myself before climbing into the pulpit. I thought it might help." He grinned. "Maybe not, sorry."

She lightly tapped his arm with her fingers. "Thank you. That is beautiful poetry. I never knew the Bible was like that."

"A love letter. That's how I think of it. Go now, with the strength of God's Word."

Juniper could breathe again. She returned to her guests.

"I'm sorry. I hope I wasn't rude. I am pleased you've come."

Her father smiled with a bit of nervousness. "You asked me to come. Do you remember?" He removed a piece of paper from his pocket, unfolded it, and laid it on the table before her. "And I've come to ask your forgiveness, although you couldn't be blamed for not granting it."

Shock registered when she saw what it was. "That was meant to be burned. I'm so very sorry. How did you come to have it? I was so young, alone, and afraid when I wrote it."

Tears formed in his eyes and his younger daughter curled her arm around him. "That was never what I planned, Juniper. Your mother, I wanted her to come to America." He refolded the letter. "St. Giles found it while remodeling and it was mailed to me."

Remembering the rector's advice earlier, Juniper kept silent, sipping tea.

Paddy squirmed on his chair. "I had hoped to build a life there, for all of us. I couldn't stay in Ireland. You see, there were things going on back then. The whole country was mad. I couldn't find a job. I left."

Juniper wanted to say something, but she must allow him to tell his story. She studied his scarred face as he spoke of the mistakes he made as a young man in America, mistakes he now realized were not too different from the choices Juniper's mother had made. She wasn't sure how he could possibly know that, but she listened.

A short while later Juniper served up a platter of chicken and potato stew just as the rector came to join them. Paddy looked puzzled, probably wondering what he had been doing in a back room but it would be explained soon. After introductions Canon Duffy blessed the meal and Paddy resumed his tale, moving through his life chronologically and arriving at the years with Mardell's mother. Then he suddenly stopped and turned toward the bedroom door.

"I'm very sorry," he said. "Someone else is here? Someone ill?" He addressed his question to the rector since he had just come out of the room.

Juniper answered. "Very ill, I'm afraid. You must go see her."

"Who?"

"Granny, of course. Your mother."

Paddy's mouth popped open. "My *mother*? Delaney Doyle, you mean?"

"Indeed. She has been living here since I left St. Giles."

Paddy put a hand on his chest. "I thought she'd died long ago." He seemed to be searching the tabletop for answers. "Will she know me? I mean, her mind's good?"

"She knows you have returned. She's wanted nothing more than to see her Paddy, she says." Juniper glanced at the rector. "She knows he's here?"

"I told her," he said. "She wants your father to come in when you're done talking."

Juniper smiled. Her father had not known his mother was alive. How many other things about them here had he not known? He should have known, maybe, but he didn't.

"And," the rector added, "she's awake at the moment. She's weakening, God bless her, so she sleeps quite a bit. She's already had a good nap, so she has."

Paddy bolted from the table and then turned back. "Forgive me."

"It's all right," Juniper said. "Go on." She rose to follow, keeping a few paces back to observe without interfering.

"Mam?" Paddy stepped into an arc of light cast on the floor by the bedside lamp.

Granny reached both arms toward him. "Paddy? Oh, my Paddy!"

Juniper realized that Granny needed her son every bit as much as Juniper had needed her. A touch, a hug, a moment to look into the eyes of someone you feared you'd never see again. She felt a hand on her shoulder. The rector stood behind her.

Juniper turned around, thanked him, and then returned to the table where Mardell Doyle sat alone. "Is this your first time in Ireland?" Juniper asked her.

"It is. You live in a beautiful country." She turned to look out the back window. "And your gardens are magnificent. I'd love to learn about them, maybe bring some seeds back with me to Ohio, if you have any."

Juniper laughed. "I have more than you could want. I'll fix up a basket for you. When do you return?"

Mardell frowned. "In a few days. I can't say I'm eager to go." Her brows arched. "I almost forgot. Before we knew you were Juniper, we were coming to see you anyway."

Juniper cocked her head to one side. "Oh, why?"

"A message. Do you remember caring for some of the American soldiers during the war?"

"Of course. A few stopped in for elixirs, especially for hangovers."

"Do you remember a young man named Leo? He had blisters on his feet."

"Oh, certainly. He had a couple of furlough days and came to see me because he could barely get his boots on. They had treated him with Friar's Balsam, which would work in time. But he was in a hurry so I cleaned him up a wee bit with vinegar I fermented from apples and then applied an ointment and he said that helped. A simple thing."

"Well, he must have thought more of your cure than *that* to have mentioned it to me years later. He was hoping we'd find you, although he didn't remember your name and we didn't realize when we first stopped by who you were. He asked me to pay you on his behalf."

Juniper held up a hand. "Around here we mostly barter. I don't want to take his money."

"Oh, but he would like you to take it. It would mean a great deal to him." She pushed a folded banknote toward her. "I have nothing to barter anyway."

"Very well. Thank you and thank him for me. I'm quite honored he remembered after all this time. Will you take some homemade soap, then?"

"Oh, that sounds delightful. Will you tell me how it's made?"

No one had ever asked Juniper to teach them. Her newly discovered sister was quite lovely.

The bedroom door opened, and Paddy and Granny appeared on the threshold. "Oh, Granny. You should be in bed."

"That's what I told her," Paddy said. "And she told me I'm her son and I'll listen to her, not the other way around."

Canon Duffy rushed over to assist and the two men settled Granny into the cushioned chair. "I want to sit with my family while I can," Granny said. She lifted one arm. "My granddaughter Mardell. Come here, child."

Mardell accepted her embrace and then pulled her kitchen chair up to sit beside her.

"Come sit here with us, Juniper," Granny said.

Juniper sat at her feet, like she so often did.

"What beautiful names my girls have. Paddy, tell us how they were named."

He sat at the table with the rector, stirring sugar into his tea. He reached into his pocket and pulled out a dented old cigarette tin, the kind soldiers carried. He opened it and removed a twig. "This here is what's left of the juniper I carried throughout the war. Have you seen the plant?" He directed his question to Juniper.

"Uh, I have. 'Tis a coniferous shrub with blue berries. Is that what I'm named for? I have some of the berries. They can be used for some applications." She turned to Mardell. "I used some of that for your Leo, as it happens."

"More common in Belgium than here, at least I never saw any in Dublin. I brought these bits home to show Róisín and she decided to give you the name, although you are called Anna?"

She nodded. "Juniper is my middle name. Unique, it is."

"No one has a name like mine, either," Mardell said. "But I can tell you where it came from, Granny Doyle."

"Aye, dear."

"I am named for my grandmothers, Margaret and Delaney. Mar and Del. My mother spelled my name with a double L so that people would pronounce it correctly."

Granny's normally pasty cheeks turned rosy. Paddy openly cried. Juniper didn't know what part these people, even the rector, would play in her future. It was too early to tell. People had moved in and out of her life like wild birds. Only Granny had stayed. And even she would have to leave Juniper soon. But Juniper had this moment. And what was her life but a wash of wee moments? This was one she'd always cherish.

Juniper learned that her sister was educated and wanted a career working in Ohio's capital city. Smart, that one. Mardell wanted to learn about Juniper's work and bring some of it back with her, she said. Paddy invited Juniper to visit them in the States. After a bit more craic, Granny needed her bed. The two men helped her and then Canon Duffy prepared to leave.

"Got an early morning appointment with the bishop," he said. "Suppose we'll be discussing my future service to the church."

"You aren't leaving Moira?" Juniper asked. A familiar hollowness spread in her chest.

"Hopefully not. I've only recently arrived." He smiled. "I'll make sure you get the pony if I do."

She didn't want that. She wanted his companionship. Especially if Granny …

Paddy stood. "If you don't mind, I'd like you to stay a minute longer. I've to tell Juniper something that may be difficult to hear and since you're her friend, she may like your support."

"Certainly." The rector sat at the table and placed his hat on his lap.

Juniper trembled inside. Could she handle any more surprises in one day?

"'Tis about your mother, Juniper."

"Róisín? What about her? Twelve years now she's been gone. I can show you her grave if you'd like. 'Tis unmarked."

He shook his head. "I thought so too. Seems your uncle is buried in that grave near the train station, not Róisín."

"What? John has been sending money."

"She didn't want you to know 'twas her. Long explanation, but she had enemies she needed to protect you from so she made it appear that she had died."

"She's alive, then?"

"Very much. I saw her myself. Circumstances have changed recently. Seems the threat is gone. She could tell you more. She'd like to see you, if you're agreeable."

Juniper rubbed an ache in the back of her neck. "Hold on. You saw my *mother*? You *spoke* to her?"

"She came to see us at the Sullivan's house. She asked me to tell you."

The room grew gray as Juniper's vision faded to make room for this news. She'd had so many questions for her mother and now only one mattered: why?

A gasp and a thud snapped her attention back to those in the room.

"Dad? What's wrong?" Mardell was leaning over someone.

Paddy was lying on the floor, groaning.

CHAPTER 43

P atrick

May 1950, County Down, Northern Ireland

He'd tried very hard to ignore it, but the pain pierced through his resolve until it knocked him off his chair like a blow from a prize fighter—but much worse than any he'd received in his days in the ring.

"Show me where it hurts," Juniper said, leaning over him.

He pointed to his lower back on one side.

"Kidneys," she said. "Get him up on my bed," she ordered.

The rector and Mardell guided him as the pain began to lessen. Patrick lay his head down on a linen pillow that smelled sweetly of dew and flowers, like Ireland herself. "'Tis better now. I'm all right."

"Let me see." Juniper lifted his eyelids and gazed at him as though she were a doctor. "Have you been making frequent trips to the toilet?" she asked.

"Not a question one discusses with ..."

"A stranger?" she asked.

He stared at both girls. "A daughter."

"Yes, he has," Mardell answered. "No sooner did he get over his cough than this started. He's fatigued too. At first I thought it was grief. My mother died recently. But this pain is something else."

"You're right. An infection I believe. Have you been to the doctor, Paddy?" Juniper asked.

A voice came from the main room. Delaney stood at the door. "I can help," she said, motioning for Juniper. "Hot water bottle for his back. Mayflower tea. And then call for the doctor."

"I don't need a doctor," Patrick mumbled. The smell of the turf fire sparked boyhood memories. "I need only my mother's cures."

Mardell brought him a glass of water. He left it on the bedside table. Drinking it would only cause him to need the outhouse.

"He's been mentioning his mother's herbal remedies ever since we came," Mardell said.

Patrick's mother clicked her tongue. "I do not need a doctor, but you, my son, do. They have pills now. What's it called, darlin?"

Juniper placed a hot water bottle behind his back. "Antibiotics, Granny."

"So 'tis. Much faster. Don't give me that look, son. You've had this infection too long. Juniper and I have seen those who can't be helped, those whose sicknesses have gone too long. We've recently had a doctor move to the village. Most things my cures are good for, but when a doctor has something that can help, you would be foolish to disregard it. Canon Duffy, would you be so kind?"

The clergyman donned his coat. "I will fetch the doctor and tell him what Mrs. Doyle said. I'll be back within the hour."

"Another lesson learned," Patrick whispered to Mardell. "Now don't you worry. I'm in fine hands."

Two days later Patrick was ready to leave Glasgleann Cottage. Mardell, who had been staying at the Sullivans and visiting during the daytime, stood waiting for him at the front door. "We're off to the Causeway, Dad."

"Are we now? To check that off your list, I suppose."

"Oh, yes." She whispered to him. "Róisín is living up there, but we don't have to ..."

Patrick whispered back. "I want to say something to her. Won't take long. Plenty of time to sightsee."

He glanced at Juniper, who was washing up breakfast dishes at the kitchen sink. She did not seem to be accompanying them. "Well, I suppose this is farewell," he said. "Thank you for your excellent care."

"You are very welcome. I'm glad you're feeling better."

"Your mother is living up there, if you'd like to come," Patrick said.

"Not now. I've Granny to look after."

He nodded and headed to the bedroom to say the most painful of goodbyes.

"Oh, my boy," Delaney said, reaching for him.

"Can you forgive me, Mam?" He came closer.

"I have nothing to forgive you for. You made a life for yourself. You had a wonderful marriage and a beautiful daughter. I know you had a rough start in Dublin, but look at you now, my American son. I'm proud."

Tears stung his recently shaved cheeks. "I'll always be Irish." He stroked the scarf around her neck with his fingertips. "Is this the one I sent?"

"Aye, 'tis. I wore it every time I went to mass. The priest is coming to see me today. One should always look one's best at church. This is as close to church as I'll get now."

A sob escaped his throat.

"Now, I'm all right, son. The Good Shepherd has led me to green pastures. I have everything I need."

All he could do was nod. She closed her eyes. He sat down on the chair by the bed and drew Colin's rosary from his pocket. Bending his head over it, he prayed for his mother. He knew all his prayers and the Apostle's Creed, but those practiced words would not come now, as though there was no time for all that. His mother would not get well, but as she said, she had all she needed. He spent a few moments contemplating the Twenty-third Psalm from which those words came. Colin roamed the green pastures of heaven now.

"That isn't yours, I'd guess."

He glanced up. His mother reached for the beads and he handed them to her. "This represents something? A heartache?"

"Remember Colin Reilly?"

"Your school chum? He died in the war as I remember."

"He did." The words came out a bit garbled with emotion.

Delaney handed them back. "You feel guilty, I expect."

"There was nothing I could do. He was shot for cowardice, but he was no coward. I don't know what was wrong with him. Shell shock or something. I couldn't snap him out of it."

"I see. And you've carried that rosary along with your guilt for ... more than thirty years."

Patrick tugged a handkerchief from his pants pocket and rubbed it across his eyes.

"I've got another cure for you, Paddy. It will work, if you allow it."

He studied her lined face, finding the mother of his youth there. "What is it, Mam?"

"Take mine." She motioned to the bedside table.

"No, Mam. You need those. You're a faithful Catholic."

"Which is why I don't need them, Paddy. You take them and remember what I'm telling you. Whatever we've done in our past is wiped away when we ask God to forgive us." She squeezed his hand. "Gone, I tell ye. Start new. Every day."

"All right." He clutched the beads in his left hand.

"And Colin's? Bury those on the grassy knoll, the place where I myself will rest when my time comes."

"Bury them?"

"Aye. Over and done. Then hug your daughters."

When she drifted off to sleep, he returned to the front room. "I'm pleased you two have had each other," he said, giving Juniper a goodbye embrace.

She didn't answer. When he pulled back, he could see she was crying too. "Wait." She retrieved a woven basket from her counter. "Take this, Mardell. I've written down my recipe for the soap. And there's some more mayflower tea for Paddy."

"Call me Dad, if you'd like. Do you mind if I take a stroll first? My mother told me about the place she's to be laid to rest."

"Of course. Would you like me to come too?"

"If you'd like."

"I'll stay here," Mardell said. "In case Granny needs anything while you're gone."

The two of them walked up a grassy lane and past the goats' pasture. The elevation slanted slightly upward until an expanse of blue sky met them.

"Nothing like the sky after the rain," Juniper said, breaking the silence.

"Didn't see a lot of the sky growing up in the city," Patrick answered. "Perhaps as a lad I just never looked."

"Really? When I was a child, and still today, I marvel at the natural world. Give me grass and trees, sunshine, and rain over an expanse of mortared manmade buildings any day."

"I'm very happy you have this place, Juniper. I do enjoy my farm in Ohio. You must come visit one day."

"I'd like that."

They paused at the top of the hill. Far out on the horizon lay a flat land he supposed was the bog where Róisín said she found her treasure. To the right lay a forested area and to the left a billowy meadow of purple, white, and yellow wildflowers. "Mam was right. 'Tis beautiful up here. I'm afraid I've forgotten a shovel." He held up the old rosary. "I've been instructed to bury my past here, Juniper."

"Oh, well, I keep some tools up here for collecting plants. Not a big shovel, but I've a wee spade if that will do."

"Brilliant."

He watched as Juniper uncovered a wooden box under a shrub. "Is that juniper?"

She laughed. "'Tis. I was quite delighted to find it here. It's not as uncommon in this area as it is in others."

"Well, fitting." He chose a spot just off the path and dug a hole with the spade. When he finished, a clear, open but not hollow feeling bloomed inside him. His mother had been right. The symbolism of burying his past had freed him. "I won't forget ye, lad," he whispered.

Examining the juniper bush, he plucked a branch and placed it in his cigarette tin. "For remembrance," he said.

His Irish daughter beamed. "Have you that letter in your pocket still? The one I wrote as a child."

"I have."

"Give it to me."

He fished around in his jacket pocket until he came up with the now crumpled piece of paper.

She held it up in the sunlight and then began to tear it to pieces.

"What are you doing?"

"Well, if we're to bury the past, I want this gone too." They watched as ivory bits of paper speckled with brown letters drifted away toward the meadow, the bog, and the forest. Separated, the words no longer held power. "You've a new letter to carry now, since you seem to have a penchant for that." She had given him something to read later. He'd placed it in his suitcase but now wanted it close.

They meandered down the hill in a lighter mood. He kissed her and thanked her for taking such good care of his mother. Then he and Mardell settled themselves into the rector's pony cart to head into town where a man would be hired to drive them to the Causeway.

Once they arrived in the village, they bid Canon Duffy farewell. "Take care of our Juniper," Patrick told him, firmly grasping the man's hand.

"I will do my best, especially since the bishop says I'm to remain in Moira for at least two more years."

"Good news," Mardell said.

Later, in the back seat of their hired sedan, Patrick reflected on the last few days. He'd been right about one thing he'd said before they came to Glasgleann. His mother knew the best cures.

"I wouldn't be surprised if something developed between that rector and our Juniper," he told Mardell.

"Oh, Dad. Always trying to marry off your daughters."

He chuckled. "I suppose I am. 'Tis a father's duty to see his children happy when he's not around." He glanced at the letter he held, planning to read it in the car. Juniper had instructed him to wait for a quiet moment.

CHAPTER 44

P atrick
   The Causeway Coast, County Antrim, Northern
Ireland

The plan was to tour the Giant's Causeway, drop in on Róisín for a few moments, and then head back on the train to Dublin. From there they'd take the bus to Cobh for the trip home. He figured they needed at least three full days to accomplish this.

"I'll drop you at Bushmills," their driver said. "Easy to make your way to the Causeway from there."

"Thank you." Patrick had paid the man a small fortune. This country needed more rails. "Bushmills is the town where Róisín lives. A wee cottage behind a church there," he told Mardell.

"Are you sure you want to see Róisín, Dad? I mean, things were not exactly cordial between you two."

"I'm sure I don't, but I'm sure I must."

"Why? Is there something you didn't say before?"

"I think so. I'm not sure what I'm going to say, but I left in a huff the first time and then again in Moira, and I don't want to leave it that way."

"Sure, Dad." She examined a brochure she had picked up somewhere.

World famous, the Giant's Causeway. He was curious to see it himself.

He didn't have time to read Juniper's letter since he and Mardell had chatted the whole way about their quest to find Juniper.

The driver pulled up to what appeared to be an inn of some type. "They have rooms here, if you'd like. And they'd be happy to direct you to the Causeway. That all right?"

"Certainly," Patrick said, exiting the car and collecting their suitcases.

"Should we stay here, Dad? Just for the night?" Mardell had been urging him to extend their visit even longer.

They would need to stow their luggage somewhere. He sighed. There would be no rushing this thing. "Let's go inside and inquire about a telephone."

It was a fine day so Patrick rented bicycles from the inn and they pedaled down a road past fields of sheep and white-washed houses. As they neared the coastline unusual rock formations began to appear at the water's edge. "Keep going," Mardell said, "we're almost there."

Thank the good Lord Patrick had recovered from his infection or he never would have been able to do this. As it was, his knees ached, but the fresh air and the smell of the ocean made the effort worthwhile. Finding a place to secure the bikes, they hiked along the cliffs looking out over the basalt rock formations. "Have you ever seen such blue water?" Mardell snapped her Brownie several times.

"I don't believe I have." The colors were so vivid Patrick could almost believe he was wearing tinted spectacles.

"My book said these rock formations were created by an ancient volcano eruption."

It pleased Patrick to be able to give his daughter this outing she had longed for.

They continued down the path, descending toward the sea. Finally, the route dropped them at the shore where the rocks piled up like stepping stones wedged together, hexagonal stepping stones. Patrick borrowed the camera and snapped a photo of Mardell standing out on the Causeway, a series of rocks stretching out into the sea behind her.

What wonders this island held! How many native-born Irish missed seeing these things, as he almost had? After wandering around like a couple of excited school children, they mounted their bicycles to make their way back to the inn.

Later, after rubbing away sore muscles, Patrick joined Mardell in the inn's pub for a meal of meat pasties, a Northern Ireland specialty. "That was so much fun, Dad. Thank you."

It would be a delightful trip if he didn't have to face Róisín again. But he must. "I sent a messenger lad over to Róisín's cottage. Told her where we were and that Juniper sent me with a message for her."

"She did? I didn't know. Do you think she'll make up with her mother? I mean, I hope so."

"I don't know, darlin." He opened the letter Juniper had given him while they ate. It was surprisingly short.

Dear Father,

It was not possible to despise you. I may have wanted to, but I realized that someone like Granny could not have raised a terrible son. You are both kind souls. Write to me when you get home. I promise to stay in touch. When I'm able, I do want to visit America.

My love to you and Mardell.

Juniper

After he read it aloud to Mardell they reflected on their journey and all the things they'd discovered along the way.

"I really like Juniper," Mardell said. "I'm going to learn how to make things with herbs when we get home."

"Ah, some Irish have the gift of gab, some the gift of poetry and literature, some have great musical talent, but my girls inherited the Celtic spirit of finding the Divine in nature. From their grandmother, so 'tis."

"It would be hard not to in this beautiful place. Oh!"

Patrick turned around to see what caught Mardell's attention. Róisín had just entered the pub and was looking around. He waved to her and she came over.

"Hello again. I was surprised to get your message," she said.

He pointed to the chair between himself and Mardell and she sat down. He scooted the letter from Juniper across the table to her. "I always keep my promises."

She reached for it but he put his hand on top of it. "First, I don't know what Juniper has written but whatever it is—"

"I deserve it."

"No, Róisín. Whatever it says, you must go to her. She will lose the only person she has close to her soon. My mother has been living with her, but now Mam's dying."

"Oh, Paddy. I'm very sorry for your trouble."

That was something the Irish said. Patrick didn't know if she was truly sorry or not, but he'd come to urge a reconciliation, so he must try.

"We've come to an understanding, Juniper and myself, but I live in America. You are here. No matter what she says, you must find a way. Promise me."

"I promise." A single tear streaked down Róisín's face. "I can't stay here in Bushmills. I'm out of funds."

"I'll help," Patrick said. "But I'm not a rich man."

"No, no. You've spent a lot on this holiday, I should think."

"Maybe Juniper would allow you to live with her," Mardell offered. "She really is a kind person."

"I don't know if she would, but I've love that. My daughter is the best soul I know," Róisín said.

"Have they pushed you out of here?" Patrick asked.

"I've been working a wee bit by cleaning the church, but they can't afford to pay me anymore. Mr. Murphy tells me the fund will be empty by the end of the year."

"It's beautiful here," Mardell said, taking a sip of water. "May I ask how you ended up in this place?"

"Oh, Mr. Murphy. He found the job for me. At the edge of civilization, he said. No one would find me here. 'Tis lovely, aye, but not home."

"You want to move back to Dublin?" Mardell asked. She always got right to the point.

"There was a time I might have, but truly those streets only hold wicked memories for me now."

"Then Glasgleann is where you should go," Mardell said.

"Belongs to Juniper now. It would truly be up to her," Róisín said.

Patrick ordered a meal for Róisín and while she waited for her food to arrive, she opened the letter. Her face paled as she read. "Well, that's that," she said, folding it up and placing it in her pocketbook.

Mardell stared at Patrick and he shook his head. Not the time to ask.

Before they parted ways, Róisín suggested to Mardell that they visit Dunluce Castle before they left the northern coast. Then she turned to Patrick. "I'm sorry. Truly I am."

"I'm sorry too. Let me help you."

She looked away. "I have made my way through many difficult situations. I will manage this too." She forced a smile. "Godspeed on your journey home."

When she left, Mardell leaned over the table to whisper. "I can't imagine Juniper rejecting her like that."

"I can't either. Neither one of us have been in Juniper's shoes. Perhaps in time she'll forgive her mother the way she forgave me."

CHAPTER 45

P atrick

June 1950, Golden, Ohio

Patrick reclined in his folding chair under the apple tree, leaning back to look up at the blue sky through its branches, an array of green and pale blue. There was no place like home.

"Hey, be careful or you'll end up like Isaac Newton when those apples fall."

Patrick glanced up to see his old friend. "No chance of that, Ernie."

The doctor marched over and shook his hand. "Why's that? In my professional opinion Patrick Doyle is of above average intelligence."

"Be that as it may, not time for the apples to fall yet."

They shared a laugh. "Always the logical one, my friend Patrick.

"The trip went well?"

"Indeed, although I'm a wee bit concerned about Juniper. She will soon lose her grandmother and she has no one else at the moment."

The sound of a car engine made them turn toward the driveway. Leo's pickup rolled up to the house.

"Well," Ernie said, "she needs to find herself a Leo. Mardell seems quite happy."

"She does, doesn't she? I wish she wouldn't take that job in Columbus."

"A job?"

"Aye, working for a politician's campaign. Hopefully after the November elections she'll come back and settle down."

Ernie collected a lawn chair from the shed and joined him. "You know, Patrick, I've never had children, but I've observed a lot of familial relationships as folks visit my office." He was a widower too. They'd talked about that. "Seems to me, you worry too much about your grown children. They have to do their own growing, you know."

Patrick chuckled. "My mother said something like that when she fussed over my decision to come to America."

"She was right. Couldn't change your mind, could she?"

"No, sir. Not any more than she could when I joined the Dublin Fusiliers in the Great War. And that new war now, in Korea? Another generation of mothers begging their sons to stay home."

"God help us," his friend said, shaking his head.

"If we ever thought we had control, or that mankind would learn its lesson, we were sadly mistaken, Ernie."

"True enough. We do what we can. Love one another. That's the lesson we all need to learn from the Good Book."

Patrick scratched the back of his head as he watched a robin hop through the tree branches. "Ah, true. Something still puzzles me about Juniper, though." Patrick was concerned and he thought it best to bring the conversation back around to something he might well have a say in, some love he might be able to help spread. "I can't quite reconcile why Juniper didn't at least try to have a wee chat with her mother once she learned she was alive. The lass was lovely to Mardell and me. A reasonable sort, she is. This doesn't make sense."

"Hmm," the doctor replied. "Perhaps one day."

"Hopefully she doesn't wait long. I'll keep hinting in my letters."

The doctor crossed his long legs at the knee and inclined his head toward Patrick. "You do that. As for you, things are better, you'd say?"

"My memories, you mean?"

"That and, well, as you know, Patrick, you've had to get used to living life without Veronica. I know how hard that is, even though it's been eleven years since my Iris passed."

Patrick drew in a deep breath, the scent of his newly mowed lawn helping to soothe him. "Don't suppose there's any getting used to that."

"No, but there is moving forward, reaching for the joy that can still be found. Be comforted by your memories, but don't neglect what you still have."

"Isn't that what I've learned most of all, Ernie. Planning a trip next year to see my Irish daughter."

"Oh, that's fine, then."

"And don't you worry. I might have a mind to try to influence my daughters' decisions, but I'll not be meddling. I truly appreciate what I have. Finding Juniper was the guidepost to sending me in the right direction, I do think."

The doctor saluted him and wandered across the yard to check on the chickens. Patrick would write a letter to Róisín tonight. Life was short. He hadn't been able to convince Róisín when they were young that they needed each other, but sometimes wisdom came with age, and she might be convinced she needed to try harder with Juniper. He wouldn't stop this time. No leaving behind the love that they all needed so desperately.

CHAPTER 46

Juniper
25 August 1950, County Down, Northern Ireland

Juniper stood at the top of the hill and looked down on Granny's grave, remembering one of her grandmother's last lucid moments.

"The bog, lass. Invite your mother. Be enough distance between you that way. A kindness you could give, and you are a caring one, my Juniper."

Earlier that day the tenants living by the bog had stopped in. "We came to live here because of the generosity of your aunt, Miss Barry," Mrs. Quigley had told her.

"Please, call me Anna," Juniper said. One step at a time, and Anna *was* her legal name.

"Miss Anna, I've come to tell you we'll be off your land."

"Oh, you don't have to. I'm happy for you to stay." She glanced at the young lad who had come with his mother. Not the one who had brought her turf but probably his brother. "Your boys have been very helpful with the turf."

"Lovely to hear that. No, no, we're off to Scotland. You see, that's where we were born, Mr. Quigley and myself. Our families are there, and my *mither*, you see she's not been well. Our place, it is, to go and help."

"I see. You won't be coming back?"

"We won't, I'm afraid. In the winters Mr. Quigley had been going back to work in the mines, and he'll have work enough. You'll find another tenant, I'm sure, and you should charge something. We are grateful for your family's generosity, but I suppose you could get some income by charging rent. The house is small, but quite nice."

"Thank you, Mrs. Quigley."

After Juniper had seen the woman out, Granny hatched her grand scheme of inviting Róisín. Earlier they'd received word from Mr. Murphy and learned that while the land and the cottage were indeed Juniper's, the flow of money had run out. Granny had supposed this would leave Róisín destitute.

Juniper surveyed the scene from the high vantage point. She could barely see the bog, and the house was further on yet. There was space to divide them physically, but could Juniper keep her mother that far from her mind? She couldn't and hadn't been able to all the time she'd thought her mother was dead. It wouldn't matter where Róisín lived, then.

Juniper laid a wreath of wild daisies on Granny's grave. "You're right, Granny. You always were. I shouldn't have written that note and asked her to stay away. She'd kept her distance all these years. There was no reason to think she wouldn't still if I wanted her to." Juniper had written that letter much the way she'd written that awful one to her father, out of fear. She'd thought if they never came around her, she could forget them, when actually the fear of being hurt again had festered a hole in her soul. The only way to heal it was to offer grace. If she didn't forgive her parents, she would be hurting herself by allowing that hole to grow and spread like a cancer.

Juniper admired the sunny faces of her flowers. "Aye, Granny. I'll make the offer. You and Paddy have pestered me enough, and I know I must."

When she arrived back at the cottage, she saw the pony cart outside her door. Inside, a fire smoldered in the hearth and the smell of tea brewing lifted her spirits.

"I hope you don't mind I let myself in," the rector said, pouring from her teapot.

"Not at all. This is so nice of you."

"And by the way, have you made a decision about your mother?"

She nodded. "I'll write the letter tonight."

"Just because you offer the tenants' house to her doesn't mean you owe her a relationship. You don't owe anything, Juniper, but a wee bit of compassion. I'll bet it will melt her heart."

"Her heart may need that, Donal." They'd agreed to use each other's Christian names. They were becoming very good friends. Very good.

"And your heart?" He winced a little when he said that, but he had a way of making her look harder at her actions.

She sipped her tea, just the right temperature to warm her inside. "I suppose it was easier to forgive my father because I knew he was going back to America. If I see my mother all the time, it will bring back the pain of being abandoned."

"Try not to think of it that way, now that you know the truth."

"You're right. You know, I have to admit that even though I don't think my mother should have hidden herself from me, she showed great care for me."

"I don't suppose that Mr. Murphy told her how much money she actually had," Donal said. "But she spent it for you and for others."

Juniper watched him stir his tea three times, an endearing habit Juniper had noticed.

"When she paid for your roof, that helped the local tradesmen," he reminded her.

"That's true."

He nodded as he spread his sermon notes across the kitchen table.

"I can always count on you, Donal, to help me see more clearly, to find the truth."

"Which is?"

"The truth is, I can disagree with my mother's bad choices, but I can't change them or force her to change them now, all this time later. Or pretend she didn't do the things she did. All I can do is try to see who she is now, look at her as though I'd never met her before."

Juniper reached for Donal's hand and instead he pulled her into an embrace. She had fallen completely for this handsome clergyman and understood that she could now move toward building a new family.

He brushed his fingers along her jawline as she stared into the depth of his gaze, tingling as he held her tighter. Donal gave her security. He'd promised never to leave her. He was patient, kind, and generous. They'd danced among the flowers in her back garden. They'd shared a laugh over her burnt potato cakes. Together they'd read books she borrowed in Belfast and pondered the meanings hidden in the Scriptures. She'd never known these feelings before, but as he pressed a tender kiss to her lips, Juniper knew for certain that she was no longer lost. She'd been found.

AUTHOR'S NOTE

I was motivated to write this novel when I heard stories about the Irish men who fought in World War 1. Many returned to find themselves ostracized and even victims of violence, simply because they'd fought for the British. While it's true that Ireland was part of Great Britain at the time, a civil war was brewing. When a group of people are angry, they sometimes lash out in the wrong places. These men, after fighting in such a horrific war, wanted to come home to the relatively peaceful existence they had left. Too many did not get that wish. Irish author Sabastian Barry's novel *A Long Long Way* inspired me to tell this story. However, I didn't want to write a novel about war. I wanted to explore that experience and how someone would recover from it, and so Patrick Doyle formed in my mind.

Juniper's circumstances were different but the longing was the same. My interest in how women were wrongly committed to asylums goes back to my novel *Annie's Stories*, published in 2014. In that book Annie had been sent to the Magdalene Laundries after her father died. There are lots of sources to read more about those laundries since they only closed in the 1990s. Here is one source: http://jfmre search.com. There were other hospitals where men and women were sent, often unjustly. These were state-operated facilities rather than religious ones. In this story, St. Giles is fictional but that families sometimes abandoned their sons and daughters in what were then called lunatic asylums is a historical fact. There are stories in my family tree about children growing up without fathers that helped me to imagine Juniper. She may not have known it at first, but she wanted to be found. Like Patrick, she struggled to find her place. This is a theme as old as time, unfortunately. In addition to that, I'm always interested in families, how they work and how they sometimes don't, and how some have created new families and found healing.

Róisín's character reflected the other side of that abandonment, a mother who had limited choices. Her determination to save her daughter from abuse eventually led her away from violent politicism. But many women were active in politics in those years, including Countess Markievicz, mentioned in the novel. Married to a Polish count, Countess Markievicz had wealth that afforded her a measure of influence, but there were hundreds of common women across Ireland who fought, with weapons and with politics, for Ireland's freedom. *Cumann na mBan*, the women's republican organization was formed in 1914. The traditional role of women clashed remarkably in Ireland with a growing number of women willing to be politically involved. Women still managed the household and sometimes were the primary breadwinners for their families while standing up for women's rights and Ireland's independence. I chose not to explore this theme in full in this novel, but there are lots of resources out there for readers who want to learn more. One recent work is ***Women and the Irish Revolution: Feminism, Activism, Violence*** by Linda Connolly.

Some historical notes:

The Great Depression is a part of history most Americans are aware of. It wasn't just America that was affected, however. There was a global economic downturn. Northern Ireland suffered nearly 30 percent unemployment as their major industries of shipbuilding, linen manufacturing, and agriculture collapsed due to the international economic crisis. It took many decades to recover. This is Juniper's environment for most of her life.

In the novel, Paddy's mother mentions dirt from Father McGirr's grave. This local legend from County Fermanagh centered on a priest's grave, Father James McGirr. Before he died in 1805, he supposedly told his flock that the dirt from his grave would heal them as much as he had done for them when he was alive. This compelled pilgrims to visit his gravesite and take a spoonful of dirt, place it in a cloth pouch, and then put it under the pillow of someone who was ill. Today there are instructions from the parish priest on the grave for pilgrims who still visit. Folks are directed to return the bit of soil after using it. Failing to do so would bring bad luck. Whether it was a toothache, a sore throat, or a flesh wound, people said it worked. And here's the fascinating part. The soil was tested in recent years and found to contain streptomyces, a form of bacteria that is used to make over two-thirds of our antibiotics today. Healing often comes from nature, as Juniper and her grandmother know in the novel.

I chose the book *A Tree Grows in Brooklyn* by Betty Smith as the source of Patrick's revelation near the end of my story. The 1943 novel's Armed Services edition was a favorite among American servicemen who read it due to a program called the Council on Books in Wartime. Betty Smith received letters from servicemen who were inspired by it, so it seemed fitting that Patrick Doyle would be stirred as well. The major theme of the book is tenacity, something Patrick needs and truly had throughout my novel. If you haven't read this classic novel, I highly recommend it.

When I think of people who lived during the time Patrick Doyle does in my novel, I'm amazed by their endurance. Those who survived two world wars (not to mention the following conflicts), the Great Depression, the violence surrounding Prohibition and the rebirth of the Ku Klux Klan, and probably more things most of us can't imagine, built the foundation we now stand on. The present has its own challenges, but the need to learn from and be inspired by previous generations is why I write these stories. Thanks for reading!

ACKNOWLEDGMENTS

This story, a long time coming, was made possible through lots of support. First of all, thanks to Jamie Chavez, friend and amazing editor. She took my wandering mess of a manuscript and helped me focus on the story. Her expansive knowledge of Ireland along with her Irish husband Gerry Hampson, helped so much. Michelle Levigne, friend and editor, helped with proofreading. If any mistakes slipped in they are mine.

The main characters' Irish stories were inspired of course by my trips to Ireland, but also by spending hours with fellow writers, especially those born in Ireland, at the Dublin (Ohio) Irish festival. Thanks for your friendship.

I also want to thank the Book Loft of German Village for their support. You many not find many mentions of bookstores in authors' acknowledgements, but I truly am thankful for this wonderful indie bookstore for continuing to stock my books and offer book signings. Readers: go support your local independent bookstores! Glen, Russ, Julie, Josh, you guys are the best!

My faithful prayer group continues to root me on and pray for me. Thank you, Gina, Judi, and Dee.

Sandy Beck, I treasure your support and encouragement, and your willingness to tell absolutely everyone about my books. We've been besties nearly our whole lives and I'll always treasure you.

My kids, my grandkids, I love you with all my heart. Our family keeps growing in numbers and in love. You inspire me to tell stories about loving families.

This, my seventh novel, would not have been possible without the support and encouragement of my husband Tom. He asks hard questions, pushes gently, and totes around heavy books to various events and festivals. I'm beyond blessed to have been married to this man for over four decades now.

To my faithful readers. Thanks for your patience. I wrote this book for you!

I'm grateful God has given me stories to tell. I keep striving to do my best with them, and I'm still learning. I'll never take for granted the opportunity and ability I have to write, and yet I believe it's a miracle it happens at all! Only God.

Visit me at https://www.cindyswriting.com

MORE BY CINDY THOMSON

Daughters of Ireland Series

Brigid of Ireland

Pages of Ireland

Enya's Son

Ellis Island Series

Grace's Pictures

Annie's Stories

Sofia's Tune

Celtic Wanderings, a 40-Day Devotional

The Roots of Irish Wisdom

Celtic Song

Finding Your Irish Roots

If you enjoyed **Finding Juniper**, please consider leaving a review on Amazon, Barnes & Noble, Goodreads, BookBub, or wherever you review books. Even a short sentence helps. Thank you! 🙏

Made in the USA
Middletown, DE
01 February 2025

70006180R00246